Shortlisted for the CWA Joh...

'A stormer of a thriller – vividly written, utterly topical, totally gripping' Peter James

'This is a remarkably well-written, sophisticated novel in which the people and places, as well as frequent scenes of violent action, all come alive on the page … This is a really excellent debut' *Literary Review*

'A page-turning adventure that grabs you from the first page and won't let go' Edward Wilson

'An exceptional debut, beautifully written, blisteringly authentic, heartstoppingly tense and unusually moving. Definite award material' Paul Johnston

'This is an exceptional and innovative novel. And an important one. Hardisty appears to know his territory intimately and describes in mind-grabbing detail its culture, its beliefs and its hopes. I can't praise it highly enough' Susan Moody

'The author's deep knowledge of the settings never slows down the non-stop action, with distant echoes of a more moral-minded Jack Reacher or Jason Bourne. A forceful first novel by a writer not afraid of weighty issues and visibly in love with the beauty of the Yemen and desert landscapes his protagonists travel through' Maxim Jakubowski

'A trenchant and engaging thriller that unravels this mysterious land in cool, precise sentences' Stav Sherez, *Catholic Herald*

'I'm a sucker for genuine thrillers with powerful redemptive themes, but what spoke to me more strongly than anything was the courage, integrity and passion with which this novel is written' Eve Seymour, *Cheltenham Standard*

'Smart, gripping, superbly crafted oil-industry thriller' Helen Giltrow

'It's a measure of the wonderfully descriptive style of writing that *The Abrupt Physics of Dying* works as well as it does. The sense of place, and the way that the climate, the landscape and the people all combine within a location very foreign to that which many of us live in is evocative' *Australian Crime*

'Wow. Just wow. The sense of place is conjured beautifully and the author's fondness and respect for the people and the region comes across in spades. If you need a point of reference think, John Le Carré's *A Constant Gardener. The Abrupt Physics of Dying* is a thriller with heart and a conscience' Michael J. Malone, CrimeSquad

'A thriller of the highest quality, with the potential to one day stand in the company of such luminaries as Bond and Bourne ... This is intelligent writing that both entertains and challenges, and it deserves a wide audience' Live Many Lives

'The story rockets along, twisting and turning amid clouds of dust from the Yemeni deserts, pausing occasionally to put aside the AK47s and take tea amid the generosity of an Islamic culture Hardisty clearly understands and admires ... An exceptional debut' Tim Marshall, The What and the Why

'*The Abrupt Physics of Dying* is compelling reading and tackles subject matter not often encountered ... it is both dynamic and different and I enjoyed it immensely' Grab this Book

'I was a big fan, in 2013, of Terry Hayes's *I Am Pilgrim* and I hadn't up to now read a conspiracy thriller which came close to it in terms of quality. But Hardisty's book was an excellent read with a similar sweep across the politics of international money-making' Sarah Ward, Crime Pieces

'Just occasionally, a book comes along to restore your faith in a genre – and Paul Hardisty's *The Abrupt Physics of Dying* does this in spades. It's absolutely beautifully written and atmospheric – and it provides an unrivalled look at Yemen, a country few of us know much about … appreciate intelligent, quality writing' Sharon Wheeler, Crime Review

'This thrilling debut opens with a tense, utterly gripping roadside hijacking … Hardisty's prose is rich, descriptive and elegant, but break-neck pace is the king … an exhilarating, white-knuckle ride' Paddy Magrane, Crime Book Club

'A great pageturner with all the elements that make a cracking thriller. There's plenty of action, twists and turns, skulduggery and an evil oil company – what more could you want? This is one of those books that makes you want to turn to Google and find out how much is fact and how much fiction' Novel Heights

'At heart this is first and foremost a cracking good thriller … a lot of good stuff here not often found in a crime novel' Crime Novel Reader

'Fast-paced and cleverly written, this novel has bestseller written all over it' Writing WA

'Hardisty details Yemen, the political climate and the science with an authority that's never questionable and with a delivery that's polished enough to make you wonder whether he hasn't secretly been publishing thrillers under a different name for years … as assured, gripping, well paced and finely detailed as they come' Mumbling about…

'For *Abrupt Physics of Dying* to be a debut novel, a brilliant debut novel, there're surely only exciting things to come from Paul E. Hardisty, starting with next year's sequel *The Evolution of Fear*. A sensational first novel for author' Reviewed the Book

'*The Abrupt Physics of Dying* is a tense thriller, the violence and corruption is vividly portrayed, yet there is nothing in the story that shouldn't be there … If you enjoy a story that is well written with a plot that twists and turns, and leads you astray, then I'd recommend this. If you want a hero that is a little bit unusual, with his own issues, but is determined and so well created, then I'd recommend this. If you want a complex and intelligent thriller, then I'd really, really recommend this' Random Things Through My Letterbox

'A well-crafted, admirably constructed, and convincing tale of modern corruption, touching on topical issues, *The Abrupt Physics of Dying* has introduced Hardisty as a serious player in the (eco-) thriller genre, and I expect impressive things from him over the coming years' Mad Hatter Reviews

'An exceptional debut thriller … well written, the prose clear and crisp, the voice clear and authentic. Tense and moving, it grabs you by the throat' Atticus Finch

'A knowledgeable and intelligent thriller which, despite being set two decades ago, feels fresh and thoroughly relevant to today's geopolitical situation … We can hear the noise, feel the heat and even taste the poisoned water. Hardisty clearly knows his stuff and has created an evocative portrait of Yemen' Louise Reviews

'It is clear that the author's background and experience has enabled him to write a thriller that is so rich and detailed in description that you can almost feel the searing heat and visualise the vast endless desert … a very powerful and compelling message of corporate greed and the deliberate destruction of life and land' My Reading Corner

'Well paced with plenty of action … I look forward to reading more from this author. Definitely a cracking debut' Bleach House Library

'Civil war, terrorism, corporate ruthlessness and corruption, and harsh global realities are examined in a thrilling, action-fuelled style that has enough authenticity and atmosphere to sink the reader into the story' Crime Thriller Hound

'Think Jack Reacher and then some. This book is adventurous and fascinatingly topical. The author brings home to us the realities of the world today with themes of global exploitation and discomfort' Tracey Book Lover

'Hardisty writes with incredible passion and technical precision and the reader can never be quite sure who is good and who is bad, which keeps the reader gripped to the end … an epic reading experience that will have them yearning to know what happens next' Segnalibro

'What I thought was going to be a forgettable pageturner actually turned out to be something far more thoughtful, both on a wider scale and at a more personal level as the story examines the dehumanising effect of conflict on Straker. The writing is beautifully descriptive, Yemen is vividly and evocatively brought to life, yet alongside this the action is often unflinchingly and brutally violent' Karen Cole

'Far from being your average pageturner, Hardisty has a superb command of language, creating evocative images of a land which many will be unfamiliar with. The issues covered are very contemporary with seemingly impossible battles against overbearing figures and organisations. It's an exciting, absorbing and provocative stormer' Kevin Freeburn

'A brilliant thriller, with so many twists and turns it will make you dizzy' Tracy Shephard

'At 430 pages it is a longer read than many other books I have read lately but is so beautifully written that you won't mind its length one bit. In fact by the end you'll find yourself wishing it was a little longer' Gunnar Davíðsson

'Hardisty portrays the milieu (its rugged topography and, in judicious glimpses, its history) so well' Detectives Beyond Borders

'The story is gritty, action packed and topical … prepare to be wowed by a new kid on the block' The Library Door

'Despite its panoramic scope – personal, political and cultural – this worthy sequel to Hardisty's gripping debut is never a difficult read. If one or two plot twists are signalled, many more are side-swipingly unexpected. Building on the strengths of *The Abrupt Physics of Dying*, it hooks you in from the start and challenges you to try putting it down before – breathless and exhausted – you reach its shocking and satisfying conclusion' Claire Thinking

'I was literally on the edge of my seat and was scared to carry on reading, as by that time there were a few characters that I was drawn to and I wanted every one of them to get out of it alive. *The Evolution of Fear* is an edge-of-your-seat thriller that comes at you fast and hard' By the Letter Book Reviews

'This is a fine action thriller that also impels the reader to consider big issues from the real world. I was emotionally hooked by the imagery, suffering a sense of loss as profit was pursued despite the cost. It is testament to the skill of the author that he can convey a difficult message whilst never compromising on the pace or excitement. Read this for the pleasure of an edge-of-your-seat adventure. You will be offered so much more' Never Imitate

'I read a lot of thrillers, and they can become formulaic after a while. Paul E. Hardisty has just set the bar impossibly high … *The Evolution of Fear* is just superbly written, taut and excellently constructed. With echoes of Terry Hayes *I Am Pilgrim*, this book just knocks it out of the park in terms of what I look for when I want to read a thriller' Bibliophile Book Club

'There is so much happening in this book that I think the phrase "action packed" was coined especially for it!' Damp Pebbles

'It's the sort of book where you can barely pause for breath … It really should come with a warning! This is a fast-paced and intelligent thriller, with a dashing hero and some cute turtles!' Northern Crime

'Feels like James Bond at his best – a perfect distilling of contemporary fears, producing a final product which is pure action. While Bond fought communists and nuclear annihilation, Straker's enemies are fundamentalism and environmental destruction. But Straker is a much more palatable hero for our times: a damaged man, who will inevitably lose something more of himself before the novel is over' Crime Fiction Lover

'The plot burns through petrol, with multiple twists and turns, some signposted, some completely unexpected' Vicky Newham

'The feelings evoked stayed with me a long time after I finished the last page and I cannot recommend it highly enough' Crime Book Junkie

RECONCILIATION FOR THE DEAD

Canadian by birth, Paul Hardisty has spent twenty-five years working all over the world as an engineer, hydrologist and environmental scientist. He has roughnecked on oil rigs in Texas, explored for gold in the Arctic, mapped geology in Eastern Turkey (where he was befriended by PKK rebels), and rehabilitated water wells in the wilds of Africa. He was in Ethiopia in 1991 as the Mengistu regime fell, and was bumped from one of the last flights out of Addis Ababa by bureaucrats and their families fleeing the rebels. In 1993 he survived a bomb blast in a café in Sana'a, and was one of the last Westerners out of Yemen before the outbreak of the 1994 civil war. Paul lived, worked and travelled throughout the Middle East and Africa for over a decade, including in Saudi Arabia, Lebanon, Jordan, Egypt and Syria. The first two novels in the Claymore Straker series, *The Abrupt Physics of Dying* and *The Evolution of Fear*, received great critical acclaim and *The Abrupt Physics of Dying* was shortlisted for the CWA John Creasey (New Blood) Dagger. Paul is a sailor, a private pilot, keen outdoorsman, martial artist, and lives in Western Australia with his family.

Reconciliation for the Dead

PAUL E. HARDISTY

**ORENDA
BOOKS**

Orenda Books
16 Carson Road
West Dulwich
London SE21 8HU
www.orendabooks.co.uk

First published in the United Kingdom by Orenda Books 2017

A catalogue record for this book is available from the British Library.

ISBN 978-1-910633-68-7
eISBN 978-1-910633-69-4

Typeset in Garamond by MacGuru Ltd
Printed and bound by CPI Group (UK) Ltd, Croydon CRO 4YY

SALES & DISTRIBUTION

In the UK and elsewhere in Europe:
Turnaround Publisher Services
Unit 3, Olympia Trading Estate
Coburg Road
Wood Green
London
N22 6TZ
www.turnaround-uk.com

In USA/Canada:
Trafalgar Square Publishing
Independent Publishers Group
814 North Franklin Street
Chicago, IL 60610
USA
www.ipgbook.com

In Australia and New Zealand:
Affirm Press
28 Thistlethwaite Street
South Melbourne VIC 3205
Australia
www.affirmpress.com.au

For details of other territories, please contact *info@orendabooks.co.uk*

Glossary

B&C gear – biological and chemical protection suits.

BOSS – South African secret police, the Bureau of State Security.

Boy – South African army slang for terrorist members of SWAPO, the South West Africa People's Organisation.

Casevac – evacuation of casualties by helicopter.

Chana – a Portuguese word for an elongated, grass-covered, natural clearing in the bush, ubiquitous throughout Southern Angola.

Doffs – Afrikaans slang: idiots.

FAPLA – *Forças Armadas Populares de Libertação de Angola,* military wing of the MPLA, the *Movimento Popular de Libertação de Angola* (Popular Movement for the Liberation of Portugal), supported by the Soviet Union and its allies.

Flossie   Army slang for C-130 Hercules four-engine military transport plane.

FRELIMO – *Frente de Libertação de Moçambique*, the major political party in Mozambique. Formed in 1962 to fight for the liberation of Mozambique from Portugal.

Lekker – Afrikaans slang: nice, sweet.

LZ – Landing Zone.

MAG – General purpose machine gun used by South African paratroopers in the border war; fired 7.62 mm rounds from belts of two hundred.

Okes – Afrikaans slang: guy.

OP – Observation Post.

Parabat – Army slang for South African paratrooper, also *vliesbom* (meat bomb).

Poppie – Afrikaans slang for doll.

R4 – Standard issue 5.56 mm calibre assault rifle of South African
   Army; the South African-made version of the Israeli Galil rifle;
   semi-automatic.

Rat packs – Army slang for ration packs.

RENAMO – *Resistência Nacional Moçambicana,*
   militant organisation in Mozambique. Sponsored by
   the Rhodesian Central Intelligence Organisation (CIO),
   founded in 1975 to counter the country's ruling communist
   FRELIMO party.

Rofie – Afrikaans slang: new guy.

Rondfok – Afrikaans slang: literally 'circle fuck'.

RV – Rendezvous point.

SAAF – South African Air Force.

SADF – South African Defence Forces.

SAMS – South African Army Medical Services.

Seun – Afrikaans: son.

Sitrep – Situation report.

SWAPO – South West African People's Organisation, national
   liberation movement of Namibia.

UNITA – *União Nacional para a Independência Total de Angola,*
   South Africa's ally in the struggle against communism in Angola.

Valk – Afrikaans for hawk, the designation for a platoon of South
   African Army paratroopers, approximately thirty men.

Vlammies – Afrikaans, short for *Vlamgat,* meaning 'flaming hole,'
   slang for French-made Mirage jets used by the South African Air
   Force (SAAF) during the war.

Vrot – Afrikaans slang: wasted, intoxicated.

1911 – Type of handgun, originally developed in the USA as the
   M1911; single-action, magazine-fed weapon whose design has
   been adopted by numerous manufacturers worldwide.

'The most incomprehensible thing about the universe is that it is comprehensible'

A. Einstein

'In times of war, the law falls silent'

Marcus Tullius Cicero

For my father

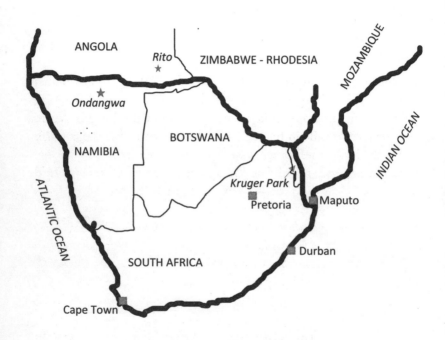

Prologue

12th October 1996
Maputo, Mozambique

Claymore Straker stood in the long bar of the Polana Hotel, drained the whisky from his glass and looked out across gardens and swaying palms to the drowning mid-afternoon chop of the Indian Ocean. For the second time in his life, he'd been forced to flee the country of his birth. Two weeks ago he'd crossed the border, made his way to the ocean, and arrived here. Back again in the land of spirits, he'd determined that, this time, he would disappear forever.

And then Crowbar had showed up.

Just how his old platoon commander had managed to find him, he still had no idea. Crowbar had simply lumbered into the little café near the *Parque de Continuadores* and sat opposite him as if meeting for coffee in Mozambique was something they did every day.

They didn't talk long. Ten minutes later he was gone, vanished into the braying confusion of the city.

And Crowbar had been right, of course. About the things you couldn't change. About the apportionment of blame. About everything. But the relics Crowbar had left on the table that day – the canister of 35 mm film now clutched hard in Clay's right fist, still undeveloped after all these years; the blood-stained notebook now thrust deep in his jacket pocket – had changed everything. History has a way of orbiting back at you; and promises, he now knew, while they may be broken, never die.

After he'd made the decision, it had taken the better part of a week to track her down. Time he didn't have. In the end it had been Hamour, a one-time colleague of hers from Agence France Presse in Istanbul, who had provided the breakthrough. Although Hamour hadn't spoken to her for more than six months, he'd heard that she'd gone to Paris. He'd given Clay the name of an associate on the foreign desk there. It was enough. Clay had been able to convince the guy that he had a story worth telling, and that only she could tell it.

He'd had her number for over twenty-four hours now, but each time he'd picked up the phone, he'd stopped mid-dial, overcome. He wasn't sure why, exactly. Perhaps it was because of the burden he'd asked to her carry once before, the guilt he still felt. Maybe it was because of what they'd almost shared – and then lost. Memory is a strange, malleable, and, he had come to realise, wholly undependable quantity. And nothing, it seemed, was immune from time's inexorable winnowing, that hollowing erosion that, eventually, pulled the life from everything.

'*Mais um*,' Clay said, pointing to his glass. One more.

The barman poured. Clay drank.

It hadn't been that long ago, really. Thirteen years. He'd arrived here in late '81, in the middle of a civil war; left in early '83. And now he was back. The place looked different, the whole city built up now – all the new peace-time buildings. Even this hotel, the grand old lady of Maputo, had undergone a facelift. The old, caged, rosewood elevator was still here; the bar with its marble tiles and teak counters; the same palm trees outside, that much older. But so much of the past had been shaken off like dust, the dead skin of years peeled away in layers. And now that he was back in Africa, it was as if he'd never left.

A uniformed bellhop approached and glanced at Clay's stump, the place where his left hand should be. '*Senhor?*' That look on the guy's face.

Clay nodded, reached under his jacket, ran the fingers of his right hand across the rough meshed surface of the pistol's grip.

'Your call is through, *Senhor.*'

Clay finished his drink and followed the bellhop to the telephone cabinets near the front desk. He scanned the lobby, closed the door behind him and picked up the phone.

'*Allo?* Who is this?' Her voice. Her, there, on the other end of the line.

He could hear her breathing, her lips so close to the mouthpiece, so far away.

'Rania, it's me.'

A pause, silence. And then: 'Claymore?'

'Yes, Ra. It's me.'

'*Mon Dieu,*' she gasped. 'Where are you, Claymore?'

'Africa. I came back. Like you told me to.'

'Claymore, I didn't…' She stopped, breathless.

'I need your help, Rania.'

'Are you alright, Claymore?' The concern in her voice sent a bloom of warmth pulsing through his chest.

'I'm … I'm okay, Rania.'

'*C'est bon, chéri.* That is good.' And then in a whisper. 'I'm sorry for what happened between us, Clay.'

'Me too.'

'Thank you so much for the money. It has made a big difference.'

'I'm glad.'

'I never thanked you.'

He wasn't going to ask her.

'Are you going to testify, Claymore? Is that why you are there?'

'I've already done it.'

'That is good, *chéri.* I am proud of you. How was it?'

As he'd left the Central Methodist Mission after the first day, the spectators had lined both sides of the corridor, three and four deep. At first, they stood in shocked silence as he walked past. But soon the curses came. And then they spat on him.

Clay cradled the handpiece between his right shoulder and chin, covered his eyes with his hand a moment, drew his fingers down over the topography his face, the ridgeline of scar tissue across his right cheek, the coarse stubble of his jaw. He breathed, felt the tropical air flow into his lungs.

'I need your help, Rania. It's important.'

A long pause, and then: 'What can I do?'

'I need you to come to Maputo.'

'Mozambique? Is that where you are?'

'Yes.'

'When?'

'As soon as you can.'

Voices in the background, the screams of children, a playground. 'Rania?'

'Clay, *cheri*, please understand, it is not so easy. I have obligations.'

'I have a story for you, Rania, one the world needs to know.'

'Clay, I … I cannot. I am sorry. Things have changed. I am very busy.'

'A lot of people have died for this, Rania.'

A sharp intake of breath.

'And it's still going on. The guy is still in his post. After all this time. It's fucking outrageous.'

'Slow down, Claymore.'

'I tried to find him, Rania. They said he was in Libya, but I know he's still here.'

'Who, Claymore? Who are you speaking of?'

'*O Médico de Morte.*'

'Claymore, please. You are not making sense. Is that Portuguese? "The Doctor of Death"?'

'That's what they called him in Angola, during the war. I never told you about it. It was too … too hard.' There were a lot of things he hadn't told her.

'What does this have to do with you, Claymore?'

'I don't have time to explain now, Rania. You have to come.'

'Let me think about it, Claymore. I need some time, please. Can I call you back?'

'When?'

'At least a few days. A week.'

'I don't have that long, Rania. They're after me.'

'*Mon Dieu*, Claymore. What is happening?'

'I can't tell you over the phone, Rania.'

'Who is after you? What is going on, Claymore?'

'I'll tell you when you get here.'

'Alright, Claymore. Call me in two days. I will see what I can arrange.'

'Thanks, Rania. Two days. This time. This number.'

Clay was about to hang up when he heard her call out.

'Claymore.'

'What is it Rania?'

'Clay, I—'

'Not now, Rania. Please, not now.'

Before she could answer, Clay killed the line. He cradled the handpiece and walked across the polished marble of the lobby to the hotel's front entrance. A porter held the door open for him. He stood on the front steps and looked out across the Indian Ocean. The sea breeze caressed his face. He closed his eyes and felt time fold back on itself.

Part I

1

No Longer Knowing

Fifteen Years Earlier: 22nd June 1981,
Latitude 16° 53'S; Longitude 18° 27'E,
Southern Angola

Claymore Straker looked down the sight of his South African Arm-scor-made R4 assault rifle at the target and waited for the signal to open fire.

For almost a year after leaving school to enlist, the targets had been paper. The silhouette of a black man, head and torso, but lacking dimension. Or rather, as he had now started to understand, lacking many dimensions. Blood and pain – surely. Hope and fear – always. But more specifically, the 5.56 mm perforations now wept blood rather than sunlight. The hollow-point rounds flowered not into wood, but through the exquisite machinery of life, a whole universe of pain exploding inside a single body – infinity contained within something perilously finite.

Just into his twenty-first year, Claymore Straker lay prone in the short, dry grass and listened to the sound of his own heart. Just beyond the tree line, framed in the pulsing pin and wedge of his gunsight, the silhouette of a man's head moved through the underbrush. He could see the distinctive FAPLA cap, the man's shoulders patched with sweat, the barrel of his rifle catching the sunlight. The enemy soldier slowed, turned, stopped, sniffed the air. Opal eyes set in skin black as fresh-blasted anthracite. At a hundred metres – less – it was an easy shot.

Sweat tracked across Clay's forehead, bit his eyes. The target blurred. He blinked away the tears and brought the man's chest back into focus. And for those few moments they shared the world, killer and victim tethered by all that was yet to be realised, the rehearsed choreography of aim and fire, the elegant ballistics of destruction. The morning air was kinetic with the hum of a trillion insects. Airbursts of cumulus drifted over the land like a year of promised tomorrows, each instant coming hard and relentless like a heartbeat. Now. And now. And above it all, the African sky spread whole and perfect and blue, an eternal witness.

A mosquito settled on the stretched thenar of Clay's trigger hand, that web of flesh between thumb and forefinger. The insect paused, raised its thorax, perched a moment amidst a forest of hairs. It looked so fragile, transparent there in the sun, its inner structure revealed in x-ray complexity. He watched it flex its body then raise its proboscis. For a half-stalled moment it hovered there, above the surface of his skin, and then lanced into his hand. He felt the prick, the penetration, the pulsing injection of anaesthetic and anti-coagulant, and then the simultaneous reversal of flow, the hungry sucking as the insect started to fill itself with his blood. Clay filled his sights with his target's torso, caressed the trigger with the palp of his finger as the insect completed its violation.

Come on.

Blood pumping. Here. There.

Come on.

The mosquito, heavy with blood, thorax swollen crimson, pulled out.

What are we waiting for?

He is twenty, with a bullet. Too young to know that this might be the moment he takes his final breath. To know that today's date might be the one they print in his one-line obituary in the local paper. To understand that the last time he had done something – walked in the mountains, kissed a girl, swam or sang or dreamed or loved – could be the last time he ever would. Unable yet to comprehend that, after he was gone, the world would go on exactly as if he had never existed.

It was a hell of a thing.

The signal. Open fire.

Clay exhaled as he'd been taught and squeezed the trigger. The detonation slamming through his body. The lurch of the rifle in his hands. The bullet hurtling to its target. Ejected brass spinning away. Bullets shredding the tree line, scything the grass. Hell unleashed. Hades, here. Right here.

The target was gone. He had no idea if he'd hit it. Shouting coming from his right, a glimpse of someone moving forwards at a crouch. His platoon commander. Muzzle flashes, off to the left. Rounds coming in. That sound of mortality shooting into the base of his skull, little mouthfuls of the sound barrier snapping shut all around him.

Clay aimed at one of the muzzle flashes, squeezed off five quick rounds, rolled left, tried to steady himself, fired again. His heart hammered in his chest, adrenaline punching through him, wild as a teenage drunk. A round whipped past his head, so close he could feel it on his cheek. A lover's caress. Jesus in Heaven.

He looked left. A face gleaming with sweat, streaked with dirt. Blue eyes wide, staring at him; perfect white teeth, huge grin. Kruger, the new kid, two weeks in, changing mags. A little older than Clay, just twenty-one, but so inestimably younger. As if a decade had been crammed into six months. A lifetime.

'Did you see that?' Kruger yelled over the roar. '*Fokken* nailed the *kaffir*.'

Clay banged off the last three rounds of his mag, changed out. 'Shut up and *focus*,' he yelled, the new kid so like Clay had been when he'd first gone over, so eager to please, so committed to the cause they were fighting for, to everything their fathers and politicians had told them this was about. It was the difference between believing – as Kruger did now – and no longer knowing what you believed.

And now they were up and moving through the grass, forwards through the smoke: *Liutenant* Van Boxmeer – Crowbar as everyone called him – their platoon commander, shouting them ahead, leading as always, almost to the trees; Kruger on Clay's left; Eben on his right, sprinting across the open ground towards the trees.

They'd been choppered into Angola early that morning; three platoons of parabats – South African paratroopers – sent to rescue a UNITA detachment that had been surrounded and was under threat of being wiped out. A call had come in from the very top, and they'd been scrambled to help. UNITA, *União Nacional para a Independência Total de Angola* – South Africa's ally in the struggle against communism in Southern Africa – were fighting the rival MPLA, the *Movimento Popular de Libertação de Angola*, and its military wing FAPLA, *Forças Armadas Populares de Libertação de Angola,* for control of the country. UNITA and MPLA were once united in their struggle to liberate Angola from Portugal. But when that was achieved in 1975, they split along ideological lines: MPLA supported by the Soviet Union and its allies; UNITA by South Africa and, some said, America. That was what they had been told by the Colonel of the battalion, anyway. The Soviets were pouring weapons and equipment into FAPLA, bolstering it with tens of thousands of troops from Cuba, East Germany and the Soviet Union itself, transforming FAPLA from a lightly armed guerrilla force into a legitimate army. As a consequence, things were not going well for UNITA, and it was up to *them* to do everything they could to help. South Africa was in mortal danger of being overrun by the communists; their whole way of life was threatened. This was the front line; this was where they had to make their stand. Everything they held dear – their families, their womenfolk, their homes and farms – all would be taken, enslaved, destroyed if they were not successful. It was life or death.

Clay remembered the day he left for active service, waiting at the train station, his duffel bag over his shoulder, his mother in tears on the platform, his father strong, proud. That was the word he'd used. Proud. He'd taken Clay's hand in his, looked him in the eyes, and said it: *I'm proud of you, son. Do your duty.* It was just like in the books he'd read about the Second World War. And he had felt proud, righteous too, excited. He couldn't quite believe it was happening to *him*. That he could be so lucky. He was going to war.

That was the way he remembered it, anyway.

Clay reached the trees – scrub mopane – Kruger and Eben still right and left, on line. They stopped, dropped to one knee. It was the middle of the dry season, everything withered and brown. Crowbar was about twenty metres ahead, standing beside the body of a dead FAPLA fighter, the radio handset pushed up to his ear, Steyn, his radio operator, crouching next to him. By now the shooting had stopped.

'What's happening?' said Kruger.

Eben smiled at him. 'That, young private, is a question for which there is no answer, now or ever.'

The kid frowned.

Eben took off his bush hat, ran his hand through the straw of his hair. 'And the reason, kid, is that no one knows. The sooner you accept that, the better it will be. For all of us. Read Descartes.'

Clay glanced over at Eben and smiled. Another dose of the clean truth from Eben Barstow, philosopher. That's what he called it. The *clean truth*.

Kruger looked at Eben with eyes wide. 'Read?' he said.

Eben shook his head.

Crowbar was up now, facing them. He looked left and right a moment, as if connecting with each of them individually. And then quick, precise hand signals: hostiles ahead, this way, through the trees, two hundred metres. And then he was off, moving through the scrub, the radio operator scrambling to keep up.

Kruger looked like he was going to shit himself. Maybe he already had.

'Here we go, kid,' said Eben, pulling his hat back on. 'Stay with us. Keep low. You'll be fine.'

And then they were moving through the trees, everything

underfoot snapping and cracking so loud as to be heard a hundred miles away, a herd of buffalo crashing towards the guns.

The first mortar round hurtled in before they'd gone fifty metres.

It landed long, the concussion wave pushing them forwards like a shove in the back. They upped the pace, crashing through the underbrush, half blind, mortar rounds falling closer behind, the wind at their backs, smoke drifting over them. Clay's foot hit something: a log, a root. Something smashed into his stomach, doubling him over, collapsing his diaphragm. He fell crashing into a tangle of bush, rolled over, gasped for breath. And then, moments later, a flash, a kick in the side of the head, clumps of earth and bits of wood raining down on him. Muffled sounds coming to him now, dull thuds deep in his chest, felt rather than heard, and then scattered pops, like the sound of summer raindrops on a steel roof, fat and sporadic; and something else – was it voices?

He tried to breathe. Sand and dead leaves choked his mouth, covered his face. He spat, tearing the dirt from his eyes. A dull ache crept through his chest. He moved his hands over his body, checking the most important places first. But he was intact, unhurt. Jesus. He lay there a moment, a strange symphony warbling in his head. He opened his eyes. Slowly, his vision cleared. He was alone.

Smoke enveloped him, the smell of burning vegetation, cordite. He pushed himself to his knees and groped for his R4. He found it half buried, pulled it free and staggered to his feet. The sounds of gunfire came clearer now, somewhere up ahead. He checked the R4's action, released the mag, blew the dust free, reinserted it, sighted. The foresight was covered in a tangle of roots. Shit. He flipped on the safety, inspected the muzzle. The barrel was clogged with dirt. He must have spiked the muzzle into the ground when he fell, driven the butt into his stomach. Stupid. Unacceptable.

Ahead, the grind of *Valk* 2's MAG somewhere on the right, the bitter crack of AK47s. Smoke swirling around him, a flicker of orange flame. The bush was alight. He stumbled away from the flames, moved towards the sounds of battle, staggering half blind through the smoke. There was no way his R4 could be fired without disassembling and cleaning it. He felt like a rookie. Crowbar would have a fit.

By the time he reached Eben and the others, the fight was over. It hadn't lasted long. *Valk* 3 had caught most of the FAPLA fighters in enfilade at the far end of the airstrip, turned their flank and rolled them up against *Valk* 5. It was a good kill, Crowbar said. And *Valk* 5 had taken no casualties. One man wounded in *Valk* 3, pretty seriously they said: AK round through the chest, collapsed lung. Casevac on the way. They counted sixteen enemy bodies.

Crowbar told them to dig in, prepare for a counterattack, while he went to meet up with the UNITA *doffs* they'd just rescued. The platoon formed a wide perimeter around the northern length of the airstrip and linked in on both flanks with *Valk* 3 and *Valk* 2. Their holes were farther apart than they would have liked, but it would have to do. After all, they were parabats – South African paratroopers – the best of the best. That's what they'd been taught. Here, platoons were called *Valk;* Afrikaans for hawk. Death from above. Best body count ratio in Angola.

Once the holes were dug and the OPs set, they collected the FAPLA dead, piling the bodies in a heap at the end of the airstrip. A few of the parabats sliced off ears and fingers as trophies, took photos. Behind them, the trees blazed, grey anvils of smoke billowing skywards. Clay stood a long time and watched the forest burn.

'Once more ejected from the breach,' said Eben, staring out at the blaze.

Clay looked at his friend, at the streaks of dirt on his face, the sweat beading his bare chest. 'Where's Kruger?'

Eben glanced left and right. 'I thought he was with you.'

'I got knocked down before we got fifty metres. Never saw anyone till it was all over. Never fired a shot.' He showed Eben his R4.

'I never took you for a pacifist, *bru*.' Eben jutted his chin towards the pile of corpses. 'You must be very disappointed to have missed out.'

Clay gazed at the bodies, the way the limbs entwined, embraced, the way the mouths gaped, dark with flies. This was their work, the accounting of it. He wondered what he felt about it. 'I better get this cleaned, or the old man will kill me,' he said.

Eben nodded. 'I'll go find Kruger. No telling what trouble that kid will get himself into.'

Clay nodded and went back to his hole. All down the line, the other members of the platoon were digging in, sweating under the Ovamboland sun. He dug for a while and was fishing in his pack for his cleaning kit when Eben jogged up, out of breath.

'Can't find Kruger anywhere, *bru*. No one's seen him.'

'He's got to be around somewhere. Crowbar said no casualties. Did you check the other *Valk*?'

'Not yet.'

Clay shouldered his R4. 'Let's go find Crowbar. Maybe he's with him.'

They found *Liutenant* Van Boxmeer towards the western end of the airstrip, radioman at his side. He was arguing with a black Angolan UNITA officer dressed in a green jungle-pattern uniform and a tan beret. The officer wore reflective aviator Ray-Bans and carried a pair of nickel-plated .45 calibre 1911s strapped across his chest. Beyond, a couple of dozen UNITA fighters, ragged and stunned, slouched around a complex of sandbagged bunkers. As Clay and Eben approached, the two men lowered their voices.

Clay and Eben saluted.

Crowbar looked them both square in the eyes, nodded.

'Kruger's missing, my *Liutenant*,' said Eben in Afrikaans.

Crowbar looked up at the sky. 'When was he seen last?'

'Just before the advance through the trees,' said Clay.

Crowbar's gaze drifted to the muzzle of Clay's R4. Clay could feel himself burn.

'Find him,' said Crowbar. 'But do it fast. FAPLA pulled back, but they're still out there. Mister Mbdele here figures we can expect a counterattack before nightfall.'

'*Colonel*,' said the UNITA officer.

'What?' said Crowbar.

'I am *Colonel* Mbdele.' He spoke Afrikaans with a strong Portuguese accent. His voice was stretched, shaky.

'Your *mam* must be so proud,' said Crowbar.

Eben smirked.

The Colonel whipped off his sunglasses and glared at Eben. The thyroid domes of his eyes bulged out from his face, the cornea flexing out over fully dilated pupils so that the blood-veined whites seemed to pulse with each beat of his heart. 'Control your ... your men, *Liutenant*,' he shouted, reaching for the grip of one of his handguns. A huge diamond solitaire sparked in his right earlobe. His face shone with sweat. 'We have work here. Important work.'

Crowbar glanced down at the man's hand, shaking on the grip of his still-holstered pistol. 'What work would that be, exactly, *Colonel*?' he said, jutting his chin towards the FAPLA men lounging outside the bunker.

As the Colonel turned his head to look, Crowbar slipped his fighting knife from its point-up sheath behind his right hip.

Mbdele was facing them again, his nickel-plated handgun now halfway out of its holster, trembling in his sweat-soaked hand. The metal gleamed in the sun. Crowbar had closed the gap between them and now stood within striking distance of the UNITA officer, knife blade up against his wrist, where Mbdele couldn't see it.

'FAPLA will attack soon,' shouted Mbdele, his voice cracking, his eyes pivoting in their sockets. He waved his free hand back towards the bunker. 'This position must be defended. At all costs.'

Crowbar was poised, free hand up in front of him now, palm open, inches from Mbdele's pistol hand, the knife at his side, still hidden. Clay held his breath.

'And what's so *fokken* important that you brought us all this way, *meu amigo*?' said Crowbar in a half-whisper.

Mbdele took a step back, but Crowbar followed him like a dance partner, still just inches away.

'I said, what's so *fokken* important?'

'Classified. Not your business,' shouted Mbdele, spittle flying. 'These are your orders. Your orders. Check. Call your commanders on the radio.'

Crowbar stood a moment, shaking his head and muttering something under his breath. 'And here are your orders, *Colonel,*' he said. 'You and your men get the *fok* out there and cover our left flank, in case FAPLA tries to come in along the river.'

Sweat poured from the Colonel's face, beaded on his forearms. '*Não, Liutenant,*' he gasped as if short of breath. 'No. We stay here. *Aqui.*' He pointed towards the bunker complex. '*My* orders are to guard this. And *your* orders are to protect us.'

Clay glanced over at Eben. It was very unusual for a UNITA officer to question their South African allies. The Colonel was treading a dangerous path with the old man. Just as odd was UNITA clinging to a fixed position. They were a guerrilla force, fighting a much larger and more heavily armed opponent. They depended on movement and camouflage to survive.

Eben frowned, clearly thinking the same thing: whatever was in that bunker, it must be pretty important.

'Our orders are to assist,' said Crowbar. Clay could hear the growing impatience in his voice. 'That means we help each other.'

The Colonel glanced back at his men. 'I am the ranking officer here, *Liutenant.*'

Crowbar's face spread in a wide grin. 'Not in my army, you ain't.' Then, without taking his eyes from Mbdele, he said: 'Straker, tell the men to get ready to move out.'

Clay snapped off a salute.

'What are you doing?' blurted the Colonel. 'You … You have orders.'

'Help us, Colonel, and we'll help you,' said Crowbar, calm, even. 'We're short-handed here. Outnumbered. Get your men out onto our flank or we *ontrek*. Your choice, *meu amigo.*'

The Colonel tightened his hand on his pistol grip. 'This is

unacceptable,' he shouted. '*Inaceitável.*' He rattled off a tirade in Portuguese.

Crowbar stayed as he was, feet planted, knife still concealed at his side. 'Try me, asshole.'

The UNITA Colonel puffed out his cheeks, glaring at Crowbar, trying to stare him down.

Crowbar jerked his head towards Clay and Eben. 'Move out in ten. Get going.'

Clay and Eben hesitated.

'Now,' said Crowbar.

Clay and Eben turned and started back to the lines at the double.

They'd gone about ten meters when they heard the Colonel shout: 'Wait.'

Clay and Eben kept going.

Then Crowbar's command. 'Halt.' They stopped, faced the two officers.

'I will send half my men to the left flank,' said the Colonel.

Crowbar muttered something under his breath. 'Tell them to report to *Liutenant* DeVries.' He pointed towards the bush beyond the bunker. 'Over there.'

For a moment the Colonel looked as if he was going to speak, but then he swallowed it down.

It happened so fast Clay almost missed it. Mbdele was down on the ground, his gun hand in an armlock, the point of Crowbar's knife at his throat, his 1911 in the dirt under Crowbar's boot heel. Mbdele wailed in pain as Crowbar wrenched his arm in a direction it was not designed to go.

'You ever *think* of pulling a weapon on me again, *meu amigo*,' said Crowbar, loud enough so that Clay and Eben could hear, 'and it will be the last thing that goes through that fucked-up up brain of yours.'

And then it was over and Crowbar was walking away, leaving Mbdele sitting in the dirt rubbing his arm.

'*Fokken* UNITA *bliksem*,' muttered Crowbar, falling in beside

Clay and Eben. 'I trust those *fokkers* about as much as I trust the whores in the Transkei.'

Eben grinned at Clay. 'Quite the get-up. Those twin forty-fives.'

Crowbar glanced at Eben, but said nothing.

'Did you see his eyes?' said Eben. 'He was wired up tight.'

'*Fokken vrot*,' said Crowbar, slinging his R4. '*Fokken* pack of drugged-up jackals.'

'What's so important about this place, my *Liutenant*?' said Clay.

Crowbar stopped and squared up to Clay. 'What's it to you, troop?'

Clay stood to attention. 'I just meant, those bunkers…'

'They're important because I say they're important, Straker.'

'They don't seem like much.'

Crowbar leaned in until his mouth was only a few inches from Clay's face. 'The only thing you need to know is right there in your hands. Understood?'

'*Ja, my Liutenant*,' said Clay, rigid.

'And that goes for you too, Barstow. Couple of *fokken* smart-arse *soutpiele*.' Salt-dicks. English South Africans. 'Now get out there and find Kruger. Take that black bastard from 32-Bat with you.'

'Brigade,' said Clay. 'His name is Brigade, sir.'

'I don't give a *kak* what his name is,' said Crowbar. 'He's our scout, he knows the country. Take him with you.'

Clay nodded.

'And do it quick, Straker. Cherry like Kruger, you don't find him by nightfall, he's as good as dead.'

Clay and Eben started moving away.

'And Straker,' Crowbar called after them.

Clay turned, stood at attention.

'I catch you again with your weapon in that state, and the commies'll be the last thing you have to worry about. I'll shoot you myself.'

**South African Truth and Reconciliation Commission
Transcripts.
Central Methodist Mission, Johannesburg,
13th September 1996**

Commissioner Ksole: And you are here, why, Mister Straker?

Witness: To tell the truth, sir.

Commissioner Ksole: The truth. Why now, Mister Straker? It was a long time ago.

Witness: Because, sir, it's killing me.

Commissioner Ksole: Do you wish to apply for amnesty, Mister Straker?

Witness: If that's possible, yes, sir. I do.

Commissioner Ksole: Can you please tell the commission, are you the same Claymore Straker who is wanted for murder and acts of terrorism in Yemen?

Witness: Those charges have been dropped, sir.

Commissioner Ksole: And, Mister Straker, in Cyprus, also?

Witness: I served time in prison in Cyprus, yes, sir.

Commissioner Ksole: And you provide this testimony of your own free will?

Witness: Yes, sir.

Commissioner Ksole: And you understand, Mister Straker, that any information provided here can, and if necessary will, be used against you in a court of law if the circumstances warrant? That this commission has the power to recommend legal action against a witness if it sees fit?

Witness's answer is unintelligible.

Commissioner Barbour: Speak up, Mister Straker, please. Do you understand the question?

Witness: Yes sir, I do. Can and will be used against me.

Commissioner Barbour: And this incident – this series of incidents – occurred on the, ah, the border, during the war in Angola. Is that correct?

Witness: Yes, sir. While I was serving with the 1st Parachute Battalion, SADF. It was my third tour, so it would have been 1981.

Commissioner Barbour: And the UNITA Colonel, Mbdele. Did you know him by any other name?

Witness: No, sir. Not then.

Commissioner Barbour: And later?

Witness: Yes, sir. The people called him *O Coletor*.

Commissioner Barbour: Sorry?

Witness: It's Portuguese, sir: 'the Collector'.

Commissioner Barbour: Thank you. Did you ever find out what was in the, ah, the bunker?

Witness: Yes, sir, we did.

Commissioner Barbour: What did you find, son?

Witness does not answer.

Commissioner Barbour: Son?

Witness: The truth, sir. We found the truth.

Commissioner Rotzenburg: It says here, in your service records, Mister Straker, that at the time of your dishonourable discharge from the army you were suffering from mental illness, including extreme instability, episodes of random violent behaviour, complex and consistent delusions, and persistent hallucinations. Do you know what the truth is, Mister Straker?

Witness does not respond.

Commissioner Rotzenburg: Answer the question, please.

Witness. Yes.

Commissioner Rotzenburg: Yes, what?

Witness: Yes, sir.

Commissioner Barbour: That's not what he meant, son.

Witness: Yes, I … I've learned to…

Commissioner Rotzenburg: Learned to what, Mister Straker?

Witness: I've learned to distinguish.

2

Death Rhumba Psychosis

The counterattack still hadn't come.

They found Brigade with *Valk* 2. He'd just returned from patrol and was reporting his findings to *Liutenant* de Vries when Clay and Eben arrived with Crowbar's orders.

'Lost?' said Brigade, looking up at Clay from under the peak of his bush hat. He was built like a mopane tree – hard withered core, dark sinewed limbs. He wore a jungle camo uniform and carried an AK-47. He had the darkest skin Clay had ever seen on a human being.

Clay nodded. 'No one's seen him since the attack.'

'It's my fault,' said Eben.

'No blame,' Brigade said in Afrikaans. 'Come.'

They searched through the afternoon, moving along the line, the parabats jumpy in their holes, answering in crisped tones: No, we haven't *fokken* seen him.

They kept going. A while later, the sound of gunfire from down the line, back from where they'd come: R4s, AKs, sporadic, gone on the breeze a few seconds later, a rumour.

They traversed all the way to the river, found a few UNITA fighters strung out there on the left flank, loose, undisciplined. They eyed Brigade warily, like hyenas, watching him until they were out of sight.

'What's their problem?' said Eben.

Brigade just shrugged.

No one had seen Kruger.

They reported back to Crowbar. He told them to widen their

search radius. Find him before nightfall. And take care. The shooting they'd heard earlier was FAPLA scouts probing *Valk* 3's lines. No one had been hurt. Yet.

They trudged back out through the browned grass, past the edge of the airfield, the FAPLA *poes* lounging around the bunkers as if on holiday, and then into the adjacent *chana,* weapons ready, scanning the bush. Where the hell could Kruger have gone? Had he been taken prisoner? Become separated and got lost? It was so easy to become disoriented out here, one *chana* so similar to the next, the sun burning in a flawless sky, the bush a brown monotony, no landmarks to guide you.

They walked on through the long dry grass, the breeze rippling the bladed sea around them, shivering through the green and yellow leaves of the mopane trees, dotted like islands. They saw no one.

A couple of hours before dusk they spotted vultures circling about a mile off. Near the edge of a small copse of mopane they found the carcass of a slaughtered elephant. Vultures scattered as they approached. There were more than twenty entry wounds in the thick grey hide. Brass scattered on the ground nearby, 7.62 mm, Russian. The tusks had been hacked off and carried away.

They moved on. A gust of wind brought a whiff of wood smoke, the lingering retch of death. They had just emerged from the copse when all three stopped and stared out across the clearing. Rotting in the sun, thick with flies, dozens of big dirt-covered bodies hulked in the grass.

'Jesus,' said Clay.

Eben doubled over, retched.

'Listen,' said Brigade.

A low moan drifted on the breeze, a whimpering that sounded almost human.

'What the hell is that?' Eben clutched his nose.

They picked their way through the slaughter towards the sound. Thick clouds of flies filled the air. Vultures hopped away as they approached, stood watching them, wings poised ready for take-off, their heads and necks red with blood. After they passed the birds went back to their work.

By the way the bodies of the elephants were grouped, it looked to be an entire extended family. Babies still close to their mothers, the big matriarch to the front where she'd faced up to the attackers, trying to protect her tribe. Her body was riddled with bullet holes. Her face had been cut away. A bloody chainsaw with a twisted blade lay discarded beside her.

When they found the source of the whimpering, Eben turned away and bent over, hands on his knees. It was a baby elephant. It had been trapped under its mother when she was killed, its little hind legs crushed under her enormous bulk. It looked no more than a few months old. Trapped and defenceless, the attackers had removed its tiny milk tusks while it was still alive. The baby elephant looked up at them with big dark eyes, called to them with its thin, end-of-life voice, the gaping bloody holes where the tusks had been hacked out already crawling with flies.

Clay staggered back. It was as if the creature was looking right at him, asking him to explain this abandonment, this end.

Brigade raised his AK47 and put a bullet through the little elephant's skull.

They kept going. No one spoke. A pair of hyenas circled off in the distance, ambling towards the feast.

'Maybe he was captured,' said Brigade some time later, when they'd stopped to drink. They were the first words he'd spoken since they'd started out.

'Maybe,' said Clay, wiping his mouth. If so, God help him.

'You are Angolan?' said Eben. Bat-32, the Buffalo Battalion, was a special unit of the SADF, based in the Caprivi, on the border. It was comprised largely of black Angolan volunteers. The NCOs and officers were white – South African regulars, Rhodesians, a few American mercenaries.

'My father is Angolan,' he said. 'I lived here as a boy. Then I moved to South Africa with my family.'

'And now?'

'My father is a doctor in Soshanguve Township. Near Pretoria.'

Clay nodded. The townships. You are a year out of high school – a private white high school, with uniforms and real-grass playing fields for cricket and rugby, and a swimming pool – and until a few months ago you lived with your parents in a big house with a big garden, and black garden-boys and a black cook and a black house-maid who lives out back in a little shack, and she has been with your family since you were a baby, but the rest of them came in every morning on a bus from somewhere and disappeared again in the evening back to that same place. What do you say to this wizened old man, easily thirty, maybe older, grey attacking his temples, out here with you now, a brother in arms, when he says he's from that very township?

Brigade looked into Clay's eyes. 'One day, I will take you there,' he said. 'You can meet my family.'

Clay nodded. What could he say? Sure, *broer*, anytime. We'll just waltz into the township and have Sunday dinner with your family, as if it were something that people just did. He stashed his canteen. 'Let's find Kruger.'

With the sun low in the sky, they looped back towards the airstrip, moved into the charred ash of the woods, the ground through which they'd advanced earlier in the day. The fire had burned itself out and smoke rose in threads from the dying embers. Ash puffed and spun from their boots and floated about them like snowflakes in the Draakensburg as they threaded their way through the skeleton lat-ticework of blackened limbs, everything here quiet after the savagery of the morning.

When they finally found his trail the sun was half gone on the horizon, big and red so you could see the solar flares dancing on its surface, hot tongues flicking at the blushing sky.

Clay, on point, walked right past. So did Eben. It was Brigade bid them halt. He reached down and, pulling something from the ash, held it up for them to see. An old canvas bag, torn and burned. It had been ripped to shreds by the exploding ammunition it had contained. It was the remains of a Fireforce vest, just like the one Clay wore now, heavy tan canvas, six pouches across the chest for 30-round R4 magazines, the remains of the pouches for M27 fragmentation grenades along the sides. Brigade dropped it to the ground.

'Could be anyone's,' said Clay.

Brigade shook his head.

It was Eben who found the R4, not far away, scorched, rendered. A bit further on, the pack, similarly charred and blistered.

He'd been hit by shrapnel, they surmised, then dragged himself some distance, trying to escape the advancing bushfire. His uniform had been completely burned away, except for one side, where he'd curled up to try to protect himself from the flames. The corpse that was Johan Kruger, 1st Parachute Battalion, SADF, lately of a small town in the Transvaal, was charred beyond recognition, like meat on a *brai*, the hair and skin gone, a charcoal foetus.

If the wind had been blowing in the other direction, he would have lived.

But it wasn't and he didn't.

They wrapped him in a poncho and carried him back to their lines, reported to Crowbar. They shook hands with Brigade, thanked him.

Under a dark continent of stars, Clay and Eben hunched in their foxholes and opened rat packs, Kruger's corpse on the ground a few metres away. Eben fired up his primus stove and heated water for tea. The line was quiet and they didn't have to be out in the Listening Post until 0400.

Eben handed Clay a cup of steaming tea.

'Why do they hack the tusks out?' Clay said, blowing steam from his dixie. 'Why not just cut them off? That poor little bugger's tusks couldn't have been longer than a few centimetres.'

'One quarter of the tusk is below the surface,' said Eben.

They sat for a long time, silent.

After a while, Eben looked in the direction of Kruger's body. 'All those people back home, his family, still thinking he's alive, going about whatever it is they're doing as if nothing's changed.'

Clay said nothing.

'I should have realised he wasn't there,' Eben whispered. 'Gone to find him.'

Clay sipped his tea, rubbed his aching feet. 'It's not your fault, Eben.'

Eben's face was in darkness. Only the whites of his eyes shone out from beneath his bush hat. 'I thought he was with you.'

Clay said nothing. What was there to say?

'Poor bastard. Lying there with the fire coming towards him.'

'Don't, Eben,' said Clay.

'And there's nothing else, Clay. Do you understand? Nothing.'

Clay reached out for his friend's shoulder, but he pulled away.

'*This* is it,' whispered Eben. 'Just this. Twenty-one years. All eternity before, forever after. And I told him it was going to be alright.'

'Stop, Eben. Just stop talking.'

'I tried to tell him. I wonder if he understood.'

'Jesus, Eben. Put it away.' It was the only recourse.

'I can't, Clay. Not anymore. There's no more space.'

Eben had been in longer than Clay, over two years – more than double Clay's time. He'd done a couple of semesters at university before joining up – English literature and philosophy. Unlike so many, Eben had volunteered. Told anyone who'd listen that he wanted to be a writer, sat up late at night in camp scribbling in his notebook, playing rock and roll on his tape deck. A warrior poet, he said, in the best tradition of Siegfried Sassoon and Robert Graves. A veteran. Old at twenty-one. They'd met the first day Clay arrived in camp. Clay had produced a cassette of Pink Floyd's *The Wall*, banned in South Africa and hard to come by. They'd been friends ever since.

'*Koevoet*'s been out here since seventy-six,' Eben said, in a monotone. 'Is it even possible? Where can he put it all?'

'Comfortably numb, *broer*,' said Clay. 'He believes in what he's doing.'

Eben looked up so that the starlight bathed his face. 'Do you, Clay?'

'Do I what?'

'Believe.'

Clay finished his tea. 'Get some sleep, Eben.'

Eben froze. 'Did you hear that?' he whispered. Eben's hearing was legendary in the battalion. He swivelled his head, reached for his R4.

Clay's senses buzzed. He reached for his weapon, faced their front, stared out into the darkness, strained his ears. All he could hear was the insect roar of the African night. He glanced over at Eben, his eyes wide – a question.

Eben shook his head, turned towards the airstrip. That way, he indicated with his finger. 'There. Did you hear it?' he said after a moment.

Clay shook his head.

'Sounds like someone screaming,' whispered Eben. 'There, again.' He pointed towards the UNITA bunker at the far side of the *chana*.

Clay twisted in his hole, listened. There it was, a muffled shriek, high pitched. It sounded like a wounded animal. 'A jackal?'

'Don't know.'

They waited, staring into the night.

Again, moments later, the same high pitched wail, clearer now.

Eben clambered from his hole.

'Where are you going?'

'Check it out.'

'Crowbar will be pissed as hell if we abandon our position.'

'We're supposed to be sleeping,' whispered Eben.

'You know what he always says, Eben. Wandering around at night. Someone could mistake you for FAPLA, shoot at you.'

There it was again, longer this time. And something else too; another sound. Shouting? It was definitely coming from across the airstrip, in the direction of the UNITA bunker complex.

'What the hell are they doing over there?' said Eben moving off into the darkness.

'Shit,' muttered Clay, scrambling out of his hole and running after his friend.

They moved quietly through the darkness. They could see lights from the bunker complex now, thin pinpoints of glowing sulphur. The UNITA fighters were sloppy. They might as well have raised a neon sign. Clay and Eben crouched about fifty metres from the bunker's perimeter trench line. They scanned the dark ground ahead, the ridge of excavated sand. There was no movement.

And then again, the same sound, softer now, as if someone were crying, the sobs coming in a rhythm. Muffled laughter erupted from within the bunker; a group.

'Looks like they haven't bothered posting sentries,' whispered Clay.

'Surrounded by parabats, why bother?'

The crash of glass. Laughter now, clear.

'Bastards are having a *fokken* party,' said Eben. 'After Kruger died saving their sorry carcasses.'

And before Clay could answer, Eben was up and sprinting towards the trench line. Clay scrambled to his feet and followed his friend.

'Eben,' he called after him, a whispered shout. 'What are you doing? Stop, *bru.*'

But Eben was in full flight. Clay saw him slow, jump, and disappear into the trench. Clay sprinted after him and jumped down into the excavation. Eben was up against one side of the slumped sand wall, R4 ready. They were alone.

'*Bru.*' Clay reached for his friend's shoulder, breathing hard. 'Crowbar finds out about this, we catch major shit.'

Another scream, louder now, a banshee wail. Sobs. A sharp crack. The pulsing rhythm of Cuban rhumba music.

'What the hell?' said Clay.

Then glass breaking. Laughter, more shouting.

Eben twisted away. 'Bastards,' he hissed. His face was contorted, covered in sweat, his eyes wild, as if gripped by some strange psychosis. 'They want to have a party? I'll give them a *fokken jol.*' He chambered a round and started down the trench towards the sound.

Clay started after him. 'Eben. Leave it *bru*,' he called.

But Eben was already out of sight, gone down a zag in the trench. Clay could see the glow of the lights, the noise of the party coming clear now. Then the sound of impact, *thunk*, a muffled grunt. Clay turned the corner.

Eben was there, a UNITA fighter crumpled at his feet. Eben looked back at Clay, eyes aflame, a lunatic grin spreading across his face. The bunker was a couple of metres away, a tarpaulin draped down over the entrance, strips of kerosene lamplight shining through the edges.

A scream pierced the night.

Eben paused, looked down at the man at his feet, up at the stars, back at Clay. For a moment, Clay thought he might turn back. But then he pivoted, whipped the tarp aside with the barrel of his weapon and disappeared into the bunker.

3

Won't Get Out of Here Alive

Clay followed Eben in.

What he saw would stay with him until the day he died, would be among the last images shuddering through his by then tortured brain.

Blinding light, after the darkness of the African night. Eben silhouetted against burning kerosene, his shoulders broad, his R4 levelled at the hip. The overpowering smell of men – close, hot – of breath and sweat and killing having been done and more to come. The unmistakable musk of semen. The naked sweating backs of a dozen UNITA fighters, the din of raised voices, a rhumba baseline of grunted chants, and above it a single, high-pitched wail. And all along the walls of the bunker, stacks of what looked like logs, some pale, long and curved, others straighter, dark, knotted. Cases, too – wooden ammunition crates. Muslin sacks about the size of apples scattered atop a small table. Eben standing there, unmoving, the men cheering now, backs turned, still unaware of their presence.

Clay grabbed one of the sacks, stood next to Eben.

'Let's *ontrek, bru*,' whispered Clay. 'Before they see us.'

Eben said nothing.

Chanting now, the men roaring in a chugging rhythm, hoarse, the higher pitched accompaniment just a murmur now.

'What the *fok* are they doing?' whispered Clay.

And then the crescendo, a roar, bottles tipped to mouths, heads thrown back. The crowd swayed, parted, and the UNITA Colonel was there, facing them, still wearing his sunglasses, hiking up his trousers, his dick swinging wet and dripping in the yellow light. He stopped dead, staring at them.

Behind him, a woman. She'd been laid on her back across a table. She was naked, her legs spread wide, ankles tied to the table legs, arms stretched above her head, wrists bound. Her vulva glistened. Semen dribbled from its dilated centre. Blood oozed from her anus. Another man, trousers at his knees, stepped towards her, penis erect, teenage hard. Her chest heaved with sobs.

Clay's stomach turned.

'*Jesus Moeder van God,*' muttered Eben.

The Colonel, recovering now, buttoned his trousers, cinched up his belt, and opened his arms wide. '*Amigos,*' he said. 'My South African friends. Welcome.' He smiled, revealing two rows of strong, ivory teeth. By now all the UNITA men were facing them, big eyed, hyper alert. All except the man who'd now taken position between the woman's legs and had begun thrusting.

The Colonel grabbed a bottle from one of his men and offered it to Clay and Eben. 'Join us,' he said.

Clay could see the veins in Eben's neck filling, hardening.

The Colonel snapped his fingers, motioned to one of his men. A bare-chested soldier held out a palm of white tablets. His pectorals and abdominal muscles were like rope, coiled, defined, slick with sweat.

'Take,' said the Colonel. 'Good shit.'

'What the *fok* is going on here?' said Clay.

'The spoils of war,' said the Colonel, smiling big. A few of his men laughed. 'You want?'

Clay raised his rifle. 'No I fucking do not want. Let her go, you animal, or I'll put a bullet in your head.'

No one moved. Silence, except for the woman's sobs, her assailant's grunts.

One of the UNITA men reached for an AK47 leaning against the cut sand wall. Eben trained his rifle on the soldier, shook his head. The man dropped his hand to his side.

'There is no need for this,' soothed the Colonel. 'We are friends here, allies.' He thrust out the bottle again. 'Please. Have a drink.'

'Tell him to stop,' said Clay. 'Untie her.'

The Colonel stood unmoving. His men, too. Confusion in their faces. Euphoria there, too. Lust. Chances were, none of them spoke Afrikaans. The man kept fucking, oblivious.

'You heard me' said Clay. '*Pare*,' he shouted in Portuguese. Stop.

The man doing the raping turned back to face them, adjusted his angle by grabbing the woman's hips, flashed a gap-toothed grin, upped his pace.

'Be reasonable,' said the Colonel. 'Two of you. Seventeen of us. Many more in the next bunker. Many.'

Clay gave him his best fuck-you smile. 'Wrong, asshole. You're surrounded by three platoons of parabats. Kill us, you're dead. Every last one of you.'

'So this is what we came here to protect?' said Eben, clearly struggling to control the tremor in his voice. 'What Kruger died for? A bunch of drugged-up rapists.' He flicked his R4 to auto, steadied it on his hip.

'Let her go and we can all walk away,' said Clay.

The Colonel dropped the bottle to his side, looked left and right. 'Then we have a dilemma, my friends. This woman is an MPLA traitor. A traitor. A political officer attached to the FAPLA battalion that's out there trying to kill us. She is our prisoner.'

Eben's R4 was up now, sighted at the Colonel's head. The woman shrieked as her assailant pounded harder.

'I don't care what she is,' shouted Eben. 'Make him stop now, or I swear you're dead.'

The Colonel said something over his shoulder. The man kept fucking.

Eben took a step forward. At that range the bullet would take the Colonel's head off. But if he was scared, he didn't show it; he just stood staring right back at Eben.

'Stop,' yelled Eben.

'He will stop,' said the Colonel.

Just then the man groaned, spasmed, stood a moment on unsteady legs, then staggered back with his trousers around his ankles.

'*Diere*,' muttered Eben. Animals.

Clay could feel the situation hovering on the boundary between states, that thinnest of lines separating liquid from vapour, right from wrong, life from death. He needed to break the cycle. Keeping his right hand on the pistol grip of his R4, finger on the trigger, he hefted the muslin sack he was holding in his left palm. It felt like a bag of marbles. 'What's this?' he said.

The Colonel removed his sunglasses. 'That is none of your concern.' He slid his glasses into his breast pocket. 'Put it down and leave and I will not report any of this to your *Liutenant*.'

'On the contrary,' said Clay. 'He will be very interested.'

The Colonel had moved his hand slowly across his chest. It now rested on the still-holstered grip of his pistol.

'Try,' hissed Eben, 'and I swear to God you're dead.'

The Colonel moved his hand away.

Using his teeth, Clay untied the drawstring on the bag and poured half the contents onto the sand floor. A scatter of clear, grey stones.

'*Kak*,' breathed Eben.

'What?'

'Diamonds,' said Eben.

That involuntary kick deep inside. Wealth. The power to shape your life, to get what you wanted, when you wanted it. It felt a lot like lust. Clay hefted what remained in the bag, a small fortune there in his palm.

The Colonel stood stiff, saying nothing, his men too.

Clay scanned the bunker. Stacks of hardwood logs – ebony, mahogany – worth thousands of dollars on international markets. And closer to the entrance, the tapered arcs, a lustrous cream, with bloodied roots. Elephant tusks, hundreds of them.

The Colonel eyed the uncut diamonds winking in the sand. 'Perhaps there is a way out of this impasse,' he said.

'Go on,' said Clay.

'You and your friend. Take that bag and go. That will be the end of it. No one will ever know.'

Clay considered it. He couldn't help it. What was this handful of rocks worth? A million dollars; two? Jesus. He swallowed.

'Two young men, still with so much to live for,' the Colonel said. 'You will never have to work again.'

Eben glanced over at Clay, a deep frown creasing his forehead. 'Keep it,' he said. And then to Clay: 'Give it to him, *bru*.'

Clay weighed the bag in his hands, tried to estimate again the mass, the worth. He closed his eyes, slid the bag into his jacket pocket. 'I tell you what,' said Clay, shifting his feet in the sand. 'Untie the woman, let us take her into custody. In return we won't mention this little hoard of yours to our *Liutenant*.'

'And we won't shoot you,' said Eben.

The Colonel's thyroid eyes bugged out, whiteless.

'I'm sure you can see the tactical situation, now, Colonel,' said Eben. 'We can take all of this, if we wish. Kill you all, blame it on FAPLA. It seems to me that, logically, you have little choice.'

The UNITA men shifted, murmuring amongst themselves. The woman was crying now, a pitiful whimper that threaded the room with guilt. The sound sent Clay's heartrate higher. Anger catalysed in his brain, pulled at its chains.

'Ridiculous,' said the Colonel.

'Really?' said Clay. 'Seems a good deal to me. We get the woman, you get to keep all of this.'

'You won't get out of here alive,' said the Colonel, his voice shaking now.

'Neither will you,' said Clay, starting to depress the trigger. 'Any of you.'

He was absolutely prepared to do it. Had seen enough death and violence over the past nine months to do just about anything. Was still able to sleep at night.

Fuck it.

☾

Commissioner Barbour: Would you say that at this point you were, ah, you were desensitised to it - to the violence?

Witness: I think we all were, yes. I didn't think about it then. But I've since come to realise that it had already started to change me, fundamentally.

Commissioner Lacy: Yes, we understand. It is important that you share your personal impressions of that time with this commission. You say the experience changed you. Can you tell us how?

Witness: All I could think about for a long time was that baby elephant. It bothered me a lot more than any of the other stuff. You lose your faith. In the government, in people, in God. I still think about it. It's hard to talk about.

Commissioner Lacy: But that is why you are here, is it not?

Witness: I suppose so, ma'am.

Commissioner Lacy: Was rape widespread?

Witness: Not in our unit, ma'am. I never witnessed anything like that from our troops.

Commissioner Lacy: But from our allies at the time, UNITA?

Witness: From what I know, yes, it was. On both sides.

Commissioner Lacy: Would you say that rape was used systematically - as a weapon of war?

Witness: It's not really like that, ma'am. I mean, both sides, FAPLA and UNITA, were using female soldiers. So I guess the distinction goes away. They're just combatants, like anyone else. They're trying to kill you. You're trying to kill them. So when they're taken prisoner, it's just another violence that you do. I mean, there's no difference. It just spills over, becomes part of the whole thing.

Commissioner Lacy: I'm not sure I understand.

Witness: There are no rules, no boundaries, for anything.

Commissioner Lacy: And yet, you tried.

Witness: I'm still trying, ma'am.

4

Damaged Neurochemistry

And of course, you never know at the time. Decisions you make, with insufficient information, on a whim, in the cauldron of a moment, pivot the course of your life entire. Equilibria that have existed for months or years shatter, and new states are entered, where perhaps, like water, conventions are upended, and exceptions to the rule become the norm, the solid less dense than the liquid, and because of it, life is possible, or for some, impossible. The laws of thermodynamics require that it be so. And so, rather than married with a beautiful wife and three lovely children, living quietly in some happy suburb, you end up alone in a hotel room on the coast of Mozambique, a decade and a half later, with the barrel of a gun in your mouth, staring out at the desert of your life, wondering where it all went wrong. And in your pain, you realise that it all started right there, with that one choice.

No one moved. The Colonel staring down the muzzle of Clay's R4. The air close and hot, potent. The woman splayed and whimpering, begging in Portuguese, *por favor, me matar, me matar*. Please, just kill me. A dozen men rooted to the ground, eyes flicking back and forth, their weapons scattered about the room. Eben talking to himself in a low whisper, a habit of the last few months: 'Come on you bastards, fucking animals, come on, just try it.' Some kind of mantra, a liturgy of hate, his R4 on full auto, at the hip, ready to cut down as many of them as he could in whatever time he'd have. Clay realising that Eben would do it – had the *bossies*, some of the troop said: bush dementia. Just the fact that they were here, now, proved it true.

Clay could see the Colonel shaking – with rage or fear or both, he couldn't know. He was staring right at Clay now, deciding.

'I'll take the right,' Eben said in English, breaking out of his trance, voice neutral.

Clay watched the Colonel registering these words, not understanding them.

'You take left. Don't hit the woman.'

'There's too many, Eben.'

'Inside out. Do it. My signal.'

Clay flicked his R4 to auto, heart rate critical. Shit.

The Colonel's eyes widened. He'd seen Clay's thumb flick the lever, knew what was about to happen.

'Give us the woman, and we go,' said Clay in Afrikaans. And then louder, in Portuguese: '*A mulher, e nós vamos*. Last chance.'

'He's not going to do it,' said Eben in English. 'He can't lose face. We have to hit first.' That's what they'd been taught, Crowbar pummelling it into their heads day after blood-soaked day. Hit first, hit hard. 'Ready?'

Clay flooded his lungs, exhaled. 'Start filling out the DD1,' he said. The SADF's punishment charge form. 'That or the death certificates.'

'On three.'

Clay nodded. How did it come to this?

'One.' *Um. Een.*

The Colonel tensed. Held his breath. Why now, here?

'Two.' Eben's voice steady now, veteran. *Dois. Twee.*

Clay tightened his finger on the trigger, a void opening up inside him. No reason for any of it.

The Colonel opened his mouth.

Eben hung on it.

'*Que a mulher ir*,' the Colonel shouted. And then in Afrikaans: 'Let the woman go.'

No one moved.

'Do it,' the Colonel shouted.

Clay felt something flood back into him.

Two men moved towards the woman, started untying her.

'You will regret this,' said the Colonel in Afrikaans, staring at Clay as if to peel back his scalp. 'Believe me. You will.'

Clay said nothing, vaguely aware of some sort of life being restored somewhere within. He kept his sight on the Colonel's forehead, where it had been for the last – what had it been? Seconds? Minutes? Half an eternity.

They had the woman up now, supported under each arm. Her hair hung over her face like a veil. Rope cuts bloomed on her wrists and ankles. Semen slicked down her dark thighs.

'Bring her,' said the Colonel.

The two men dragged her across the sand. She was limp, lifeless.

The Colonel straightened, pulled down the hem of his uniform jacket. 'I formally remand this prisoner into your custody.'

The men threw her to the ground at Clay's feet. She lay in a heap, unmoving.

Eben hissed between his teeth.

'You have what you wanted,' said the Colonel, gaze fixed on Clay's jacket pocket. 'Now return what is mine.'

Clay reached into his pocket, closed his fist around the bag of raw diamonds. Looking back, he wasn't sure what had motivated him. It may have been avarice or greed; revenge perhaps – a need to inflict hurt. Whatever the reason, Clay withdrew his hand, left the diamonds where they were.

The Colonel's eyes bulged. 'Give it to me,' he hissed.

Clay raised his rifle. 'Consider it payment for services rendered,' he said.

The Colonel took a step forwards but Eben checked him with a jerk of his R4.

'That is my property,' shouted Mbdele. 'Mine.'

'Cover me, said Clay,' slinging his R4, kneeling beside the woman.

'Your *Liutenant* will hear about this,' screamed the Colonel, his whole body shaking.

'Your best friend,' said Eben, smiling big.

Clay lifted the woman, cradling her in his arms like a bride.

Eben indicated the entrance with his head, his R4 still trained on the men. 'Get her out, back to our lines. I'll stay here until you're clear. Go.'

'We go together.'

'No way, *bru*. You carrying her? Too slow. We'd be easy targets. Get her out and back, I'll follow.'

Then Clay realised: Eben was going to do them. He could feel it, see it in his friend's eyes. Take out as many of them as he could.

'Don't do it, Eben. It's not worth it.'

Eben stood, whispering to himself again, gibbering like some drugged-up township preacher.

'Race war, *broer*,' said Eben. 'Not my doing. Been put here, *bru*.'

'They'll kill you. You can't get them all.'

'Go. Now.' Eben was shouting now. 'Go, damn it. There's no other way.'

The Colonel and the other UNITA men stood motionless, as if sensing the tottering pile of stones on which their future was built, their fate if the thing tipped the wrong way.

'I'm not moving, *bru*. Not until you promise me. Walk away. No shots fired.'

Eben stood muttering to himself, finger twitching on the R4's trigger, shaking his head to the cadence of some opaque philosophy playing in his mind. 'Go. Get her out of here.'

'We go together.'

'Consequences,' Eben said. 'I am only what I believe and what I do. Nothing more.'

Clay shook his head. 'Promise me, *bru*.'

Eben glanced at him, at the woman, back at the soldiers. 'Fuck me, Straker. Okay. Fine. Whatever you want. Just go.'

They were out of time. All of them. 'Okay, Eben. Okay. No shooting.'

Eben sighed, as if letting go of something. 'Okay.'

Clay turned, swung the tarpaulin aside and emerged into the star-lit clarity of night, some strange kind of threshold just crossed.

He ran as fast as he could, this stranger's naked body heavy and close in his arms. Her eyes were closed but she was breathing. After a few steps she raised her arms, wrapped them around his neck, held on tight. Halfway across the airfield he stopped, turned back towards the bunker, listened, peered into the darkness. No sound. No Eben. What the hell was he doing?

It took Clay a few minutes to find his hole. As he approached, a voice rang out in the darkness.

'Password.' Afrikaans.

Clay stopped. '*Fokken rooi gevdar*,' he shouted back. The red danger. The reason they were all here. 'It's Straker.'

'*God verdoem*, Straker, what are you doing out there?' It sounded like de Koch.

'Went for a *kak*. Eben's following.'

De Koch muttered something.

Clay jumped down into his hole. Holding the woman with one arm, the weight of her on his knee, her arms tight around his neck, he fumbled with his groundsheet, spread it over the sand. He tried to lay her down, but she wouldn't let go of his neck.

They stayed holding each other in the cold for a long time. He listened for Eben, to her breathing, felt the warmth of her, the smell of tears and sweat and dirt and sex and blood coming to him as catalysts, reactants bonding with his own damaged neurochemistry. She was shivering.

After a while her clench loosened. Clay whispered to her, gently laid her down. He grabbed his field blanket, wrapped it around her. She was awake now, eyes open.

'*Está certo*,' he said. It's okay.

She nodded. Sat up. Brushed her hair from her face. He handed her his canteen. She took it in a trembling hand and drank. He gave her a biscuit from his rat pack. She took it and sniffed at it. He fired up Eben's stove and boiled some water, made tea. She wrapped her hands around the steaming dixie and sipped.

A few minutes later, Eben jumped into the hole. He stood a moment catching his breath. 'Jesus,' he said.

'Jesus,' repeated Clay, handing him a dixie of hot tea.

Eben sipped. 'That was close.'

Clay said nothing. There had been no shooting.

'How is she?'

'Alive.'

'Like us.'

'For now.'

'Do you think he'll tell Crowbar?'

'No idea. Maybe.' Clay looked at his watch: 0345. 'Now what, *bru*? We have to be at the LP at 0400.'

Eben sank down in his hole, drank his tea. 'We go out on LP. Towards dawn, we fire a few shots. Come back, say we captured her.'

'What, naked?'

'I'll go get a uniform from one of those FAPLA dead.'

'Jesus, Eben. You've gone *bossie, bru*. I swear it.'

'"No promise has been given you for this night".'

'What?'

'Seneca.' Eben shot off a smile, clambered back out of his hole, slung his R4. 'Back in a bit,' he said, and disappeared into the starlit darkness.

Clay hunched down in his hole and glanced at the woman.

'*Obrigado*,' she whispered.

He nodded, wondering if she'd try for his gun; try to kill him, escape. The thought turned confused and uncomfortable inside him, at odds with everything he'd been taught growing up: a woman something sacred, to be protected always. And now she was so close, him having just carried her, as naked and vulnerable as ever a creature was. So to think of her as an enemy ... He swallowed hard. The UNITA Colonel had said she was a political officer, whatever that meant.

'*O que você vai fazer?*' she said, handing him back the empty dixie. What will you do?

Clay hunched his shoulders. They could just let her go. Let her run off into the bush. No one would ever know. But she could be important, could have information that might save lives. And if Colonel Mbdele did tell Crowbar about what had just happened, they'd have to explain what they'd done with the prisoner.

'*Que está fazendo aqui?*' said Clay, his Portuguese poor. 'What are you doing here?' he repeated in Afrikaans.

'Fighting for my people,' she replied in Afrikaans.

'Me too.' That's what they tell me, anyway.

She pulled the blanket around her shoulders. 'I am not a soldier.'

'MPLA?'

She looked down for a moment, then back up at him, her face now just visible in the pre-dawn retreat of constellations. Bruises, a cut on her swollen lower lip, big, dark eyes. 'No.'

'FAPLA?'

'I said no.'

'SWAPO?' The South West Africa People's Organisation, Namibia's left-leaning independence movement, aligned with the MPLA.

The woman shook her head. 'My name is Zulaika. I am from a small village near Rito.'

Rito, an Angolan town not too far from here, about 180 kilometres from the border. 'What are you doing here, Zulaika? Tell me.'

She grabbed his sleeve. 'Please,' she whispered. 'Let me go. I am not a soldier.'

'You said you were fighting for your people.'

Slowly, she reached her hand towards Clay's R4.

He pulled it away.

'Not with this,' she whispered.

Clay checked his watch. Eben had already been gone ten minutes. If they didn't relieve Cooper and Bluey in the LP at 0400, they'd be screwed, put up on charges.

'I don't understand,' he said.

'Those men…' she stopped, hid her face in the blanket.

'UNITA.'

'These are not soldiers,' she hissed. 'They are criminals.'

Clay said nothing.

'And you help them. Give them weapons and money. Protect them.'

Clay shook his head. 'Not me.'

'South Africa. You.'

Clay looked down at the ground. 'What they did was wrong.' He could barely hear himself say it.

'You must help me,' she said.

Clay straightened, shook his head. 'You're a prisoner of war. We'll hand you over to military intelligence. You'll be well treated.'

The woman shook her head, wrapped her arms around herself.

Minutes passed. Eben was still not back. Clay scanned the length of the airstrip, the dull hulk of the UNITA bunkers just visible in the distance.

'They are using drug weapons,' the woman whispered.

'What did you say?'

'*Drogas,*' she said. '*Catalisadores.* For killing people. Black people.'

'What are you talking about?'

'You must let me go. Please.'

'Drugs for killing? Chemical weapons? Is that what you mean?' There had been persistent rumours over the past several months that FAPLA had acquired mustard gas from the Cubans and Russians, and intended to use it against UNITA, and, if necessary, South African forces.

She shook her head quickly, two, three times. 'No. Not that. Drugs. *O Médico de Morte*, he gives them.'

'What?' She was still in shock from what had happened. She wasn't making sense.

She repeated it in Portuguese. 'That's what we call him. The Doctor of Death.'

Clay shuddered. 'Who?'

The woman swivelled her head, put her finger to her lips. 'Please. They will kill me. You must let me go.'

Clay was about to ask her what the hell she was babbling about when Eben jumped back into the hole. He was breathing heavily. Sweat poured from his face. He dropped a blood-stained uniform jacket and trousers on the woman's lap. A cap with a bullet hole through the side.

'Put those on,' Eben said. 'We've got to get going.'

The woman held up the trousers, looked at them both.

Clay and Eben turned their backs as she dressed.

'What took you?' said Clay.

'Ever try undressing someone suffering from rigor mortis?'

Clay said nothing.

'I'll go and relieve Cooper and Bluey,' Eben said, clambering out of the hole. 'Hang back out of sight. Join me at the LP when they're clear.'

A few minutes later Clay and Zulaika followed in the darkness, Clay leading her along by the wrist. He found the LP and pushed her inside. A shallow depression scraped in the sand, a double row of sandbags out front, the thing covered over with mopane branches. Eben said that Bluey had reported no activity overnight. The woman cowered in the corner, knees pulled up to her chest, arms wrapped around her shins. Clay stood to next to Eben and gazed out into the night, watching the sky lighten. Somewhere out there, a battalion of FAPLA soldiers was intent on killing them.

'We should let her go,' said Clay after a while.

'She's a prisoner.'

'She told me she's not MPLA. Or anything else for that matter. Just a villager.'

Eben shook his head. 'What's she doing out here, then?'

'If we let her go, now, no one will ever know. No *rondfok*. Like nothing ever happened.'

'What if she is MPLA, gives away our position? No. It's too risky.'

The woman was listening to all of this, silent there in the back of the hole.

'She speaks Afrikaans,' said Clay. 'Well.'

'Just a villager?' said Eben. 'Not a chance.'

'That's what she said.'

'Crowbar will know what to do.'

'And that UNITA Colonel,' said Clay. 'What about him? What if he comes out and starts bitching to Crowbar? If we have the woman, it proves the Colonel's story. We'll be so deep in the shit we'll drown.'

'We'll say we captured her. Tell Crowbar the UNITA Colonel is a lying sonofabitch. Who's he going to believe?'

Clay looked down the length of his R4, out into the bush as the sun's edge bled into the morning sky, torching the horizon.

'Listen, *bru,*' said Eben, playing his R4 back and forth as he scanned the bush. 'We did what we did out of *principle*. This place is so fucked up I'm surprised I even remember what that looks like. She's a prisoner. We turn her in. It's the right thing to do.'

And before Clay could answer, Eben fired off three quick rounds.

Clay hung his head. The woman sobbed.

Seconds later, the radio crackled. It was Crowbar.

Eben tagged the handset. 'Wait one,' he said in Afrikaans.

Time slipped away. The sun rose red and angry over the Angolan bush. The heat came, and with it the flies.

Eben looked at Clay a moment, raised his eyebrows, keyed the handset. 'Contact,' he said. 'One prisoner. Appears to be a lone scout.'

5

Toronto Maple Leafs

By the time Clay and Eben reported to Crowbar's command post – a hole scraped into the sand at the northern end of the airfield – the sound of gunfire filled the morning stillness. Crowbar was standing in the open, radio handset to his ear, turning left and right as he gauged the sounds of battle surging across their front. He glanced at Clay, pointed to the ground near his feet, turned away, talking calmly in Afrikaans even as the first mortar rounds started to land.

Clay and Eben put a knee to ground where Crowbar had indicated they do so. The woman crouched between them in her bloody FAPLA uniform and cap. Stray rounds cracked over their heads.

Crowbar passed the handset to his radioman, stood looking down at them. 'This your prisoner, Barstow?'

Eben stood to attention. 'Yes, my *Liutenant*. A scout. She stumbled into our position.'

Above the sound of rifle fire and the scattered thump of grenades came a drone of engines, still far-off, to the south. Helicopters? Their extraction? It would be a good time to clear out. Clay searched the already too-blue sky.

Crowbar once-overed the woman, humphed. 'Weapon?'

'Forty-seven,' said Eben. 'Back in my hole. I was thinking of keeping it, if that's okay, my *Liutenant*.'

A surge of gunfire to the left: *Valk* 3 pouring on the fire. The whump of a mortar round exploding near the UNITA bunker.

'Probes on the right flank,' said Crowbar. 'FAPLA is hitting us hard on the left. We may be next. Barstow, get back to your position. Straker, stay here with the prisoner.'

Eben glanced at Clay, doubled away towards the firing.

'*Kak*,' said Steyn, the radioman, pointing across the airfield. '*Fokken* look at that.'

The UNITA Colonel, Ray-Bans glinting in the low-angle morning light, was striding towards them through the smoke.

Clay's insides twisted to a new level of anxiety. The woman reached up for his hand but he pushed her away.

'What the *fok* does *he* want?' said Crowbar.

Colonel Mbdele was still thirty metres away but he was already shouting, pointing at Clay and the woman. Clay couldn't make out his words over the roar of the firefight, but he knew the meaning.

Clay grabbed the woman by the arm and started back towards his hole.

'Where the *fok* are you going?' said Crowbar.

'I should be up on the line, sir. The attack's coming.'

Crowbar pointed at the ground next to him. No words. Your father indicating precisely where you were to stand. Clay obeyed.

The Colonel was with them now, cheeks puffing in and out, his face running with sweat, white dust covering his uniform. He was about to speak when the sky flashed, exploding in a roar. Burned kcrosene settled over them as a big silver Hercules banked away over the trees, wingtip close, turboprops screaming.

The Colonel glanced up at the aircraft, across at the woman, at Clay. He squared up to Crowbar, handgun pointing at the ground, and puffed out his chest. 'You must attack,' he said. 'Now. Tell your men to advance.'

Crowbar looked at the Colonel as if he'd come trying to sell him bibles or copies of the Koran.

'You must secure the airfield so the plane can land,' the Colonel continued. 'FAPLA is too close. You must push them back.'

As if to prove his point a mortar bomb sailed in over their heads, an 82 mm round. They could see it arcing through the air, dark and finned, a wingless bird. It seemed to hang there a moment at its apex, then fell and exploded harmlessly in the middle of the *chana*. Smoke and dust drifted over them.

Crowbar's previous calm was gone. He stepped to within a pace of the black man's face, jabbing him in the solar plexus. 'What the *fok* do you mean, coming in here in the middle of a firefight and telling me my job?'

The Colonel rocked back on his heels. 'I am telling you to secure this landing strip. Get on your radio, *Liutenant*. Check with your superiors, if you need confirmation.'

'Get me battalion,' Crowbar shouted to his radioman. 'Now. I've had enough of this *fokken* idiot.'

'And that is my prisoner,' the Colonel hissed, pointing at the woman. 'Hand her over to me now.'

The C-130 circled away to the south, a speck above the trees.

'This is our prisoner,' said Crowbar.

The Colonel reached into his pocket and pulled out a document. 'Here are her identity papers, *Liutenant*. This man,' he pointed his pistol at Clay, 'came into our position last night and took her from us at gunpoint.'

Crowbar grabbed the paper, stared down at it a moment, then at the woman, comparing the photograph to the dishevelled, bruised, dust-covered reality. He jammed the paper back into the Colonel's hand and wheeled on Clay, eyes wide. 'Ridiculous. Tell him, Straker.'

Clay looked down at his boots. Either the woman had been lying, or the Colonel was bluffing, was using some other person's papers. If he had to choose who to trust, he'd go with Zulaika. 'We captured her at dawn, sir, like Eben said, outside our LP. She must have been probing before this attack.'

The radioman passed Crowbar the handset. 'Battalion, sir.'

Crowbar keyed the handset, spoke, listened, looking off towards where his men were fighting for their lives. He kicked the dirt a couple of times, paced, talking again, the veins in his neck straining, the radioman following, twisting and turning as Crowbar wandered.

The Colonel glared at Clay then smiled at the woman. Clay could feel her shudder.

Finally, Crowbar thrust the handset back towards the radioman.

'Straker,' he said, eyes flashing high-altitude blue. 'Get back to *Valk* 5. Tell Sergeant DuPlessis to get ready to attack. Manoeuver left. Roll up the bastards' left flank. Wait for my command. Leave the woman here.'

Clay hesitated, Zulaika holding tight to his arm.

'I said get going, Straker,' Crowbar raising the handset to his ear.

'Don't hand her over to those bastards,' Clay said over a surge in gunfire from the left. 'Please, sir. They'll kill her.'

Crowbar stopped mid-sentence. 'Get back to DuPlessis with my message,' he said, as if meeting on the street, in a corridor somewhere. 'Now.'

The Colonel smirked.

Clay shrugged off the woman's hand and doubled back towards the line. There was nothing more he could do. That's what he told himself.

☾

It didn't take long.

FAPLA had concentrated their attack on the paras' left flank. When *Valk 5* surged up the middle and wheeled left, they caught FAPLA's main attacking force in enfilade, started rolling up their flank, just as Crowbar had planned. When it was over, what remained of the FAPLA battalion was in full retreat. They counted twelve FAPLA dead scattered in the bush, as many blood trails. De Koch had been clipped by an AK round when his MAG jammed, and Wessels had been hit in the arse by some shrapnel, but otherwise there had been no casualties. This time Clay hadn't fallen over, hadn't jammed his barrel into the ground. His R4 was clean, well-oiled and functioning perfectly, and for the third time in his life he'd used it to kill a human being. No doubt this time: the FAPLA soldier close, front on. Clay had sent two rounds into the man's torso, watched the bullets shred through the tissue, the explosion of red mist, the body crumpling lifeless to the ground, limbs twisted awkwardly beneath the weight of chest and head and shoulders. It had been a clean kill. He'd felt good. Excited. And alive, so alive.

Only much later would this same murder fill him with dread – nightly tremors carrying the sure knowledge of having done something so fundamentally wrong that good would forever escape him, and bad luck would thereafter be his shepherd. His best friend would die, as a result, after years in a coma. Others that he called friend would lose their lives. And so, too, the daughter he would never have.

Once the position was secure, Clay found Sergeant DuPlessis and volunteered to report back to the CP. He'd raced back to the airfield, the world so quiet after the cacophony of battle, just the sound of his footfall in the long grass, his breathing, the beating of his heart, and now, the whine of four big turbines approaching from the west. Crowbar was at the far end of the *chana*, checking on de Kock and Wessels, talking to the medic. The big C-130 thunked down onto the grass not far from where they stood, careened along the makeshift airstrip in a tornado of dust, the reversed props sending a cloud of debris billowing skyward.

The woman was gone. So was the UNITA Colonel. Clay's battle glow faded. He stood before Crowbar, reported the success of the action and passed on DuPlessis' message: low on ammo, water critical. Resupply or extraction needed soon. Crowbar nodded.

The C-130 was at the far end of the *chana* now, pivoting, taxiing back towards them, the sound of the turboprops modulating on the breeze, landing lights blinking through the dust.

'Our evac, sir?' said Clay, already somehow anticipating all those future times, good and bad, when these big four-engine brutes would signal the beginning and the ending of things, bring him home, take those he had tried to love away.

Crowbar didn't answer. He started towards the UNITA bunker, striding quickly to where the Hercules was rolling to a stop. The big transport swung around in a tight 180 until it was head to wind, the take-off length of the *chana* before it, engines idling, props turning, ready to take off. The pilot would know how vulnerable they were here, would be itching to get airborne again.

Clay followed Crowbar at a run.

The Hercules's rear ramp lowered. A man stepped out onto the grass and stood surveying the scene: the FAPLA bodies from yesterday's assault stacked like cordwood, the UNITA bunker, sunlight angling in the swirling propwash, dust, leaves and chaff spinning in the air. He wore faded blue jeans and a tight black t-shirt, a blue American-style baseball cap and tinted aviator glasses. A sidearm was strapped to his right thigh. He started towards the bunker with long, sure strides. He wasn't SAAF, that was sure.

A moment later a second man appeared on the aircraft's rear ramp. Shorter in stature, noticeably overweight, balding, with a thick black moustache, he wore a dark suit that looked a size too small and a white-collared shirt that bulged over his belt. The man hesitated at the edge of the ramp, pulled a handkerchief from his pocket and held it over his nose and mouth, looking out at the trampled, battle-scored *chana* as if it were a pit of boiling sulphur.

By now, Colonel Mbdele had emerged from the UNITA bunker and was walking out towards the plane. The man in the baseball cap waved to him and they met and shook hands. By now, the man in the suit had left the safety of the Hercules and was puffing his way across the browned grass towards Mbdele. He walked with a noticeable lurch, head down, as if suspicious of every square inch of this tortured country. With every step his dark suit seemed to lighten in colour as it accumulated a layer of fine, white dust.

Mbdele stiffened as the man in the suit approached. They spoke a moment and then Mbdele handed him something – a small, fist-sized bundle. The man in the suit inspected its contents, closed the bag and thrust it into his pocket.

Clay was beside Crowbar now, heard him mutter 'What the *fok*' as they approached Mbdele and the two white men. As they slowed to a walk, the man in the cap turned to face them, smiling through a short-trimmed fair beard, and thrust out his right hand. He was powerfully built, about six foot, taller than Crowbar. A tattoo of a coiled cobra flexed on his left bicep. 'Good to see you,' he said in Afrikaans. 'Well done securing the LZ. Nice flanking manoeuver, too, *ja*.' Strong Free State accent. Crowbar's part of the world.

By now, black UNITA soldiers had emerged from the bunker and were filing towards the plane. They struggled across the *chana*, each pair and trio loaded down under the weight of a thick, dark log. Some carried underhand, some with the logs hoisted onto their shoulders. The man in the suit stopped each pair, inspected the load, jotted something down in a small notebook, and then directed the men towards the Hercules' rear ramp.

Mbdele stood behind him, watching the process.

Crowbar shook Cobra's hand. 'Van Boxmeer. First Parachute Battalion.'

Cobra nodded. 'Yes, I know. Your reputation precedes.'

'And you are?' said Crowbar.

'That's classified,' said Cobra with another big smile.

'How exciting for you,' said Crowbar. 'Well, Mister Classified, I have wounded. We're low on ammo, water and food.'

Cobra looked back over his shoulder at the UNITA soldiers filing past, disappearing into the Hercules, then straggling back out without their loads.

'What the *fok* is going on here?' said Crowbar.

'Ebony,' said Clay.

'I know what the *fok* it is,' said Crowbar. 'And I didn't ask you, Straker.'

Now the tusks were being carried out of the bunker and onto the waiting plane. They were huge. By the wear at their tips, they'd been taken from big bull elephants, twenty, thirty years old. Some of them took four soldiers to carry. Clay had counted fifty-eight pairs so far.

'Did you hear what I said?' Crowbar took a step towards Cobra. 'We have wounded. They need casevac. Now.'

Cobra stood before them, implacable. The ivory kept coming. Seventy-two pairs now, including several tusks no more than half a metre long.

'Is this what it looks like?' said Crowbar.

'What does it look like?' said Cobra.

'Like you have no intention of getting my men out of here.'

'You're smarter than you look.'

'Just who the *fok* are you?' Crowbar was angry now, his eyes flashing dangerous fire-blue.

Cobra smiled again, that same distant cool, didn't answer.

They were almost finished the loading, now. The last of the UNITA fighters filed onto the Hercules then back out. Ninety-six pairs of tusks. The radio hissed.

Steyn, Crowbar's radioman, held out the handset. 'Sir, you'd better take this.'

Crowbar put the handset to his ear, listened a moment, spoke quickly, then passed it back to Steyn.

'Counterattack coming,' Crowbar said. 'Tanks. Looks like half a dozen T55s.'

Clay's heart wobbled, spiked. He'd never been up against tanks before, but he'd heard the stories from some of the older *okes*.

As if to prove the report correct, the tree line held by *Valk* 5 erupted in high explosive flame. The shock wave hit them a fraction of a second later, dissipated at that distance, but tangible, a push in the chest. Then the sound.

'*Jesus*,' muttered Steyn.

The man in the suit dropped to his knees and covered his head with his arms as the smoke and debris from the explosions washed over them. His face was dripping with sweat and the folds of flesh stacked above his collar wobbled as he gasped for air. His suit was now almost the colour of the *chana* itself. Slowly he got to his feet, brushing the dust from his trousers.

'*Dit is alles hier*,' he said. It's all here. The words shattered in his throat like broken masonry.

A surge of gunfire broke along the tree line. Mbdele frowned, nodded. By now the last of his men had scrambled back to the bunkers.

The man in the suit reached into his breast pocket and retrieved a small metal box about the size of a cigarette packet. He turned it over in his fingers a moment. 'But there is something missing, no?' he said in Afrikaans.

Mbdele hunched his shoulders, puffed out his cheeks 'No, it's all here,' he said, his eyes focused on the box. 'You counted.'

The man in the suit closed his fist around the box and shook his head slowly from side to side.

Mbdele looked like he was going to have a seizure. 'Please,' he cried. 'It's all there in the plane. You counted.'

'No,' shouted the man in the suit. 'Something is missing.'

'God damn you, Botha,' the Colonel yelled above the roar of the engines and the rising din of battle.

The man the Colonel had called Botha paused a moment, and then with a quickness that belied his bulk, turned and started walking back to the Hercules.

Mbdele stumbled after him. '*Por favor*,' he shouted. Please. '*Ela está aqui.*' She is here. Please.

Botha stopped and turned to face Mbdele. Mbdele signalled towards the bunker. Two UNITA fighters emerged from a trench and started across the open ground towards them. One carried a Belgian-made FN rifle slung across his shoulder, his right hand gripped hard around the other soldier's upper arm. The other soldier was smaller, barefoot. He looked up from under a peaked FAPLA cap.

Clay started. It was the woman, Zulaika. Fresh bruises blossomed on her cheekbones. Blood flowed from her nose and a cut on her upper lip.

Mbdele looked Clay straight in the eyes, grinned and wiped the sweat from his eyes. Botha handed Mbdele the box. Mbdele opened it, stared a moment at its contents, then snapped the metal lid shut and thrust it into his trouser pocket.

'Take her to the plane,' said Botha.

The UNITA soldier jerked her arm, started her towards the waiting C-130.

Before they'd gone three steps, Zulaika screamed, went limp, fell to the ground. The soldier wrenched her arm, pulling her to her feet.

Clay took a step forward, levelled his R4 at Mbdele. 'You're not taking her anywhere.'

Even as he did it, Clay knew he had crossed a threshold. After, he would come to see it not as a distinct line, but as a broad no man's land of decisions and circumstances, some within his control but most not, a boundary of shifting dimensions; time, space, circumstance, emotion and principle all swirling in an insoluble constellation. He watched it unfold as if disembodied, looking down at himself, rifle in hand.

Cobra had unsheathed his sidearm and was pointing it at Clay's head. It was a black Z88 Beretta 92: standard SADF issue. 'Control your men, *Liutenant*,' he said.

Another explosion ripped through the tree line, the sound of small arms shivering along the line, Steyn's radio going crazy now, sitreps coming in from every unit, Mbdele's nickel-plated handgun out now, too, pointed at Clay's face.

'What the *fok* are you doing Straker?' barked Crowbar.

'They'll kill her, Koevoet,' said Clay. 'Or worse.'

Crowbar breathed a sigh, looked back over his shoulder, and then whipped his R4 around, levelling it at Cobra. 'None of you are going anywhere until someone tells me what the *fok* is going on here.'

Steyn and the other UNITA soldier stood face to face, rifles pointed muzzle to muzzle. No one moved. Botha, who, until now, had seemed to ignore the presence of the parabats, directed his dark gaze at each of the soldiers, as if taking photographs of them.

The radio hissed, the word 'tank' coming across the frequency now, the voices stressed, insistent. Three deep lines creased Cobra's forehead. He glanced over towards the sounds of battle, the din terrific now, decibels louder than the Herc's engines, and then back at the plane. The pilot was waving frantically from the cockpit's open side-window. The engines cycled up. The propwash blew Zulaika's hair horizontal, sent Cobra's cap spinning away across the grass.

'Shit,' Cobra said. 'That was my favourite hat.'

Crowbar and Clay glanced at each other.

Cobra ran his hand through his hair. It was the colour of a Kru-gerrand, newly minted, four nines pure. He looked at Crowbar, at Clay, at the rifle pointed at his chest. 'Got it in Toronto a few years ago,' he said. 'Maple Leafs. You know – ice hockey.'

Clay could *feel* the 9 mm round in the chamber of the pistol now pointed at his head. Could see in everything about the man holding it that he was a marksman, a killer, some kind of Special Forces type, that he would have no hesitation in blowing Clay's brains across the dust of the *chana*.

The parabats were falling back, the tanks getting closer.

'I don't have time for this,' said Cobra, exhaling. He said it as if he were filling in a form at a bank.

'Make time,' said Crowbar. 'I've got all day.'

A shell screamed over their heads, detonated beyond the Herc.

'This mission comes from the top, *Liutenant*,' said Cobra. 'Radio your battalion commander if you like.'

Crowbar exhaled long. He'd called HQ earlier, when Mbdele had challenged him, and had been rebuffed, told to do everything he could to assist UNITA. 'My wounded,' he barked. 'Take them out.'

Cobra shook his head. 'No room.'

'Assholes like you give this war a bad name,' said Crowbar.

Cobra smiled. '*Dankie.*' Thanks.

Crowbar lowered his weapon. 'Go. I've got a real battle to fight.'

Clay kept his rifle aimed at Cobra's chest. 'Please, *Oom*,' – uncle, the Afrikaans word of respect – 'you can't let them take her.'

Another shell screamed in close overhead, ploughed into the ground just beyond the C-130. Debris pelted the aircraft's aluminium skin.

A bead of sweat tracked down the bridge of Cobra's nose.

Crowbar glanced at Clay. It felt like a punch in the head.

The Hercules' engines were powering up. The plane started to move forward. Cobra and Mbdele looked at each other and then back towards the plane.

As they did, Crowbar raised his rifle and fired. It happened so quickly no one had the chance to move, let alone register the action. The UNITA solider holding the woman spun to the ground screaming, his left thigh holed. Crowbar grabbed the woman, flung her towards Clay, flicked his R4 to auto, daring anyone move.

'You've got what you came for,' he shouted above the engines and the staccato of rifle fire. 'Now, unless you want to miss your flight, I suggest you piss off and let me do my *fokken* job.'

Mbdele and Cobra stood a moment, unsure what to do. The UNITA soldier lay whimpering, clutching his leg. Then Cobra shrugged, flashed a smile, and holstered his weapon.

'What are you doing?' screamed Botha. 'That is my prisoner.'

'Correction,' said Crowbar. 'This is my prisoner. Now, piss off before anyone else gets hurt.'

Cobra reached into his satchel, pulled out a half-litre plastic bottle, tossed it to Crowbar. 'Some water for you,' he said. 'See you around some time.' Then he turned and jogged off towards the now-moving Hercules. Mbdele glared at Clay, holstered his pistol and ran after Cobra.

Botha – if that really was his name – still hadn't moved; he stood alone now with three rifles pointed at his chest. He stared at each of them in turn and then leaned forwards at the waist. '*Jy dooie mense*,' he said above the noise of the battle. You're dead men. Then he turned and lumbered towards the plane, struggling in the Herc's propwash. He stumbled once, looked as if he wasn't going to catch the plane, but scrambled back to his feet and closed the gap, stepping onto the aircraft's rear ramp just as the pilots gunned the engines.

Soon the Herc was accelerating down the length of the *chana* in a cloud of dust. Clay stood watching as it clawed its way into the sky, tracers arcing up green and pretty behind it.

☾

Commissioner Ksole: And this man, the one who appeared to be making the exchange with the UNITA Colonel, were you aware of his identity?

Witness: At the time, I had no idea. Just the name, Botha. I … I only learned later who he was, who he worked for.

Commissioner Ksole: This was Botha?

Witness: Yes.

Commissioner Ksole: Are you sure?

Witness: I think that was his name, yes. One of his names anyway. May I ask: have you heard this name before, in these enquiries?

Commissioner Ksole: You may not.

Witness: Thought I'd ask.

Commissioner Ksole: So it was your commanding officer who initiated the confrontation with Botha?

Witness: No, sir. It was me. Crowbar, Liutenant Van Boxmeer, took a big risk, not letting them have the prisoner. He paid for it later. We all did.

Commissioner Lacy: And was this when you were wounded, Mister Straker, during this operation?

Witness: For the first time, yes.

Commissioner Lacy: Tell us about it, please, Mister Straker.

Witness: I'd rather not. It's not why I came here.

Commissioner Lacy: Please, indulge us.

Witness does not respond.

Commissioner Lacy: Are you alright, Mister Straker?

Witness does not respond.

Commissioner Barbour: Mister Straker, are you unwell?

Witness: Sorry? What was the question?

Commissioner Lacy: Tell us what happened, when you were wounded. The commission would like to know, for the record.

Witness: We had to fight our way back to the border. FAPLA was too close to airlift us out. They sent an armoured relief column instead. I was hit by a rocket fragment before we RV'd with the relief column. Cooper was killed. The guy from Valk 2 who was hit through the chest died, too.

Commissioner Lacy: Your service record shows that you were
    decorated as a result of this action.
Witness does not respond.
Commissioner Lacy: Mister Straker?
Witness: If that's what it says.
Commissioner Barbour: I think we should take a recess.
Commissioner Lacy: Thank you, Mister Straker.

Part II

6

1-Mil

25th June 1981,
1 Military Hospital, Pretoria, South Africa

When he opens his eyes he sees her for the first time.

Someone he could have loved, maybe, in some different world where people were free to indulge in such things. Someone he will think about, now and again, for the rest of his life.

This may hurt a little, she says, pulling away the bandages on his forearm. Her voice is gentle. He imagines her speaking to her children this way. If she has any. There is a ring on her finger.

How was that, she asks. Gentle, he says. You're gentle. She smiles, likes this, he thinks. It feels good that she likes it.

It looks a lot worse than it is. She tells him that he is very lucky. The fragment missed the ulnar artery. He is luckier than Cooper. The same rocket took off his legs. He died crying for his mother in a pool of blood so big Clay couldn't believe it had all come from one man.

He asks where this is. He remembers being stretchered onto a C-130 at Ondangwa, the medic slipping him a dose of morphine. Number 1 Military Hospital, Pretoria, she says. They brought you in yesterday. We operated right away.

He looks down at the scar running lengthwise along his forearm, then back up at her face. She has a delicate face, fair, with sun freckles across the bridge of her nose. Her nose is small, slightly upturned. You have beautiful eyes, he tells her. She does.

She seems not to react. There is no flutter of eyes, no reddening across her prominent cheekbones. She hears this all the time, he supposes. She checks his IV.

Like a Cedarburg river bed, he says. He will always remember saying that, thinking immediately after that he sounds like a twenty-year-old in love with his attractive nurse.

She stops and looks into his eyes, showing him inside hers. He sees sun-dappled currents, muscled water shifting clear and cold over smooth river stones. It jolts him. Chemicals jostle. He feels weak. Something inside him hollows out.

After a moment she tells him that they will keep him here for two weeks. He can report back to his unit after that. He tells her he'd rather just go back right away. He says it because he wants her to think him brave. And because he means it.

She picks up his chart, flips pages. It says here that you are engaged to be married, she says, looking up over the edge of the clipboard. You are entitled to receive visitors, you know. He knows. We can arrange some privacy for you. He knows, has heard the stories of conjugal visits. He repeats that he would rather just get back to his unit. She appears not to understand. His fiancée is in Bloemfontein. She lives with her parents. A twelve-hour train journey away. For what? What would he say to her? That he'd killed at least two human beings since he'd last seen her; that he'd seen women raped and men burned alive, friends die waiting for the casevac, the sand soaking up their blood like so much rain? Despite the promise of sex, he doesn't *want* to see her. He feels strange, confused. He doesn't say any of it.

She tells him he cannot be released sooner. He must heal. They must observe him. I'll ask the doctor, he says. She crosses her arms across her chest. I am the doctor, she says. She is also a Captain. He splutters some apology, swears as if he were still out in the bush, apologises again. He repeats that he would rather just go back as soon as possible. He says please, addresses her as Doctor for the first time. She is very pretty for an officer, he thinks, in that older-woman kind of way. He guesses she is thirty. Thereabouts.

She looks down at him for a long time. You want to go back, she says. Yes. Why? she asks. Why what? He feels stupid. Why do you want to go back there? He stares down at his arm a moment, so carefully cleaned and stitched, then back up at her face. I just do, he tells her. She looks angry. Her tone changes. That's not an answer, soldier. He considers this. He feels threatened in some vague way he can't place. He asks her is this an official medical question, ma'am.

She smooths her hair, looks away. No, she whispers. He can barely hear her. She looks around the ward, at all the other wounded soldiers in their beds, back at Clay. The anger is gone, replaced by something else. I don't understand, she says. I want to understand. He thinks he sees pain in her expression, some kind of bewilderment. He is not sure. She seems easy to read, but she is not.

He tries to explain. It is difficult. He cannot look into himself in a way that makes anything clear enough for words, let alone sentences. That's where I belong, he finally comes up with. She stands a while, some sort of calculus spinning in her brain. He will never forget what she says then and what comes after.

This war is not what you think it is.

What do I think it is? he replies immediately, without thinking.

The *rooi gevaar*, she answers. That's what you think it's about. He can tell from the way she says it that she is not a native Afrikaans speaker.

So tell me, he says. It's a race war. Plain and simple. She whispers this, glances over her shoulder. He remembers Eben saying this same thing, that night in the UNITA bunker. He tells her they have black soldiers fighting with them. He thinks of Brigade. They are volunteers. Ask them.

You're all being duped, she says, whispering still. She waves her arm towards the other beds. All of this suffering, for a *lie*. She stresses the last word like this. A *lie*.

Something inside him goes cold. As if a part of him has been cut out and what replaces it is not at body temperature. He thinks of how Kruger felt as they lifted him onto the poncho, so heavy. Why are you telling me this, he asks her. She is an officer. What she is saying is treason. People are being shot for less.

I am telling you because you love this war, she says. Maybe you don't know it now, and you're too young to articulate it, but you do. You love it. And I hate it. There are many who feel this way. And then she turns on the balls of her feet, like a dancer, and strides away between the rows of beds. The soldiers who are awake watch her go, and some of them – the ones who can – smile at each other.

☾

Next afternoon she comes and helps him into a wheelchair, although he says he can walk, and she pushes him along the corridor and out into the big garden at the back of the hospital and parks him in the shade of a big pine tree. She says she is on her break. She brings him paper and a pen and sits in the grass beside him, reading some book in French while he tries to write a letter to Sara.

He writes *By the time you get this letter I will be back on the Border. I was here in Pretoria at 1-Mil just for a small thing no time at all and please don't worry*. And that was it. Two lines. A line for each day they'd spent together during his leave a month ago. He folds it and puts it in an envelope and writes Sara's name and her father's address on the front and gives it to the doctor. She takes it and puts it in the pocket of her dress.

What are you reading, he asks her. Jean-Jacques Rousseau, she tells him. *Les Confessions*. She says it in French, with an accent. I don't know this writer, he tells her, and she asks him do you like reading and which authors do you like? I have a friend who reads all the time, he says, carries books with him even on operations. He is a philosopher, and a writer, too. One day he will get something he's written published, maybe after the war.

What about you? she asks, sitting there on the lawn bent over her book with her knees up and her dress hiked up above her knees so he can see her calves, slender and smooth and white. The sight of them sends a quiver through him that catches in his throat, and when he speaks his voice is lower and he wonders, can she hear his arousal? I like to read, he says, sure. She smiles at him and it only makes it worse and he realises he is hard, aching hard, and if there weren't rules about such things he'd tell her and maybe she'd do something with him, knowing how close he'd just come to dying and that he could be dead in a few days. Such are the ways a twenty-year-old thinks, he would realise years later. Thinking that people other than your parents actually give a shit about you and what might become of you, and sometimes not even them.

I'll bring you something, then, she says after a while, standing and smoothing the front of her white doctor's dress and wheeling him back to the ward.

That night a parallel life complete opens to him. Perhaps it is the drugs, the morphine and the antibiotics and whatever else they are putting into him. Maybe it's just that his brain has had some time to process what he's done and seen and felt and heard and smelled these past months. Whatever the cause, it's a life he never wanted. And over the years, he will come to fear it to the extent that escaping its nightly inevitability will become an obsession.

That night, it is a simple one. Vivid and so real he swears he is there. He checks himself to see if it is a dream. He thinks this: It is not a dream. It is happening. He is standing in the bush, his R4 pointed at a FAPLA soldier. The man is unarmed, bewildered, close enough to spit on. He holds his hands out, palms up, pleads with him in Portuguese. Clay pulls the trigger. The rifle does not fire. He tries again. The man turns away, tries to make himself small, draws his arms up around his face as if that might somehow protect him. But it is as if a piece of hard rubber has been lodged behind the trigger and is preventing its depression. He squeezes as hard as he can, but the trigger depresses only slightly, not enough to trip the firing pin. Still the man stands there, whimpering, pleading. He does not run. Why doesn't he run? Clay puts his left index finger inside the trigger guard, on top of the other finger, pulls as hard as he can.

His arms quiver with the effort. Still he cannot get the trigger to move that last half-millimetre. The man stares at him with wide, pained eyes washed in terror.

Clay wakes with a start, his heart hammering in his chest, his face and arms and torso covered in sweat. The bedsheets are soaked. In the darkness he hears one of the other soldiers shift in his bed, call out something he cannot decipher, the others breathing in their own parallel places. He runs his good hand down along his chest to his abdomen, the muscles lean and hard after weeks in the bush, the sweat slick on his skin, until his hand reaches his penis. It throbs in his hand. He pushes away the dream and any thought that it may have been associated with his arousal. He lies as quietly as he can in the sleeping ward and he thinks of the doctor. She comes to him in the night, takes off her clothes, whispers to him that it's okay and just be quiet I'll do everything, but before she can do anything he comes; it shoots thick and hot and heavy all over his chest and he can feel it running down his sides and he wipes the sweat and the cum from his body with the bedsheets and lies there in the darkness not wanting to sleep and feeling like there is nothing inside him and he is a shell.

He dreams again, vivid, real, as if his eyes are open. The fat, balding man with the suit – the one who was inspecting the tusks at the *chana*; the one the UNITA Colonel called Botha – is there in the hospital. He walks the ward, dressed in a doctor's coat, inspecting the wounded men, checking them off in his notebook. He is wearing a face mask, like the doctors do when they operate, but Clay *knows* it's him by his dark, expressionless eyes.

The next afternoon she takes him out to the garden again, parks him under the same tree. She hands him a book. Something you might like, she says. A paperback edition of *For Whom the Bell Tolls*, battered, faded. He riffles the pages, smells the book. It reminds him of his father, now dead. That was a war worth fighting, she says. He asks her the question with his eyes. The Spanish Civil War, she says, 1935. Robert Jordan, the hero, is fighting against tyranny. You are fighting for it.

He looks at her for a long time. She looks back. She is deadly serious.

The next day, out in the garden, he tells her he is halfway through the novel. It's good, he says. She smiles, goes back to her book. She is reading something else today, doesn't tell him what. For some reason that he will not understand until much later, he tells her about the UNITA Colonel and his men loading the tusks and the wood and diamonds onto the unmarked Hercules, about the fat, ugly man in the suit inspecting the cargo, and how strange it was seeing him there, so obviously out of place. He tells her about seeing him again in his dreams, walking the corridors of the hospital, about Cobra leaving them there with the FAPLA tanks bearing down on them. He tells her about the woman prisoner, what they'd done to her and what she'd said about the drugs, how Koevoet had finally decided to let her go during the retreat to the border. She listens, says nothing. She looks pale, as if his words have stolen the blood from under her skin. She takes him back to the ward. Something has changed.

☾

Commissioner Rotzenburg: And the diamonds, Mister Straker. What did you do with them?

Witness: When I was wounded, I gave them to Eben. Eben Barstow, my friend. I told him to keep them safe for me.

Commissioner Rotzenburg: What did he do with them?

Witness: He buried them in a hole under the floorboards of our tent at the airbase, Ondangwa.

Commissioner Rotzenburg: And were you aware of their value?

Witness: No, sir. Not at the time.

Commissioner Ksole: And later?

Witness: Yes, sir.

Commissioner Ksole: And can you share that with us, please: What was their value?

Witness: Something like half a million US dollars, at the time. A lot more now.

Commissioner Rotzenburg: That is a lot of money. What did you do with them?

Witness does not answer.

Commissioner Rotzenburg: What did you do with the diamonds, Mister Straker?

Witness: This is not what I came here to talk about.

Commissioner Rotzenburg: You acquired those diamonds illegally, Mister Straker, of your own admission. At gunpoint. Are you a thief, Mister Straker? Is that why you do not want to tell us?

Witness: Yes.

Commissioner Rotzenburg: Yes, what?

Witness: Yes, I am a thief. And I am a murderer.

Commissioner Ksole: A murderer?

Witness: Yes.

Commissioner Lacy: You were a soldier. Soldiers have to kill.

Witness: Not … Not like I did.

Commissioner Ksole: We will get to that. Did you have any visitors in hospital?

Witness: Yes, sir. Captain Wade, our company commander came to see me.

Commissioner Barbour: Were you surprised?

Witness: A little, I guess. I mean, I was just an enlisted man. He was a good officer.

Commissioner Ksole: What did you talk about?

Witness: He asked me about the operation. He knew about the prisoner, the woman. He wanted to know what I'd seen.

Commissioner Ksole: And did you tell him?

Witness: Yes, sir.

Commissioner Ksole: Everything?

Witness: No, sir. Not everything. I didn't tell him about the diamonds. Or about Crowbar – Liutenant Van Boxmeer, I mean – shooting the UNITA soldier.

Commissioner Lacy: Did you tell him about the rape?

Witness: Yes, ma'am. I did.

Commissioner Barbour: And this young woman, the, ah, the doctor. Can you tell the commission her name, please?

Witness: There weren't many lady doctors around back then. It shouldn't be hard to find out.

Commissioner Ksole: You don't have to tell us. We know. This is for confirmation, Mister Straker. I am sure you understand.

Witness: I'm not here to speak on her behalf.

Commissioner Rotzenburg: Do you not wish to proceed with your testimony, Mister Straker?

Witness: Why do you think I'm here?

Commissioner Rotzenburg: Frankly, Mister Straker, I don't know.

Commissioner Barbour: Please, gentlemen.

Commissioner Ksole: Coming back to the doctor. There was something in the book she gave you, was there not?

Witness does not answer.

Commissioner Ksole: Mister Straker?

Witness: How do you know that?

Commissioner Ksole: Answer the question, please.

Witness: Yes. Yes, there was.

7

Life Set to Music

It was a story they'd tell many times over the coming months. The time Crowbar – already holder of the Honoris Crux, the SADF's highest award for valour, the equivalent of the Victoria Cross or the American Medal of Honour – led three platoons of parabats, low on ammo, food and water, out of Angola. They were fewer than a hundred men and were pursued by an entire communist battalion, at least a thousand strong and backed up by a dozen T55s (the number grew with the telling). It was a story that became legend on the border, but that too soon no one would want to hear; a heroic act for a bankrupt cause in a war that few had heard of, and everyone who had, wanted to forget. It was Eben who told the story that night, staring into the fire, Pink Floyd cranked on his tape deck, one of the rare times they were allowed beer in camp, the other *Valk* and some of the aircrew there, too.

Low on ammunition, the tanks threatening to break through and cut them in two, the UNITA *dofs* having run away, Koevoet works out a plan. They collapse the flanks, Coetzee's *Valk* 3 folding in behind *Valk* 5, de Vries's *Valk* 2 in the rear. They are deep in Angolan territory, 185 kilometres from the border. Evac by air is ruled out. The enemy is too close. The parabats will have to fight their way out.

So begins a three-day fighting retreat. They meet the advancing FAPLA troops with disciplined, concentrated fire, then fall back, hour after hour. Night falls, and they keep moving. By daybreak, they've put ten kilometres between themselves and the communists. Crowbar calls in airstrikes, Mirage jets pounding FAPLA. The

250-pound bombs shake the teeth in their heads a mile away. The *vlammies* report two tanks knocked out.

By now Eben was pacing around the fire in some kind of bushman's war dance, beer bottle in one hand, the other timing the jet's swooping bomb runs to the beat of the music. The troops roared with delight as each tank went up, their faces bathed in firelight, eyes blazing raw youth, the joy of being alive and able to tell such stories. Life set to music.

Crowbar finally manages to get a casevac in to take out the wounded and deliver badly needed supplies. Later that day, FAPLA catches them again, rushing troops forwards in Russian-built BTR armoured vehicles. *Valk* 3 reports contact with a Cuban unit, their first such encounter. They are well trained, disciplined. *Liutenant* Coetzee and his radioman are killed when a Cuban rocket hits their position.

Heads dropped around the fire. Coetzee was a favourite with the men.

They fight on until nightfall, when again they put distance between themselves and the relentlessly pursuing communists. By now they have been fighting and running for fifty hours without a break. Men fall asleep standing up. An armoured relief column has been organised to relieve them, but they are still at least a day away.

Eben paused, drained his beer, threw the empty into the fire, everyone waiting for him to continue. Dressed in a FAPLA-zippered jumper and SWAPO short-peaked cap, he stared out at them with those madman's eyes, held them there, hanging. Cock tease, someone shouted. Laughter. Eben put his finger to his lips. All you could hear was the crackle of the flames and the hum of the big camp generators.

Then Crowbar does something unexpected. He tells de Vries to take *Valk* 2 and 3, drop their heavy gear, mortars and machine guns, extra ammo, and make for the border as fast as they can go. *Valk* 5 picks up whatever they need, blows the rest. Right, says Crowbar, the twenty-odd remaining members of his platoon clustered around him.

Eben stood with his hands on hips, chest thrust out, imitating the old man. Now we attack. *Now*, he said, Eben doing Crowbar's thick Boer accent. This is *our* time. Ours.

The men roared into the night, clapping each other on the back. So many smiles. Someone threw a near-empty bottle of vodka into the fire. It exploded with a blue flame. The men cheered, whistled. Clay, just two days back from 1-Mil, thought: I am happier than I have ever been in my life.

The rest of it everyone knew.

Valk 5 turns 180 degrees and closes on the communists in the night. They catch FAPLA sleeping, the Cubans, too, exhausted after two days of fighting pursuit, their vehicles being serviced, dealing with scores of wounded, never imagining that the small force of South Africans would turn and attack. They hit hard and fast, just before dawn, penetrating the FAPLA perimeter in seconds. They cut through the camp, scything down everything that moves, demolition parties following up, destroying vehicles and equipment with C4 charges.

And as Eben told the story, Clay saw it all as if it were now, the images sharp and clean, not as they would later become in his dreams – looping back in incomplete shards, a jumbled kaleidoscope of death. Now he was there, step by step with Eben. He remembered the little FAPLA soldier standing before him, bare chested, seconds awake, blinking in the light from the burning vehicles, and how he doubled over as the bullets from Clay's R4 ripped through his lower abdomen. He remembered the sounds, too, the screaming, the gunfire, the concussions as the first charges went up, the terrified shouts of those surprised, Eben whooping like a Confederate as he blazed away on full auto, his eyes like now, crazed firelight dancing on his retinae. And Clay remembered his surprise at seeing his friend like this and wanting to ask him of what philosophy this insanity was born.

It doesn't take long. They are in and out in less than half an hour. That's when Straker and Cooper are hit by the same rocket.

Eben said it in a whisper. Faces swivelled towards Clay in the firelight, nodded in acknowledgement.

The morning sky burns red as they pull Cooper – what's left of him – along the ground by his webbing. They can't find his legs. They wait for him to die, then start back towards the border, a towering pillar of black smoke testament to their night's work. Dozens lie dead; more. The communists have no idea of the size of the force that has hit them. Crowbar calls in an airstrike. Can't miss it, he says into the radio handset. We've popped smoke for you. Big smoke.

The men around the fire roared with laughter, Eben swooping his free hand again, bombing run after bombing run. *Vlammies*, Impalas. Shine on You Crazy Diamond.

The next day air recon estimate more than a hundred enemy dead, at least as many wounded, four tanks knocked out. All three platoons make it back safely. But de Jager, one of *Valk* 5's new privates, is killed after the link up with the relief column. He steps on a SWAPO mine along the cut, dies instantly. He is nineteen.

☾

The next day, *Valk* 5 was back on Fireforce standby. They lounged shirtless in the sun by the plastic-lined pool, drinking cold Cokes from the canteen, always in boots and trousers, webbing and weapons and Fireforce vests close to hand, ready to jump onto the helicopters at a moment's notice. The other platoons, meanwhile, conducted foot and vehicle patrols along the cutline.

Clay lay in his bunk in the four-man tent he shared with Eben, de Koch and the new *rofie*, Cronje. The sound of jets taking off and landing, the occasional helicopter hammering past, the canvas rippling in the hot dry breeze. The smells of burned avgas and sweat and woodsmoke mingled with the dry-season burnishing of umbrella thorn, bushwillow and moringa. Clay closed his eyes, let these chemicals dance through his brain and cut incisions whose scars, a decade and a half later – back in Africa for the first time since he'd left the war – would transport him instantly and specifically back to this very moment when, lying on his bunk, the book the doctor had given him open face down on his chest, Crowbar walked in.

Clay jumped to his feet, stood to attention. The book fell to the floor, lay cover up on the plywood floor.

Crowbar glanced down at the book, harrumphed. 'How's your arm, Straker?'

'Good as new, my *Liutenant*.'

Crowbar reached into his pocket, withdrew a small, black case about the size of a pack of playing cards. 'For you,' he said, tossing it onto Clay's bunk.

Clay stood, said nothing.

'And mail.' Crowbar stuffed two letters into Clay's hand.

'Thank you, sir.'

Crowbar scanned the tent. 'You lied to me, Straker.'

Shame burned through Clay, as if it were his father standing there.

'You think I'm stupid, Straker?'

'No, sir.' No.

'You're lying to me now.'

'No, sir.' Absolutely not.

'It was her, Straker – in the identity-card photo that UNITA Colonel showed me. It was that woman you said you'd taken prisoner out on LP.'

Clay stared straight ahead. He'd been expecting this, was surprised it had taken so long.

Crowbar raised his arms, clasped his hands behind his head, and exhaled. 'What the *fok* were you two doing? Tell me.'

'It was me, *Oom*. Just me.'

'Don't *fokken oom* me, Straker.'

'They were raping her, sir. All of them.'

'I don't give a God damn what they were doing.'

Clay stared into his commander's eyes. 'Then why did you let her go, sir?'

Crowbar stared right back, didn't answer. His eyes were like a spring-morning sky, when everything is clean and the sun prisms through the moisture in the air. 'You're messing in things that aren't our business, Straker; you and that dreamer, Barstow. Our job is to kill commies. Nothing else.' He ran his hand through his thinning hair. 'Do you understand me?'

'Yes, sir.'

'Full pack and weapons, Straker. You will march the base perimeter until I tell you to stop, or until we get called out on Fireforce.'

Clay nodded.

Then Crowbar leaned in towards him. Clay could feel his commander's breath hot and wet under his chin. 'Lie to me again, Straker, and I'll transfer you out of this unit so fast you'll be gone before you know I've done it. Understand me?'

'Yes, sir.' Clay knew he meant it, too.

Crowbar stormed out.

Clay threw on his vest, hefted his pack and helmet, grabbed his R4 and started towards the eighteen-kilometre-long perimeter fence.

He'd gone a hundred metres when Eben, similarly loaded, fell in next to him. 'Think I'm going to let you have all the fun?' he said.

'Kocvoct nail you, too, *broer*?'

'Volunteered.'

Clay smiled. This was why he'd wanted to come back. 'I thought it'd be a lot worse.'

'Such a pussy, our Koevoet.'

'No telling when he'll let us stop, *broer*.'

'All night.'

'Wonder if they'll bring us breakfast.'

Eben grinned. 'So how was 1-Mil? Get anywhere with those pretty nurses?'

'I got a book.'

'Always good.'

'Hemingway.'

'Not so good.'

'I like it.'

'Try Tolstoy.'

'Next time I get hit maybe.'

Eben smiled. 'You get mail?'

Clay nodded, pulling the letters from his shirt pocket. One from Sara: proper stationery, perfumed, still unopened; the other stamped Pretoria, four days ago, his name and unit scrawled longhand with a ballpoint, no return address. He opened the Pretoria letter, staring at the page as he walked. 'Jesus,' he said.

'What is it?'

He passed the letter to Eben.

'What the hell?' said Eben, looking up from the paper. 'Who's it from?'

'Someone I met at 1-Mil.'

Eben read: '"If you want to know more about what we talked about, read the book." A bunch of numbers. "Your woman friend told you about a doctor. This is his operation. Observe. Come see me if you can."'

Eben replaced the letter in its envelope and handed it back to Clay. 'What the hell did you tell her, *bru*?'

Clay marched on, in time with his friend. With each step his sense of dread, of having made a serious error, deepened.

After a while he said: 'I told her everything.'

'Shit.'

'I don't know why I did it. I shouldn't have. There was something about her.'

'I hope she was worth it.'

'It's not that. Nothing happened.'

'That's too bad.' Eben flashed him a smile.

'Do you think the censors read it?'

'They don't usually read the incoming mail, but you never know these days, *broer*.'

Clay shook his head. He'd been stupid.

After a while Eben said: 'What's in the book?'

'It's a story about the Spanish Civil War. You know, 1935.'

'I know when it was. I mean, is there a message inside, an inscription, anything like that?'

'Nothing that I can see.'

Eben considered this a while. 'Be careful with this, *bru*.'

It took them just under four hours to complete the first circuit of the sprawling, twenty-square-kilometre airbase, encircled with earth berms and barbed wire. As they approached the canteen, the sky was fading to that particular shade of pink that, for Clay, would always be Ovamboland. *Valk* 5 was waiting for them, lining both sides of the road as they passed. De Koch handed him an ice-cold Coke, told him to suck it up, smiled. Slaps on the back, laughter, the usual comments: we'll keep dinner for you; time you did something useful; Bluey, destined to die a few short days later, saying: I was going to chuck a couple of grenades over the wire so they'd think we were under attack and we'd have to go out on Fireforce.

Clay grabbed Bluey by the arm. 'Do me a favour, Blue. There's a book on my bunk. Get it for me, would you?'

Bluey nodded and smiled. He had a great smile, a mouth that stretched and then stretched wider again, and a laugh to go with it.

They kept walking, started their second lap, chucked the empty Coke tins back at their platoon mates. Soon they were passing the officer's bivouac area. A lone figure stood outside one of the tents, smoking a cigarette. Clay and Eben straightened their backs, saluted. Crowbar watched them go without acknowledging them.

A few minutes later Bluey ran up and handed Clay the book. 'Did you see the old man back there?' he said.

Clay nodded.

'He sure is pissed at you, my *broers*. What the *fok* did you do?'

'Don't ask,' said Clay.

Bluey clapped him on the back and started back to the platoon.

'I know what it is,' said Clay, handing Eben the letter. 'It's a cipher.'

Eben laughed. 'A cipher. Sure, *broer*. Sunstroke, that's what it is. I'll tell Koevoet to put you in the infirmary.'

'What else could it be?' said Clay. 'This doctor, I'll tell you *broer* she was saying some seditious things. About the war being a sham, about us all being manipulated. She sounded like some kind of revolutionary. She sounded like you, actually.'

'Sounds like a smart *bokkie*.' Eben opened the letter and read the first set of numbers: 'One: forty-nine.'

Clay leafed through to the first chapter, counted out the first forty-nine words. 'The.'

'Three: ten.'

'It's okay, I've got it,' Clay said, the sequence already locked in his head, a photograph of the page that he could read as plainly as if it were in his hand now. He'd always been able to do it, especially with numbers. At school it was his best party trick, his best smile-getter from the girls.

'Carefully,' he said aloud.

He flipped through the book, found the chapters and counted out words from the start of each. Night had fallen quickly and it was almost too dark to read.

'"*The carefully girl said head*". Makes no sense.'

'Was she your "carefully girl", the person you met in 1-Mil?'

Clay smiled.

'Did she say head? Did she give it, perhaps?' Eben smiled. 'Maybe I should get hit next time.'

'What? No. I wish. She's married.'

'Try backwards, from the end of each chapter.'

Clay did it, quickly, as the light faded. 'Makes even less sense.'

'Try letters instead of words,' said Eben.

Clay leafed through the pages, counted out the letters.

'"*C-O-A-S-T*". That's what you get. "*Coast*".'

'I like the other meaning better.'

'Me too.'

'Maybe it's her way of giving you her phone number,' said Eben.

They grinned at each other in the dark, adjusted their packs, kept walking..

They tried other combinations, but none produced anything

intelligible. Even so, her words kept spinning through Clay's brain. Hundreds of sick and wounded men passed through the hospital each month; why give him the book? Why the letter? It was clearly from her. Was it really a cipher? What else could it be? Some kind of elaborate joke: an experienced woman having some fun with a naive young soldier? Or was it something more sinister? He'd heard the stories of BOSS operatives approaching unsuspecting soldiers, fishing for evidence of anti-regime sentiment. Could this be a trap? Could the *oke* on the Hercules, Cobra, have reported him, denounced him to the Bureau of State Security as a troublemaker, a communist sympathiser? And what about the fat man in the suit, Botha – the one who was haunting his dreams? You're dead men, he'd said straight-faced to three combat-hardened paratroopers. Clay's stomach tightened. What had Zulaika said? Doctor Death. Drugs for killing? Was Zulaika the woman the doctor's note referred to? Clay shook his head. Something seriously screwed up was going on. Besides the war. He folded the envelope and thrust it deep into his trouser pocket. He was going to do exactly as Crowbar had said and stay as far as he possibly could from whatever it all meant.

They were halfway through their second circuit, not far from the main gates, along a stretch of the perimeter berm where scrub acacia grew in a dark thicket, screening the road from the rest of the base, when a lone figure appeared ahead of them.

Clay raised his rifle. The man put up his hands, approaching them at a slow walk, a cigarette burning between his lips. It was Brigade, the black 32-Bat scout.

Clay lowered his weapon. 'Sorry, *broer*,' he said. 'Didn't recognise you. What are you doing in Ondangwa?'

Brigade exhaled a lungful of smoke, nodding to them both. 'Come with me,' he said, pointing towards the main gate. 'There is someone wants to talk to you.'

Clay looked over at Eben, back at Brigade, smiled. 'Sure thing, *broer*. Just walk off base. I'm in enough trouble as it is.'

Brigade handed them each a piece of paper, flipped on a small torch and played the beam across the documents. Official orders, naming each of them specifically, attaching them to someone called Captain Blakely, 32-Battalion. Legitimate.

'What the hell?' said Eben.

'We'll have to check with our CO,' said Clay.

'Already done,' said Brigade, poking the paper with a long, bony index finger. The orders were countersigned by Captain Wade, their company commander. 'You must come now.'

'No way, *bru*,' said Clay planting his feet. 'I don't care what this says, I'm not going anywhere unless Koevoet tells me to.'

'Who is it wants to talk to us?' said Eben.

Brigade looked over his shoulder, checked his watch and shuffled his feet in the sand. 'Zulaika.'

'Jesus Christ Almighty.'

'Carefully, girl,' said Eben.

☾

Commissioner Lacy: Was this the first time you became aware of the Bureau of State Security's interest in you?

Witness: No. That wasn't until later.

Commissioner Ksole: After the Roodeplaat break-in?

Witness: How do you know about that?

Commissioner Ksole: Please answer.

Witness: Before that.

Commissioner Barbour: And did it not strike you as … strange, the orders coming this way?

Witness: Yes, sir. It did.

Commissioner Barbour: But you went all the same?

Witness: I was a twenty-year-old soldier, sir. With respect, what else was I going to do? They were written orders. I did as I was told. We all did. It was a long time ago.

Commissioner Barbour: But that changed, didn't it?

Witness: Later on it did, yes, sir.

Commissioner Ksole: When did you first realise the connection with Torch Commando?

Witness: Not until after.

Commissioner Ksole: After what?

Witness does not respond.

Commissioner Ksole: After what, Mister Straker? Was it the massacre?

Witness: Yes.

Commissioner Ksole: Please speak up.

Witness: Yes. The massacre.

Commissioner Lacy: Surely you were aware that this kind of thing was going on, Mister Straker?

Witness: I'd heard the rumours. We all had. But I thought they were crap; communist disinformation. That's what our officers told us.

Commissioner Ksole: You grew up in a privileged part of Johannesburg, did you not? Your family was well off. You had black servants.

Witness: Yes, sir.

Commissioner Ksole: And you never considered the situation of these people?

Witness: No. Not until later. I was just a kid. That was just how it was.

Commissioner Ksole: So you tell us.

Commissioner Barbour: So why are you here, son?

Witness does not answer.

Commissioner Barbour: Son?

Witness: Sir. For the dead, sir. They need the truth to be
   told.

Commissioner Barbour: And for the living?

Witness: Time, sir. They need time.

8

So Much He Could Not See

It was only once they were on the helicopter that Zulaika finally spoke.

'Thank you both for what you did…' she said, her voice coming thin and pulsed over the helicopter's intercom. She hung her head. '…Before.' She looked different now. Without the bruises and the swelling, her face was leaner, the cheekbones more pronounced, the nose smaller. Her eyes looked bigger, darker.

Clay adjusted his headphones, swivelled the microphone pickup closer to his mouth and hit the transmit button. 'Where are we going?'

'There is something you must see.'

The scattered orange pinpoints of village cooking fires flashed beneath them. Clay imagined the people clustered around, sharing the evening meal, telling stories, distracted for a moment as the helicopter sped over close and fast, some glancing up into the night sky before turning back to gaze into the flames, the sound of the rotors fading into the night. Soon the fires were gone and there was nothing beneath them but the star and quarter-moon silvered bushland.

'We're in Angola,' said Eben.

Brigade nodded, his face lit by the red-green glow of the cockpit instrument panel.

Clay still couldn't believe that Wade had signed the order; that they'd just walked out of the front gates of the base like that, fully kitted out, and jumped into a waiting helicopter. And now they were back in Angola.

Brigade reached into a pack and pulled out what looked to be a collection of rags. He handed Clay a stained grey sweatshirt and a red-and-white Palestinian-style bandana.

'Put these on,' said Brigade. 'No uniform markings.'

Clay pulled off his Fireforce vest and unbuttoned his uniform tunic. He pulled on the sweatshirt, tied the scarf around his neck and pulled his vest back on.

'Welcome to long-range recon,' said Brigade over the intercom.

They sped through the night, the cool air whipping their faces through the open doors, all of Africa below them dark and, for the moment, without war.

Soon the helicopter's engine changed tone as the pilot cycled down and started to descend. Clay's heartrate jumped as it always did when they were about to go in. He fought to control it, to breathe, to focus.

And then he was out, the hard, dry ground beneath his boots and the sound of the rotors retreating into the night. He followed Brigade and Zulaika through the short grass, Eben beside him, the stars shot like miracles in the limitless darkness above him. A thorn caught his trouser leg, ripped the brown canvas open; a dulled pain signal blooming momentarily and vanishing in a torrent of adrenaline.

They walked for an hour, maybe more, under the wide, turning night sky, Brigade and Zulaika in the lead. A couple of times Zulaika held them up and they went down on one knee and gazed out into the night, then continued on. After a time, they came to a small clearing. Brigade signalled halt. They stood in the shadows thrown by the moon and the stars, and waited. Clouds the size of cathedrals drifted in low-blown ranks above them and the shadows they made passed over the land so that it was like standing on an ocean.

Zulaika's hand touched Clay's elbow. He looked out across the clearing to where she was pointing. The figure of a man appeared just inside the tree line, silvered in light. Clay raised his rifle.

'No,' she whispered, putting her hand on his weapon. She stepped out of the trees into the clearing. Fully illuminated, she stood there a moment, and then raised her hand.

The man did the same then started towards them.

'Well, will you look at that,' said Eben.

The man was very small and wiry, with a long beard, naked except for a flap of hide covering his genitals. The spear he carried was short handled with a hammered metal point. He was barefoot.

Zulaika and Brigade greeted him in !Kung, the click language of the bushmen. They spoke for a long time, the plosive ejective and nasal-aspirated clicks and consonants of the Ju'hoan dialect hard and distinct against the background of a million sawing insect legs and vibrating wings. And then, above all of it, coming on the night breeze that pushed the clouds over the land, the deep-chested moan of a lion.

Clay glanced over at Eben.

Eben shrugged. 'Wake me when I stop dreaming,' he whispered in English.

Later, it would be as real as a dream, and the memory of it the thing imagined. But right now he could feel the place the thorn had cut into his leg, touch the blood, viscous like rapeseed oil between his fingers, the sweat channelling down his spine, pooling cold between his legs and in the backs of his knees, the R4 familiar in his hands almost as if it were part of him, a fused prosthetic.

And then they were up and moving again, single-file through the wide, dry savannah country, the diminutive bushman leading, his feet sure and quick, soft on the land. They skirted a copse of mopane, spread like oversized parasols on a Durban beach, then sprinted silent across a narrow clearing. They came to a place where the bush became suddenly dense with thickets of scrub acacia and leadwood, umbrella thorn and close-sprung mopane and wool bush – country favoured by dik-dik and giraffe.

Zulaika stopped, waiting for them, put her finger to her lips then pointed into the dense bush. 'One kilometre through here,' she said. 'Be as quiet as you can.'

'When we get there, we will set up an OP,' said Brigade.

'What are we observing?' said Clay.

'You will see,' said Zulaika.

'Why do you ask such questions, Straker?' Eben said in English, so the others couldn't understand. As he said it one of the big cloud shadows slid away and Clay could see Eben grinning so that his teeth and his eyes shone in the moonlight. 'You don't need to know. Always works the same, no matter whose army you're in.'

'And whose army are we in now?' said Clay.

Eben adjusted the sling of his R4 so that the magazine and pistol grip rested on the front pouches of his Fireforce vest. 'You tell me, *broer.*'

They followed the bushman into the trees.

It took them the better part of two hours to thread their way through the close-spaced trees and the dark, spreading undergrowth. Clay was much bigger than the others, weighed down with over a hundred pounds of ammunition and water, ten M27 grenades, and two eponymous command-detonated M18 anti-personnel mines that Brigade had given him in the helicopter. While the bushman, Brigade, and the delicately boned Zulaika slid along the barely perceptible trail with stealth, Clay crashed through the underbrush like a buffalo. Eben, sweating behind him, wasn't much better. Though they were upwind, he couldn't imagine how whatever lay at the far edge of this forest wasn't already alerted to their presence.

They came to the edge of a long, broad *chana*. The bushman signalled down. Clay, Eben and Brigade dropped their packs. Prone, they snaked forwards until they could see clearly across the short, open grass. The clearing must have been more than a kilometre long, about as wide as a rugby pitch. They were close to one end, tucked into a thick patch of silver brush, wedged between two big old ironwoods. From where they lay they could see along the whole reach. The flat, dead grass was bright against the dark of the surrounding trees, and the scuttling clouds made dark patches that drifted over the illuminated ground.

The bushman pointed to the closer end of the *chana*. About a hundred and fifty metres away, some sort of wire enclosure glinted in the dull liquid-mercury light. A cattle pen of some sort. Nearby, a makeshift shelter – log uprights, palm-frond roof. Beneath it, a few upended wooden packing crates and a couple of stools.

'Now we wait,' said Brigade in Afrikaans. 'Four-hour shifts. The rest of us move back into the forest, set up there. I will cover our rear with the Claymores.'

Clay retrieved the M18s from his pack and passed them to Brigade. 'Are we expecting company?'

Brigade shrugged. 'We could be here for some time.'

'What, exactly, are we expecting?' said Eben, violating his own rule.

'With luck, we will see,' said Zulaika.

'Luck?' said Clay.

Zulaika looked at him square. 'I am sure they will come.'

'Who, Zulaika?' said Clay. 'Tell us. We're here. Trust us now.'

She looked out across the *chana* a moment, seeming to consider this as one might consider a proposition of marriage, or of doing violence.

'It is not trust,' she said. 'You are here exactly because of trust. It is not that.' The words caught in her throat, the Portuguese strong in the Afrikaans. She closed her eyes and Clay could see tears clinging to the tips of her dark lashes like dew on sweetgrass, each a blown-out star field.

Clay waited.

She blinked away the tears, the drops running silver across the dark skin of her cheek and guttering in the linear beauty scar that ran from the highest point of her cheekbone to the corner of her mouth. She captured the moisture on the glistening underside of her tongue.

'It is because of what it is that I cannot say. I cannot explain because I am not sure what it is. I can only say that it is of the greatest evil.' She turned away, hid her face in her hands.

Clay decided not to push her. He nodded. 'I'll take first watch.'

Brigade handed Clay a pair of binoculars and a starlight night-vision scope. 'If you see anything, wake me.'

Clay looked a moment at Brigade. A fever had ignited inside him somewhere, suddenly and without warning, and he could feel it running hot through his chest and come burning to his face. It felt a lot like shame. He took the gear. And then he realised: he was taking orders from a black man. 'Yes, Sergeant,' he said.

The others moved back into the thickness of the understorey. Clay settled into a position where he was well hidden but could see out along the entire clearing. He arranged his pack as a back rest, checked his R4 and set it on the ground beside him with the binoculars and the night scope.

An hour gone and the Southern Cross had risen over the far tree line, the ranks of cloud more widely spaced now, the breeze lighter. The *chana* was still empty and quiet. Clay drank from his water bottle and was replacing the cap when a rustle in the undergrowth stopped him dead.

Zulaika emerged from the shadows. 'I cannot sleep,' she whispered.

Clay offered her the water bottle. She shook her head.

'All quiet out there,' said Clay.

She settled in beside him and scanned the *chana*.

'Why are we here, Zulaika?'

'I told you. To observe.'

'No. I mean, me. Why am *I* here? Me and Eben.'

'You have orders.'

'I've seen them.'

She looked out across the clearing. 'You are a soldier. You follow orders.'

Yes, even from a black man; and when I did, I felt shame, even though I know him and know he is a good, experienced fighter and outranks me. 'So do you.'

She nodded. 'This is my country.'

'You lied to me. You are MPLA.'

She said nothing, just sat there for a long time on the ground, obscured in the darkness.

Clay let the silence of the African night reign.

Finally, she said: 'Please, you must trust me.'

'Not for a second.'

She shook her head, picked up the binoculars, scanned the close end of the clearing where the shelter and the wire pen were. 'Yes, I am MPLA.'

Clay eased his sidearm from its holster, pointed it at the woman. 'I should kill you now.'

She moved the binoculars from her face and glanced at the handgun. 'Do it,' she said. 'I welcome death.'

Clay said nothing.

'This war has taken everything from me.'

Clay lowered the handgun but kept it in his hand.

Zulaika placed the binoculars on the ground next to the night scope. 'Until a year ago, we had only heard of the war. It was in Namibia. It was nothing to us. At night, sometimes, we could hear the bombs, but only if the wind was right – they were very far away.'

She lived with her husband and his family and her four children – two boys and two girls. Her village was small and even during the war of independence from Portugal they were so far away from Luanda and the big towns that they saw nothing of the government or the other factions. And then, after 1975, everything went quiet and for a long time they thought peace had come. And indeed, for them, it had. Her husband tended their cattle and goats, and she worked in the fields and in her family home. The rains were good and her children grew and were happy and no one in the village was hungry.

And then one day armed men came into the village. They said they were fighting for the freedom of the people. She thought they were already free, but she was a woman and was not part of the discussions. At first all they did was take the men into the forests to cut wood and carry the tusks from the elephants they had killed. After a while the men returned to the village, and the soldiers disappeared. They all thought that the soldiers were gone for good. But after a time they returned, wanting men for soldiers. Her husband and her eldest son refused, but they took them anyway.

Not long after, a different group of soldiers came. Foreigners were with them. They said they were from a place called Cuba. They told the villagers that they were communist – that it meant that everyone should share everything, which is what they already did in her village. The new soldiers stayed for a while and gave out food and medicine and then left. Her husband and son had still not returned. She cried for them every night. The pain and worry inside her was too big.

And then, one night, the other soldiers came again – the 'freedom' soldiers – and this time they took some of the older boys, thirteen and fourteen years old. This time she decided she would do something. She followed them into the forest and watched them use the boys and men to cut and carry wood and hack the tusks from dead elephants. They called themselves UNITA. She watched them give the men and boys pills instead of food. She followed them for days, hiding, eating from the land, her feet raw. They went north to the diamond fields, where she watched the men and boys work in the muddy gravel rivers until they fell exhausted, hoping always for a glimpse of her husband and son. But hope was not enough. She walked back to her village, her worst fears growing. And the next time the other soldiers came to her village, the MPLA communists, she told them what she had seen and pointed to the places she had been on their maps. The foreign soldiers spoke in Spanish, which sounded like Portuguese, but was impossible for her to understand. The Angolan MPLA commander was her age, and very kind. He gave her food for her family – small delicacies, like chocolate and Cuban cigars for her father-in-law. He was kind and cultured and did not treat her with disrespect, as the UNITA soldiers had.

'We will find your husband and son,' the MPLA commander told her. 'Help us. Be our eyes and ears.'

Of course, she agreed. What else could she do? They gave her a radio and an identity card, which she hid in a hole that she dug inside her hut and covered with a piece of planking and woven mats. The next time the UNITA men came she followed them with her radio and told the MPLA commander where the enemy soldiers were and how many they numbered and what they were doing, for by now they truly were the enemy in her mind. As the UNITA forays into her country became more frequent, finding the missing village men and boys became her reason for living. Each time UNITA returned to her village she scanned the faces of the men but could see none of her village kin. She came to recognise some of the UNITA soldiers, though. The commander who called himself Colonel and would take young village girls to use, returning them swollen, bruised and afraid. *O Coletor*, they called him. Then some of the other soldiers started taking the girls and even some of the married women, too. They were mean and drugged-looking and treated the girls and women very badly. Some of the girls became pregnant. Once, one of the young men of the village tried to resist. He stabbed a UNITA soldier in the kidneys. The soldier died eventually, and when he did the young village man was shot in the head with a pistol by the UNITA Colonel. The whole village was forced to watch.

Zulaika said: 'Now I have only my hate.'

She begged the MPLA commander to protect their village. He told her he would do what he could, and for a while the UNITA men did not come back. The MPLA commander told her that there were rumours about the missing men, although no one could confirm them. But he was sure the same fate was befalling those of his own soldiers who had been captured by UNITA during the increasingly bitter fighting.

Zulaika looked at Clay. Her face was set hard in the patchwork of slanting moonlight. 'I was following them, the night you rescued me. I was careless. They caught me. I managed to call my commander just before they took me.'

A long time later, when all of this had become clear, and Clay was able to use the perspective of time and distance to make sense of some of it at least, he would come to see this woman as one of the bravest he had ever known, and, equally, would see the essential evil so readily unearthed in men. But now, here under the setting moon somewhere in the southern Angolan bush with only the compressed and limited experience of a boy of twenty years, there was so much he could not see.

'And that was why we were called in to help.'

'Yes. I am sorry.'

'Tell it to Kruger and Coetzee.'

'Who?'

Clay was about to answer when something shifted in the periphery of his vision, off to the right, at the close end of the clearing. He touched Zulaika's hand, signalled quiet, pointed towards the wire cage and the shelter. He grabbed the binoculars, scanned the *chana*, the shelter's near-white frond roof, its moon-shadow trembling long across the zinc-metal clearing.

'What did you see?' whispered Zulaika.

'I don't know,' he said. Forever, perhaps. What would still be here after all of this they were doing and they themselves were gone?

'It could have been a cat,' she whispered. 'There are caracal here. They hunt at night.'

'Maybe.' He kept scanning, ran his hand over the back of his neck, felt the sand gritty in the film of sweat on his skin. He was about to put the binoculars down and try the starlight scope when something moved in the trees beyond the wire enclosure.

'There,' he whispered. 'If it's a cat, it's a big one.'

He focused on the place he'd registered the movement, a faint but perceptible straight line change against the random shimmering of the wind-blown forest.

'Do you see anything?' She was close to him now, pressed up against his side, and he could feel the warmth coming from her body, the softness of her full hips.

He scanned the tree line both sides of the place he'd seen the brief change in shadow pattern. 'Nothing,' he said, passing her the field glasses. 'Have a look.'

Zulaika took the glasses and scanned the near end of the clearing and back along the length of it to where the moon was now low over the trees. She handed him back the binoculars. 'There is no guarantee,' she said.

He was about to ask her exactly what in life was guaranteed and then thought that surely she knew this much better and more sadly that he ever could. And then the movement came again, clear and definitive. He watched as two men emerged from the trees, lit up against the darkness of the forest. They halted a moment before moving towards the thatched shelter. They were carrying G3 rifles, the South African-made version of the Belgian FN.

'UNITA,' whispered Zulaika. Her voice was deep, constricted. 'I will tell the others.'

9

Men and Boys

The men moved carefully, deliberately, weapons at the ready. They stopped a moment at the shelter, then crossed to Clay's side of the clearing and disappeared into the trees. If they were working their way along the tree line, it would only be a matter of minutes until they stumbled into his position. Surely, he had nothing to fear; these men were supposed to be their allies. But dread moved through him, hard and cold. He reached for his R4.

A few moments later Brigade, Eben and Zulaika joined him. Clay signalled quiet, pointed in the direction he'd last seen the men and raised two fingers. As he did, more men emerged from the trees. A ragged column was moving into the clearing, some of the men armed, others not.

Zulaika gasped, loud, involuntary. Clay, Eben and Brigade all turned to face her. She shook her head, hand over her mouth, pointed.

Clay grabbed the binoculars. The unarmed men walked with heads bowed, their hands roped behind their backs, tied one to the other in single file, their naked bodies shimmering in the pale monochrome.

'Jesus,' said Clay, passing the glasses to Zulaika.

The prisoners were being herded into the wire cage, a dozen of them, maybe more; black men. One of the armed men closed the gate. The prisoners huddled together in the far corner like Takoradi slaves.

'What are they doing?' asked Eben.

'That is what we are here to learn,' said Brigade.

'They are our allies,' said Eben.

'Our allies don't always tell us what they do,' said Brigade.

'So why not just go and ask them?' said Eben.

Brigade shifted his AK in his lap. 'We have our orders.'

'I count fifteen fighters,' said Clay, 'including the two scouts, who could be moving our way right now.'

'The bushman will warn us,' said Brigade. 'If we need to, we can move back into the forest.'

'I don't like it,' said Eben glancing over at Clay. 'We're too exposed.'

'We stay here and observe,' said Brigade.

Just then Zulaika shifted, turned the focus wheel on the binoculars, glassed the edge of the trees. 'More are coming,' she whispered over her shoulder. 'More prisoners.' She returned to her surveillance, adjusting the focus with tiny movements of her fingers. She gasped. 'Some of the prisoners, they are from my village.' Her voice was hoarse. 'There are boys. Young boys.' And then: '*Mãe de Deus.*'

All Clay could hear now was her breathing, tripped and shallow like a wounded animal's.

He touched her elbow. 'What is it?'

She moved the binoculars away from her face, stared at him, eyes wide, desperation there. 'My son,' she said, almost choking on the words.

Clay counted a dozen more fighters, another string of ten prisoners, boys and men, bound, naked. The pen was filling up.

'You have seen what they do to the women,' said Zulaika. '*Meu Deus*, what will they do to these boys?' She hid her face in her hands and sobbed quietly.

No one spoke.

Clay picked up the binoculars, scanned the pen, the soldiers. And then Clay saw him. He straightened, refocused. 'Jesus Christ.'

'What is it?' said Eben.

Clay passed him the glasses. 'There, to the right of the hut.'

Eben raised the binoculars. '*Fok* me. The *poes* from the bunker. Colonel what's his name.'

'Mbdele.'

At the sound of his name Zulaika spun round. Her face was hidden in the darkness, but Clay could feel the hate flow from her.

'Quiet,' said Eben. 'Everyone down.'

Clay lay silent, scanned the clearing. Two soldiers had left the hut and were now moving along either side of the *chana*. They each carried a large sack. Halfway towards where Clay and the others were hiding, both men came to a halt, aligned themselves at right angles to the long axis of the clearing, stooped, and started hammering something into the ground. The sound of the twin hammer blows reverberated across the open ground, one very close, no more than fifty metres away, the other at the far tree line.

'What are they doing?' whispered Zulaika.

No one answered her. The men had finished hammering and were moving along the length of the *chana* towards them. Clay hugged the ground.

The man on the near side of the clearing was only a few metres away now. They could hear his footfall in the grass, his breathing as he laboured under his load. They heard him stop, drop the sack. He was right there. Clay could see him through the light screen of brush that separated them, the FN strapped across his back, the South African webbing across his midriff. The man reached into the sack, withdrew a stake and hammered it into the ground. From the other side of the clearing, the same noise, steel on steel, like a downwind echo.

Then the man moved on, down the edge of the long, narrow clearing. Clay looked out at the stake. It was within touching distance. Something was taped to its side, just below the crown, long and cylindrical.

Clay looked at Zulaika, at Brigade. 'And what are we supposed to do here, exactly?'

'Just see,' said Brigade. 'Observe.'

'That's it?' said Eben.

'And report back,' said Brigade, frowning.

'And it's Blakely and Captain Wade who ordered this?' said Clay.

'Yes,' said Brigade.

'I don't believe it,' said Eben. 'Not for a goddamned minute.'

'A little late now, *bru*,' said Clay. 'We're here. So what do we do?'

Zulaika sat as if in some kind of trance.

Clay ground his teeth. 'You heard Zulaika. Her son is in there.'

'We're outnumbered at least five to one,' said Brigade, 'probably more. We are here to observe. We will stay hidden, then exfil before they detect us.'

The sound of hammering from both sides of the *chana* as another pair of stakes went into the ground.

'What the hell are they doing?' said Eben.

Just then, the faraway drone of aircraft engines came shifting on the breeze.

Zulaika raised her eyes to the sky. 'No,' she said. 'We must stay.'

'Orders,' said Brigade.

Whose orders exactly? Clay could not help wondering. 'She's MPLA,' he said to Brigade. 'Did you know that?'

The sound of aircraft engines was louder now. More hammering, down towards the far end of the clearing. Brigade looked towards the sound a moment, back at Clay. 'My orders are to come here, with her, and to observe. Not to engage.'

And then from the far end of the clearing two cracks and a steady hiss, like water spraying on concrete. A red glow burst over the *chana*.

'Flares' said Clay. 'That's what's on the stakes.'

Another pair of cracks, the hissing louder now. The men were running back along the length of the clearing towards the hut and the wire enclosure, setting off the flares as they went. A red glow bathed the grass of the clearing and the tree line.

'They'll fire up this one next,' said Clay. 'We have to move. Now.'

'Back into the trees,' said Brigade, up already, moving.

Clay scrambled to his feet, grabbed his gear and followed Zulaika into the denser bush. They'd just reached an ancient ironwood surrounded by a thick clump of thornbush when the flare ignited. Red light shot though the bush.

Clay grabbed Eben's arm. 'Jesus, doesn't any of this strike you as strange: working with our enemy, doing surveillance on our allies?'

'If that's who they are,' said Eben.

Just then a loud crack from the clearing, a climbing hiss. High above them, a red starshell flare exploded in the night sky.

'They're calling in air,' said Brigade.

'Come on,' said Zulaika. 'We must go back.' She started running towards the *chana*. Brigade followed her.

Clay and Eben watched them go.

'I don't like it,' said Eben.

'Neither do I.'

'What do you think they're doing?'

'Maybe it's the same thing as before. Wood, ivory, diamonds.'

'Maybe. You see any?'

'No.'

'Could be just inside the tree line.'

'Could be.'

The sound of an aircraft slowing, engines pitching in the night.

'C-130,' said Clay.

'Definitely.'

'What do you want to do, *broer*?'

'We could walk out.'

'It's a long way.'

'Four days, I reckon. Nothing we haven't done before.'

'Desertion, *broer*. They'd shoot us.'

'Not a chance. We got separated. Fought our way home.'

'We could call in an evac.'

'Brigade has the radio.'

'Do you trust him?'

'I thought I did.'

'And the woman.'

'Yes,' said Clay. 'I trust her. Not sure why, but I do.'

'Just like that lady doctor. You sure can pick 'em, Clay.'

'We stay.'
'What the hell, then,' said Eben.
'What the hell,' said Clay.

10

The Way He'd Remember It

By the time they got back to the edge of the *chana*, the men – the armed and the unarmed – were looking up into the sky. The eastern sky hinted at dawn. The stars died. Strung out along the length of the clearing, twin rows of red flares marked a landing strip over fifteen hundred metres long. And on the breeze, the drone of an approaching aircraft grew louder.

Clay and Eben lay with the others in the thick bush at the edge of the clearing and listened to the aircraft's engines throttling into a final-approach trim, the surge and wane as the pilots gauged the distance from touchdown. A bright light flooded the *chana*, like a premature dawn. Just above the tops of the far trees, some new close planet shone big and clear in the night sky. The thing seemed to hover a moment, strobing time with the engines. And then it was streaking groundward, a meteor. The plane thumped hard onto the grass, bounced and settled again. The engines roared as the pilots reversed pitch, the props throwing up a storm of dust that careened towards the place where Clay and Eben and their companions lay obscured in the bush.

The plane flashed past them. The cloud of dust – fine sand and the dry clay of the *chana* – engulfed them, and for a moment they were blinded, as within a whirlwind, dead grass and the white Ovamboland powder settling over them. And then it had cleared and they could see the big hulking thing bathed red and grey in the dull pre-dawn light, rolling towards the waiting men, the big, square-cut propeller blades of the outer engines feathered already.

It all went quickly after that. When he was finally able to excavate those things so long buried and consider them, his recollection was of speed. Perhaps, he'd think, looking back, it had been speed born of fear, of impending guilt. For, without evidence, is there crime? Or was it some eclipsing of the senses, some adrenaline-fuelled rush, a speedball of wilful ignorance obliterated with a single touch, palm on wrist?

The Hercules taxied towards the men waiting by the enclosure, swung its big fin tail so that it was facing along the length of the runway, and lowered its rear ramp. The turbines wound down and quiet descended.

Men jumped from the plane, running towards the UNITA fighters waiting by the shelter. Clay grabbed the binoculars and focused on them: half a dozen, armed; irregulars by the look of them – caps and jeans, bandanas pulled up over their mouths and noses so that only their eyes were visible.

'Whites,' Clay said.

No one said anything. They'd all seen the ghostly forearms, pale in the moonlight.

There was a brief conference. Some of the UNITA soldiers walked over to the wire cage. One of them opened the door and a group of prisoners was led from the cage and lined up next to the palm-roofed shelter. Five of them, naked, shackled. The white men stood before the prisoners, weapons at the ready.

'Bloody hell,' said Eben.

'Look,' said Clay.

A pair of men had emerged from the back of the C-130 and were walking towards the shelter. One of the men was small, soft-looking, as if unused to the rigours of the outdoors. He wore dark trousers and a white lab coat. The other was taller, athletic. He wore old-style khaki shorts and a camouflage-pattern jacket, and carried a scoped R4 in one hand and a military issue satchel in the other. Both men had headlamps strapped across their foreheads, beams of light jerking across the grass before them as they walked.

The pair stopped and stood before the line of prisoners. From this angle, Clay could now see the faces of the two men. Both wore surgical masks.

Eben muttered something Clay could not make out.

One of the armed white men barked out something in Afrikaans. A pair of UNITA soldiers grabbed one of the prisoners from the line, guided him to where the man in the lab coat and his companion stood. He was silent, walked with his head bowed, his hands still tied behind his back. One of the UNITA soldiers placed himself behind the prisoner and withdrew a sidearm. Then he pointed his pistol at the prisoner's head.

Zulaika gasped. Clay went cold.

The UNITA soldier jammed the pistol hard into the base of the prisoner's skull so that it pushed his head forward. Then he kicked the prisoner in the back of the legs. The prisoner crashed to his knees.

The man in the lab coat stood looking down at the prisoner. He was bearded, wore a dark bush hat with the strap cinched up tight under his chin so that the loose, pale flesh bulged out in parallel ridges. A stethoscope hung around his neck. His face mask jumped as he spoke. He bent at the waist, reached his hand under the prisoner's bowed head, lifted his chin and looked into the prisoner's face a moment. Then he held his hand out. His companion reached into his satchel and withdrew what looked like a syringe, and handed it to him.

And then the needle raised to the night, a finger's flick to the side of the syringe, the glint of moonlight on surgical steel. That was how Clay would remember it, anyway, years later when the involuntary slipstream of his mind threw him back to these places that he'd tried for so long to obliterate. He would remember, too, how quiet it was, as if the insect kingdom, too, were watching, waiting.

The needle was pushed into the man's deltoid. The plunger was depressed. It was like that – passive, the man's body taking the chemicals, the other prisoners and their minders all watching this occur, the night so quiet, as if in some sort of stasis, a halfway place between understanding and not, Clay and the others hidden on the edge of the *chana*, watching as if this were a demonstration, an entertainment of some sort.

The man convulsed, his body shaking uncontrollably. The spasms seemed to go on and on, the man's limbs flailing at his sides, his head twisting and lolling. Then he voided his bowels and collapsed. One of the white soldiers laughed. A pair of UNITA fighters grabbed the incapacitated man by the wrists and ankles and dragged him away. Another prisoner was brought forward, pushed to his knees. Another injection. Same result.

'Holy Mother of God,' Eben whispered.

Soon, all five prisoners were lying on the ground in a neat row, naked, unmoving. The man in the lab coat walked slowly along the row, head bowed, shadowed by his assistant. The prisoners looked like patients now, ranked out like Clay had been a few days before in 1-Mil. Clay followed with the glasses as the man in the lab coat stopped and crouched next to one of the patients. After a moment, he flicked the ear pieces of his stethoscope into place and placed the detector onto the patient's chest. He turned to his assistant and said something. The assistant scribbled in his notebook, the headlamp beam juddering across the naked bodies of the black men as he wrote.

Something tugged at Clay's sleeve. It was Zulaika. She rolled towards him and placed her lips on his ear. He could feel the humidity of her breath on the cold of his cheek, smell the tears' enzymes reacting with her skin. 'It's him,' she gasped. '*O Médico de Morte*.' The Doctor of Death.

Clay turned to face her, looked into her eyes.

'It is him,' she repeated.

'Bloody hell,' whispered Eben in Afrikaans.

Zulaika pulled back her hair, her tears shining like blood in the flare-light. 'I don't know what they are doing. But these men they take are never seen again.'

'Did you see the way that *oke* spasmed out when they injected him?' said Eben. 'What the hell are they doing?'

'They're not dead,' said Brigade. 'The doctor is listening to their hearts.'

'No, you are wrong,' said Zulaika. 'He is checking that they are dead.'

They watched as the doctor called over to the soldiers standing near the wire cage. Clay could hear his voice on the night air: gruff, thickly Afrikaner. More prisoners were brought from the cage and lined up as before.

'Maybe they're military intelligence types,' said Clay. 'We know that they fingerprint and catalogue every enemy prisoner – give them medical checks. Maybe they're just vaccinating them.'

'Are you joking?' said Eben. 'Did you see how they reacted?'

The second group of prisoners was lined up before the doctor. These men had seen what had happened to the first group. Their heads were not bowed. They stared at the doctor, eyes wide with fear. Several were shaking. There was one boy. He was crying.

Zulaika scrambled to her feet. 'Adriano,' she cried. She was about to break cover, but Brigade grabbed her, held her by the shoulders.

'You cannot,' he said.

'*Meu filho*,' she sobbed. Her entire body was shaking. Her lips quivered. Tears poured down her face. She looked at Brigade a moment, and in the time it took to blink she'd transformed. She slapped Brigade hard across the face and pushed him away. Then she pulled her sidearm, and pointed it at Brigade's face. 'Don't,' she hissed, backing away towards the clearing.

As she turned and began to run Clay rugby tackled her, his arms around her waist, bringing her down. The pistol spilled from her hand. Clay rolled her over, clamped his hand over her mouth and looked her in the eyes. 'If you go out there, you're dead,' he whispered, knowing that she didn't care.

Fury poured undistilled from her eyes as she struggled beneath him.

'If one of us works our way around onto the flank, we could get them in a crossfire,' said Eben. 'Maybe scatter them before they realise what's going on.'

'No,' said Brigade. 'We have only four weapons. It would be suicide. And our mission will fail.'

Zulaika struggled, mumbling something under Clay's hand.

'As soon as we open up, the pilots will get out as fast as they can,' said Eben. 'The whites will leave with the plane, they won't wait around.'

'That will leave only UNITA,' said Clay.

'A firefight against UNITA, our allies?' said Brigade. 'No. We cannot.'

'If they're our allies, what are we doing here in the first place?' said Eben. 'Fuck 'em. I hate the bastards.' He pointed out towards the men lying in rows on the ground. 'Look what they're doing, for fuck's sake.' He grabbed his R4 and stood. 'I say we take them out.'

Brigade raised his AK and pointed it at Eben. 'Stand down, troop,' he said. 'If we shoot now, we kill the prisoners in the crossfire, too.'

Eben stared at the black Sergeant, disbelief in his eyes. 'What the *fok*?'

'That's an order,' said Brigade.

Eben didn't move, just stood there bathed in the fractured flare-light, shadows twitching on his face, chest and hands.

Clay felt the tension drain from Zulaika's body. She took a deep breath through her nose. He loosened his grip and took his hand away.

'Brigade is right,' she said. 'We are too few. It is too dangerous.' She rolled away from Clay and resumed her position.

Brigade lowered his weapon. Eben still stood unmoving in the darkness.

Clay lay beside Zulaika and picked up the binoculars. 'They're probably just injecting them with something that will make them sleep, or make them docile. If they wanted to kill them, it would be a lot easier just to shoot them.'

Zulaika nodded, looking at the ground. 'Probably you are right. I am sorry. It is my son.'

Clay said nothing. He knew the men and the boys were dead, that she knew this, too.

One by one the remaining prisoners were led before the doctor.

This time they were not forced to their knees, but remained standing. Each was injected. This time, the reaction was altogether different. Rather than the almost immediate spasm and collapse of before, the men stood for a long moment after being injected, seemingly unaffected. Clay could see the looks on their faces change as they realised that they were going to be alright, relief flooding into them, only to be replaced moments later with a kind of wide-eyed drowsiness. It took several minutes. They swayed, gently at first, as if fighting off sleep, then more violently, as if drunk. Then their legs gave way and doubled beneath them and they made to sit on the ground and then to lie down. Soon they were still. And in all of this, the movements seemed half controlled, robbed of dignity.

When it was the boy's turn, Zulaika turned away. She curled up like a foetus on the ground, whimpering. After a moment, she jammed her right fist into her mouth, stifling her moans. For the boy, slumber came quickly. He collapsed to the ground moments after being injected and was carried away like the others.

The doctor moved slowly among the supine bodies, examining his work, occasionally stopping to touch a man's neck, or crouching to place his stethoscope on a man's chest. His assistant followed, writing in the notebook.

And then it was over. The enclosure was empty and the doctor and his assistant were walking back to the Hercules. The white paramilitaries and some of the UNITA soldiers slung their weapons, and working in pairs, started to pick up the bodies.

'They're carrying the bodies to the plane,' said Clay.

'That's why we never see them again,' said Zulaika, her voice strangled. She pushed herself to her knees. 'We thought that they were being shot and buried somewhere. We never imagined this.'

'Jesus, Zulaika,' said Eben. 'Your hand.'

She looked down. Blood poured from the second knuckle of her right index finger. She shrugged, slumped back to the ground.

Brigade broke out the medical kit, inspected her hand. 'She almost bit right through,' he said, dousing her wound with disinfectant.

'Where will they take them?' she murmured.

'I have no idea,' said Clay.

'Hold still,' said Brigade, splinting the finger and wrapping her hand in a bandage.

'Only one way to find out,' said Eben, getting to his feet. His face glowed red in the flarelight, the whites of his eyes red, too, everything stained. He wrapped his bandana over his mouth and nose, slung his R4 across his back, broke cover and started walking towards the Hercules.

'What the hell?' said Clay.

'Come back,' hissed Brigade.

But Eben kept walking steadily towards the Hercules. He was in the open now, plainly illuminated by the red of the flares and the silver moonlight.

Clay didn't really think about what he did next. By then it was just instinctive, – a pup following the older dog. He grabbed his R4, jumped up and ran after Eben, falling in beside him, slinging his weapon as Eben had and pulling his bandana up over his face.

'Come all the way out here,' said Eben as they walked towards the place where the bodies were laid out. 'I'm going to bloody well find out what these assholes are fucking around at. I'm getting so god-damned tired of it all, Clay. You know what I mean, *broer*?'

Clay was only starting, then, to understand what drove Eben. By the time he had finally worked it out, years later, everything that had made Eben the man he was had been lost forever.

Now they were close enough to the C-130 for Clay to see the pilots' faces bathed in the glow of the cockpit. Men scurried in and out of the aircraft's open rear ramp.

'It's the same one,' said Clay.

'The same what?'

'The same *flossie* that landed in the *chana* that day we got hit by the FAPLA regiment near Rito. The one they took out all the ivory on.'

'Shit,' said Eben. And then: 'What's that smell?'

Amongst all the comings and goings, the noise of the Hercules' engines starting up, the darkness and the swirling flarelight, no one paid them any attention. They walked to the plane, under the wingtip and through the dust of the propwash to the shelter.

Three rows of men and boys lay in the grass, covered in dust. The smell was overpowering. Excrement pooled around the bodies.

Clay and Eben merged into the swirling chaos, unremarked, did as the other armed men were doing. Clay grabbed the feet of one of the bodies, Eben the arms. They half carried, half dragged, the naked, shit-covered man to the plane and up the ramp, just one more pair of white men toiling in the red-lit darkness. As they reached the cargo deck, one of the white paramilitaries scrambled past them, jumped to the ground and hunched over, hands on his knees, spewing vomit onto the grass.

Clay and Eben laid the body out next to the others, two parallel rows forming along each side of the aircraft's wide cargo deck, feet towards the middle of the deck. Three more times they returned for another body, the other men around them huffing and coughing, heads down in the dark, faces covered, the carrying exhausting, the dead always so much heavier than the living.

This would be the last one. Clay set the man's feet gently on the deck, stood and wiped his shit-smeared hands on his trouser legs. The plane was vibrating now as the pilots tested the plane's inboard engines. He looked at Eben. 'Let's get the hell out of here,' he said.

'Not until I find out what the hell they're doing,' said Eben.

Clay turned towards the rear ramp just as a pair of soldiers laid out the last body. They were between Clay and Eben and the exit ramp. The two outboard engines spun to life. Clay nudged past the men, head down, stepping between the shit-smeared legs of the bodies. One of the men jostled Clay as he passed, muttered something. Clay now stood at the edge of the ramp, the trampled grass and safety only a few short steps away. Outside he could see the last of the black UNITA soldiers assembling, moving off into the red-fringed forest from where they'd come. Brigade and Zulaika were out there, too, still hidden, waiting. At any moment, one of the white paramilitaries would do a head count and realise that they were plus two. It was time to go.

Clay looked back. Eben was still there on the cargo deck, talking to the pair of white soldiers. One of them laughed at something Eben said. The other was fidgeting with his weapon, eyeballing Clay. The inboard engines were spinning up. They were out of time. Clay was about to signal to Eben when the forward bulkhead door that led to the cockpit opened. A powerfully built man in a black t-shirt and combat trousers stood with his hand braced on the bulkhead. Unlike the men who stood facing him on the cargo deck, his face was uncovered. He stood there a moment, surveying the cargo bay. His gaze moved from one man to the next, along the rows of bodies. For a second and a half he looked right at Clay. Then he raised his right hand and made a twirling motion with his index finger. A coiled Cobra flexed on his bicep. Then he turned and closed the bulkhead door. Everyone scurried for their seats. All four turbines roared. The ramp started to close. The aircraft was rolling.

☾

Commissioner Lacy: We have heard persistent rumours about
    such activities, Mister Straker. But this is the first
    time the commission has heard first-hand testimony
    describing an actual event. Is your colleague – the one
    you say was with you that day – able to corroborate this
    testimony?

Witness: No.

Commissioner Lacy: Why not?

Witness: He's dead.

Commissioner Lacy: I'm sorry.

Witness: I'm not.

Commissioner Lacy: That's a very strange thing to say,
    young man.

Witness: It's a long story.

Commissioner Ksole: If corroborated, this testimony could
    constitute a case for bringing a charge of war crimes
    against the perpetrators. I will ask this straight out,
    Mister Straker. Were you a member of Torch Commando?

Witness: Torch Commando? No. I had never even heard of it
    at the time.

Commissioner Ksole: But you did come to know of it?

Witness: Yes, sir.

Commissioner Ksole: Surely you realised what was going on?

Witness: I knew then that something was very wrong. I
    hadn't started putting the pieces together, though. That
    came later.

Commissioner Lacy: After you were wounded again?

Witness: Yes, ma'am.

Commissioner Lacy: At 1-Military Hospital?

Witness: Yes, ma'am. And after.

Commissioner Ksole: And where did you think the plane was
    going? What did you think they were going to do with the
    prisoners – the men and the boys?

Witness: I had no idea.

Commissioner Ksole: It is very important that you answer
    this truthfully, Mister Straker. This is pivotal.

Witness: I thought they might be military intelligence
    people. That maybe they had been interrogating the
    prisoners, that they were taking them back to South

Africa for fingerprinting and processing. Or burial. I had
seen them doing that before, on other operations. I could
never have imagined what they were going to do.

Commissioner Rotzenburg: Can you provide evidence that
corroborates your claim that you were on that plane
clandestinely?

Witness: Sorry, sir. I don't follow.

Commissioner Rotzenburg: Can you prove that you weren't
actually working with this doctor and his men?

Witness does not answer.

Commissioner Rotzenburg: The witness will answer the
question. Can he prove he was not complicit in the crime
he describes, if indeed it actually occurred?

Witness: _____. You think I was part of it?

Commissioner Barbour: Please, Mister Straker. You will
refrain from using that kind of language.

Witness: I'm sorry, sir.

Commissioner Rotzenburg: I repeat the question. Can you
prove you were not complicit in this crime?

Witness: Why would I be telling you this if I was?

Commissioner Barbour: Many are coming forward, Mister
Straker, admitting their crimes, seeking absolution,
reconciliation. We have heard some heinous things, some
terrible things.

Witness: I came here to tell the truth.

Commissioner Rotzenburg: You helped load the prisoners onto
the plane?

Witness: I … Yes, I did.

Commissioner Rotzenburg: Can you prove that you were not
actually one of the perpetrators?

Witness: No. I can't prove it.

11

Enemies and Friends Alike

The plane rumbled over the sand of the *chana* and gained speed. Men scurried to the fold-out canvas seats ranged along the forward bulkhead and the sides of the fuselage, strapped themselves in. Clay grabbed Eben by the arm and pulled him towards the aft-most seats. The two men Eben had been speaking with sat on the facing side of the deck, staring at them. Clay and Eben buckled in, their movements automatic.

The Herc rotated and climbed into the troposphere. After a while they levelled out. The aft ramp was lowered, and fresh, cool air flooded the cargo bay. In a few minutes the stench from the bodies had dissipated somewhat.

The plane droned on through a lightening sky, the new sun showing red through the gaping rear exit. As they climbed again, the temperature dropped and soon Clay was shivering.

An hour and a half in and they were still heading west, the paramilitaries dozing in their harnesses, some speaking quietly, their words lost in the harmonics of the engines vibrating through the airframe and their own bones. The bodies of the prisoners lay open-mouthed in their slave-ship rows, heads ranked a few inches from the fuselage, the feet of the boys ranged up level with the knees of the men, the two constituencies, the black and the white, the living and the dead, segregated even here, so far above the surface of the earth, the morning sun slanting through, red and pale and magnanimous.

Clay nudged Eben. '*Broer*,' he said. 'Look.'

Through the aft exit bay, far below, a line of white foam ran like a frontier between wedges of dune-red desert and Atlantic blue.

Eben jumped out of a shallow doze. 'What the hell?'

'The coast. Heading west.'

'Where are they going?'

'You mean where are *we* going.'

Eben frowned. 'We.'

'Maybe they want to fly south along the coast, enjoy the view.'

Eben glanced down at the rowed bodies. 'I'm sure they'd appreciate that.'

'Cape Province, maybe? We should be turning south pretty soon, then.'

'The absurdity of the situation we find ourselves in, my friend, is beyond measure,' Eben said in English.

'What were you saying to those two *okes*?'

'I told them we were Special Forces, long-range recon, attached to UNITA.'

'Jesus, Eben.'

'I said we had orders to get to the LZ and exfil with them. It was either that or admit we were spying on them.'

The two men Eben had been speaking to were staring at them again from across the cargo deck. Clay could see their mouths moving under their bandanas. One of the men pushed his scarf from his mouth. He had a thick black moustache and lambent eyes. His chin was covered in dark stubble. He looked at Clay a moment then nodded, professional. Clay nodded back, his stomach cold.

'That won't stack up if Cobra gets a look at me,' said Clay. 'He saw me plain and clear that day near Rito.'

'So we better make sure he doesn't.'

Clay tightened the bandana around his face. 'Thank God for the shit.'

'Poor bastards,' said Eben.

'Poor bastards,' repeated Clay.

'Next time I'm at mass with my mum I'll do just that, *broer*. Dear Lord, I'll say, thank you for the shit.'

Clay smiled, felt the bandana cinch up around his nose. He hoped the men across the cargo bay noticed it.

'Do you really think old Wade signed those orders, Clay?'

'Who the hell knows?' He'd been wondering just that for more than an hour. Why would their CO have signed an order sending two relatively junior soldiers out on a covert mission into a neighbouring country with a known enemy to conduct surveillance on their ally? 'Maybe the order was a fake,' Clay said.

Eben nodded. 'Why would a 32-Bat Sergeant forge an order? Unless he's a mole.'

You've been reading too many spy books, *bru*.'

'There's one way to find out. As soon as we get back, we go talk to the CO.'

Clay nodded.

'If we get back.'

'Seneca.'

Eben smiled. He had a great smile. Even said so himself.

They fell into silence. Time slowed. The rising sun painted the cargo bay roof red. Clay watched the rear door's shadow retreat across the forward bulkhead, that knife-edge of now-yellowing light warping over the faces and blinking eyes of the paramilitaries, then flowing like a tide across the landscape of rowed-out bodies. Ten-thousand-foot air flowed thin through his lungs. Anoxia toyed with his senses, brought strange visitors, offered fleeting illusions of clarity. Still heading west, out to sea, somewhere over the Atlantic.

Clay was about to speak a prayer of his own – and mean it – when the engines throttled back. Instantly everything was a little bit quieter; the whine of the servos as the flaps came down, the adjustment of pitch as the aircraft was trimmed up.

'We're slowing to drop speed,' said Clay. They had both done enough jumps from C-130s – *flossies* as the parabats called them – to know the sequence well enough.

'Out here?' said Eben. 'I don't see any chutes.'

Clay scanned the cargo bay. 'Over there, near the ramp controls.' A dozen parachutes packed away behind strapping.

Clay figured they were about two hundred kilometres offshore now. Below, the deep, cold blue of the Benguela current, which ran north along the western edge of Africa, and the darker upwelling of nutrient-rich waters that brought fish and seals teeming to the Skeleton Coast. The men were unbuckling their shoulder straps now, standing, checking their webbing. Clay and Eben did the same.

The forward bulkhead door opened. Cobra appeared, a cigarette burning between his lips. The sharp smell of tobacco whirled through the cargo bay. The rear ramp was coming down now. Beyond the rows of bodies, the deep blue of the ocean filled the yawning cargo-bay door. Even from this altitude the surface was alive, duned with long ribbons of darker water that shifted with the currents, sculpted by shearing winds and squalls, scattered over with pearl-strings of low cloud. Clay imagined all the life below that surface, the creatures varied and multitudinous.

Once, sailing with his uncle in the Indian Ocean off Durban, he'd caught a yellowfin tuna. It had taken him more than an hour to bring the fish close enough to the boat to see. He remembered looking through the water and seeing him so big, far down still, magnified by the lens of the water, the beautiful silver of the broad flanks, the flashes of deep yellow, a shade like none you could see in the city, in anything made by people, and below him that dark-blue Indian Ocean depth.

Cobra closed the bulkhead door behind him and stood facing the men. He took a long pull on his cigarette, poured the smoke back out through his nostrils. 'You know what to do,' he shouted in Afrikaans. 'Make it quick. Cold beer and a *brai* when we get back.'

A few grins and nods as the men paired up as before and started moving towards the rear of the plane. Clay and Eben followed.

The first pair stood next to the aft-most body. Each man tethered himself to the aircraft with one of the big nylon straps, clipping it into his webbing. Then together they lifted the body, wrists and ankles, and dragged it across the ramp. They stood like that a moment, silhouetted against the blues of the ocean and the atmosphere, the body between them. Then they swung it over the edge.

Clay gasped, choked. Someone laughed.

The next pair lifted a body, carried it to the ramp, swung it out into the slipstream. Six pairs of men performed the same act, and then it was Clay and Eben's turn. The man at their feet was of average height. His ribs showed through greying skin. He had a short grey beard, a pinched nose. The eyes were open but dead, empty. Clay took the man's hands in his own. The skin was cold, the arms already stiff. Eben lifted the man's legs. Clay looked at his friend. Eben's eyes were stretched wide above the edge of his bandana. Clay met his gaze, fixed it a moment – a second perhaps, two, trying to convey what he didn't know how to say: all of the things that later he would come to imagine he had managed to process then, there, as it was happening.

Many years later, when he had finally unearthed all that he had buried inside himself, in the deepest ocean trenches, he would come close to a realisation. And it was this: that he had become one of those soldiers in the documentaries he'd seen about the Nazi atrocities during the war – laying and stacking the bodies of murdered Jews, rows upon rows in the pre-dug mass graves. Only now it was the sea, and even though he did not agree with it, he was, nevertheless, a part of it, a cam in the machine, spinning asymmetric on his axis and doing his job as the whole thing whirred around him and consumed and killed and grew. And much later, as a witness testifying about these atrocities, he would be asked about this man standing opposite him, the best friend he'd ever had; and when the lady commissioner expressed her regret at his death, Clay would say he was glad and she would be truly shocked. He would see it on her face, in the colour coming up under her powdered cheeks, the moistening of her cracked, old-woman's lips. Can you imagine living a year, let alone a decade, with the knowledge of this act locked away in a body as immobile and unresponsive as the one they'd just thrown from the door of an airplane travelling at ten thousand feet into the ocean below? And what if you were unable to drown it in alcohol, dim it with sex or drugs, mute it with the epinephrine of combat or fear; or even, if you were lucky – and then only for the shortest of times – kill it with love?

Clay did what the others before had done: tethered himself with one of the big nylon straps, hooking the d-ring to his body webbing. Eben did the same. They started towards the ramp, the body heavy and rigid between them, the excrement now hard and dry on the man's legs. They stood at the edge of the ramp. Clay stared down at the ocean far below, the pure-white clouds drifting across its surface.

This cannot be happening.

This is not me doing this.

I am looking down on someone else and some other ocean.

And whether he had thought these things then, the flesh of the man's arms cold against his, or much later, he would in the end no longer be able to distinguish.

They swung the body. Clay watched it fall, a man and then a black speck against the limitless blue. And then nothing.

Clay turned, unclipped, started walking back to the rows of bodies as another pair moved to the ramp's edge. Another body was flung out. Clay's insides were shuddering as if they would liquefy at any moment and come up through his throat, as if he would vomit out his liver and heart and stomach and his shit-wormed intestines. His hands were shaking. Someone clapped him on the back, laughed.

The next one was a boy, not much more than ten years old. Curly dark hair fringed around a delicate face, the skin lighter than some of the other men, more like the bushmen – a warm caramel colour. The boy was not nearly as heavy as the man they had just thrown into the void. Clay clamped down hard around the boy's wrists, lifted. The skin was warm to the touch, almost feverish. Eben lifted the boy's legs, shuffling a moment with the weight.

Then Eben stopped dead, wide eyed. 'Jesus *fokken* Christ,' he said.

Clay looked down at the boy's face. It was a face he would remember for the rest of his life, a face that would come to him, there in that hotel room on the coast of Mozambique so many years later, after he had lost the only woman he had ever loved and there was nothing left for him in the world.

Clay staggered. A bolt of lightning shot through him, blew apart his circuits.

The boy's eyes were wide open, staring right at him. These were not the dull, lifeless eyes that Clay had seen before on enemies and friends alike. There was depth, movement. And in the boy's wrists, even and strong like time, a pulse.

It was Adriano, Zulaika's son.

☾

Commissioner Rotzenburg: I remind the witness that he is under oath.

Witness: I understood. I understand.

Commissioner Rotzenburg: This is a very serious accusation.

Witness: It's not an accusation.

Commissioner Barbour: With respect, Mister Straker, this sounds fantastic. I mean, it's very hard to believe.

Witness: It happened.

Commissioner Ksole: And you participated.

Witness does not answer.

Commissioner Ksole: I repeat, Mister Straker. You participated.

Witness: There was nothing else we could do.

Commissioner Ksole: You could have stopped it.

Commissioner Rotzenburg: If it actually happened. I remind the witness and this commission of the findings of the Cyprus Prison Service's evaluation of his mental state, in its report of 1995. On this basis, how can we be sure that your testimony is in any way accurate, Mister Straker?

Commissioner Barbour: The commission already has this information. We are all aware of it.

Commissioner Rotzenburg: In the opinion of the Chief Psychiatrist of the Cyprus Prison Service, Mister Straker, you are an extremely unstable individual. He concluded that you have a tendency to confound the past with the present, that you muddle places and events. In short, Mister Straker, your internal chronometer does not function as a normal person's does.

Witness is silent.

Commissioner Rotzenburg: So, I repeat the question. How can we be sure that these details are accurate?

Witness: I guess you can't.

Commissioner Barbour: Gentlemen, please.

Commissioner Ksole: May I repeat my question, please? Could you have stopped it, Mister Straker, what happened on the plane?

Witness: With respect, sir, there were two of us; over a dozen of them. We were two miles above the Atlantic.

Commissioner Ksole: You could have tried.

Witness: What would you have done, sir?

Commissioner Ksole: I would have at least tried.

Witness: Truly?

Commissioner Ksole: Of course.

Witness: Then you would have ended up out the door, too.

Commissioner Barbour: Please, Mister Straker. You are walking very close to the edge, here.

Commissioner Ksole: You don't know what might have happened.

Witness: I don't know anything anymore.

Commissioner Lacy: Mister Straker?

Witness: What can one man do, alone?

Commissioner Ksole: His best, Mister Straker. His best.

Witness: My best was never good enough. I know that now.

Commissioner Lacy: But you are here, Mister Straker. This is a brave thing you are doing, and the commission commends you for it.

Witness does not answer.

12

Looking Straight into Him

'Jesus Christ,' said Clay. 'He's alive.'

Eben stared at him. 'What?' he shouted, trying to out-decibel the noise from the open doorway.

Clay tipped his chin at the boy he was holding by the wrists, the pulse clear there now, an unmistakeable nudge he could feel all the way through himself. 'He's alive. Breathing.'

Eben's eyes widened.

Next to them, another pair of men had hoisted a body and were waiting their turn to move towards the doors. It was the *okes* Eben had been speaking to before take-off.

'Get moving,' barked the man with the dark moustache.

'This one's alive,' shouted Clay.

'All these ones are,' the man shouted back, glancing at the row of bodies at their feet. 'Get moving.'

'He's only a boy,' said Clay. 'Just a villager.'

'How the *fok* do you know that?'

'We were there with UNITA when they took him from the village,' bellowed Clay. Eben's story was all they had now.

Some of the other men were looking at them, muttering.

'A little late, now, *broer*,' shouted the man with the moustache. 'Should have taken it up with UNITA. Now either get going or get the *fok* out of the way.'

'*Fokken* recon pussies,' shouted the other man.

'What's the hold up?' someone called from further forward.

Cobra was moving towards them, weaving his way between those standing and those not.

Clay looked at Eben. It was all there in his eyes.

In the months and years to come, in the time that was left to him, Clay would imagine other courses of action they may have chosen to take that day; and even as the memory of the thing itself was subsumed and interred, the imagined alternatives began to establish themselves as possibilities, and a salve of doubt came to be brewed and applied to the wound. Maybe it hadn't happened the way it had. Maybe he and Eben had put the boy down, refused to help with the dumping of bodies, had picked up their weapons and in righteous fury dispatched every one of the executioners, then entered the cockpit and commandeered the plane and brought the leaders – Doctor Death and Cobra – to justice. Or, maybe they'd somehow convinced them all, including Cobra and Doctor Death, through strength of argument, through force of will, to desist and turn back to the makeshift airstrip in Angola, let the prisoners who were still alive go. And along the way, Clay and Eben had convinced the doctor to abandon this murder altogether and seek a more righteous path. And in their gratitude for the saving of their souls, the doctor and Cobra and his men had allowed Clay and Eben on their way, too, some perhaps with admiration in their eyes. But of course rationalisation was more powerful than any of these twenty-year-old's fantastic reconstructions. If they hadn't done what they'd done, they wouldn't have survived, and the story would never have been told, and the possibility of justice would have been lost forever. After all, when they'd first embarked on this journey they'd had no idea what would happen and were thus completely unprepared. Faced with few viable options, they'd done the best they could at the time. And as with all rationalisations, it didn't help much.

Clay and Eben let the other pair pass and watched as the man they carried was thrown alive into the ten thousand feet of air that was all he had left.

They laid the boy down on the deck, towards the rear of the cargo bay, out of the way of the other pairs of men dragging bodies towards the ramp. Cobra was halfway along the length of the cargo deck now, eyes narrowed.

'We're screwed,' said Clay.

Another pair passed with a body. The man they were carrying was big, heavy, and they could only drag him, his back scraping across the ridged aluminium decking. 'Kaffir lovers,' one of the men said as he passed.

'Stay here,' Eben said. 'And whatever you do, don't let him see your face.' Then Eben pulled away his bandana, turned and paced towards Cobra.

Clay crouched next to the boy, his back to the fuselage. He kept his head lowered, took the boy's wrist in his hand, felt the pulse there steady still.

Eben was standing with Cobra now as the men worked around them. One by one the bodies, dead and living, were thrown tumbling into the slipstream, as if to measure time. Eben and Cobra continued talking. Clay looked at the boy. Like the others, he had voided his bowels when injected, and his legs were coated with dried excrement. His breathing was shallow and laboured, as if his lungs were being compressed by a great weight. His pulse was regular but slow, and he seemed incapable of movement. His facial muscles, too, seemed unable to contract, voluntarily or otherwise. Only his eyes retained a hint of life, an almost imperceptible flicker of the retina. The boy was looking straight at him. Straight *into* him.

The deck was clear of bodies now.

All except the boy.

Clay glanced up to where Cobra and Eben were standing. Cobra signalled with his hand and the rear ramp started to close. Clay could hear the flaps coming up and the surge of power to the engines and then the Hercules was banking steeply so that some of the men standing on the deck stumbled and braced against the turn. Soon they were level again and Clay could see by the light in the half-open rear door that they were heading east, back towards Africa.

Cobra turned and started back towards the cockpit. Eben returned and crouched beside Clay and the boy.

'How is he?' said Eben.

'Alive. Barely. Whatever they put inside him has caused almost total paralysis. His lungs and heart are working, but only just.'

'Truly fucked up,' said Eben.

The other men were clustering at the forward bulkhead, where the doctor's assistant was dispensing soap from a gallon jug. Water splashed to the deck from a thirty-gallon container balanced on a tubed platform. The men were washing their hands and faces, drying themselves with towels that they threw into a plastic bin lashed to the forward bulkhead.

Clay looked at his friend. 'What did you say to him?'

'I told him that the boy was the son of an important Angolan politician – a man with connections high up, someone our politicians were dealing with on the inside in Luanda. I told him we had orders to infiltrate UNITA, posing as advisers, and get him back.'

Clay shook his head, amazed. 'Did he buy it?'

'Not sure.'

'You're a hell of liar.'

'I'm going to be a hell of a writer someday, *broer*.'

Clay didn't doubt it one bit. 'If this kid doesn't get medical attention soon, he won't be anything. Did you find out where we're going?'

'No idea.'

'Do you really think they're just going to land and let us walk off the plane with the boy?'

'I have no clue, *broer*. It's all minute by minute right now.'

Clay glanced at the parachutes racked up behind the canvas webbing. 'We could jump.'

'Over the ocean?'

Clay shook his head. Stupid. They were still more than two hundred kilometres from the coast. They'd drown.

'We're just going to have to bluff it out,' said Eben. 'Keep your R4 close.' Then he turned and walked forwards to where the other men were washing up. Clay watched him queue up for soap and wash his arms and face and rinse himself with the water and towel dry. Soon Eben was talking to some of the men, and this was the way that Clay would always see him, his face lit up, a raconteur spinning the story out with his infectious smile and the big movements of his hands and arms, his whole body moving to the rhythms and paces of the story. Clay could see the men he was speaking to warm to the story, laugh at some well-placed word, some punctuation. He had a gift, Eben did, out on his lunatic fringe.

Clay stayed with the boy. Dared not leave him. Feared that, if he did, even for a moment, he would disappear from this deck just as all those other souls had vanished, become just another echo.

As the plane droned on, Clay held Adriano's hand, timing his pulse and the almost imperceptible rise and fall of his small chest. The boy seemed stable. He wasn't good, but he wasn't getting any worse.

Eben came back, handed Clay a cup of water and a blanket, turned and went back to where the other men were sitting. Balls. That's what Eben had. Elephant balls. He knew it then, sitting there on the *flossie's* cargo deck with the boy's pulse echoing frail in his own veins. And much later, after Eben was gone, Clay would allow himself to realise that his friend was one of the bravest men he'd ever known, and how unfortunate it was that his death had not been a brave one.

Clay spread the blanket over the boy, sat beside him and watched the Atlantic drift past far below, shrouded now in afternoon mist, the horizon a blurred diffusion of sea into atmosphere, water into air.

And then the forward bulkhead door opened.

A man stood for a moment in the doorway, a plastic-gloved hand gripping the bulkhead. He seemed to sniff the air, scanning the cargo bay. Some of the paramilitaries, the ones who weren't sleeping in their harnesses, looked away. Others busied themselves with equipment, weapons.

It was the man Zulaika had called *O Medico de Morte*. Doctor Death. His assistant, bareheaded now, was following him.

They were heading straight for Clay.

13

Benguela Sky

Clay let go of the boy's hand and dropped his head slightly, feigning sleep.

He'd been about the same age as this boy, a little more, when he'd last done this. He'd pretended to be asleep in the car that time when he'd driven to Durban with his mother and father, the summer they'd visited his uncle at his place near the beach. They'd arrived late at night, and he remembered smelling the warm sea smell and feeling the salt already on his skin and the way the air felt heavy and full of water. He'd been awake when they arrived but he wanted his father to carry him. Maybe it had been because he'd realised, then, that this might be the last time his father would ever carry him from the car, through the door and then strong and smooth up the stairs to lay him on the bed. And the whole time he could hear his father's voice and smell the heavy tobacco smell on his skin from the cigars he smoked, and feel his strong miner's arms around him like nothing would ever be able to hurt him.

'I would move away from him, if I were you, trooper.' The voice was cracked, as if scarred by some adolescent illness, Skeleton Coast dry.

Clay looked up. Dark eyes peered out over a white hospital mask. Doctor Death.

Clay didn't move.

'Cholera.'

Eben was there now, standing beside Clay.

'I heard you boys were sent to bring this kid out,' said the doctor. 'I'm afraid that will not be possible. Quarantine rules apply. That's why we are burying at sea, so to speak.'

'He's still alive,' said Clay.

'He won't be for long.'

'Are you a doctor?' said Clay.

The man nodded.

'Then help him.'

The doctor shook his head. 'I've already done all I can, for all of them.' The doctor fixed his gaze on Clay. 'You look dubious, trooper.'

'They…' Clay hesitated. 'No one said anything about cholera.'

'What did UNITA tell you?'

'Nothing,' said Eben.

The doctor closed his eyes a moment, reopened them. 'It has become very serious,' said the doctor. 'We have been helping UNITA combat the disease for some months. We believe MPLA is deploying it as a biological weapon.'

'Jesus,' said Clay.

'We are working on some experimental treatments for those who have already contracted the disease, and we have been vaccinating the healthy.' He pointed at the boy. 'This one, I am afraid, must be disposed of.'

Clay stood, trying to reconcile what he'd just heard with what he'd witnessed back at the makeshift airstrip. If the communists were using biological weapons, as had been persistently rumoured over the past few months, the war was entering a deadly new phase. 'You're not touching him.'

The doctor adjusted his mask. 'You are in danger yourselves of contracting the disease.' He looked back at his assistant. 'We could inoculate you now, if you like.'

'We'll take our chances,' said Eben.

The doctor coughed. 'I am sorry, trooper. We cannot land until the body is safely dealt with.'

Outside, Clay could see the red dunelands of the Namibian coast, the blue ocean beyond. 'Our orders are very specific, sir.'

'Whose orders?' said the doctor.

'Can't say, sir,' said Eben. 'Classified. I'm sure you understand.'

The doctor stared hard into Eben's face, coughed into his mask then turned away and shuffled back across the empty deck and through the bulkhead door, assistant in tow. Every one of the paramilitaries was staring at them now.

'Do you believe him?' said Eben in English. 'All this bullshit about biological weapons?'

'He was trying it on. Fishing.'

'What about all the rumours?'

'If it was true they would have issued us B&C gear,' said Clay.

Eben raised his eyebrows. 'You think so?'

'Yes I do, damn it.'

'If he's in radio contact with Mbdele, he'll know pretty soon that our story is bullshit.'

Just then the bulkhead door reopened and the doctor appeared with Cobra beside him.

'*Kak*,' said Eben. 'Didn't take him long.'

'Not going to be able to talk our way out of this one, *broer*,' said Clay in English, just loud enough for Eben to hear.

Eben adjusted the sling of his R4, palmed the pistol grip. 'Just don't let him see your face.'

Cobra, flanked by two paramilitaries, the doctor and his assistant, stopped about five metres away, hands on hips. 'You men,' he shouted in Afrikaans. 'Whoever you are, move away from the boy and lay your weapons on the deck.'

Eben and Clay stayed where they were, saying nothing.

'Step away,' said Cobra again, louder this time. 'Lay down your weapons.'

Looking back, they never really had a choice. Earlier, of course, there had been all kinds of options – other decisions which could have been made, each with its own trajectory of action and result and consequence. But as soon as they'd decided to set foot on that plane, they'd carved away almost every alternative. Clay raced through the possibilities in his mind. Most ended with them both dead. The boy, too.

It was Eben who acted first.

Cobra was filling his lungs, preparing for a third and, most likely, final vocal challenge when Eben raised his R4 and flicked it to automatic.

'We'll do it the other way around, gentlemen,' Eben shouted.

The doctor's eyes bulged. He looked like he was going to shit himself.

Clay raised his rifle too.

'Drop your weapons, please,' said Eben, 'and take a step back.'

Cobra held his ground. The doctor's mouth was pursed tight. Clay was pretty sure no one had ever pointed a gun at him before.

'Now,' said Eben.

Cobra raised one hand, pulled his sidearm from its holster at his waist, laid it on the deck. The other two paramilitaries did the same. The doctor's assistant stood motionless.

'You, too,' said Eben, motioning to the doctor's assistant with the muzzle of his rifle.

The assistant slumped his shoulders, placed his sidearm on the deck.

'Grab two chutes,' said Eben in English out of the side of his mouth.

Clay was already doing it, one hand still on the R4's pistol grip. By now the other men had seen what was going on, were collecting their rifles and moving aft.

'Tell your men to stay back and put their weapons on the deck,' shouted Eben in Afrikaans. 'Or your doctor friend here gets it first.'

The doctor was trembling now. Sweat beaded on his forehead and above his pursed lips. He swayed a moment and flexed at the waist. A look of surprise came over him as a dark stain spread down both trouser legs.

Cobra glanced at the doctor, frowned, held up his hand. 'No shooting,' he said. 'Put down your weapons.'

His men stopped where they were, about halfway along the cargo bay, and placed their weapons on the cargo deck.

Clay hoisted a parachute onto his back and started securing the straps.

'There is no need for this,' said Cobra. 'We have no quarrel with either of you, or your mission. But the boy cannot go back.'

Clay tossed the other chute onto the deck at Eben's feet, went to the aft loadmaster RECP control panel, R4 still aimed at Cobra. Beyond, ten men faced them, weapons at their feet. At this range, even on automatic, Clay and Eben might be able to take out four or five, no more, before the rest returned fire. He keyed the RAMP/DOOR switch to ON, grabbed the pendant control and started lowering the ramp. At cruise speed, the noise from the slipstream was deafening. They were going too fast.

'We're not going to let you go,' shouted the doctor at the top of his voice, barely making himself heard over the buffeting from the open rear door. 'You know that, don't you?'

'Cover me,' shouted Eben.

Clay secured the ramp in the DOWN position, stood with the wind whipping at his trouser legs and through his hair, two hands now on his R4. Eben threaded on his chute and tightened the straps.

Just then, one of the pair standing with Cobra reached to his back and pulled out a handgun. It was small, compact, designed for concealment. Clay reacted first, fired just as the man was raising the weapon for a shot. The 5.56 mm round cut through the man's shoulder and he fell to the deck in a heap. The pistol clattered across the deck.

No one moved. Cobra's men were all poised, ready to pick up their weapons. The doctor was down on the deck now, too, beside the wounded man. At first Clay thought he might have hit him by mistake. But there were no wounds that he could see, no blood. The doctor was curled up, whimpering in a puddle of his own piss.

Eben was backing towards the ramp.

Cobra held up his hand again. His men tensed, line abreast.

'Grab the kid and jump,' Eben yelled in English.

Clay reached for the boy with one hand, the other still on the R4. 'We go together.'

'Go,' yelled Eben. 'You need two hands to hold the boy.'

Eben was right. At this speed, the force of the slipstream might rip the boy from his arms. Clay picked up the boy. As he did, his bandana fell away from his face. He stood. Cobra was staring right at him.

For a moment their gazes locked. Cobra's eyes flashed with recognition. His hand was still raised, as if waiting to give the signal to his men to grab their rifles and open fire. Clay let his rifle hang from its strap around his neck and shoulders, clutching the boy in his arms.

And then Cobra lowered his hand. He did it slowly, backing away. 'Stand back,' he shouted to his men.

'What are you doing?' shouted the doctor's assistant.

Eben stood blinking, R4 still at the ready.

'Let them go,' shouted Cobra.

'You can't do that,' shouted the assistant, crouching beside his boss. 'You don't have the authority.'

'I'm not risking a firefight,' said Cobra. 'Not here. We could all end up dead.'

Clay took a last look at Cobra, those strange gunmetal eyes flashing in the light from the open cargo-bay doors, and jumped.

The slipstream hit him like a speeding car and he tumbled out of control, the world spinning red and blue around him. For a moment he thought he was going to lose his hold on the boy, but he clamped down hard, fighting to right himself.

For an eternity he spun earthwards, the boy's naked body clutched to his chest. Then slowly he managed to stabilise himself. He pulled the rip cord and heard the drogue deploy, and then the jerk as the main chute opened. Below, the ochre and haematite dunelands of the Namibian coast, and high above, the solitary white puff of Eben's chute opening out against a blue Benguela sky.

Part III

14

Even Up the Scorecard

13th August 1981,
Latitude 24° 19'S; Longitude 14° 57'E, South-West Africa

The dunes rushed up to meet him, sculpted walls of red-and-gold sand as high as Johannesburg's tallest buildings. The sea breeze was carrying him inland fast, across the long, crested peaks, the light and shadow of afternoon casting the troughs in darkness. He could feel the reflected heat of the crests rise up to meet him in pulses between the coolness of the troughs. And then he was down, his feet piercing the lit, upwind side of a steep, red dune just beyond the line of shadow, sand billowing all around him as the chute carried him forward. He held tight to the boy, trying to protect his head as they tumbled over the rippled surface in which it was entirely probable that no human had ever before stood. He jammed his boots into the sand, grabbed the chute's cords, collapsed the canopy and finally ploughed to a halt.

He lay a moment, breathing hard, looking up at the sky. Through the din still filling his head – the shouts of men, the mechanical drone of aircraft engines, the sheared fluid scream of the slipstream, the rush of thickening atmosphere past his ears as he fell to earth – now, another sound: the wind's whispered caress of the dunes, the feathering of sand grains, too many to ever be counted.

Clay looked at the boy. His eyes were closed. Sand crusted his lashes, patched his face, his torso and his smooth, hairless arms. He reached for the boy's wrist, felt for a pulse, but his own heart was beating so fast he could distinguish nothing. He reached a hand under the back of the boy's head and lifted his face to his own, listening. But there was just the breeze sighing along the spine of the dune, the sand shivering like skin on its back and naked flanks.

Clay shed his harness and put his ear to the boy's chest. Nothing. God damn it, after everything. He kicked out a ledge on the flank of the dune, put the boy on his back, pulled off his R4, laid it cross-slope on the sand, pulled the kid's head back and opened his mouth, making sure the air passage was open. Then he pinched the boy's nose, placed his mouth over the boy's and exhaled. He watched the chest expand, counted three. Again, pushing air into the boy's lungs, watching the response, the inflation, the collapse. Still no pulse. Again and again he flooded the boy's lungs with air, to no avail.

Clay jammed the heel of his hand down hard onto the boy's chest, leaning in with as much weight as he dared. He'd seen men crack the ribs of casualties they were trying to revive, so hard did they push. Three, four sharp thrusts, and back to the artificial respiration, alternating now, three and three. How long had the boy been gone? In basic training they'd been told that the onset of brain damage was three minutes without oxygen. With all of the shit they'd pumped into him, who knew? Perhaps his brain was gone before they'd jumped. Almost surely.

They were in shadow now, the sun still in the sky but hidden behind the next dune.

Let him go now, he said aloud. Let him go. Clay put his lips to the boy's mouth for the last time, watched the chest rise, fall. And then he sat back on his heels and looked up at the sky.

And it was clear to him, at that moment, that he had been put on this earth not for the giving of life, but for the taking of it. He had already killed three men that he knew of definitively. Probably more. They had all been strangers – men who in another time he would have passed in the street without a glance or thought. And much later he would realise that everything he had done – refusing to dump the boy into the sea and jumping with him – had not been because he was intrinsically good, but because he was selfish. He'd done it for himself, to somehow even up the scorecard. But at that moment, at that point in his life, he had neither the time nor the self-awareness to reach such an understanding. All he knew was that, when he looked back down, the boy's chest rose, then fell. Once. Almost imperceptibly.

In fact, no, it was just the light.

He reached for the boy's wrist, closed his eyes. There it was, the faintest of pulses, a rumour. Another rise of the chest, stronger now, no trick of shadow. And then the boy opened his eyes.

☾

Darkness came.

Clay dug a ledge in the side of the dune. Then he cut away some of the parachute silk, wrapped it around the boy and laid him on the ledge as the air cooled. The first stars appeared, strobing in the heavy sea air. Clay opened his canteen and dribbled water into the boy's mouth, but the boy could not move his lips or tongue. Clay took a swig himself, felt the water lave over his mouth, almost painful. He didn't have much left.

Alone, without water, carrying the boy, his chances of finding his way out of the dunes and reaching help were small. As he'd fallen from the Hercules, he'd been tumbling so violently he hadn't had time to examine the territory. By the time he'd deployed his chute, he'd been too low to see much except a corded landscape of dune crests stretching away in every direction. He knew the dunes ranged parallel to the shore, roughly north–south, but not much more. Travelling across the dunes would be extremely hard work, especially carrying an extra thirty kilos. Much better to strike north or south, follow a crest, and find a draw or drainage that would lead inland. It could mean a hundred kilometres or more, on foot, with little water and no food. And in a few hours it would start getting hot.

He sat a long time and watched the stars brighten, felt the dune's heat radiating back into him. He looked at his watch. Ten hours until sunrise. He needed to find Eben. He knew that Eben would have been looking out for his chute, would have tried to land as close to them as possible. He was half surprised that Eben hadn't already found them. Clay looked up to the crest of their dune. In the darkness he guessed about fifty metres of climbing. He'd get to the crest, pop a flare. Eben would see it. Clay ran his hands across the pouches of his Fireforce vest. One flare. Two smoke grenades. A couple of M27 frags. Lots of ammo for the R4. But heavy. He picked up his R4 and started up the slope, feet ploughing through the loose sand.

Halfway up he stopped, realising his mistake. What if that wasn't Eben who'd followed him out of the C-130? What if they'd killed him, or captured him, and the chute he'd seen was one of Cobra's men, sent to track them? Dispose of them. That was the word the doctor had used. Dispose. Jesus. Clearly they didn't want the boy around as evidence. Otherwise why would they have gone to all that trouble to dump the bodies at sea? As soon as he popped the flare, he'd be as good as dead. But, at the same time, he was sure that Cobra had recognised him, there on the deck of the Herc, just before he'd jumped. Had Cobra nodded to him? Or had Clay imagined that? What he was sure of was that Cobra had *let* him jump. But had Eben followed? And if Cobra had decided to send someone after him, would he have sent a man alone? The rule was you always sent men in teams. Pairs at least. Only assassins worked alone. Would Cobra really have sent a lone hyena to hunt him down, kill him and dispose of the boy? Clay sat on the slope, laid his R4 across his knees and caught his breath, looking out into the darkness. Somewhere out there, close by, was either his best friend or a deadly enemy.

Commissioner Barbour: Mister Straker, welcome back. I must inform you, before we begin, that yesterday, ah, yesterday evening, Commissioner Rotzenburg tabled a motion to end your testimony and disallow what has already been committed to record. The commission has considered the matter, and, ah, despite the misgivings of some of our members, has decided to allow you to continue your testimony.

Witness does not answer.

Commissioner Barbour: Do you understand, son?

Witness: Yes, sir. I … Thank you, sir.

Commissioner Barbour: On the condition that you please stick to answering the questions asked of you, and refrain from any more outbursts or invective.

Witness: I understand.

Commissioner Barbour: Good. Now, yesterday, you told us that this … this doctor, the one on the plane, claimed that FAPLA was deploying biological weapons against its own people.

Witness: Yes. That's what he said.

Commissioner Barbour: And you also told us that he was in Angola, working with our allies to protect them against this weaponised disease.

Witness: That's what he said. Cholera.

Commissioner Lacy: These are extremely serious allegations, Mister Straker. I am sure you understand that.

Witness: I am not making any allegations, ma'am. I'm just telling you what happened.

Commissioner Rotzenburg: This was fifteen years ago. How sure are you that you have recalled these details accurately?

Witness: How am I supposed to answer that?

Commissioner Ksole: Truthfully, Mister Straker.

Witness: Why would I come here, of my own volition, and do anything else?

Commissioner Barbour: Please, Mister Straker. Restrict
   yourself to answering the questions posed by the
   commission.

Witness: Sorry. Yes. I am sure that I have recalled the
   events accurately.

Commissioner Ksole: And did the boy – the one who you
   jumped from the plane with – did he show symptoms of
   cholera?

Witness: He was sick, that's for sure. He almost died. But
   I would say no; no he didn't have cholera.

Commissioner Rotzenburg: Are you a doctor, Mister Straker?

Witness. No, I'm not.

Commissioner Rotzenburg: And can you describe the symptoms
   of cholera?

Witness: No, I can't.

Commissioner Ksole: And did you contract the disease at any
   point after these events?

Witness: No, sir. I did not.

15

Mathematics

Clay surfed back down the dune to where the boy lay, the sand hissing under his feet. Nestled into the flank of the dune, the boy looked peaceful, his chest now rising and falling in a slow but regular rhythm, all of him covered over with a thin layer of blown sand so that, in the pale starlight, Clay almost missed him. He realised that, in a few more hours, if he didn't move him, the dune would take the boy into herself; he would disappear forever.

He brushed some of the sand from the boy's face, hair and chest, hoisted him over his shoulders in a fireman's carry, adjusted the weight, and started south. Clay had to assume the worst, proceed as if an enemy were out there, stalking them. There was no other option. If Eben had jumped, there was nothing Clay could do for him. He could only hope that Eben would find them, despite the fact that Clay would now have to do everything he could to stay hidden.

For the next two hours he followed the trough between the two great dunes, the sand thick and heavy beneath his feet, the boy a live weight through his shoulders, spine and legs. The air was cooler here, but it was hard going and he was sweating hard. At the rate he was losing fluid, dehydration wasn't far off. Once, he thought he heard a voice in the darkness, a word only. He stopped and listened for a long time, alert, ready, but all he could hear was the whispering of the dunes. He kept going, blanked his mind to the ragings of his body, all the autonomous signals of survival.

Three hours before sunrise, with the faintest hint of dawn lightening the eastern edge of the sky, he stopped and laid the boy on the sand. He stood and looked back the way they'd come. His tracks were clearly visible in the starlight, snaking along the base of the trough. Down here, his footmarks would persist for much longer than on the more exposed flanks of the dune, days perhaps. He estimated they'd covered about thirty kilometres, maybe less. In this landscape, thirty kilometres was nothing; a ripple. Clay sat, felt the exquisite relief in his legs, the thirst deep in his brain. He shook his head, checked the action of his R4 and blew sand from the sights and the trigger. If it came down to a fight, he would need his weapon in working condition. Come dawn, he would have to decide: keep going, visible to anyone on either crest, walk as far as he could until the heat became unbearable, or build a hide near the crest of one of the dunes, now, in what remained of the darkness, and wait out the day. At least up there, he'd be able to see what was coming. Just thinking of a whole day without water, waiting out the sun's progress, took on a physical dimension, as if the mental and physical parts of himself were fusing, driven together by the imperative of thirst. But they were too exposed in the trough. They might cover a few more kilometres this morning, but at some point the heat would force them to stop, and they'd end up needing to do the same thing – build a shelter, rest. And if they did, the dune crest would be the best place.

He pushed himself to his feet, feeling the effort in every sinew, and also the deeper, more concentrated challenge of will required to overcome the twin voids of thirst and hunger. He slung the R4 over his shoulder, took a long look at the night sky, so dark, like liquid, the river of stars running through it cold and clear, as if he could drink it in. But there was no slaking his thirst, only the mute aeons of sky, an infinity of time.

He reached down to pick up the boy. As he slid an arm under the boy's shoulders and another under his legs and lifted gently, he heard a voice. He stood perfectly still, listened. Nothing.

Jesus, he was starting to hear things, hallucinations brought on by extreme thirst. He hoisted the boy up over his shoulder and started up the slope. He was almost to the crest when he heard it again. This time he knew it was no hallucination. Three words, in Portuguese: *Agua, por favour.*

Clay kicked out a ledge just below the crest of the dune and laid the boy down. His eyes were closed, lids dusked over with sand. But his lips were parted. And then again, frail over the hiss of the waking dune, the same words, drifting up from between the parted lips: Water, please.

Clay pulled out his canteen, felt the absence of weight, the thin sloshing. Perhaps a quarter-litre left, less. He opened the bottle, held it to the boy's mouth and dribbled in a thin stream. The boy coughed, spluttered, lips moving now, but with effort. Whatever they had given him was wearing off. Muscle control was returning. Clay could see it in the way the boy's breathing had regularised, in the colour of his lips where the water had washed away the sand.

And then the boy's eyes opened.

And for a moment, as Clay knelt on the sand and watched this rebirth, he could see the boy's mother – in those irises the colour of Kunene river water, brown mud with flecks of wood and leaf, in the whites clear and pure and the round shape with the upturned, almost European corners.

The boy nodded and swallowed.

'*Está bem,*' Clay said, putting one hand on his own chest. It's okay. '*Mim. Amigo de sua mãe.*' Me. Friend of your mother.

The boy nodded.

Clay gave him more water.

The boy started to say something.

Clay put a finger over the boy's mouth, shook his head. '*Quieto,*' he said. 'Don't speak, little guy. Save your strength.' You may be thinking you've woken up from a nightmare, but you may have just landed in another. Quiet now. I need to think. An hour till dawn. Clay scanned three-sixty. From where they sat, they had a good view in every direction. In the faint, grey pre-dawn he could see the dune crests sculpted to knife edges, one after the other, ranking away seemingly forever. They were alone.

Clay dug another notch out of the seaward side of the dune crest for himself: big enough that he could curl up comfortably against the sand; deep enough that his body and head were below the crest. Then he cut a wedge in the crestline so that he could see out landward, along the ranks of serried dunes, their sharpened edges just starting to bleed red in the morning sun. Day was coming fast. He pulled off his boots and placed one close to the boy's head, and then arranged a panel of parachute silk so that it covered the boy, the boot propping up the silk like a tent pole, creating a space around his nose and mouth. Clay anchored the silk around the boy with deep handfuls of sand and pulled the panel taut. Hunching down into his part of the excavation, he positioned his R4 in the crest wedge and pulled the rest of the parachute silk up and over himself, using his other boot to prop open a viewing port on the seaward side. Anchoring the edge of the silk around himself, the panel was good and tight, allowing breathing space and circulation of air. Now he had cover from the sun and good views of both adjacent sets of dunes, and to the south. His only blind spot was longitudinally north. He pulled out his knife and cut a rip in the silk. By pushing on the taut surface of the silk he could open up a viewing slit that gave him a full view along their dune and down into the trough below. He took a small sip of water and settled himself into the sand, felt it shift and contour to his body. Already he could hear the grains of quartz scurrying across the taut silk above them, pushed along by the quickening breeze. Cocooned, man and boy, they breathed the close, warming air and waited for their fates; waited for God to pass judgement on them, on their actions past and future.

The sun rose, flicking angry red tongues into the void, pulsing in a cloudless sky, atomising the morning's fallow brume until there was nothing except the air and the sand and the heat broaching from the dunes.

Clay looked out through narrowed eyes across the heating mirage. Already the sea breeze had drifted the sand up and over their shelter, and other than the three openings that he had to continually keep clear of sand, the dune had swallowed them up. They were invisible.

As he had started to do on the long patrols, Clay played games in his head. He'd found that it kept him awake, sharp – prevented his mind from wandering into the dark places he did not want to go. He started with the simple stuff, counting out prime numbers, stalling in the high hundreds, counting back again, branching out along multiples of primes, deconstructing those same numbers by subtraction. In school he'd always been good at maths, had been able to get top marks without ever studying, something in the innate logic of numbers that his brain seemed to process naturally. And then the mathematics were gone, and he was thinking about this boy lying nearby, and the other boys and men swallowed by the ocean.

Hours passed. The sun turned above them, the heat so intense now that it seemed to atomise the very air they breathed, to scour it from their lungs, and with it, precious fluid. He dosed the water carefully now, small sips for himself, dribbling the water carefully into the boy's mouth.

Slowly, the day burned on. The zenith came, blistering. And then, somehow, the dune shadows lengthened. A hint of a sea breeze wafted over them, and the heat relented. Not much, perhaps just a few degrees, but he could feel it. A measure of relief.

The boy was recovering rapidly. Already his breathing was stronger and more regular. Clay was sure now that this had nothing to do with cholera. He reached out and touched the boy's tightly curled hair, felt the delicate smoothness of the top of an ear, the curve down to the lobe, softer again, exquisite almost. He considered again all that the boy's mother had told them. He had just begun to extrapolate towards what she had been surely hiding, when a flash of movement stopped him blank.

Two dune crests away, something emerged from the heat haze. At first he wasn't sure what it was. The shape dematerialised into a disembodied mirage, wavered there, all in pieces, then reformed.

It was a head, poked above the dune crest.

He watched it swivel left and right, then emerge from the dune, body and arms and legs swimming in the distortion, fully silhouetted now against the sky. Clay lay motionless, his breathing shallow, slow. Was it Eben? One of Cobra's men? He couldn't tell.

The figure stood a moment, seemingly scanning up and back, and then started down the face of the dune, moving seaward, in Clay's direction. Within seconds the figure had disappeared behind the crest of the intervening dune. A few minutes later the figure reappeared; the same cautious, almost predatory behaviour, pausing at the crest, partially hidden, the top of the head only visible, scanning the terrain, about a hundred metres away from Clay's hide, with just the broad red trough separating them. Then it was up again and moving. The man wore a wide-brimmed bush hat with a coloured bandana wrapped around his eyes and mouth, and a brown canvas Fireforce vest. He was armed, R4 at the ready. It was Eben.

Years later, Clay would wonder at what impulse, what luck or intuition had made him look away at just that moment. Perhaps it had been the boy stirring, maybe it had been his subconscious reasoning out what should have been so obvious, what he would have realised sooner had he been more experienced and had he not let his fear and thirst dull his thinking. Perhaps it had just been his training. By then he could not remember. Whatever the reason, at just that moment, Clay poked open the slit in the sand-covered silk and looked along the knife edge of his dune to his left.

And there he was, prone against the seaward side of the dune, rifle aimed at Eben.

In his memory it had all happened so quickly, a blur. Bursting from under the cover, whipping his R4 around towards the threat, Eben's name flying from his lungs and across his parched vocal chords, emerging as a hoarse grunt, the man glancing up and towards Clay, Eben spinning towards the flash of parachute silk and flying sand. They all fired at once.

16

No Illusion Come

Clay rolled the man over with his boot, leaned forwards and pulled the bandana away from his face.

'*Moeder van God*,' said Eben.

It was *O Medico de Morte*'s assistant. Clay's bullet had shorn away half his throat and the meat gaped pink and strangely bloodless in the sun. Clay crouched and unhooked the man's canteen. It was almost empty. He passed it to Eben.

'You go ahead, *bru*,' said Eben.

'How much you got left?'

Eben shook his head. 'Not much.'

'Me either.'

'Save it for the boy.'

Clay nodded then went through the man's pockets. He found a small notebook and a few rand. No ID of any kind. Clay stashed the book and the cash in his inner vest pocket. There was no trace of the satchel the man had been carrying back at the landing strip.

Eben kicked at the dead man's rifle, a scoped R4. 'I saw his chute open not long after mine. He was arguing with Cobra just as I jumped.'

'Alone?' said Clay.

'I only saw one chute. I've been trying to find you, and avoid him. Not easy.'

Clay clapped him on the back. 'Tell me.'

'How's the boy?'

'See for yourself.'

Clay led Eben back to where the boy lay. He was awake now. As they approached he pushed himself up onto one elbow, rubbing a hand across his face.

'Still think it's cholera?' said Clay.

Eben ran his hands through his hair. 'I don't know what to think anymore.'

'Way out?'

Eben pointed south. 'A big draw through the dunes, inland to the sea. Ten, maybe twenty kilometres. Hard to tell. There has to be some sort of track or road there. It's the only way through.'

'Sunset soon,' said Clay. 'Better to travel at night.'

'Walking in the dark with a friend, *bru*. Better than alone in the light.'

Clay shook his head. 'More Seneca?'

Eben grinned. 'Hell no. Something a blind person said once. Let's go.'

They took turns carrying the boy. Even so, it was slow going – the sand heavy around their feet, as if the dunes were trying to suck them in, the sun gone now but the sand throwing back its stored heat like an echo.

In the end it was a lot further than twenty kilometres. More like thirty. By the time they emerged from the dunes into the broad gravel and salt-pan wash that Eben had seen from the air, it was day and the sun bore down on them like a curse. The dunes gave way to searing white alluvium and the flat, scoured braiding of river channels, so ephemeral as to be dead.

By now, Eben's canteen was empty, and there were only a few drops left in the dead man's bottle. Whatever water they had, the sun claimed. Sweat vaporised from their bodies before it had time to bead. Saliva thickened in their mouths, viscous as tar.

They trudged across the lifeless plain, still taking turns carrying the boy, the heat reflecting from the coarse white gravel, the shoals of pure-white sand and the slabbed beds of crystal halite. Clay wrapped his bandana tight around his face against the glare, leaving only a narrow slit for his eyes. Mirages appeared, flash floods shimmering across the plain before vanishing into the heat, only to reappear moments later as pools and lakes, shifting inland seas of indefinite proportion, ungoverned by laws of any kind. And in this landscape they were entirely separate, three souls alive in a world where nothing lived and everything was without thought or feeling.

Scanning the ground before him, Clay felt as if his retinae were being seared away, his eye sockets welded shut. Heat came through the soles of his boots and up through the calluses and bones of his feet. The boy's head lolled against Clay's chest with each step, the rhythm of it steady with the crunch of his soles against the baked ground, the beating of his heart thin and fast in his chest, the air moving thin and hot through his lungs — all of it a trance state of sublimation, of things boiled away to residue.

They stopped, threw up the parachute silk as a makeshift awning and huddled under the small patch of shade to rest. The boy was in bad shape. Clay patted his cheeks, tried to wake him.

'He's in some sort of coma,' Clay whispered through cracked lips.

Eben did not respond, just sat with his head between his knees. Clay watched the slow rise and fall of his shoulders as he breathed.

'You okay, *bru*?'

No answer.

Clay nudged Eben's shoulder. '*Bru*?'

Nothing.

Clay checked his watch. Still six hours until dusk, until some respite from the sun. They'd seen no trace of the track Eben had thought he'd seen from the air, no sign of habitation or movement. Turning inland now wouldn't help. Without water, they wouldn't get far. They had to reach the track. Clay lifted the edge of the chute panel and gazed out across the shimmering plain.

He nudged Eben. 'Come on, *broer*. Let's *ontrek*.'

A groan from Eben.

Clay pushed him, harder this time. 'Get up, troop.'

Eben turned away and curled up on his side, pulling the silk away with him.

Clay made sure the boy was covered then sat in the full glare of the sun. 'God damn it, Eben,' he whispered to himself.

He stood, brushed some of the sand from his trousers, hoisted his R4, looked back from where they'd come, the dunes now just a rumple of oxide red above the flowing silver-black mirage. He took a few steps, feeling the fatigue in his limbs, thirst clawing at him from the inside. He knew they needed to keep going, that every hour they rested here was another hour their bodies would be without water. The centre axis of the valley, if that's what you could call it, was still a couple of kilometres away, judging by the apparent size of the far dunes.

Clay shuffled back to where Eben and the boy lay under the parachute silk. He was about to kick Eben when something he'd seen made him stop.

There, on the horizon, snaking above the haze, barely visible – a thin weft of dust.

A dust devil? There was no wind. He strained to see, fumbling in his vest for his binoculars. Raising the glasses, he scanned the abraded mirage of the horizon. Nothing.

Clay pulled away the silk, kicked Eben in the side.

'Let's go,' Clay said, rolling the silk up and stashing it in his pack.

Eben stared up at him through narrowed slits. 'Water,' he whispered through swollen lips.

'Sorry, *bru*,' said Clay. 'Gave the last of it to the boy.'

Eben closed his eyes and dropped his head. 'I can't feel my legs.' The words came out thin and cracked, as if over rusty wire.

Clay reached down, threw the boy over his shoulder, and then grabbed his friend's arm and pulled him to his feet. Eben swayed unsteadily. He was still wearing his Fireforce vest. Clay unclasped it and pushed it off his shoulders. Its twenty-five kilograms thudded to the ground, raising a puff of dust. They'd been taught never to lose their gear. This would have to be an exception. With the boy over one shoulder, and supporting Eben with the other, Clay started walking.

They hadn't gone far when he saw it again. A thin tendril of grey-white dust spiralling into the sky, closer than before.

'Eben, look,' he said. 'What is it?'

But his friend did not answer. His eyes were swollen shut, cauterised by the glare.

Clay strained to see through the shimmering distortions thrown up from the pan. But all he could see was the halite glare, the liquid mercury of the horizon and above it the cloudless sky. The dust devil was gone.

He kept going. He didn't have a choice. Keep going until the end.

Eben's steps were barely a shuffle now, his weight collapsing into Clay's side, his boots dragging across the salt. Clay looked at his watch. Gone midday. They'd covered perhaps three hundred metres in the last ten minutes. He looked up.

There it was again. That curlicue of dust.

He eased Eben to the ground, then the boy, and reached for his binoculars.

It was no mirage. No illusion come of hope and dehydration. It was a dust plume. He followed it. Whatever it was, it was moving. Fast. And it was moving inland, towards them. Clay estimated about ten kilometres distant, maybe more. It could only be one thing.

Eben and the boy lay motionless on the hardpan. Heat poured from the ground, shimmering distortions that enveloped their bodies as if to assimilate them whole. Salt crusted their faces white, rimed their lashes. Eben's lips were cracked, little red scars against the white. The boy was barely breathing. Blood trickled from his nose. Soon, the desert would claim them.

Clay searched the horizon again, half expecting the dust devil to have disappeared. But it was still there, closer now, still moving towards them. It was their last chance. Clay covered Eben and the boy over with the parachute silk. Then he dropped his Fireforce vest and his R4 to the ground, and, reaching deep inside himself, he started to run.

17

Survive This

After a few hundred metres, his body rebelled.

There was nothing left. He'd lost too much fluid. His tongue seemed to have grown to twice its normal size. His mouth and throat were sand dry. Despite the heat, his hands and feet were dead-man cold, his system shunting its remaining fluids to the most vital organs. His body was starting to shut down.

He gazed out across the mirage, the heat coming in waves now, roiling across the pan in great cresting breakers, sweeping all before it. For a moment he lost sight of the dust plume, and again doubted its existence in anything but his own mind. But just as quickly it was there again, much closer now, riding the surf. He stumbled forward, each step an act of will.

As he went, mysteries emerged. Illusions spun in the torsion like ashes in the wind – blunt hallucinations that he knew he ought to recognise, ascribe some meaning to. But materialisation and disaggregation were coincident, their lifespans as brief as the agonised contractions of dehydrating cells, gone before they were born. And then, through the turbulence, a single black body, there, close to the ground – a dark, shifting planet.

He staggered towards it, vision tunnelling down onto this single point, this pulsing dark attractor. But it wasn't a planet. Of course it wasn't. And even as he recognised it for what it surely was, in part of his mind it was a comet, an asteroid, hurtling towards him, its gaseous wake streaking skyward.

Clay stumbled up the gravel shoulder and collapsed onto the hard-baked surface just as the vehicle flew past. He lay with his cheek against the road and watched it speed away in a cloud of dust.

He closed his eyes. He'd been too slow.

Coma beckoned. He could feel it. Feel his heart slowing. His breath shallowing. The scorching air so thin, a gasping partial vacuum. The final stage.

He forced his eyes open. Wished to see the world one more time.

And there it was, emerging from the dust. A vehicle approaching.

☾

And then a hand behind his neck, pulling him up. Water flowing across his tongue, down his throat. He clutched at the bottle, drank, spluttered, choked most of it back out.

He opened his eyes. A face he would never forget. Kind, grey eyes. Deep, sun-cut lines. A big smile shining out from beneath a thick russet beard. Hair to match. And then that deep tenor, like Bach, so unexpected, talking to him in a language he could not understand, but which was so familiar.

'*Dankie*,' Clay rasped, in Afrikaans.

The man nodded, smiled. '*Ja, ja. Afrikaans.*' And then, in Clay's own language: 'Drink, then talk.' He tilted the water bottle, and Clay drank.

Finally, Clay wiped his mouth. 'We've been lost for three days.' He raised his arm, pointed back in the direction he'd come. 'My friends are out there. Two of them.'

The man nodded. 'Can you stand?'

Clay reached for the man's arm. He pulled Clay to his feet. He wasn't tall, but he was sturdy.

'I am Jürgen,' he said. 'Come. We will find your friends.'

Jürgen walked him to the vehicle. It was an old Land Rover with a roof rack loaded with gear. Three blond heads peered from the open windows, staring at Clay with wide eyes. Two children, a boy and a girl, and from the front passenger seat, a woman with an oval face and long hair braided in tresses that hung from the window and halfway to the ground.

'My family,' said Jürgen.

Clay tried a smile, felt his skin crack as it stretched.

Jürgen leaned Clay up against the front of the Land Rover. 'How far are your friends?'

'A couple of kilometres,' Clay said, his voice barely a whisper. 'Maybe more.'

'In this case, we must detach the trailer,' said Jürgen. 'Wait here, please.'

Clay watched as Jürgen disappeared behind the vehicle. The woman stared at him. Her eyes were the colour of water. Her hair shone like ripe wheat. He realised he was staring back, looked away.

'We are ready,' said Jürgen, opening the woman's door. 'Astrid, my love, please.'

The woman stepped to the ground. She wore a short summer dress in some feminine pattern. Her legs were long and tanned the colour of springbok hide.

Jürgen put a hawser-rope arm around her shoulders. 'This is Astrid, my wife,' he said.

She nodded, smiled.

'And I'm Otto,' said the boy, fighting with his sister for space in the open rear window. 'Are you a soldier? Is he is soldier, Papa?'

'Are you not going to introduce your sister?' said Jürgen.

'I am Ingrid,' said the little girl. She had her mother's face and hair, the same long braids.

Clay steadied himself against the vehicle, put out his hand. 'I'm Claymore. Clay.'

Jürgen's grip was powerful. 'Clay. Good. Now we know each other. Let us go and find your friends, yes? Before it gets dark.' He helped Clay into the front passenger seat and closed the door. Astrid got into the back with the kids.

Soon they were moving north, trundling across the salt pan. Out of the sun, Clay let the breeze flow over him, felt his body begin to stabilise.

'Are you a soldier, Mister Clay?' said Otto from the backseat. 'He has soldier's boots, Papa.'

'Yes, I'm a soldier,' said Clay. 'A South African paratrooper.'

'I told you so,' said Otto. 'It was me who saw you, Mister Clay. That's why we came back.'

'And very well done, Otto,' said Jürgen.

Clay scanned the flat, dry ground before them, heat haze rippling across it, distorting everything. It would be so easy to miss them. Twice he directed Jürgen towards some apparition, only to have it dematerialise. He looked back to the road, no longer sure of the direction he'd come. He'd been so weak, he hadn't thought to take a bearing. Christ, they could be anywhere.

They searched for almost half an hour. Every minute that passed, Clay knew, put his friends that much closer to the end. 'I can't see them,' he said, running his hand across his face. 'I don't know where they are.'

'Don't worry,' said Jürgen. 'We will keep looking until we find them.'

They drove on.

A short time later, Otto stood, hooked one arm over the seat and tapped his father's shoulder.

'What is it, Otto?' said Jurgen.

'There,' said the boy. He pointed across his father's shoulder. 'There, Papa. Do you see?'

'Yes,' said Jürgen, turning the vehicle. 'Well done, son.'

And suddenly, much closer than Clay had imagined, there they were. Eben and the boy, lying under the parachute silk where he'd left them, Clay's R4 and Fireforce vest in the dust nearby.

The boy was unconscious, Eben not much better. Clay and Jürgen carried Eben to the vehicle, set him on the ground in a wedge of shade thrown by the roof rack. Astrid carried the boy in her arms and laid him out on the back seat. She washed his face and then sponged water over his body, washing away the salt, dripping water into his open mouth. The two children had scurried into the Land Rover's back cargo area and hung over the seat back, watching, whispering to each other.

At first, Adriano did not respond, but Astrid continued her gentle work, and soon the boy's lips were moving and she gave him water in tiny sips from a green plastic cup.

Clay and Jürgen tended to Eben. Soon he was sitting up, back against the vehicle, drinking down cup after cup of water.

'I have beer,' said Jürgen after a while.

Eben looked up at Clay through salt-crusted lashes, smiled. 'Is this heaven?' he rasped. 'Am I dead?'

Jürgen called to Otto in what Clay now knew was German. The boy rummaged in the back and scurried out to his father, holding three dripping tins.

The Windhoek lager was ice cold. Clay's throat burned as it went down, and his head ached from it, but it was wonderful.

They squeezed into the Land Rover, the three men in the front, weapons between their legs, Fireforce vests at their feet, the woman in the back with Adriano and the children. Soon they were back on the track, heading inland as the sun set behind the dunes.

☾

That night they set up camp in a copse of trees not far from a small village. Clay helped Jürgen pitch two big tents. Astrid and the children lit hurricane lamps and set out cots and bedding. Soon Jürgen had a fire going.

Adriano was still weak, and Astrid insisted on getting him to bed right away. She sat with him for a long time, spooning Coca-Cola into his mouth, cooling him with wet towels. When the coals were ready, Jürgen broke out eggs, bacon and thick, dark bread, and started frying everything up in a big cast-iron pan. The smell of the food made Clay dizzy. He realised he hadn't eaten for four days.

'We farm near Windhoek,' said Jürgen, passing a heaped plate to Clay, another to Eben. 'We come here every year.' And then to his son: 'Otto, bring these gentlemen knives and forks, please.'

The boy, who, since finishing his chores, had been orbiting Clay like a faithful pup, jumped up and quickly returned with cutlery and three more tins of beer.

'We camp on the beach and fish, and we play in the waves and the dunes. It is very quiet.'

Eben glanced at Clay. 'You're on holiday,' he said, his vocal chords still taught.

'*Ja*. We were on our way home when Otto saw you on the road.'

'Aren't you worried about SWAPO?' said Eben. 'They have been known to operate in these parts.'

Jurgen smiled. 'We can adapt to much, young man. But we will not compromise on our Skeleton Coast holiday.'

'Live as brave men,' said Eben. 'And if fortune is adverse, front its blows with brave hearts.'

'I like this,' said Jürgen.

'It's Cicero,' said Eben.

'Who is Cicero, Mister Eben?' said Otto.

'He was a Roman philosopher,' said Eben, smiling at the boy. 'He died almost two thousand years ago, but the things he thought and wrote live on.'

'Mister Eben is an educated man,' Jürgen said, turning to face his children. 'All the world's knowledge is there for you. Study hard, and you will honour yourselves and God.'

Otto and Ingrid nodded.

'How can we thank you?' said Clay, knowing that there was nothing that could in any way meet the measure deserved.

Jürgen smiled, waving this away with a big hand. 'Please. It is our great pleasure.'

Astrid emerged from the darkness and slid into the camp chair next to her husband. He reached for her hand and squeezed it.

She smiled. 'He is sleeping,' she said. 'He is very lucky. Much longer, and he could have died.'

Clay watched her as she spoke. She was pretty, in that wind-burned, hard-working way that farm women sometimes were. After some time she glanced up at him and smiled. He lowered his eyes. It was too hard to look.

Jürgen said grace. They ate. Gazing into the fire, they talked of farming, of family and friends, of Africa and its troubles. Never once did Jürgen or Astrid ask about how they had come to be alone on the Skeleton Coast with a black child, lost and near dead.

Eben finished his meal and excused himself, wandering off to the tent. After a time, Astrid stood and led the children to the vehicle, whispering to them in German.

Jürgen placed another log on the fire. Sparks rose into the night, a funnel of glowing fireflies. Clay watched the flames leap and fall. It was very quiet now, and it was as if they were alone in the world.

'Otto likes you very much,' Jürgen said.

Clay looked at his host and now saw the years in his face, the hard work. Guessed him at late thirties, early forties perhaps.

'I fear for him,' said Jürgen. 'And for Ingrid.'

'The war.'

Jürgen nodded. 'They are African.' He motioned towards the tent with his chin. 'As much as that boy. I was born here. My father and grandfather, too. Astrid's grandparents, also, all of them. What kind of Africa will my children inherit, young man?'

Clay did not know if he expected an answer. 'I don't know, sir.'

Jürgen smiled. 'You are not in the army, here, young man.'

'Sorry,' said Clay, finishing his beer. 'Jürgen.' He said it, but it didn't feel right.

'We will not win,' said Jürgen.

'Sir?'

'History is not with us. You know that, don't you? Despite your efforts, your sacrifice. Despite all the money and the technology, it is not for us, anymore. It is for them.'

Clay did not answer, just stared into the fire, contemplating the meaning of these words.

Soon after, Astrid reappeared with the children. Otto and Ingrid were scrubbed and combed and dressed in pyjamas. They kissed their father, and then, to his surprise, they kissed Clay. They reached up on their toes and planted little kisses on Clay's bearded cheek, whispering *gute nacht*. They smelled of soap and shampoo. He mumbled a reply and watched them as they trundled off into the darkness with their mother.

'I am blessed,' said Jürgen after a time.

Clay thought that yes, he surely was.

They drank another beer together and then Jürgen kicked the fire out and they said goodnight to each other. Clay washed his face in the basin Astrid had set out on a tripod next to an ancient ironwood, dried his face on a towel she'd hung from one of its branches.

Eben and Adriano did not stir when Clay pulled back the tent flap. Eben had left the lantern burning on a low flame, and the golden light now flickered over their sleeping faces. A third cot beckoned, covered with an open sleeping bag and a big feather pillow. Clay killed the flame, peeled off his clothes and sank naked into the cot. He was asleep before he had time to think.

☾

Sometime in the night, Clay woke. It was very quiet. He pushed himself up, pulled on his shorts, grabbed his sidearm, and went outside. It was cooler. Stars filled the sky. The faintest breeze stirred the leaves of the trees. He walked some way from camp, found a suitable tree and had a piss. The first in days.

He started back to camp. Starlight illuminated the two tents, threw shadows filtering across the ground, the camp chairs set around the fire pit, the Land Rover and the unhitched trailer. He was about to pull back the tent flap when he saw something twitch near the vehicle.

Clay stopped, senses firing. He peered into the semi-lit darkness, but all was still. He waited, watched. And there it was again, a definite movement. He let the tent flap fall, took a few steps forwards, moved into shadow. There on the ground, underneath the vehicle, two dark shapes. Not shadows.

Clay worked the Berretta's action, chambered a round. Between him and the vehicle were the two tents, the fire pit and open ground to the right. He decided to flank left, towards a clump of trees, and circle in behind the trailer.

He moved quickly, keeping to the shadows. Within seconds he was poised behind the trailer. He stopped, listened. Nothing. He raised the Beretta, stepped towards the vehicle.

There, on the ground beside the vehicle two dark shapes. Intruders.

Clay was close now, nearly upon them. He trained the weapon on the closest target and braced his trigger hand. As he did, the target twisted towards him. A pair of big, pale eyes stared up at him from the darkness. Clay staggered back. It was Otto.

Beside him, *Jürgen's* square-cut face, ghost-white in the starlight, nestled in the hood of his sleeping bag. His eyes were closed and his chest rose and fell in a deep, regular rhythm.

Clay lowered the handgun and put a trembling index finger to his lips.

Otto nodded, pulled his sleeping bag up around his shoulders and closed his eyes. As Clay turned away, he glanced inside the Land Rover. Stretched out across the back seat, snuggled deep into her sleeping bag, Ingrid.

Clay stood watching her sleep, tried to calm his breathing. Of course. They only had four camp cots. He hadn't even considered it. He walked back to the tent and slipped into his cocoon. After a long time his heart slowed and he slept.

When he woke again, the sun was high and it was already hot. Eben and Adriano were still asleep. He looked at his watch. He'd slept twelve hours.

The events of the last days came flooding back: the red night of the landing strip, the tumbling bodies, the dunes and the blinding salt pan, Otto's eyes staring up at him in the starlight. And now here. Alive. He thought of Jürgen and his wife, the way they were with each other, of their hospitality, of what he'd said about Africa.

And in all of this, trepidation walked; and it was as if happiness was something to which he had lost all claim.

They stayed two more days at the camp. They ate, drank, slept. Played cards under the big tarpaulin Jürgen rigged between two trees and the vehicle. Eben and Adriano got stronger. Clay convinced Jürgen to take back two of the cots, that he and Eben were well used to sleeping rough. At Otto's insistence, Clay field-stripped his R4 as the boy watched, reassembled it, banged off a few rounds. At night, Eben told stories around the fire: tales of knights and ladies, of monsters and shipwrecked sailors, that delighted the children. Adriano, isolated by language and race, kept to himself and seemed to respond only to Astrid.

The next morning, Jürgen took them as far as Palmvag and the crossroads with highway 43 – the main north-south trunk road that snaked down the spine of South-West Africa. Astrid gave them a plastic bag of oranges, bread, a couple of tins of tuna and some hard-boiled eggs. They filled their canteens from one of the family's ten-litre jugs of water. Clay tried to offer them money but Jürgen pushed it away with a smile and apologies for not being able to take them further.

Clay and Eben shook hands with Jürgen. Astrid kissed Adriano. He hugged her back. As the Land Rover disappeared in the distance, Otto was still waving from the backseat.

And that was it.

Eben kicked the ground with his boot. 'Makes you want to survive this, doesn't it?'

☾

Commissioner Lacy: So you saved the boy. You should be proud of what you did, Mister Straker.

Witness: How do you mean, ma'am?

Commissioner Lacy: Well, I mean, you brought him to safety.

Witness does not answer.

Commissioner Barbour: Continue, please, Mister Straker.

Witness: From there we hitched a ride north to Opuwo. There was an army post there. We decided not to turn the boy over to military intelligence. Instead, we put in a call to Captain Blakely of 32-Battalion – the officer who had signed the order for us to accompany Brigade into Angola. We figured that was the best way to get Adriano back to his mother. And we wanted some answers.

Commissioner Ksole: 32-Battalion. They were known as 'the terrible ones', were they not?

Witness: By some, yes, sir. The commies – sorry, the communists – were terrified of them. They had a reputation.

Commissioner Barbour: And was Captain Blakely surprised to hear from you?

Witness: More like relieved, I guess. He said we'd been reported missing, presumed killed. He sent a transport to pick us up. When we got to the 32-Bat base on the Caprivi, he met us outside the main gates. Brigade was with him. And so was our CO, Captain Wade.

Commissioner Ksole: Did that not strike you as strange, Mister Straker, at the time?

Witness: No, sir. Not at the time. We worked pretty closely with 32-Bat, so our CO being up there didn't seem out of the ordinary.

Commissioner Ksole: What did you tell them?

Witness: They asked us about what we'd seen on the plane. We told them.

Commissioner Ksole: Everything?

Witness: Almost everything.

Commissioner Ksole: Did you tell them about killing the man who followed you into the dunes?

Witness: No. No we didn't.

Commissioner Ksole: And why not, Mister Straker?

Witness: We were scared.

Commissioner Ksole: Of being court-martialled? Of being accused of murder?

Witness: Yes, sir.

Commissioner Ksole: And what was their reaction?

Witness: How do you mean, sir?

Commissioner Ksole: What did the officers say when you told them about what happened on the plane?

Witness: Just that we'd done well.

Commissioner Ksole: Did they seem surprised?

Witness: I can't say, sir.

Commissioner Ksole: And did they say anything else?

Witness: They ordered us not to tell anyone what we'd seen.

Commissioner Ksole: You were sworn to secrecy.

Witness: Yes, sir.

Commissioner Lacy: And the boy?

Witness: Captain Blakely and Brigade took the boy. Blakely promised to get him back to his mother.

Commissioner Barbour: And as far as you know, did he? Get the boy back to his mother, I mean.

Witness: Yes.

Commissioner Barbour: You are sure, Mister Straker?

Witness: Yes, sir. Absolutely sure.

18

The Final Accounting

They'd been on the road for more than an hour before Captain Wade spoke. Hunched over the steering wheel, a Cuban cigar smouldering between his lips, Wade finally replied to one of the questions Eben had been throwing out at regular intervals since leaving 32-Bat's Caprivi headquarters.

'I sent you boys because there was no one else I could trust.'

The Land Rover rattled over the rutted track that served as the main east-west artery paralleling the border. Wade slowed and pulled to the side of the track to let a convoy of four supply trucks rumble past in the other direction. They continued on in a choking plume of dust.

'And does the Colonel know about this?' said Clay.

Wade was quiet a long time, staring out at the road. His sandy hair was cut bristle short and frosted with road dust. There were deep lines in his sun-burned face. He was early thirties, but looked forty.

'Look,' he said, pulling the cigar from between his teeth. 'You boys know what you saw out there. So I don't need to tell you that there is some very bad shit happening. I'm sorry I dragged you boys into this, but I didn't have a choice.' He was a native English speaker, a salt-dick, like them. 'We've been watching UNITA for a while now, and when this opportunity came up, we had to act.'

'Who is "we", sir?' said Eben.

'*We* is us, Barstow. You, me and Straker, here.

Eben shot that sarcastic grin he used whenever confronted with military doublespeak.

'Yes, sir,' said Clay. 'But who can *we* trust?'

'Do not talk about any of this to anyone. Do you hear me? Both of you. I need your word.'

'You have it, sir,' said Clay.

'So the answer is, trust no one,' said Eben.

'That's right.'

'Who is this Zulaika woman, sir?' asked Clay. 'Is she really MPLA?'

Wade nodded. 'She is. But only as a matter of convenience.'

'So then why are we working with her, against UNITA, our allies?'

'Look, Straker, the more I tell you boys, the more dangerous it is for you. You're just going to have to trust me.' Wade crushed the butt of his cigar against the top of the steering wheel and dropped it into the breast pocket of his battle tunic. 'She told me about what you boys did in the bunker. That's why I picked you. You get it. Most of the people here, they don't...' Wade trailed off into silence again.

'Get what?' said Eben.

'What this whole thing is really about.'

'Not the *rool gevdar*,' said Clay. Just what the lady doctor at 1-Mil had said. As he said it, something opened up inside his chest. It felt like treason. And something else: it felt like futility.

'No, not the fucking *rool gevdar*,' said Wade, his composure momentarily gone, his eyes flashing as he turned his head to stare right at them.

Eben was smiling now, broad and wide.

'And the Colonel, sir?' said Clay. 'Is he one of the people that doesn't get it?'

'Especially the Colonel.'

Clay swallowed hard, glanced over at Eben. Now he looked scared.

'What about *Liutenant* Van Boxmeer, our platoon commander?' said Clay.

'God damn it Straker, I said no one. Crowbar knows nothing about this. Keep it that way. He's just a good soldier who does what he's told.'

Clay nodded. 'So who is this Doctor Death?' said Clay, pressing. 'He's one of ours, isn't he?'

Wade frowned, drove on.

'You might as well tell us, sir,' said Eben. 'By the sounds of it we're already fucked anyway.'

Wade whipped his head around and glared at Eben. 'You're in the middle of a war, son,' he said, swerving to avoid a pothole. 'Of course you're fucked.'

☾

By the time they reached Ondangwa, the sun was low in the sky, and the bush took on that golden, late-afternoon glow that reminded Clay of summer days playing cricket and lounging in the back garden of his family home in Jo'berg. In straight-line time it wasn't that long ago. But it felt like forever.

Wade had steadfastly refused to speak anymore of the incident and instead fell into the usual superficial conversation an officer has with his men: home, food, sleep. He dropped them five kilometres from the main gate and told them to walk the rest of the way in, and then report directly to Crowbar with the agreed story. They hadn't seen him and he hadn't seen them. It was for their own protection, he said.

'Sometimes it feels wholly as if I'm living inside one, long, interrupted dream,' said Eben as they walked back alone along the wheel-churned road, watching the sky light up flamingo pink and blood orange. 'As if my life is not, you know, *rational*.'

Clay didn't reply. He reached into his trouser pocket and pulled out the notebook he'd taken from the body of Doctor Death's assistant out in the dunes. 'Maybe this will tell us something.'

He opened the notebook to the first page. It was a ledger of some sort: columns of handwritten numbers and a strange shorthand of letters and Greek symbols. He flipped through the pages. The same unintelligible stuff: numbers, symbols, the occasional scrawled chemical or medical term. Inside, towards the back, was a folded sheet, typewritten. He passed Eben the notebook and opened up the paper. It was an official document, under the seal of the South African Army Medical Service, SAMS.

'Listen to this, *bru*,' said Clay, reading from the document. 'Subjects injected with formulation 13B – muscle relaxants: methylqualone and hydroxyl pheylbenzenacetic acid (60%); anaesthetic: etomidate (20%); central nervous system depressants (sleeping agent): phenobarbital (20%). Subjects exhibited rapid interference with motor function, immediate loss of coordination and muscle control, and confusion and lethargy, followed by seizures and terminal respiratory failure. Reduced dose and potency recommended.'

Clay stared at his friend, the coldest shiver creasing the length of his spine. 'That's what those *poes* were doing out there that night. They were injecting those poor bastards with this shit. Did you hear that: "Immediate loss of muscle control."' He shook his head. 'Can you fucking believe it?'

Eben grabbed the paper. Clay walked on in silence, the weight of his rifle and the ordnance filling his Fireforce vest suddenly an almost intolerable burden.

'Holy Mother of God,' said Eben. 'Listen: "Lower dosage. Formulation 14C. Substitute neuromuscular blockers with MDMA one for two. Subjects display slower onset of paralysis. Respiratory failure delayed or prevented. Total loss of muscle control temporary. Recovery expected within twenty-four hours."' He looked up at Clay.

'Adriano,' said Clay.

Eben nodded.

'Lab rats,' said Clay. 'That's what they were using them for. No wonder they wanted to get rid of the evidence.'

'*Moeder van God*,' said Eben. 'Our own medical corps.'

'Look at the header,' said Clay, cold creeping through him now, despite the searing tropical heat. 'Operation COAST.'

Eben grabbed the paper. 'Holy shit.'

'The doctor's message, from 1-Mil. The doctor's operation.'

'She knows.'

'Or she suspects. That was why she used a cipher. She must be under surveillance.'

'BOSS.'

'It would make sense. Can you imagine if this got out? We're already an international pariah.'

'Well deserved,' said Eben.

'And what about Cobra?' said Clay.

Eben threw a questioning look.

Clay pointed to his bicep. 'On the *Flossie*.'

Eben nodded. 'You think he recognised you?'

'*Ja*, definitely.'

'Then we're in deep shit.'

'First thing tomorrow we talk to Wade. Tell him the whole story.' Clay grabbed the paper back, folded it back in the notebook. 'Show him this.'

'Everything?'

'Everything. The way I see it, we don't have a choice.'

Eben frowned. 'Admit to killing one of our own? We could be shot, *bru*. You know that don't you?'

'What do you mean, *we*, Eben? I was the one who shot him.'

'Don't even say it. We're in this together.'

Clay shook his head. 'Wade isn't telling us the whole story. He said so himself. He's trying to protect us, but he doesn't know how far we're already into this thing. Cobra knows who I am. And if he does, Doctor Death does, too. It won't be hard to track us down.'

They walked on in silence as darkness came.

☾

An hour later and they were being waved through the main gates of the airbase. They walked the mile and half to their bivouac area feeling not so much like returning heroes as suspects in a crime. They slung their R4s and marched in step, noticing the glances of the airmen and the other parabats, knowing that the word would have gone around that they were missing, believed killed.

When they reached *Valk* 5's bivouac, Bluey and the others were there to meet them with cold cokes and pats on the back, wanting to know all about it. Clay and Eben told them the story they'd rehearsed and agreed with Wade. Long-range recon patrol with 32-Bat into Angola to report on FAPLA movements near Rito. They had become separated after a firefight and had walked back out on their own. No worries.

Later that night, Clay lay on his bunk and opened the box that Crowbar had thrown there almost three days before. Inside, pinned to a black-felt background, was an MMM – Military Merit Medal – the blue, sky-blue and orange striped ribbon rumpled against its brass bar and twelve-pointed brass star. Clay looked at it for a long time in the half-light, wondering what his mother and father would have felt if they were still alive. Proud, he said to himself. They would have been proud. His mother would have told all her friends and neighbours, had everyone round to tea, showed them photographs. My son won the MMM, she would have said. We are so proud. But now they can't be, because of a stupid, fucking pointless car crash.

He picked up the medal and held it to his chest a moment. There had been no ceremony. The Colonel hadn't pinned it to his chest in front of the Battalion on parade. It was just tossed onto his bunk like a tin of beer or a spare mag. Here you go, troop. Three kills. Three men dead because of you. And one boy saved. Would one saved cancel out one killed, he wondered, when the final accounting came? Was there to be such a thing? Or was it all, as Eben claimed, just a one-way trip to nothing.

Clay put the medal back in its box and dropped it into his foot-locker. He was alone in the tent. He checked the entrance and then got to his knees, reached under his bunk and levered up the floor-board, exposing the Ovamboland sand beneath. Quickly he dug away the earth. The heavy polypropylene bag he'd stashed the dia-monds in was still there. He pulled it free and opened it up. The pouch was inside. He took it out and tipped the stones into his palm. Such small things, dull and clear against his skin, the bigger one about the size of a 7.62 mm round, with its pinkish tinge and uncharacteristic sharp edges.

After a while he funnelled the diamonds back into the pouch and dropped it into the bag along with the bloodstained notebook, and then covered it over again with handfuls of sand before replacing the floorboard.

Clay lay back on his bunk, crossed his arms under the back of his head and stared at the canvas above him. Somewhere in the distance: the clatter of gunfire, the fading sound of an outbound chopper. Did these objects change things, he wondered? Could some stones, a few sheaves of paper, change lives, directions? Were they a means to a future, or the end of one? For the first time in a long time he thought about Sara, his fiancée. He hadn't written to her in weeks, now, not since the hospital. He'd tried a couple of times, but the words he needed were too hard to find, and those he didn't were too banal. And the more he didn't tell her, the harder it became to write anything at all, until it seemed simply an irrelevancy, and he knew that he didn't love her and never had and that he'd only asked her to marry him because it was what she'd wanted, even though they'd only spent two days together and didn't know anything about each other and never would.

Tomorrow, he'd go to Wade. He'd tell him everything. He'd tell him about the diamonds and about killing Doctor Death's assistant in the dunes. He'd show him the documents, the notebook. He was now convinced that the 1-Mil lady doctor's cryptic note was somehow linked to the events he'd witnessed in Angola, the SAMS experiments on unarmed black prisoners, and that UNITA – or at least the element of UNITA that Colonel Mbdele ran – was part of it. What had Zulaika said? Drug war. What he'd seen certainly qualified. She was telling the truth. MPLA or not, Wade trusted her. He trusted Wade. And Operation COAST? He'd mention the word to Wade, see how he reacted.

Clay thought again of the diamonds; Mbdele's diamonds. He remembered the night in the bunker, Mbdele's offered handful of pills, and the way the UNITA fighters' eyes flared and danced – that drugged-up, euphoric, sex-crazed, primal look in each tortured face. He'd heard of people taking pills to get high, but never seen it or experienced it. Not with his background. Not from a proper, white middle-class Johannesburg suburb. Not a boy from a respectable white private school with its own pool, and rugby and cricket pitches, and the compulsory military training after school. Not him.

All of that – home, school, friends, his parents, even Sara – seemed a long way away now. Gone. Obliterated, and never coming back. He was someone different now; or maybe it was just that he had finally become the person he was always supposed to be.

Sleep came. That deep blank born of physical and mental exhaustion, of the exquisite relief of just being alive.

When he awoke it was dark. He walked to the enlisted man's mess building with Eben to get some dinner. Above them, the sky was clear. Stars covered the night so that there was no black, only shades of starlight, distant and unimaginable. The diesel generator hummed in the distance, barely audible over the insect din. The mess hut was set in a small earth revetment just off the main base track. It was the last sitting of the day and they could hear men's voices, the clink of cutlery on metal trays. The windows glowed yellow. The officer's mess was not far – less than a hundred metres down the road, past a small thicket of Mopane trees. They had just turned onto the staked pathway that led to the enlisted men's mess when Eben stopped dead, grabbed Clay's shoulder.

'Look,' he whispered.

Wade was standing alone on the road near the mopane thicket with his hands on his hips. The light from the officer's mess shone through the trees and struck Wade in dappled, moving patches.

'What's he doing?' whispered Eben.

Clay was about to answer when Wade took a step forward. Another man emerged from the edge of darkness and stood facing him. Wade took a step back. The sound of raised voices came clear now in the African night – the two men were arguing about something.

'Do you recognise him?' asked Eben. People came and went from the big front line airbase on a regular basis, so it was not unusual to see strangers.

'No,' said Clay. The man's back was turned to them, and he was still partially obscured by the fractured mopane shade. But there was something about the way the man stood, about the size of him, that was vaguely familiar.

The man was questioning Wade now, his tone increasingly insistent.

'Come on,' said Eben, starting towards the two men.

'Wait.' Clay grabbed his friend's elbow.

Just then, Wade turned away from the man and started walking back along the road, towards the officers' bivouac area. The other man stood in the road, watching him go, silent now. After a while he stepped out into the floodlit part of the road and started towards the mess. As he did, Clay caught a glimpse of his face.

'Jesus Christ,' said Clay.

'What?' said Eben. 'Who is it?'

It was him: the same fleshy dark jowls, the ravaged skin, that same lumbering gait. 'It's the *poes* from the *chana*, the one I told you about – tallying all those UNITA tusks,' whispered Clay, the man's final words that day echoing in his head: *You're all dead men.*

Botha.

'Shit,' said Eben. 'Do you think he's come to report us?'

More like kill us, thought Clay. 'Didn't take him long. Let's get out of here.'

They started back to their tent.

'We better tell Crowbar,' said Clay. 'The bastard threatened him, too.'

'Who's he with, anyway? He can't have any jurisdiction here, can he?'

'Who the hell knows,' said Clay. 'Just stay alert. We'll take turns keeping watch. Anything moves outside the tent, shoot it. If he's stupid enough to try to come after us here, we'll plug him and tell everyone we thought he was a *terr*.'

Eben nodded, muttering to himself.

Crowbar wasn't in his tent. Someone said he was up at command for a briefing – something big apparently. Clay and Eben waited around for a while, but he didn't come back. They went to bed hungry, Eben taking the first watch.

Deep in the night Clay was awoken by a loud explosion, how far off he couldn't tell, followed by the usual moment of silence before the scurrying reaction of shouting men and grinding vehicles. But to these ragings he was now so inured that he was soon asleep again.

At 0430 he was shocked awake by the screaming of NCOs: Parade in five minutes. Full kit. Draw extra ammo, food and water. We'll be away a while this time. Get moving.

They stumbled out into the cool half-darkness of morning, formed up by section and platoon. Crowbar stood before them, stern faced, waiting as the NCOs dressed the ranks and called the men to attention.

'*Valk* 5 is going back into Angola, men,' said Crowbar. 'This time as part of a divisional-scale effort against FAPLA. Operation Protea they're calling it. We will be putting over four thousand men into Cunene Province. Our orders are to destroy a major concentration of FAPLA and Cuban troops massing around Rito. We will be supported on the ground by elements of 32-Bat, SAAF gunships and *Vlammies*.'

Crowbar paused for a moment, looked down at his boots, then back up at the men. 'Last night, we suffered what is believed to have been a mortar attack by SWAPO terrorists. A single mortar round fell inside the compound, destroying one hut. A patrol was sent out in pursuit of the attackers, but no contact was made. I regret to inform you that Captain Wade was killed. There were no other casualties. *Liutenant* de Vries will be acting CO of the company until further notice.'

☾

Commissioner Ksole: Operation Protea. The SADF's Provost General's records show that this is the operation that resulted in the massacre near Rito, in Angola, on 23rd August, 1981. Is that correct?

Witness: *(Coughs)*

Commissioner Ksole: Mister Straker?

Witness: Yes. Yes, sir.

Commissioner Lacy: The records also show that this was the day that you and your colleague – Lance Corporal Eben Barstow – were seriously wounded. Is that also correct, Mister Straker?

Witness does not answer.

Commissioner Lacy: Mister Straker?

Witness: I, ah. May I have a moment, please, ma'am, I've … I need … Ah. Sorry.

Commissioner Barbour: Take your time, son.

Commissioner Ksole: Mister Straker, the question was put to you previously about your wounds. Please can you confirm that this was the date – 23rd August, 1981 – on which you were seriously wounded?

Witness: That is correct. Eben was hit before we reached the village. I was hit not long after.

Commissioner Barbour: Tell us what happened, son.

Witness: It started right after we airlifted into the *chana*. We started taking fire as soon as we hit the ground. I was leading the section that day. I was on point. We were in pursuit of the enemy. There was contact on our right. I could hear AK47 fire close by. I emerged into a clearing. At the far side of the clearing I saw a flash of movement just inside the tree line. I fired. We crossed the clearing. We found a boy, lying in the long grass. Shot through the stomach.

Commissioner Ksole: You shot a civilian, a boy?

Witness does not answer.

Commissioner Ksole: Mister Straker?

Witness: Yes. I shot him. It was an accident. I thought it was an enemy soldier. I panicked. I didn't take time to verify the target, I … Oh, Jesus.

Commissioner Barbour: Was he dead?

Witness: He was still alive. I put Eben in charge of the section and carried the boy back to the LZ. I tried to put him on a casevac, but by the time I got there, he was dead.

Commissioner Lacy: And your friend, Lance Corporal Barstow?

Witness: He was hit a few minutes later, before I re-joined the section. A bullet to the head. I helped carry him to the casevac.

Commissioner Lacy: And he survived.

Witness: You could call it that, I guess.

Commissioner Ksole: And all this happened just outside the village?

Witness: Yes, sir. About half a kilometre from the church and the edge of the village. I re-joined the platoon just as we started advancing towards the church. That's when we started taking heavy fire from a twenty-three.

Commissioner Barbour: A twenty-three? Please can you explain to us what that is, son?

Witness: A 23-millimetre gun. It was designed as an anti-aircraft weapon, but the commies learned that it was hugely effective against men on the ground. There was one in the village.

Commissioner Ksole: And then what happened?

Witness: There is something else, sir. Something I need to say.

Commissioner Barbour: Proceed.

Witness: The little boy. The one I … the one I shot. He. He. It was…

Commissioner Barbour: Take your time, son.

Witness: It was Adriano, sir. The boy we saved from the plane. Zulaika's son.

Commissioner Barbour: Good God.

19

And Quiet Came

The piece of Kingfisher's skull that had opened up Clay's cheek was safely in his pocket.

He could hear de Kock's MAG pumping out rounds somewhere up ahead and to the right of the little white church, and now the slower concussion of the 23 mm anti-aircraft gun that had taken Kingfisher's head off. Rounds whipped over his head, little frissons of death. He crouched low and ran towards the village, Crowbar just visible up ahead through the shifting ground-smoke. Clay's heart was pounding as if it would blow its valves. The dull ache in his cheek had now spread to his whole head, and he could feel his left eye starting to swell shut. He kept running.

He had just passed the church when he heard a mine go up, that distinctive, muffled *whump*, and then the inevitable screams of men. By the time he joined the rest of the platoon, Bluey was dead. The mine had taken off his right leg and most of his left, and he lay, grey and gone, in the short, burned grass.

In Clay's memory, what happened next would always remain shrouded in that thick, grey battle smoke that seemed to rise from the earth like vapour from a mass grave, as if the pounding of battle had opened crevices and wormings in the soil, allowing all that lay dead and rotting within to rise again. It was through this hell of swirling mists that he stumbled, half blind from the hole that had been ripped in his face, the sounds of the fight drumming inside his head, his soul by now tortured to the finest point of regret.

He was in the village. He could see the mud huts, the small vegetable plots, the animal pens fashioned from mopane branches. Some of the huts were on fire. He could hear the sound of the enemy's weapons: AKs and the big 23 mm. Bodies littered the ground, uniformed FAPLA soldiers, villagers, too. An old bushman, slack-skinned and naked with a long grey beard, lay sprawled in the middle of the main square, a big red hole in his chest. His eyes were open. Nearby, a woman lay face down in the dust, bundled in her dirt-covered cloth. The back of her head was missing. Clay stumbled, ploughed into the ground as a mortar round exploded close by. Gunfire raged all around, an insane, crackling laughter. Screams thickened the air, the cries of women, the hoarse barks of men and dogs. The gun that killed Kingfisher roared to life again. It was close. Its detonations banged in his chest like a second heartbeat.

Clay staggered to his feet, fired his rifle into the smoke, towards the sound of the 23 mm gun. For a moment the smoke shifted and he could see the big anti-aircraft gun on its wheeled mount, flame erupting from its elongated muzzle as it banged out deadly projectiles. Just as quickly, it was gone, shrouded in smoke. Clay emptied a magazine on full auto in the direction of the gun. Then another. The gun fell silent. He stumbled towards the gun. When he got there, the crew were dead, three of them, sprawled in the dust. He stood looking at them for a long time, the battle raging all around him.

And then it was over.

Quiet came.

That's when he was hit.

20

Easier Than Living

He'd known right away that it wasn't good.

He'd seen enough to know when a guy was bad. Something about the tone in everyone's voice, the look on their faces as you waited for the casevac, glanced at where you were hit and then turned away, fear in their eyes.

He remembers being lifted onto the Puma, Crowbar telling him he'd be alright, everything light and hazy as the morphine started to hit. And then just glimpses, like looking out through his mosquito net as a child in summertime, the morning sun coming through, flat and diffuse and shot through with promise. And then an operating theatre, the surgeon's masked face, his mouth moving beneath the white, blood-spattered mask. Bright lights. The interior of a Hercules, the drone of engines, the rows of stretchers laid out on the cargo bay floor and him thinking even then of Adriano and Eben and Zulaika and Otto and Bluey and Kingfisher and of the old busman's dark, cloud-strewn eyes staring up at the sky.

And now here, the same hospital as before. Everything in rows, always in rows. He reaches down and runs his right hand over the bandages that encase his chest. His whole right side is heavily swaddled. There is a tube running from an incision in his chest, another down his nose. Slugs of yellow fluid are sucked slowly from his body. He feels short of breath, as if someone is standing on his chest. He runs his tongue over the inside of his cheek. The hole is gone, sealed with a ridge of dangling threads. He rolls each stitch around the tip of his tongue until he has memorised every trough and tendril of this jagged new landscape. The stitches are incomprehensibly large. The outside of his face is heavily bandaged. He feels no pain.

Night comes. Nurses, too, turning and folding, adjusting, whispering. One of them pumps his IV full of morphine. He sleeps. Morning floods the ward. The pain in his side returns, intensifies as the shadows contract and glide across the floor in ghostlike geometries. Fever transports him. The nurse ups the morphine dosage, but the pain returns quickly, grows. Dreams come, violent and impossible to grasp. A man standing at the end of his bed. He is broad shouldered and overweight, balding. His dark eyes are without depth. Looking into them is like staring into the void. He wears a doctor's white coat and facemask but he is not a doctor. The man hovers there, staring down at him. It is the fat man in the suit – Botha. The one who was tallying the tusks in the *chana*; the one they'd seen at the base the day before Wade was killed. When Clay opens his eyes Botha is gone.

Another morning comes bright and shadowlike. The pain is a living thing inside him now, growing. That's when he sees her again. She is standing at the foot of his bed, facing him, like the man in his dreams. Other doctors are with her, men with grey hair and glasses. There is a hushed conference. Fear blows through his chest, a swallowing gale that leaves him gasping for breath. After they are finished talking the other doctors leave and she comes and sits next to him.

Do you remember me, she asks. He nods, yes, how could I forget? She tells him that his wounds are not healing. They have missed something. I could have told you that, Doctor, he says. She nods, looks down at the floor a moment. The shrapnel shattered several ribs, tore through your left lung. Pieces of shattered bone and metal are still lodged in the lung. They did not get it all out first time around. Do you understand? she asks. He nods. She touches his hand and it is better than morphine.

We are going to have to operate again, she says. I am going to do it myself. He tries to smile. It is hard to breathe, to speak. She squeezes his hand. Her smile is beautiful. The freckles on the bridge of her nose are beautiful. How is Eben? he asks. His own voice sounds far away, like a memory. Who? she says. Eben Barstow, from my unit. Is he here? He was hit in the head. He would have come in not too long before me. She shakes her head. I will try to find out for you. Are you ready? We have to take you in now.

❨

He awakens in post-op. Soon the pain is worse than before. His body is aflame. Fever transports him. He is in the house he grew up in, the pool and the big garden with the hut in the back where their maid lived, and it is somehow the murdered village; the faces of those massacred alive again, the living blank-eyed and cold. She appears once more, hovering above him, her voice disembodied, echoing through dreams and half-imagined illusions. Botha is there too, standing at the foot of his bed like an undertaker sizing him up for a coffin.

Twice more he is wheeled into the operating theatre. Each time he awakens, and the doctors come, and for a while he seems stable. And then the fever returns. He has no sense of time passing. There is just the bed and the bandages and the slowly pulsing fluids and the pain advancing and receding in concert with the flow of chemicals through his body. He can feel himself tiring, wearing down. It is as if he is coming apart. Dreams and reality coalesce. She is there by the bed most times he wakes.

The next morning – is it the next morning? – she is there again. She looks at his chart, sits beside him, holds his hand. The damage was very extensive, she says. Do you understand? We are doing everything we can. One rib was shattered into very small pieces. Some pieces are so small we can't see them on the X-ray. I am having to do it by feel. I've gone in three times, now. I don't think I can do it again. There is too much damage. I'm sorry, Claymore. She uses his name for the first time. Claymore. He thanks her. It comes out as barely a wheeze, but she seems to understand, smiles at him.

That's when he knows he is going to die. He knew it when he'd first been hit, but now he knows it for sure. He is not sad. There is justice in it, he tells himself. At least six men he has killed, maybe more. And one boy. He tries to tell her this as she sits beside him, but his voice is gone, his vocal chords frozen. Spikes of pain drive through his chest. She stands, looks down at him a long time. He knows she is saying goodbye. She turns and walks away.

He misses Eben more than he has ever missed anyone in his life. This is a surprise to him. He is not prepared for it. The power of it.

Time becomes a blur. There are vivid dreams. He is falling towards the ocean. The fat man in the suit is there again, standing at the end of his bed, smiling as he falls. He is so far up that the clouds beneath him look like strings of his mother's pearls against the shifting blue of the ocean. He can see the longshore currents, the deep blue of the cold upwellings, the pale, sky-coloured shoals of warmer water, the emerald blush of sandy shallows and reefs. As he falls he reaches for his rip cord but he realises he has no parachute. As the ocean rushes towards him, he sees the bodies of men on the water. They float face down, arms and legs spread like the points of a star. The bodies are black against the vivid blue.

He wakes just before he hits the water. Sweat covers his body. How can a heart beat so fast? He is still alive.

☾

'Hi.'

She was sitting beside his bed in her white coat, a clipboard in her hands. She was smiling. 'How do you feel?'

'Better than I look.' Clay tried to sit up, but she reached out her hand and gently pushed him back down.

'Rest,' she said. 'That's what you need now.' She has an unusual accent. South African, yes, but with something else leavening the vowels. American?

'How long was I out?'

'It's been almost two weeks since the last operation.'

'Two days?' His hearing must have been damaged by the explosion.

She moved her head slowly from side to side. 'Two *weeks*.'

'Not possible,' he croaked.

She walked to the end of the bed, unhooked his chart and handed him the clipboard. There it was. He'd been in the hospital three weeks.

'Jesus,' he mumbled.

'Thank whoever you like. You are a very lucky boy.' She ran her gaze over him. 'Sorry,' she said after a while. 'Man.'

'Did you find out about Eben?' he managed.

'Your friend. Yes.' She frowned. 'He is here at 1-Mil. In the head trauma ward.'

'How is he?'

She pulled in her lower lip. 'He is in a coma. But stable.'

'Jesus.' Clay closed his eyes, bit down on the fact. An image of his friend's face came, blood pouring from the wound in the skull, pooling in the eye sockets. The bullet had taken away part of his skull and beneath the matted hair the brain glistened in the sun.

'Can I see him?'

'You are healing quickly, but right now you are in no condition to be visiting anyone. Perhaps, in a week or so, if you continue to improve, you might be able to receive visitors. But right now you're not going anywhere, soldier.'

Clay lay back. 'Tell me, Doctor. No bullshit. Will Eben make it?'

She looked over her shoulder, back along the length of the ward, then gazed into his eyes. A tear welled in her left eye, brimmed at the underlid, receded. 'There is a good chance he will live, yes. But he …' She stopped, sat staring at him. 'Were you close?'

'He is my best friend. *Is*, doctor. Present tense.'

Her cheeks blushed pink. 'Of course, sorry. I get so used to … to having these conversations. I apologise.'

'But what, Doctor?'

'I spoke with the attending surgeon. Your friend was in critical condition when he arrived, but stable. But there were complications.

That's what the surgeon said. Complications before the operation. Something went wrong.'

'What do you mean, complications?'

'I'm not sure. I only spoke briefly with the surgeon. Something about a foul-up in pre-op. Your friend suffered extensive brain damage. The operation was only partially successful. He is alive, but he has lost all motor function.'

Clay said nothing.

'Your friend is quadriplegic, Clay. I am sorry.' She looked at the floor. 'And there is little chance he will regain cognitive function.'

Something was pushing down hard on his larynx. He was choking. Tears flooded his eyes, hot, unbidden. Shame welled up inside him. He gasped. He hadn't cried since his parents died.

He felt her hand on his shoulder.

'Don't,' he snapped, pushing her hand away. 'What does that mean – won't regain cognitive function?'

'Those parts of his brain that control speech and movement have been badly damaged. He can hear, see, understand, but he cannot move or in any way acknowledge communication.'

Anger bloomed inside him now. Fury. If he'd had his R4 he would have blown out the windows and shredded the walls, kicked over the beds. 'Are you saying that they could have saved him, but someone screwed up? Is that what you are telling me?'

'Look, Clay, I'm sorry. Please understand. He was in a very bad way when he came in. That kind of trauma, it almost always—'

Clay cut her off. 'Answer my question, God damn it.'

She straightened, crossed her arms. 'Calm down, soldier,' she said, stern now. 'Bullying me is not going to change anything.'

But he couldn't hear what she was saying. 'They told me to leave him,' he shouted. 'They fucking told me.'

She recoiled, shocked at the vehemence in his voice. 'Please, don't—'

But he didn't let her finish. Remorse crashed through him. 'I should have left him out there. Let him die. God, what have I done?'

She sat another moment and then said, 'I'm sorry. I shouldn't have told you.'

Clay said nothing, lost inside his own pain.

'You need rest. I am going to give you a sedative.'

He looked up at her. 'How long until I can go back to my unit?'

She frowned, just an inflection of the mouth. 'Are you serious?'

'Of course, I'm serious.'

She winced. Her gaze hardened. 'You are not going back, soldier. Not for a long time.'

'How long?'

'Six months, at least.'

Clay swallowed. 'Might as well be forever.'

'If it was up to me, it would be.'

Clay looked at the soldier in the bed facing him. He had lost his right leg just above the knee. 'Dying is easier than living,' he said.

Her eyes ignited. It was as if she was trying to look right into him – into places he dared not go.

'Stupid boy,' she breathed.

21

All You Can Do

Many years later, after London and Yemen and Cyprus, after finding love and losing it, after the Truth and Reconciliation Commission's final verdict on his testimony and application for amnesty, he'd sit in the Polana Hotel in Maputo and think about those days in the military hospital and marvel at how time dulled the senses, ripped out all intensity and left only a palimpsest of dreamlike impressions. The way the shadows slid across the floor and the whitewashed walls, the smells of the veldt coming like memories of memories on the breeze that blew through the big, open windows of the recovery ward, the other odours – hospital antiseptic and soap, urine and sweat, the occasional waft of smoke from the incinerator. Sounds, too: the squeak of bed springs, the clip of nurses' shoes on the polished floors, the voices of men lost in a thousand dreams, a thousand worlds that no one would ever know or see. He'd think about all that was lost and undone, the waste of lives entire, and try to place all of this into some kind of equilibrium between cost and benefit, between good and insane. And in this futile calculus, staring out at the vastness of the Indian Ocean, its changing blue serenities and violent slanting storms, there was no succour.

'You *fokken* slacker.' Crowbar stood at the end of Clay's bed dressed in his best uniform and maroon paratrooper's beret. The blue Honoris Crux ribbon topped out a rack of decorations that blazed on his chest. 'Lying here while the rest of us to do all the hard work.'

Clay smiled with the good side of his face, saluted with his left hand. 'My *Liutenant*.'

'The doctors say you are improving.'

Clay tried to push himself up. 'Good to see you, sir.'

'Lie at ease, troop,' Crowbar said, pulling up a chair. 'We have to talk.' Crowbar looked right and left along the ward and sat. 'The enquiry is in three days.'

Clay nodded; he'd been told by the head doctor that he had been ordered to appear at the inquest, that he had been cleared to attend for one day only.

'I'm here to push your wheelchair, Straker.'

'How are the boys, sir?'

'We stayed in-country for two weeks after you were hit. We lost de Koch. Killed a lot of *fokken kaffirs*, though. FAPLA and Boy.'

Clay closed his eyes; de Koch had been a friend. They all were.

'Eben's worse.'

Crowbar straightened. 'I saw him.'

'I should have…' Clay began, stumbled. 'I didn't—'

'Don't, Straker,' Crowbar interrupted. 'No good can ever come of it. It's not for you to decide.'

Clay lay quiet. Many years later, in the wilds of Yemen, another good man would try to teach him exactly this, and would give his life proving it.

Crowbar leaned in close and dropped his voice. 'Look, Straker. This inquest is total bullshit. A complete *rondfok*. The boys and I have all agreed what happened.'

'I understand, sir.' Of course, he understood. He listened, heard, memorised. It was the truth. Of course, it was. What other truth was there? What other could there be?

'Good.' Crowbar slid a steel hipflask into Clay's hand. 'Something for the pain,' he said. 'Don't drink it all at once.'

'Thank you, sir.' Clay slid the flask under the bedsheets. 'Can I ask a favour, sir? It's important.'

'Of course, *seun*.'

'There's a package buried under the floorboards of my tent at Ondangwa, under the upper left foot of my bunk. Can you bring it to me?'

Crowbar frowned. 'Personal effects?'

'You could say that.'

'I'll see what I can do.'

'Thank you, sir.'

Crowbar shuffled his feet, waited until a nurse passed. 'And Straker, just so you know. Wade wasn't killed by a SWAPO mortar.'

'Sir?'

'You heard me.'

'But the Colonel sent out a patrol after them.'

'No, son. Wade was killed by an M27 frag. Didn't you hear it?'

'No sir, I was asleep.'

'I was the first one there. He was killed by someone inside the base. One of our own.'

Clay shook his head, realisation flooding through him now.

'Who?'

'Could have been anyone.'

Not anyone. 'I know why they did it, sir.'

'I don't want to hear it, Straker,' Crowbar snapped.

'But, sir…'

Crowbar drilled a withering stare into Clay's eyes. 'No, Straker.'

'Wade knew, sir. That's why they killed him.'

Crowbar leaned in very close, until his chin was almost touching Clay's cheek. 'Don't say another word. I don't know what you're talking about and I don't want to. And neither do you. Do you understand me, troop?'

'But—'

'This is my army, Straker. My country. As fucked up as it is.'

'Do you think that justifies—'

'Shut the *fok* up, Straker.'

'Then why tell me about Wade.'

Crowbar sat back in the chair, raised his thick, hairy forearms, clasped his hands behind his head. 'I'm not any happier about it than you are. Wade was a good officer.' He closed his eyes.

'You're part of it aren't you?' Clay regretted it as soon as he'd said it.

'Part of what?'

'You ordered us to attack the village. Kill all those people.'

'I *fokken* follow my orders, Straker. I don't decide what happens. I do what I'm told and try to bring as many of you limp-dick amateurs back alive as I can. *Fok jou*, Straker.'

'So you admit it.'

'I don't have to explain myself to you, Straker.'

'And now Wade's dead.'

Crowbar stood wrenching his beret between two massive hands. 'You think *I* killed Wade?'

'No, I…' Clay stumbled. 'That's not what I meant.'

'I hope the hell not.'

'I'm sorry, sir.'

Crowbar leaned back in. Clay could smell the booze on his breath. 'Look, Straker, let me give you some advice. Just forget anything you might think you know about any of that *kak*. It's not for us. Get better. Get through this. With that wound they're not going to let you redeploy. You've done your part. Go home. Find yourself a good woman and have half a dozen kids. Try to live. It's all you can do.'

Clay said nothing.

Crowbar stood, replaced his beret and adjusted its rake across his brow. 'I'll be back in three days. Just remember what I told you. You know what to say. Every one of your brothers is counting on you. I'm counting on you, Corporal. So are Barstow and de Koch and Cooper.' And then he turned smartly and strode out of the ward.

☾

Commissioner Ksole: So, you lied to the military tribunal?

Witness: Yes, sir.

Commissioner Ksole: The report I have in front of me indicates that over fifty civilians were killed that day – a whole village wiped out. It also says that most of those killed were old men, women and children. Is this true, Mister Straker?

Witness: Yes.

Commissioner Ksole: And were you responsible, Mister Straker, for what happened that day?

Witness: I … I don't know how to answer that, sir. I was there. I … (*Coughs*).

Commissioner Barbour: The Provost General's report into the massacre, based on the inquest in which you and members of *Valk* 5 testified, found that your platoon was not responsible for the murder of the civilians in the village. Based on the testimony of the Bosbok pilots who overflew the village the day after, and of the members of *Valk* 5 themselves, the inquest found that FAPLA carried out the slaughter in reprisal for the loss of their own men.

Witness: Yes, sir.

Commissioner Ksole: So you falsified your testimony to the Provost General's enquiry of 1981?

Commissioner Barbour: Think carefully before you answer, son.

Witness: Yes, sir. I lied. That's why I've come back. To set it right.

Commissioner Lacy: That is why we are all here, Mister Straker. For the truth.

Witness: Thank you, ma'am.

Commissioner Barbour: It sounds to me as if you engaged the enemy. How can you be sure that FAPLA themselves didn't kill the villagers, or that they weren't simply caught in the crossfire? The way you describe it, it seems to me, that … ah, well, that is the most likely interpretation. Did you actually see any of your own men killing civilians?

Witness: No, sir. No, I didn't.

Commissioner Barbour: And did you, to your knowledge, aim
   your weapon at a civilian, with the intent to kill?
Witness: No, sir. No, I didn't, as far as I can remember
   it. Except for the boy. I did that.
Commissioner Rotzenburg: But isn't that exactly the issue,
   Mister Straker? That you can't remember. You now dispute
   the official version of events, to which you yourself
   originally contributed, and now you are unsure about what
   you actually saw.
Witness: I am trying to tell you that I didn't see anyone
   kill civilians. We were in the middle of a firefight. Both
   sides were shooting. It was all a blur.
Commissioner Rotzenburg: So, it is entirely possible that
   the official version of events is correct, as my colleague
   suggests?
Witness: I can't remember it clearly. I don't remember
   killing civilians, but I am sure I did. That we all did.
Commissioner Lacy: How can you be so sure?
Witness: Because the village we destroyed, that we were
   sent to destroy – ordered to destroy – was Zulaika's
   village. The woman I saw with the back of her head shot
   off, that was her. It was her.
Commissioner Barbour: Jesus wept.
Witness: It wasn't an accident. Not a crime of passion. It
   was planned. They wanted her dead. We were sent there to
   kill her and everyone she knew.

22

Drowning

Seeing the boys from the platoon again had been nothing like he'd expected. He'd only been away a month and by now was one of the veterans of the unit, but there was already a distance there, an unspoken separation. They were going back to the fight, and he was not. It put aeons between them. He knew it and so did they. Only Crowbar, who'd been in long enough to see hundreds come and go, seemed unchanged.

After the enquiry, Crowbar delivered him back to the hospital, wheeled him back to his bed. They shook hands.

'Please, sir,' said Clay. 'Don't forget.'

Crowbar nodded. 'Your personal effects. No worries, Straker.'

'Under my bunk. It's important, *Koevoet*.' He knew he was taking a chance, but there was no other way.

Crowbar stiffened a moment. 'Anything else, Straker? *Fokken* breakfast in bed, perhaps?'

Clay smiled. 'I get that already.'

Just an inflection of the brow. '*Ja, ja, fokken* smart arse.'

'*Dankie, Koevoet.*'

'Oh, and I thought you might want to know,' said Crowbar, straightening his beret. 'That black scout of ours, Brigade. He's missing in action. Didn't come back from a long-range recon patrol about a week ago. I know you liked him.'

Clay looked deep into his commander's hard blue eyes and nodded, another little void opening inside him.

'Look after yourself, *seun*,' said Crowbar. 'And don't do anything stupid.' He handed Clay a paper shopping bag, and leaned in close.

'Get out, Straker. Leave South Africa. Do it fast. I don't expect to see you again.' Then he straightened up, saluted, turned about face and walked away before Clay could say another word.

After everyone had gone and the ward was quiet, Clay opened up the bag. Inside, a dog-eared copy of *Catch-22*, a copy of the previous day's *Sunday Times*, and at the bottom, a loaded Beretta 92 with a spare mag. There was also a small muslin pouch held closed with a drawstring. Clay snatched a shallow breath, opened the pouch and tipped the contents into his palm: a single stone a little bigger than one of the seven hundred steel balls packed inside an M18 Claymore mine.

Clay's stomach bottomed out. A diamond, uncut.

Clay turned the stone over in his fingers. Was it one of *his* – one of Mbdele's? It was a particularly unremarkable example, tinged brown from defects in the tetrahedral bonded lattice. He couldn't tell. Just minutes ago, Crowbar had stood right there next to Clay's bed and told him that he would send on his effects when he could. Had he lied? Had Crowbar somehow managed to get back to Ondangwa, retrieve the bag from under the floorboards in Clay's tent, and then get back to Pretoria in time for the inquest? And if so, where were the other diamonds – the big pink one? Why would Crowbar have picked out just one stone and kept the rest? For the money? He couldn't imagine Crowbar doing something so dishonourable. And what about the notebook they'd taken from *O Medico de Morte's* assistant? Clay had buried it with the diamonds. Surely if Crowbar had dug out Clay's 'personal effects', as he'd called them – Clay hadn't specified what was in the bag – he would have seen the notebook, looked inside, realised its significance. And if he had, what had he done with it? The very existence of those documents was proof that Clay had committed murder. And if this stone in his hand wasn't one of the diamonds he'd buried under his bunk, then where the hell did Crowbar get it? Was he, as Clay had begun to suspect, more involved in this thing than he was admitting? Clay's mind raced through the possibilities, but there was no way to disentangle them, no way to know.

Clay slipped the diamond back into its pouch and set it on his bedside table. One thing was sure: Crowbar had told Clay to get out and given him the means to do it.

(

Days passed. He still needed morphine – would reach for the little bell on his side table that brought the nurse and her gift of bliss. But he was healing. He could feel it. Breathing was a little bit easier every day. He slept for big parts of the day: long periods of prescribed hallucination that left him reeling at the vivid insanity of the images conjured up by his brain. Periods of lucidity were there, too, and terror walked through them.

Then one day, Sara came.

She sat beside him. He could tell she'd been crying. Her eyes and the tip of her nose were pink and inflamed. She wore the same dress she'd worn that day she'd met him at the airport, when he'd come back home on leave after his parents died in the car crash. She looked heavier than he remembered her.

She smiled at him and placed a bouquet of flowers on his bedside table. 'I didn't know what else to bring,' she said, staring at the bandage on his face.

'Sara,' he said, not looking at the flowers. 'What are you doing here?'

'Oh, Clay,' she whispered. 'They told me that you'd been wounded, that you were here. I wanted to come and see you.'

Clay said nothing.

Sara fiddled with her hair. 'Are you alright, Clay?'

'I'm fine.'

'What happened?'

'Nothing.'

'Mother said I should come down. That perhaps we could talk about plans for the wedding.'

'Wedding?'

'We never set a date, Clay. Mother says we should start making arrangements, booking a church, thinking about the guest list.'

An emptiness blew through him, cold and come over a great distance. He couldn't quite believe that he was even having this conversation.

'We're all so proud of you, Clay. We read about your medal in the newspaper. It's wonderful what you are doing, keeping us all safe from the communists.'

Clay looked away.

'Just think, it will be so grand. You in your uniform with your medals, me in my dress. I have something picked out already.' She rummaged in her handbag, withdrew a piece of paper. 'What do you think?'

Clay looked back at her. She was holding up a page from a bridal catalogue – a pretty model in a demure, high-necked white gown.

'I don't know,' he said.

'There are loads of styles,' she said. 'I know it's bad luck for you to see the dress before the wedding, but there's no harm in you seeing pictures.' She pulled out a magazine. 'I wanted something sexier, low cut, but mother…' She flipped through the pages, found what she was looking for, put it in front of him. 'Something like this?'

Clay stared at the picture. 'I don't know.'

Sara looked up at him. Her face had crumpled, her smile gone. 'Don't know what, Clay? Are you alright? Should I call the nurse?'

'I don't know.'

Sara was silent. Clay matched her.

After a while, she said: 'Don't you want me here?'

'No,' he said. 'I don't want you here.'

Shock in her face, surprise. 'What are you saying, Clay?'

'Get out, Sara.'

And that was it.

Many years later he'd replay it all in his head, and the guilt would come, raw still despite the scarring. She'd be sitting there, tears flowing across her face, not saying a word, and it would last a long time. Twice more he would tell her to get out. Like this: Get out, Sara. I don't want you here. I don't want to talk about weddings or medals or anything. I just want to be alone. And then she'd be standing next to his bed and he would know he'd hurt her in the most fundamental and unforgiveable way, and ever since that day he'd never found the courage to call her or write her to tell her he was sorry, that he wasn't the man she thought he was; that he'd thought he was.

She stood and walked out.

Later a nurse came and gave him an envelope. Inside was the ring they'd bought her while he was on leave; the little, flawed diamond, solitary in its abandoned gold band.

☾

The doctor came by to check on him at least once a day, but she seemed distracted and distant. One night she gave him a copy of *Crime and Punishment*, told him it belonged to her husband.

'What does he fly?'

She said nothing, just sat staring into the darkness of the ward.

'Doctor?'

She looked up at the ceiling, took a few shallow breaths. 'Mirage,' she said.

Clay nodded. 'Those *Vlammy* pilots, they keep us alive, you know.'

Her eyes brimmed a moment then flashed as she turned her face away. 'Stupid fucking war,' she hissed.

She checked his chart. He could see that her hand was shaking. She stared down at the clipboard, the shadows glancing from the pale panels of her uniform, stretching across the polished floor and warping over the ranks of parallel beds. Then she hooked the chart to the end of his bed and walked away.

The next day she was silent, withdrawn, went about her work with grim efficiency. She checked his pulse and blood pressure, examined the place where she'd cut open his body and then closed it back up again, all without a word. She wrote something on his chart and made to leave.

Clay reached for her arm. 'Please,' he said. 'I have something to tell you.'

She glanced along the length of the ward.

'You asked me about Operation COAST,' he whispered. 'That's the message you sent me, wasn't it? In the book? The cipher?'

She looked both ways, nodded and leaned close.

'The guy I killed, out in the dunes,' said Clay, whispering close into her ear. 'The one who was helping to administer the injections to those poor bastards…' Clay tailed off, the memory wrapping its hands around his throat.

'Go on,' she whispered.

'He was carrying some documents. They mentioned Operation COAST.'

Her mouth opened, a small, perfect oval, as if she were about to blow out candles on a birthday cake.

'It was a list of chemicals and their effects on human test subjects,' he said.

Clay watched her eyes widen and a deep frown crease her forehead.

'Do you have the documents?'

'I did. I tried to get them for you. I don't know what's happened to them.'

Can you remember any of the details?' she whispered.

He started to speak.

She shook her head, rearranged the papers on her clip board and handed him a pencil from her breast pocket. 'Write it for me,' she said. 'As much as you can remember.'

Clay scribbled out the contents of formulations 13B and 14C, the accompanying clinical observations, and handed her back the clipboard.

She stood reading. 'Are you sure this is correct?' she whispered. 'It's very detailed.'

'I think so,' he said. 'I have a good memory for things like this. I'm better with numbers, but I'm pretty sure it's right.'

She pulled the paper from the clipboard, folded it and slid it into her pocket.

'What are you going to do?' he asked.

'I'm not sure yet. Don't tell anyone about this.' She squeezed his hand. 'Try to rest. I'll speak to you tomorrow. I must go.' She hurried away.

Unable to sleep, having again refused morphine, Clay read deep into the night. The ward was dark, Dostoevsky's words semi-obscure in the dim moonlight, shrouded in veils of pain. The story took on the rhythms of the hurt flowing through him, paragraphs rising up to crest and break into foamy troughs of half-relief and partial understanding, only for the turbulence to gather again and rise so that at each peak he could see across an endless sea of breaking waves. And in each of these cyclings he searched for some meaning, for answers to his questions. But there were only glimpses of land on a shifting horizon, distant coastlines obscured by shoals of low cloud.

Around midnight a nurse came and asked if he wanted morphine. He took a small dose. Clay read on as the drugs took effect, his mind wandering now, rereading the same paragraph three times, something about two kinds of men – those that want to be controlled and those that transgress the law because they can. Raskolnikov was hurtling towards self-destruction. Clay closed the book and shut his eyes.

He'd just drifted to the edge of a dream when something shunted him back. Someone was standing next to his bed, fumbling with his IV. Clay opened his eyes. It was a doctor. He was holding a syringe, preparing to inject something into the IV line. The doctor turned and smiled under his facemask, the white cotton bunching up under his nose.

'Straker,' the doctor said, his voice grating like rusty hinge. 'Good. You are awake.'

'What are you doing?' said Clay, groggy from the morphine.

'Don't worry,' the doctor said. 'It will all be over soon.' He smiled with dark, seemingly depthless eyes and inserted the needle.

Those eyes. That voice. 'I don't want morphine.'

A strangled laugh emerged from the doctor's mouth. 'Don't worry. It's not morphine.' He started depressing the plunger.

Clay shook his head. A thick vapour had now flooded the ward, wisped around the doctor's head. 'What…?' he gasped. Something was wrong. Very wrong. 'Who are you?'

'What did I tell you in Angola? Do you remember?'

'Angola? You were in Angola?' Clay tried to push back the chloroform shroud collapsing in on him. He could feel the peripheries of his consciousness dissolving. None of what was happening made sense. Was it another dream?

The man's mouth moved underneath the mask, the dark eyes narrowed. 'You are a traitor, Straker, to your country and your race.'

Clay's heart lurched from rest to terror as realisation hit. Adrenaline flooded his system. He threw out his arm, reached for the bell. A bolt of pain pierced his ribcage. The man grabbed his arm, wrenching it outward. Clay grunted as the whole of his injured side lit up like fire, despite the anaesthetic. The bell hit the floor with a loud clang. The man cursed, lost his hold on the syringe as the IV stand crashed to the floor. He reached to right it but by now lights had come on at the end of the ward. Without another word, he sprinted to the other end of the room and disappeared through the double doors.

The effect on Clay's body was almost instantaneous. He grappled for the catheter in his arm, but it was as if his hands were made of foam rubber, the fingers thick and spongy. He was vaguely aware of someone rushing towards him, of voices raised. Spasms racked his body. His arms fell limp, then his legs. He felt as if he was drowning. And then she was there, looking down at him. He tried to scream, but nothing came.

Part IV

23

Straight to the Heart

19th September 1981,
Pretoria, South Africa

She had left the windows open. And through them came Africa.

Came the warm caress of the breeze, laden with a continent's fertile beauty, all of its dark, warring despair. Came the earth-red smell of laterite, the sweet tang of wood smoke and the blossom of wildflowers, that unmistakable redolence of rain in the distance. Sounds, too, flooded in. Sounds that would always be home. Thunder rumbling on the horizon, like a faraway waterfall. A woman's Zulu lullaby drifting through razor wire and the green hanging boughs of suburban trees. Birdsong.

And the absence of things too. Missing, the sting of burning rubber, the acrid shove of cordite, the stink of death. Absent the wail of jet fighters and the rip of gunfire, the screams of the wounded and the cries of dying animals. Here, now, there was no war.

Clay pushed himself up in the bed.

The room was big, with a high ceiling and shuttered French doors that opened up onto a polished stone veranda. Morning sun streamed through the mosquito net in thick beams heavy with pollen. Hardwood floors gleamed. A ceiling fan spun quietly overhead. Opposite, a young couple smiled out at him from within a silver frame set on an antique chest of drawers. It was – he realised he'd never asked her name – the doctor from the military hospital. She had her arms around a young man's neck. Their hair was tousled, sun-bleached. They looked happy, their beauty captured in that moment forever.

On the bedside table was the standard-issue Beretta Crowbar had given him, the copy of *Catch-22*, the muslin pouch with the diamond in it. A glass of water, too, a box of some kind of pain medicine, the copy of *Crime and Punishment* she'd given him in the hospital, and a note. The bedside clock showed twenty-nine minutes after ten in the morning. He reached for the paper, wincing in pain as his side stretched out. *I will be back soon*, it said. *You're safe here. But don't leave the house. Stay away from the front windows. Keep quiet. No music! If you are up to it there is some soup on the stove, bread and butter on the counter, water in the kettle for tea. My shift finishes at 3 pm. I should be home by four. I will explain everything then. Vivian.*

Vivian.

Clay levered himself up and swung his feet to the floor. Pain burned through his side. Sweat bloomed from his pores. He sat panting, hands propped on his knees. An image of Botha standing above his bed came to him, the last thing he remembered: that dark malevolent stare, those words. A cold chill bit a long way inside him.

Maybe Botha was right. Maybe Clay *was* a traitor. He'd killed one of his own, had known he was doing it. He'd disobeyed orders. He'd lied at the inquest. They all had. They'd court-martial him, probably shoot him.

Sitting here on this marital bed, none of it seemed real. He'd wake in a moment and he would be back at the war with Eben, and it would all have been an echo in his mind, fast receding, soon forgotten. The thought of his friend brought it all rushing back. That glimpse of brain through the opened skull, the weight of him in his arms as he hoisted him onto the casevac's deck – all of it too real, none of this a dream.

He pushed himself slowly to his feet, took a first tentative step and found that he could walk without too much pain, as long as he kept his strides short and didn't try to twist at the waist. She – Vivian – had done a good job.

He wandered the rooms, through the big archway into the sitting room with the river-rock fireplace, the big mullioned windows letting out onto the leafy garden, then into the library, back through to the kitchen. A hardwood-floored corridor led from the main room to the front of the house. The planking underfoot was old, worn, creaking under his weight. A formal sitting room and dining room flanked the front door. He checked every room, determined possible entry and exit points. Every interior door but one was unlocked.

Why was he here, in her house? For it *was* hers. Everything about the place spoke of a life of order and learning, of love and hope for the future, of compassion and beauty. But it was also his – the man in the photograph, her husband. The 1:72 models of aircraft ranged across the wooden shelf by the bookcase, each one carefully painted and decaled; the painting of the Spitfire climbing through the clouds; the SAAF dress uniform with captain's insignia and campaign ribbons carefully pressed and hanging in the closet; the weight bench out on the patio, the bar still loaded up with a hundred kilos of rusting iron.

Clay sat on the back patio step and looked up at the sky. He felt like an intruder. He turned his face to the sun. Photons rained over him, swam red across his retinae, warmed the scar on his cheek. A bird landed on the patio, hopped towards him and stopped just beyond touching distance, looking at him, waiting for something. It was a ring-necked dove, so common here, grey with a dark collar and white lilac-tinted breast. It crooned, those three familiar syllables that transported him to another house in another suburb in Gauteng province, where, as a boy, he'd lain in his bed under the eaves and listened to the doves cooing in the big jacaranda outside his window in the early hours before school. And, as these memories came, that empty place opened up inside him and he could not close it or hold on to it so as to describe it any way that he could understand. And much later, he would reflect that his life had been divided into two halves, whether by accident or by design of fate. One, a period of belonging, the other of loss. And he would try to calculate that point at which the loss had eroded the treasured store of belonging such that, for a short time, an equilibrium had been reached, a point at which the sum of his life had balanced to zero. And in this he came to realise that, with each passing day, the essence of him was further reduced, become negative, a gravity so powerful as to swallow light, crush matter.

The dove, tired of waiting, flapped up to a high branch. As it did, another sound, this one from inside the house, made Clay start. He froze, listened. It couldn't yet be past eleven. Vivian wasn't due back until four. There it was again: a creak, then a click.

Jesus. Someone was inside the house.

Pulse jack-knifing, Clay reached to the small of his back for the Beretta. It wasn't there. He'd left it on the bedside table. He cursed and pushed himself to his feet. He shuffled to the edge of the open patio door and hid behind the outside wall. From here he could see through into the main sitting room. He waited. Then the sound of a door being pushed to, slowly. The slightest click. Without a weapon, unable to run, he was defenceless.

Footsteps approaching now, creaking over the hardwood. A rustling sound, like crunching paper or plastic. Then another door opening and closing, with stealth. Clay looked back towards the garden. Through the shrubs he could make out a high back wall lipped with coiled wire. There was a garden shed, but no obvious exit. He cursed himself for not having reconnoitred the garden too, identified at least one exfil route. He started moving along the back patio towards the bedroom. If he couldn't run, he would fight.

The French doors of the bedroom were still open. He stepped over the threshold, holding his breath. He picked the gun up from the bedside table and eased back the action, wincing at the sound. It was loaded. He moved towards the open bedroom door and flattened himself against the wall just inside the doorway, listened for a moment, then glanced into the sitting room. It was empty. Whoever it was, he had to assume that there was more than one of them. The sound of footsteps again, coming from the hallway that connected the main sitting room with the front parlour and front door. The footsteps were getting louder. He cycled a few breaths and raised the Beretta.

He'd never seen her out of uniform before.

She wore a pretty, knee-length dress that swayed as she walked. Her hair was down, wisped about her head in the breeze blowing through the open windows. She'd put on some lipstick. Her eyes looked bigger than he remembered, very blue, even from here. She was carrying a paper shopping bag in one arm. He watched as she turned away and disappeared into the kitchen, heard her open and close the fridge, run the tap. He didn't move, stayed hidden. A moment later she emerged from the kitchen carrying two mugs and started walking across the big sitting room, past the bookcase and the expensive-looking hi-fi system. Her dress clung to her body as she moved. It was of some thin material, tied about the waist with a belt of the same cloth, patterned in hues of blue, like the sea from altitude, ripples and waves and currents and the frisson that surfed up Clay's spine and foamed through his groin.

She stopped in the middle of the room and glanced outside, as if she'd heard something. Her forehead knitted into a frown.

When she turned back, Clay was standing in the open bedroom doorway, the gun still in his hand.

The look of worry on her face disappeared into a big smile. 'Good morning,' she said.

'*Howzit*,' he said, aware that she probably knew he'd been watching her, feeling it come as heat to his face. 'You're home early.'

'I told my boss I wasn't feeling well.' She walked up to him and handed him a mug. 'You shouldn't be up,' she said, looking down at his torso, bare except for the bandage around his midriff. 'That wound hasn't healed yet.' She took him by the hand and started guiding him back to the bed. 'And put that horrible thing away.'

'Didn't your ma tell you that you should knock before you enter?' he said, putting the Beretta on the chest of drawers next to the photograph.

'Sorry. Next time, I will.'

He sat on the bed.

'How do you feel?' she asked.

'I'm good.'

'Well you look good,' she said. 'For a dead man.'

Clay stopped, frowned, started to form a question.

'I'll explain,' she said. 'Now, come on. Listen to your doctor.'

He lay back and propped his head up on a couple of pillows she arranged for him. She sat on the edge of the bed next to him.

'So tell me,' Clay said.

When she'd found him in the ward, he'd been unconscious, his respiratory system in the process of shutting down. A nurse had been administering CPR, but to no effect. She'd been on duty in another ward when one of the nurses had come running. A man had been seen fleeing the hospital, dressed as a staff member. Beside Clay's bed they'd found the partially depressed syringe still stuck into the IV line, and a single empty phial on the floor nearby. He was going into cardiac arrest. There was no other option. She'd administered adrenaline, straight to the heart.

Clay's heart was pounding now as the realisation hit him.

'After everything we'd been through trying to save you, I was damned if we were going to lose you like that,' she said, brushing a wisp of hair from the bridge of her nose.

'It was Botha,' said Clay. 'The guy I met in Angola.'

Her eyes opened wide. 'What do you mean?'

'I saw him standing by the bed trying to inject something into my IV. He told me he was going to kill me.'

Vivian went white behind the dusting of earthy freckles. 'Are you sure?'

Clay nodded.

'What did he look like?'

'Big, broad, overweight. Dark moustache, balding. Skin like the pox. Ugly as hell, if you ask me. The guy in my dreams – the ones I told you about.'

She shook her head. 'Are you sure you weren't hallucinating?'

Clay thought back. 'That's what I saw.'

She rubbed her thumb across the knuckles of her index finger, staring at the bedclothes, lost somewhere. After a while she looked up at him. 'If it is the same man, then we are all in real danger.'

'It was him. I'm sure.'

She was quiet a while, thinking this through. 'What did you do out there, Clay?'

'What I was told.'

'I mean, what did you do that would make them want to kill you?'

He told her about the rendezvous with the C-130, about Botha's apparent role in taking delivery of the tusks and diamonds from UNITA, and their confrontation over the prisoner, about seeing him again on the Ondangwa base the night Wade was killed.

'Botha argued with Wade, there, outside the mess hall. I couldn't hear what they were saying.' Clay raised his hands to his face, pressed his fingertips into his forehead. 'I should have tried to get closer. I was scared.'

She put her hand on his head, ran her fingers across the rough brush-cut stubble. She did it absentmindedly, as if by habit. 'Everyone is scared, Clay.'

Clay said nothing, felt her fingers travelling through his hair.

'Someone is making a fortune out there,' she whispered.

That hole opened up inside him again. It wasn't enough that SWAPO and FAPLA were trying to kill him. Now it was his own goddamned people. People who were profiting from the very conflict Eben had just been sacrificed to. The hole gaped like an unfilled grave.

Her face darkened. 'Did Botha pay UNITA? For the tusks, I mean. Did he give them money, weapons?'

'I couldn't see everything. But there weren't weapons – not on that flight, anyway. He did give Mbdele a small box. I have no idea what was inside, but it was too small for cash. More like a pack of smokes.'

She nodded. 'Drugs, perhaps?'

'I don't know. Maybe.'

'Maybe.'

'Who is he?' said Clay. 'Botha. Who does he work for?'

'I have no idea. But he used this.' And from the pocket of her dress she withdrew an empty phial.

Clay read the three characters on the label, the only markings. 'Jesus Christ,' he whispered.

'Formulation 13B. As soon as I saw, I knew. It was only because you'd remembered what was in the stuff that I knew how to counteract it.'

Clay pursed his lips, exhaled.

'You've seen what it does to people. You've felt it.' She shook her head. 'It's outrageous.'

Botha had been there with Cobra when they'd taken away the hardwood and the tusks, but not over the Atlantic with Doctor Death and the dead and dying blacks – not that Clay had seen, anyway. But the implications were clear: it proved some sort of connection between Botha's dealings with UNITA, and Doctor Death's fucked-up experiments in Angola. The common element was Cobra. He'd been there both times, with his dozen or so Special Forces types.

Clay's head was spinning now, trying to make sense of the pieces. Then he remembered. 'The document I told you about,' he said. 'It was on SAMS letterhead.'

She recoiled visibly. 'What did you say?'

'Formulation 13B – those notes were typed on South African Medical Service letterhead.'

She sat for a long time without speaking. After a while she stood and walked to the still-open doors and out onto the back patio. He could see her standing in the sunshine, hands on hips.

After a while she came back in and sat back down on the edge of the bed. 'That would be how he got access to the hospital,' she said, composed again. 'If it was him you saw.'

'It was him.'

'Okay. It was him.'

Clay thought back to the clearing in Angola, the men and boys collapsing to the ground, voiding themselves, the laughter of Cobra's men as they stepped over the bodies. He shivered. 'What the hell is our medical service doing with drugs that are designed to do this to people? It doesn't make sense.'

'That's what we have to find out.'

'Is that what Operation COAST is?' he said. 'Some kind of medical testing project?'

'Here,' she said, unfolding the hand-rendered reproductions he'd made for her in the hospital. 'Look again.'

Clay took the paper.

She jerked three shallow breaths. Clay thought she was going to cry, but instead she took his hand in hers. 'Is there anything else you can remember, Clay? Anything at all?'

He searched his head for the image of the originals, compared the copy, character by character, line by line. They were identical in every way. He didn't understand most of it, but he knew it was the same. 'Everything's there,' he said. 'I'm sure.'

'How, Clay?'

'My memory works like that. Not for everything, but definitely for numbers, strings of characters. The more random and meaningless, the easier it is. It's been like that since I was a child.'

The doctor nodded, clinician again. She looked at his scribblings. 'What about the logo – the letterhead?'

He looked at the papers. No letterhead. He'd left that out, missed it completely. 'The SAMS crest was top centre,' he said, indicating with his index finger. 'Here. And you're right. There was something else.' He moved his finger to the top right corner of the page.

'What was it?'

He scanned the beam of his memory over the page, trying to focus. 'There was something in fine print. A block of text. Part of the letterhead. I didn't pay it much attention.'

'Try to remember Clay. Top right. What was it?'

He dredged. 'An address block,' he said.

'Where, Clay?'

Some of the words sharpened. 'Pretoria,' he said. 'Definitely. And something else.' He scanned, focusing. '*Roodeplaat Laboratories*, something like that.'

'I've heard of it,' she said. 'It's not too far from the hospital, I think. Was there anything else, Clay?'

He shook his head, tightened down on her hand. Questions spun in his head. 'Why did you call me a dead man, Doctor?'

She placed her index finger onto the note she'd written earlier. 'Vivian,' she said. 'Please. That's my name.'

'Vivian,' he repeated. 'Please, Vivian. Tell me.'

She attempted a smile. It didn't come out as one.

Over the next half-hour, Vivian recounted how, after she'd restarted his heart, she'd cleaned him up and wheeled him out of the ward and to an unused operating theatre. Swearing the other nurse to secrecy, she'd filled out a death certificate for Claymore Straker, 1st Parachute Battalion, SADF, indicating death due to wounds received in battle. Making sure he was stable, she'd covered him over with a sheet, and, enlisting the help of a trusted friend – Joseph, a black orderly she'd worked with for years – they'd wheeled Clay to the ambulance. Under the veil of darkness, the streets empty, they'd driven him to the morgue.

'I was sure that we were being watched,' she said, putting her empty mug on the floor and crossing her legs. 'Joseph wheeled the gurney into the morgue, but we kept you in the ambulance. The chap who runs the morgue is a colleague. He took delivery of a couple of pillows.' Again she tried a smile.

They'd returned to the hospital, parked the ambulance in the big garage, and, leaving Clay with Joseph, she'd left through the main doors and walked to her car. The main parking area was quiet but she was frightened, aware that her life had just changed forever. She drove out of the main gates as usual, as if she was driving home. After a while she doubled back. Keeping to the side streets, she approached the hospital by the rear service entrance. Joseph was still waiting with Clay. Together they got him to her car and she'd driven him here.

'Joseph and I carried you to the bed.' She rubbed her shoulders. 'Dragged more like. How much do you weigh, anyway?'

'Not as much as I did three weeks ago,' he said.

She flicked a smile, a real one this time, but there was sadness there, too. 'I just hope no one was watching,' she said. 'It was dark, and I parked as close to the back doors as I could, but still...' She trailed off into silence.

'You said before, when I first met you, that you thought BOSS was watching you.'

She nodded. 'I'm not sure. I've never seen anything specific. It's more a feeling. Random things. A person I've never seen before passing me in the corridor in the hospital, a click on the phone just after I pick up. I don't know, Clay. Maybe I'm being paranoid.' She untied her pony tail and shook her hair free. 'They're cracking down on us, all over the country.'

'Us?'

'Not now,' she said.

'What do you mean, not now?'

She looked around the room, towards the open windows. 'Not now.'

'You're right,' said Clay. 'Not now.' He pushed himself up and swung his feet to the floor. Pain grabbed his side, twisted hard.

'What are you doing?' she said. 'You must be careful. There was a lot of damage. If you move quickly like that, you could rupture something.' She made to lie him back down but he resisted.

'You've all put yourselves in danger because of me,' he said. 'I have to leave.' He pushed himself to his feet, wobbled, straightened. He was naked except for a pair of loose-fitting, hospital-issue boxer shorts and the swath of white bandage across his midriff.

She was standing now, too, hands on her hips. 'Lie down, Corporal.' It was not a request. 'You're in no shape to stand, let alone walk out of here.'

'I can't ask you to do this,' he said. 'Any of you.'

She shook her head. 'Stupid boy.'

Clay reached for the Beretta, trying to hide the effect of the pain shooting through him. He stood, wincing involuntarily, the gun in his hand.

'Don't bend at the waist,' she said. She was much smaller than him, the top of her head barely reaching his collar bone. 'You have to keep your core as still as possible, for a few more days at least.'

Clay started towards the closet, opened it and started rummaging through the drawers.

'His clothes are on the right side,' she said.

Clay opened one of the drawers. Underwear and socks, neatly pressed and twinned. He grabbed a t-shirt from the second drawer, a pair of trousers from the third. They looked about his size. He put the handgun on a shelf and started threading on the trousers.

'Do you really think that you are the only one?' she said, still standing by the bed. 'There are thousands of us, across the country.'

Clay faced her. 'Us?'

'People who want change. Whites.'

Clay zipped up the trousers, put the Beretta into the waistband at the small of his back. 'Traitors, you mean.' He wasn't even sure if he meant it, but the words came anyway. 'We've heard about you, supporting the communists while we risk our lives defending the nation.' It was what Crowbar would have said, what they all talked about, out there on the front lines. The slackers and traitors. By the time he'd finished saying it, he'd regretted every word.

She frowned, holding his gaze a long time.

Clay hung his head. He could feel the power of this woman, her conviction. 'Look, I'm sorry,' he whispered.

She didn't answer, just stood there boring through him with those river-bed eyes. A Shona melody danced in through the open windows, a woman's voice, a song of loss and hope.

They listened. Listened right through. And then it was over.

'My neighbour's cook,' she said.

'Our housemaid used to sing.'

She was walking towards him now. 'If you're going to go, you'll need some shoes,' she said, stepping past him and reaching into the closet. 'And a decent shirt.' She handed him a pair of tan desert boots and a khaki-coloured button shirt. 'These should fit.'

'Thanks.'

She stood close. 'Do you really think that you're protecting us by leaving? The minute they identify you, they'll know we were involved. Joseph and I signed the death certificate. My friend who runs the morgue has already confirmed cremation and shipped the remains to your next of kin. You might as well just turn us in yourself.'

Clay rocked back. Of course, she was right. He couldn't go back to his unit. He couldn't go home; soon his uncle and Sara would receive the news of his death – died of wounds received in combat. Botha had wanted him dead. And now he was. Whoever Botha was working for, he was clearly able to move through the system at will – into Angola, onto military bases and into hospitals. Who had that kind of reach? Suddenly Clay felt very, very alone. Crowbar's words replayed themselves in his head: *I'd get out if I were you.*

Vivian reached for his hand. He let her take it.

'Please,' she whispered. 'I know you're frightened. I am, too. But we need to work together. There is something more than the two of us at stake, Clay. And you know it. You've *seen* it.'

'Is that why you sent me the letter?' he said, after a while.

She nodded. 'After what you told me the first time we met, I knew that you were seeing first-hand what we suspected was going on out there. And I knew it troubled you. That you had a conscience. We need your help, Clay.'

'Who is "we", Vivian? Tell me.'

She looked up at him. Her lips were close to his chest. He could feel her breath gentle on his skin as she spoke. 'Torch Commando. It's a groundswell, Clay. A loose network inside the services. No one knows its full extent. We limit contact to a few points so that if one part is exposed, the damage can be contained.'

'Jesus,' said Clay. 'We'd heard the rumours, but I never really believed them. I thought Torch died out in the fifties.'

'It's the regime that's dying, Clay. You may not be able to see it yet, from where you are, but it's happening.'

'How far does this thing go? I mean, is it the army, too?'

'It's everywhere.'

He glanced at her husband's uniform. 'The air force?'

She nodded.

Clay thought back to his conversation with Wade, that day in the Land Rover with Eben; Crowbar's assertion that Wade had been killed by one of their own. 'I need to sit down,' he said.

She led him back to the bed.

He sat, stared at the veins in his hands, the scar on his forearm. After a while, he said: 'So what do we do now?'

She picked up the empty mugs, stood by the bed. 'You get better, stay hidden. Stay dead. I go to work, as usual. And we try to figure out what the hell is going on.'

Clay pointed to the photograph on the dresser. 'Is that your husband?'

She breathed in slowly through pursed lips. 'Was,' she said. 'He was shot down and killed thirteen months ago.'

**South African Truth and Reconciliation Commission
Transcripts.
Johannesburg, 15th September 1996**

Commissioner Lacy: And you never fought again. Is that
correct, Mister Straker?

Witness: I never went back to my unit, that's correct,
ma'am.

Commissioner Lacy: And your friend, Mister Barstow?

Witness: He never came out of that coma, ma'am. Thirteen
years he was like that. Thirteen _____ years.

Commissioner Barbour: Please, Mister Straker.

Commissioner Ksole: So, he didn't testify.

Witness: No, he didn't. But Eben wouldn't have lied, I can
tell you that. He would have told the truth.

Commissioner Barbour: Are you saying, Mister Straker, that
the regime attempted to assassinate you, while you were
still on active duty?

Witness: Yes, sir. Me and Eben.

Commissioner Barbour: Are you absolutely sure, Mister
Straker. You said yourself that you were heavily sedated,
that you were having dreams; having, ah, hallucinations.

Witness: All those times in the hospital I saw him looking
down at me, I thought they were dreams. I was so drugged
up. But it was him. Botha. He was there in the hospital,
making sure I was going to die. When he found out that I
was going to make it, he tried to kill me.

Commissioner Rotzenburg: This person that you call Botha -
the man you claim tried to kill you - do you know who he
was, who he was working for?

Witness: I'm pretty sure he—

Commissioner Rotzenburg: No, Mister Straker. Not
conjecture, please. Did you ever see any identification?

Witness: A friend of mine did.

Commissioner Rotzenburg: Second-hand information and
conjecture have no place here, Mister Straker. Did you
see any identification yourself?

Witness: No, I didn't.

Commissioner Rotzenburg: You suggest this person was

working for the government. Could he not just as easily
have been working for private interests, or even for one
of South Africa's enemies?

Witness: I suppose so, yes.

Commissioner Rotzenburg: The truth is, you have no idea who
he was, who he might have been working for or with, or if
he was even real. Is that not the case, Mister Straker?

Witness: I have no proof. But he was real.

Commissioner Barbour: And why do you think he – whoever he
might have been – wanted you dead, son?

Witness: Botha was there with Colonel Mbdele at the bunker
in Angola. He must have known that we were on that
C-130 over the Atlantic, too, that we'd bailed out with
Zulaika's son. All of that. He knew we were close to
revealing the truth. But I don't think he wanted to kill
us to keep us quiet, sir.

Commissioner Barbour: Then why, son?

Witness: He wasn't afraid of being brought to justice. It
wasn't a cover-up. He was the system. He was justice. We
were enemies of the state. He said it himself. We were
traitors to our nation and to our race. Eben, me, Vivian.
All of us. We had to be eliminated. Truth is for the
dead. The living can't afford it.

24

Animals

Days passed.

Days in which he limped between denial and acceptance and back again, a journey through sun-scorched plains and starless nights, where the only sounds were the rush of blood in his head and the dirges of a dying continent. Vivian would come and go, he only half aware of her wax and wane, of her regular ministrations – the morphine injections, the changes of dressing. And in all of this she was gentle as summer wind, as welcome as a cool katabatic from the Draakensburg. She spoke to him sometimes when she thought he was asleep, and he could hear her voice as if over hills and across deep-cut valleys, words disconnected and lost.

In the middle of the day he would wake with the warm air caressing his face through the open windows and he would lie there a long time thinking about Eben and Crowbar and the war, and wonder what was to become of them all. And in some way he could not quite grasp, none of it seemed real. It was as if it had all happened so fast that he had never had the time to properly register any of it: leaving his parents' house; jump school; the missions into Angola. All of it now seemed to blur one into continuum: the deaths faked; the bodies floating down towards the ocean in some half-forgotten nightmare; the hospital a film set; this haunted house from something he'd read in school.

But the pain was real. The throbbing ache in his torso that seemed to spread up through his shoulders and neck and to his head, and that deeper dolour that could only be described as a hole, an emptiness, a growing absence.

He'd push himself up from the bed, throw on Vivian's husband's trousers, a shirt, fix some breakfast, wander the house, out onto the back patio with a cup of steaming coffee. He would stand in the sun a while, feeling the stitches in his side, each day twisting his torso through a few more degrees, getting stronger, bit by bit, cell by cell. By late afternoon she'd return from the hospital, shower and change into a dress, fix supper for the two of them. They'd talk for a while, play cards as the sun set and the room darkened. She was intelligent and serious, just old enough to be his mother. After, she'd lead him to the bedroom, check his dressing, give him morphine, and then disappear.

He'd been there for a week when he finally summoned the courage to ask her where she had been sleeping.

'In the spare bedroom,' she answered, her tone curt.

He hadn't seen a spare bedroom on his wanderings. But before he could enquire further she'd gone, closed the door behind her. He lay in the darkness and thought about her, imagined her here with him, naked and warm.

Later that night he'd risen and gone to find her. She wasn't on the settee in the main room, or in the front parlour. He searched the house, even the half-moon-filtered back garden. She'd disappeared.

He turned and started back to the bedroom. He was halfway across the main room when he heard it: muffled sobs coming from the corridor. He followed the sound to the door that had always been locked. He put his ear to the frame. Nothing. He waited. And then some time later more sobs. He tried the knob, but the door was locked.

'Vivian,' he whispered.

The sobs stopped.

'Vivian, it's me. Are you alright?'

No reply. He stood there in the darkness for a long time, but no answer came. After a while, he went back to bed. His watch showed gone two in the morning.

Nine days after being declared dead, Clay stood naked in the bathroom, looking in the mirror. It was mid-afternoon, a couple of hours yet until Vivian was due back from the hospital. The house had warmed. He pulled the dressing from his torso and dropped the stained bandages onto the tile floor. The scar ran from just above his hip to his lowest rib and then dog-legged towards his solar plexus. He traced the line with the tip of his finger, felt the stitches furrowing the swell of knitting flesh. There were the other scars, too, the one in his cheek glowing with the same deep bruising, the forearm showing what these new violations might become over time.

He thought about Eben, still back there in 1-Mil. Some things heal. Some never will.

He turned on the shower and let the water warm. He stepped under the stream, a hot shower still such a luxury after so many months on the line. All of them would be back there now, Crowbar and the boys, back in Angola, perhaps. And even though he now knew, somewhere deep inside himself, that the war was fundamentally wrong, that something incredibly sinister was happening in his country, something that had been hidden to him all the years of his childhood, hidden in plain sight every day, he wished with all of himself he was back there with them. And in this desire, he recognised that there was something fundamentally warped inside him, and whether it had come because of all that had happened, or if he had been born like this, he could not tell.

He turned off the water and reached a towel down from the curtain rail. He was drying his hair when the shower curtain slid open. He jerked his head back, almost slipping on the wet surface of the tub.

It was Vivian. She was standing before him, staring at him from dark sockets haloed in thick, black makeup. She wore a black high-necked evening gown and had pulled her hair back tight across her scalp. Her lips were black, as if she'd used the eye makeup on her mouth. Her bare arms were thin and pale, her feet bare on the wet tile.

'Get out of my tub,' she said. Her voice was like hard-trampled ground.

Clay stepped onto the floor mat, wrapped the towel around his waist. 'What's wrong, Vivian?'

'Give me my towel,' she said.

'What?'

'You heard me,' she slurred.

Clay could smell alcohol.

'I'm sorry, I was just…' He started towards her, towards the door. 'My clothes are just outside,' he said.

'Stay there,' she said. 'Don't move. Give me my towel.'

Clay stared back at her. He could see the guttering in her makeup, the angry red veins gripping the whites of her eyes. 'Are you alright, Vivian?' The same words he'd whispered through the locked door three nights ago.

She closed her eyes a long while, didn't answer. When she opened them again she took a step towards him and held out her hand.

Clay unwrapped the towel and stood naked before her. She took the towel and dropped it on the floor behind her. He made to move to the door but she shook her head. 'Don't move,' she whispered, hoarse.

His heart was racing. 'Vivian, please. What's happened?'

'Move your hands away so I can see,' she said.

He stayed as he was, covering himself.

'Do it,' she whispered. Tears welled in her eyes.

He pulled away his hands.

She stood watching as the tumour between his legs grew, unbidden.

Clay stared into her face, watched the flip of her eyes as she scanned from her handiwork to his face and back down towards his groin. He made to speak but she raised her finger to her lips. He was aching now, weeks of frustration and anger and raw fear bursting inside him, straining for release.

He took a step towards her, opened his arms.

'Don't move,' she hissed.

Clay stopped.

'There it is,' she said, her voice hoarse, as if she was choking. 'The reason for all our pain.'

He took another step, not understanding. For a moment he thought she might accept him. But then she looked up into his eyes. Fury swirled there.

'No,' she shouted, jerking back and away from him. 'Get back. Don't touch me.'

Clay stopped dead, a cold spline piercing his chest. He raised his hands, backed away. Heat drained from his body, leaving him cold and shrivelled. Inept and inexperienced, he'd read the signs all wrong. He grabbed another towel from the rack, covered himself.

'I'm sorry,' he whispered. 'I thought…'

She looked as if she'd just been pulled back from the edge of some deep chasm, her eyes stretched wide and red-rimmed. Dark veins pulsed beneath the pale skin above her cheekbones, spread brittle across the surface of her bone-thin arms. She looked as if she'd been living on starvation rations. She was shivering.

'Jesus, Vivian, what's wrong?' he whispered, stupid, clumsy. As if there was an answer that could be put into words. As if the answer wasn't entirely evident.

He closed his eyes and moved towards her and this time she didn't push him away. He wrapped his arms around her and felt the tremors birthing deep inside her and held her tight. And when she started to cry he could feel her relax into him and then she was sobbing hard and deep, the shudders ripping through her body. He stood and tried to absorb them all. And this time it was he who would help her. He let her collapse into his arms, scooped her up and carried her to her bedroom, laying her carefully on the bed and covering her with the blanket. He looked down at her for a moment as she curled up like a child, and then he turned away, picked up his clothes and left her there, closing the door behind him.

☾

Vivian slept through the evening and all through the night. By the time she emerged from the bedroom, it was morning. Clay was fixing breakfast using a few eggs he'd found in the fridge.

She'd showered and changed. Gone was the black makeup, the funeral clothes.

'You okay?' he said, knowing she wasn't.

'Where did you sleep?'

Clay pointed to the couch.

She sat at the kitchen table. 'You bandaged yourself.'

'Not very well.' Clay flipped the eggs.

'How is the pain?'

'Getting better,' he said.

'You heal fast.'

'Hungry?'

She nodded, a little bob of her chin.

'Good.' He wasn't going to ask her about what had happened the previous night. Everyone breaks. He knew that now, had seen far too many examples of it already. And everyone does it differently.

Of course, he wouldn't learn until much later that the breaking usually comes as a delayed reaction, a time bomb hidden away in some dark corner of yourself, waiting to go off when you least expect it, when you are least prepared. For him, it was more like a slow leak than an explosion, a drip-feed of poison that eroded every part of him, the half-life of the toxins measured in years, the release steady and continuous. And it would be with him still, all those years later, closer to the end than the beginning, even after he'd done the one thing that he'd thought would end it.

Clay poured her a cup of tea and one for himself. She sipped in silence. He put a plate in front of her, deciding not to apologise for his cooking, and sat across from her.

After a while he said: 'What's in that room, Vivian? The locked one.'

She looked at him as if deciding what to tell him. Then she placed her knife and fork carefully side by side in the middle of the plate, folded her hands in her lap, and took three quick shallow breaths. 'Botha came to the hospital yesterday,' she said.

The words grabbed Clay by the throat.

'He had your file, Clay. Your service record. He said he wanted to see your death certificate and interview those who had signed it. Me.'

'Jesus,' breathed Clay.

'I asked him for identification.'

Clay held his breath.

'He's BOSS, Clay.'

Fear took a trek down Clay's spine, down through his legs. Unlimited access, unlimited mobility. 'What did you tell him?'

'I showed him the hospital records. Told him that we'd tried to revive you but couldn't, that you'd died of your wounds.'

'Did he speak to the nurse, too?'

Vivian nodded 'She told me she'd stuck to the story.'

'Do you believe her?'

'I have to, don't I? She was terrified.'

'We can't take that chance, Vivian. We have to assume she talked.'

She continued as if she hadn't heard him. 'He also went to the morgue and demanded to see the ashes, the documentation. My friend told him he'd already shipped the remains to the next of kin. Botha checked all of the manifests, everything.

'Do you think he believes it – that I'm dead?'

Vivian shook her head. 'I don't know, Clay. He seemed satisfied. He thanked me and everyone, then he left.'

Clay pondered this, but the fear held tight.

'I've been doing some checking into Roodeplaat Research Laboratories,' said Vivian.

Clay leaned forwards.

'The building used to be occupied by a contract medical lab. They did blood work, that kind of thing. I think I may have even used them once or twice, years ago. Apparently, a little over a year ago, the lab was sold to RRL. It does work exclusively for the government. Eight months ago, it was declared a secure facility, restricted access. No one I spoke to seemed to know what its purpose is, or who runs it.'

'I hope you're being careful.'

'I went there yesterday on my lunch break. I sat in my car across the street, watched the entrance.'

'And?'

'There was razor wire all around. Armed guards posted at the front entrance. Everyone who came and went was ID-checked, searched, and sent through metal detectors.'

'Seems unusual for a lab.'

'Not if they're producing stuff like formulation 13B.'

Clay said nothing.

'After a while I went around to the back service entrance. There was the same high security.'

'Jesus, Vivian. Did anyone see you?'

'The building backs onto a wooded ravine. I hid in the bush.'

Clay looked into her eyes, new respect budding inside him.

'Just before I was going to leave, a lorry arrived. The guards checked the driver's documents and then they opened the back of the lorry and inspected the cargo. I was close enough. As they opened the doors, I could hear them. I could *smell* them, Clay.' Her face disappeared behind her hands.

He reached for her. 'What was inside?'

She looked up at him. Tears brimmed in her eyes. She opened her mouth but nothing came.

Clay waited, squeezed her hand.

'Animals,' she gasped through a constricted windpipe. 'Monkeys, apes.'

'Jesus.'

Vivian wiped her eyes. 'And there's one more thing. After what you told me about Botha, I decided to check your friend's effects before I left the hospital.' She reached down beside her. 'I found this,' she said, placing a book on the table. 'He had it with him when he was brought in.'

'Eben.'

She nodded.

Clay caught a breath. It was the notebook he'd buried under the floorboards in his tent – the one they'd taken from *O Medico de Morte*'s assistant in the dunes.

25

A Part of Who He Was

They didn't really have a choice. And they both knew it.

Later that same evening they'd decided. If they had any hope of finding the truth about Operation COAST, they needed to get inside that laboratory.

But they were running out of time. The longer they waited, the worse their position became. How long until someone cracked, went to the authorities, succumbed to Botha's probings? As soon as they learned that Clay was still alive – and it seemed to him almost certain that they would – he and Vivian would both be in mortal danger, her coconspirators too: Joseph, the other nurse, her friend who ran the morgue.

There, in her kitchen, they went through what they knew (not much) and what they didn't (a lot). Cleary, UNITA, South Africa's erstwhile allies – or at least that part of UNITA run by *O Coletor*, Colonel Mbdele – were doing a lot more than fighting a guerrilla war in Angola. The diamonds, ivory and hardwoods Clay had seen them loading onto Cobra's C-130 were evidence of that. But what were they getting in return for the plunder? Weapons and ammunition, military support to continue the fight? It was certainly plausible; in Africa, commonplace. But Zulaika had been convinced there was more to it. The poor bastards they'd seen injected that night at the temporary airstrip in Angola probably would have had the same view. Eben, too. The only thing that linked any of this to Operation COAST was the document he'd found on Doctor Death's assistant out there in the dune-lands. Formulation 13B, the same foul shit Botha had used to try to kill Clay that night in the hospital. Vivian's Torch cell inside SAMS had suspected for some time that experimental drugs were being shipped to combat zones and used for unauthorised field trials. Until now, they had been uncertain about exactly what was being tested. Based on anecdotal evidence, Vivian and her colleagues had surmised that the drugs were most likely designed to aid in the pacification and interrogation of prisoners. Certainly, there were much more effective ways to kill people. But every time they had tried to trace these activities they'd come up against the same wall: a classified military operation code-named COAST. All they knew about COAST's structure was that it was run by one Doctor Grasson, an ex-cardiologist, apparently well connected within the upper levels of government. When Vivian had heard Clay's stories the first time they'd met in 1-Mil, she had immediately made the connection and decided to cultivate him as a source. She'd tried with others before, but they had never yielded any useful information. It was about that time that she started to suspect BOSS was watching them.

Vivian's analysis of the contents of the notebook, matched with Clay's observations from the night at the makeshift airstrip in Angola, confirmed that the tests were both systematic and extensive. The details of trials on more than two hundred test subjects were catalogued in the blood-stained pages. And Formulation 13B was the link between Cobra, Botha, Doctor Death (were Grasson and *O Medico de Morte* the same person?) and Colonel Mbdele – the first real breakthrough they'd had. Were *they* Operation COAST? And was this thing legally sanctioned, as it appeared – supported by the Bureau of State Security and thus the government itself, or was it a private operation, run for profit by some kind of fucked-up consortium? Based on the documents and the information in the notebook, the Roodeplaat Research Laboratories were where the stuff – some of it anyway – appeared to originate. That's where they had to go.

They both knew, there and then, that from here on their lives would be very different, that everything they had come to know as normal, as *theirs*, would be lost. Was already lost. Gone like childhood. And there was no route back, no way to reverse the flow of time and events.

That night Vivian slipped out the back way, told Clay to stay at the house, to keep alert. Clay offered her the Beretta, but she refused. 'I'm a doctor,' was all she'd said.

A doctor.

An activist.

A rebel.

A widow.

And Crowbar and Steyn and DuPlessis, all of them – out there somewhere tonight in the Angolan bush, staring deep into death's enchanting eyes – would call her a communist, a traitor. Her, alone here in this place of ghosts, this shrine, every night curled up small and so vulnerable in that big, cold bed. He thought back to their encounter in the bathroom, her in mourning, even her hair now the colour of the longest night, the years and miles between them, despite his nakedness. And then the way she'd held him there, as if on some threshold, deciding perhaps, before crushing his arousal. Had it been an attempt to break free, to fight her way back to warmth and connection? Or was she trying to pull him into her vortex, into that dark ocean already lapping at his knees? Did she even know?

And now here he was, dead, seduced, plotting against his country, the country he'd sworn to defend against all enemies, the country of his birth. He filled his lungs, stood, walked to the kitchen and got a glass of water. Maybe he could still get out. If he left now, under the cover of darkness, he could hitch his way north, make his way back to the platoon. He'd tell Crowbar the death certificate had been an error. He'd be safe there, with his fellow parabats. Crowbar would protect him. All he'd done was follow orders. Sure, they'd rescued Zulaika from UNITA that night in the bunker, but they'd just been doing the right thing. Wade had ordered him and Eben on the recon patrol with Brigade. Yes, he'd killed Doctor Death's assistant out there in the dunes, but no one could prove it. By now the body would be buried under thousands of tons of shifting sand, and the only witnesses were dead; or dead enough. He could burn the note-book, destroy the evidence. Crowbar would know what to do. They needed good soldiers. There would have to be an enquiry, of course. If he stayed quiet about what he'd seen – the rape, the injections, the bodies thrown into the ocean – BOSS would have no reason to question his loyalty. He might get a few months confinement, lose a stripe, but he'd be okay, be allowed to stay with his unit. Vivian had a network, contacts. She could look after herself.

He had to force the lock to get into the room. He pushed the door open and stepped inside. The first thing that hit him was the smell: must, old books, undertones of rust, steel, pinewood, brown-ing paper. And something else. The lightest of perfumes. Her.

He switched on a lamp, cast its light around the room. A thick layer of dust covered every surface: the ceiling-to-floor bookshelves, the old Corona typewriter on the paper-strewn oak desk, the ranks of model airplanes lining two, long pine shelves against the inside wall. Framed photographs covered the other part of the wall. Dust ridged the tops of each frame. A younger version of the man in the photograph on the bedroom chest of drawers stared out into the lamplight. He was all in white, holding his cricket bat aloft. To his left, a dozen young men in flight suits and sunglasses giving the thumbs up. John grinning in the cockpit of a Mirage, helmet on, oxygen mask dangling open beneath his chin. Vivian in a bathing suit, smiling big, one hand up as if waving the photographer away, blue sky and bluer ocean behind her. A Bianci racing bicycle was propped up against the bookshelf. Next to it on the floor, a set of dumbbells loaded up, fifty pounds each, a stack of aero-nautical supplements. And there, nestled cocoon-like between stacks of books and flight manuals, a sleeping bag laid out on an inflatable mattress, a head-dented pillow pushed up against the desk.

Clay opened the big cupboards. Inside, another sleeping bag rolled into its sack, a pair of backcountry backpacks, ropes and carabiners, climbing boots, ice axes and pitons. A 35 millimetre camera with extra lenses packed into a snug black case. Clay grabbed one of the backpacks and started loading it up with everything he might need.

When she returned a few hours later, just before dawn, Clay was sitting in the main room, the backpack next to him in the big lounge chair, the Beretta in his lap, the copy of *Catch-22* folded open, cover-up on one knee.

She stood before him. She looked as if she'd spent a night in the wilderness. Her coat was torn in two places. There were red scratches on her face and hands, leaves in her hair.

'Where are you going?' she said.

'Wherever you are,' he said.

Loyalty is a crazy thing. He'd already been out the front door, halfway to the street, when he'd decided. Loyalty isn't exclusive. Being true to a person, to a country, to an idea, does not preclude other equally valid loyalties. And it can't be blind. This woman had not only saved his life but had brought him back from the edge of a death apparently prescribed by the authorities of his own country. If Botha was acting legitimately in the name of the nation – and something deep inside him still doubted this – the nation was wrong. He could see that now. His loyalty to this place, this beautiful land, was absolute. But this system, a system that would do such things, did not deserve his loyalty. In fact, he could see now, as clearly as a high-veldt sunrise, that his loyalty to this place demanded that he rescue her from this corruption, this travesty. Crowbar would understand. And Eben would be proud.

She sat next to him and explained the plan.

She'd met an associate on the edge of town – someone high up in the medical service. *One of us*, she called him. He'd been nervous, twitchy, not his usual composed self. He'd been surprised when she'd asked him about Roodeplaat, questioned why she'd called him, used the emergency code word, for something so inconsequential. He had made to leave, but she'd managed to convince him to listen, had assured him it was important.

There were, they'd determined, only two ways in – through the front door, or perhaps the rear service entry. But it had to be in the open. Any sort of break-in would jeopardise more people, expose more of their network. Her contact had made a few calls. Evening was the best time, he reported. Most of the staff would be gone. Late-evening deliveries under the cover of darkness were common. He could provide her a high-level SAMS identification badge, and a special pass that would get her through security and into the building. It would take him a day, perhaps two. She would have to get in and out quickly, leave everything as she found it.

She sank back into the couch, hugging her arms around herself. 'So, that's it,' she said. 'As soon as he gets me the badge, I'm going in.'

'I'm going with you,' said Clay.

She looked at him a moment, open mouthed. 'You can hardly walk,' she said.

'I'm fine,' he said. 'I'm not letting you do this on your own. What if something goes wrong?'

'If I'm not back by dawn, run.'

'Where to?'

'Same place I'm going to right after. Soshanguve.'

Clay thought he'd heard wrong. 'What did you say?'

'You heard me – the township.'

'Jesus,' said Clay. 'You're serious.'

'We have friends there. It's the one place that the authorities don't control. Well, not fully anyway. The perfect place to hide.' She scribbled a name on a slip of paper, a Pretoria address. 'Show him this.' She handed him the paper. 'He can get you in, keep you safe.'

Clay nodded. 'Like I said. I'm going with you.'

She leaned towards him, reached for his hand. 'I know what you're trying to do, Clay. You want to protect me. It's very sweet of you. But he's only organising one badge.'

'I'll go, then.'

'You don't know what to look for.'

'Explain it to me. I've told you. I've got a good memory. You have a camera. I can take photos.'

Vivian shook her head slowly from side to side, glanced at her wristwatch. 'No, Clay. I have to do this.' She stood. 'I'm already late.

I have to get to work. If I don't show up it will only raise suspicion. We have to sit tight until I get word.'

☾

Clay sat up in bed. The bedside clock showed just gone eleven in the morning. After Vivian had left he'd slept for a couple of hours, a fitful half-sleep haunted by shadow and uncertainty. The pain came. He'd refused Vivian's offer of morphine that morning, had wanted to stay sharp, wanted to start weaning himself from its dulling thrall. He tried to read, but the few pages of Crowbar's copy of *Catch-22* jarred him like a shattered mirror. He'd just reached for the glass of water on the bedside table and was raising it to his lips, when he heard it.

Over the hours and days here, lying in this bed, he'd come to know the sounds of this old house: the sharp cracks from the north-facing pantry in the early afternoon, when the sun's warmth caused the shelving to expand; the skittering of the doves' talons on the roof tiles above the patio; the way the back windows creaked in their casements when the warm afternoon winds blew over the city. And now, this familiar sound that signalled Vivian's departure every morning, her return in the afternoon: the creak of the hardwood floorboards just inside the front door, the noise carried along the hallway into the living area, through the open bedroom door.

Someone was inside the house.

He hadn't heard Vivian's knock. Had he missed it? No. Every other afternoon since that first day he'd heard it, clear and distinct. And it was too early.

Adrenaline flooded his system. Clay pushed himself up, swung his feet to the floor, grabbed the backpack – ready to go now, with extra bandages, water and food – and the Beretta from the side table. He was breathing hard. He stood, listened.

Nothing. And then, seconds later, a click. The front door closing. Another squeak of the floorboards. Two of them, then. Definitely not Vivian.

Clay shouldered the bag, winced as the abrupt movement stretched his side. He breathed away the pain, moved to the patio door, slipped outside, closed the door behind him. He scanned the back garden, the wall along the back lane. No one. He moved barefoot along the back wall of the house towards the shuttered windows of the main room. Vivian had cracked the louvres halfway before she'd left the house, as she did every morning. Crouching low, Clay peered through the lowermost slats. From here he could see the main room, the entrance to the kitchen on the right, and the doorway to the master bedroom he'd just vacated on the left. He could feel the gun shaking in his hand. He pushed it against his thigh, tried to control his breathing.

More sounds. Two sets of footsteps, clear now. Whoever it was, they were moving through the front rooms. Jesus. He should run, along the side of the house to the front hedge, out through the side gate onto the street. But there could be others out there, too, watching the front of the house. He glanced back over his shoulder, across the garden, certain now that they would have people positioned in the back. He pulled back the Beretta's action, chambered a round, filled his lungs and prepared to move.

That's when Clay saw him. That same pitted face, those eyes that seemed to draw in light but let none escape. Botha stood surveying the main room. A second man – taller, fair, armed with a handgun – appeared behind him. Cobra.

Botha raised his arm and Cobra stopped where he was, stood perfectly still. Clay held his breath.

Then Botha raised his chin and sniffed the air like a hyena. Clay could see his nostrils flaring, drawing in the scent of the place. Could he smell him? The blood, the sweat, the maleness he'd left on the bedsheets the night before, dulling his frustration by his own hand? Jesus. The bastard was tracking him.

Botha pointed to the kitchen. Cobra moved in the indicated direction, to Clay's right. Botha started towards the master bedroom, to Clay's left. Both rooms had direct access out onto the back patio. In a few seconds he would be trapped between them.

Clay crouched low and moved towards the kitchen. His side was screaming now, as if he could feel every stitch Vivian had so carefully sewn, inside and out. He stopped just before the doors, hugging the wall. The sounds of cupboards opening, the fridge closing, muffled through the window glass, and now that same Shona melody drifting through the trees, the woman's voice soft as a lullaby.

And then footsteps, Cobra walking back towards the main room.

Clay counted three and peered through the kitchen door. Cobra was gone. Clay grabbed the door handle, pushed and stepped into the kitchen, Beretta ready. There was no sign of disturbance. The breakfast dishes were as he'd left them in the sink – two plates, two coffee cups. Shit. If Cobra was observant, they'd know she wasn't alone.

Clay padded across the kitchen towards the main room, pushed himself hard up against the wall. A cough, and then a click and those squeaky hinges Vivian had complained about – the doors leading from the main room out onto the back patio opening. Now the sound of boot soles on the patio tile. Clay crouched behind the kitchen table. There was nowhere else to hide. If Cobra came to the kitchen door, looked in, Clay would have nowhere to go. He would have to fight. And he knew that Vivian was right: as soon as the authorities learned he was still alive, they were all going to disappear, one way or another.

Clay readied the Beretta, took aim. The moment Cobra stepped in front of the kitchen window he'd have a clear view of Clay. As soon as he did, Clay would have to kill him.

Panic came. He was falling down a deep well, the sides rifled like a gun barrel, the surface wet and slick, with no edge or fault to hold. He fell deeper, the circle of light above him growing smaller to vanishing. He tried to push it back, as Crowbar had taught them. *Breathe. Focus. Your life depends on this.*

Looking back, he realised that this was the start of it. Right there, crouched on that kitchen floor in a suburban home in Pretoria, naked except for a pair of shorts and a handgun, feeling the first symptoms of what would become a lifelong companion, constant only in its unpredictability, predictable only in its year-by-year worsening, until it would become as much a part of who he was as where he was born and who his parents were.

'Check the rubbish.' Botha's voice, raised.

The words broke Clay free. He breathed, cycled air through his lungs. The rubbish. Here, in the kitchen?

Through the kitchen window, he could see Cobra running across the lawn towards the back wall. Cobra pulled off the lid of one of the metal bins and peered inside. He sniffed at the contents, looked up towards the house.

'Anything?' came Botha's voice again, close. He was standing on the back patio, only metres from Clay.

Cobra reached into the bin, pulled out an empty tin, then a bulging, dripping plastic bag, which he held between thumb and forefinger. He stood staring into the bin.

'No one here now,' said Botha. 'But he's not dead. He's been here. I can smell him.'

Clay's heart rate climaxed, all that this meant starting to cascade through him.

Cobra reached into the bin again, almost up to his shoulder this time, and withdrew what appeared to be a long strip of white toilet paper. It was covered in what looked like shit smears. He kept pulling until several metres of the stuff lay on the grass.

'What is it?' called out Botha.

'A bandage. Covered in blood.'

'I knew it,' said Botha, walking across the grass towards the bins.

And then Cobra, barely audible: 'What do you want me to do?'

'Cut off a piece with blood on it and bag it. Put the rest back and let's get out of here.'

26

Presumption of Superiority

Clay waited until he was sure Botha and Cobra were gone. Then he picked up the phone. Fear coursed through him thick and hot.

A nurse answered.

Clay spoke her name – Doctor Russell.

'She's on the ward at the moment, I'm afraid. You will have to call back.'

'No, wait. Please. Tell her it's urgent. This is her father. I need to speak to her.' It was the emergency code they'd agreed earlier.

Hesitancy. 'I'll try to find her, Mister Russell. Please hold the line.'

The hospital was a twenty-minute drive from the house. Botha would be on his way there way now, of this Clay was certain. He had to warn her.

And then what?

Clay stood in that strange room, the telephone in one hand, the Berretta in the other, and tried to comprehend what was happening. The realisation came hard and caustic – a reaction deep inside his core; a change of state so abrupt that he felt as if his blood had solidified in his veins. Three weeks ago he was in Angola fighting for the country of his birth, surrounded by those he would always be closest to. He'd come to accept the possibility of his own death – at least he thought he had, in an abstract, read-about-it-in-the-papers kind of way. And he'd comforted himself with the thought that, whatever happened, his body would be returned to the red soil of the veldt, next to his parents. Now he knew there was a good chance he would never see South Africa again.

The line burned empty. Clay looked at his watch. He'd been

holding for almost five minutes. What was happening? Had the nurse been distracted by a patient, forgotten about him? Had Botha radioed ahead, sent his men to the hospital to arrest Vivian? Had they already arrived? He was about to hang up and try again when the line rattled.

'Hello? Are you still there?' The nurse.

'Yes.'

'Doctor Russell is in surgery. She asks me if you have a message for her?'

'Tell her we've had visitors. I'm going to the beach.'

The nurse repeated the message.

'And tell her she has less than ten minutes.'

'Sir?'

'She has less than ten minutes. Tell her.'

'Yes, sir.'

'It's very important. Do you understand?'

'Yes, sir. I'll tell her right away.'

Clay put down the phone. Shit. What else could he do? He didn't have a car. Even if he stole one from the street he'd never get to the hospital in time. They'd agreed the night before on the emergency message – I'm going to the beach – as the signal for immediate danger. The beach: the address on the outskirts of Soshanguve. The plan was to rendezvous there, and escape into the township.

It was a long way, at least four hours on foot. Bus would be the best bet, one of the old diesel-belching relics the blacks used for the daily trip to and from the city for work. Nights were white. Clay dressed, swung the backpack onto his shoulders, pulled Vivian's husband's green bush hat down low over his eyes and started towards the back door. He'd just turned the handle when the phone rang. He stopped, waited. It rang three times. Silence echoed through the room. He pushed the door closed, walked to the phone. A few seconds later it rang again.

'It's me.' She sounded scared.

'They know I was here. They're coming for you.'

Silence. And then: 'Go to the beach. I'll meet you there in two days.'

'Two days?'

'There is something I have to do.'

'Don't, Vivian. You have to get out, now.'

'The pass is ready. I'm going in this evening.'

'You're crazy. They were here. They know I'm alive. They know what you did.'

'Go. I'll catch up with you if I can.'

'I told you. I'm not going without you.'

Dead air on the line, her thinking about it.

'There is a park at the end of my street. Go out the back, turn left. It's not far. Joseph will pick you up there in twenty minutes.'

'How will I know him?'

'He'll know you.'

And before he could reply she'd gone.

Clay took a last look around the room, and started for the back. He trudged down the laneway. Jacarandas wept over him, spread their fluttering shadows across the wheel-rutted gravel. The pack wasn't nearly as heavy as the loads he was used to carrying in the bush, but the weeks in hospital had weakened him and it wasn't long before he was breathing heavily. Still, he longed for the familiar weight and security of his R4, felt somehow incomplete without it.

The park wasn't far, less than a kilometre. He reached it in just under ten minutes. It wasn't big – about the size of a cricket pitch. Jacarandas and big, old ironwoods shaded a coarse lawn of buffalo grass that sloped up to a wooden bandstand set at the top of a small rise. The place was quiet. A young white woman pushing a pram along the footpath, her black maid in tow; a black gardener pulling up weeds from a flowerbed near the road. Clay walked up the rise to the bandstand, set his pack on the wooden bench and stood looking out over the park and the well-tended suburban gardens spreading out all around him, this neighbourhood so like the one he grew up in, the presumption of superiority as much a part of the place as the large, fenced gardens and the pools and the little backyard shacks for the black help.

Half an hour since he'd left the house, and Joseph still hadn't appeared. Clay scanned the surroundings for the hundredth time. The park was empty. What if something had gone wrong? What if Joseph had been arrested, or gone to the authorities of his own accord? He'd give it another fifteen minutes, no more. If Joseph hadn't show by then, he'd head to Roodeplaat on his own.

A car approached, slowing as it neared the park. Clay stretched, careful of his side and checked the Beretta in his pocket. The car pulled to a stop near the park entrance. It was a white Chevrolet – ubiquitous in South Africa. Through the window glare Clay could make out the silhouettes of two men.

The driver's side window lowered and a smoking cigarette butt spun to the pavement. The passenger-side door opened. One of the men got out and stood with his back to Clay, looking back along the road, a cigarette burning in one hand.

Something jabbed into Clay's ribs.

'Easy.' It was a voice he'd heard before.

Adrenaline surged through him, a kick in the chest. Clay froze, heart hammering. He'd let himself be distracted by the car, allowed the bastard to walk right up behind him. 'Jesus Christ,' he muttered.

'Not exactly,' said the voice. 'Give me the gun.'

Clay reached into his pocket.

'Slow.'

Clay put the Beretta on the bench. A hand grabbed it.

'You certainly have fucked things up, Straker.'

Clay could hear the man backing away.

'Turn around and sit.'

The man was sitting on the other side of the bandstand, one knee crossed over the other, one arm thrown across the wooden railing, a black handgun levelled at Clay's stomach. It was Cobra.

27

The Vast Improbability of Life

Cobra threw Clay a plastic zip tie. 'Hands together in front,' he said.

Clay threaded the tie, put it around his wrists.

'Go ahead,' said Cobra with a jut of his chin.

Clay made himself big, wedged open his wrists as far as he dared, pulled the strap tight with his teeth.

Cobra smiled. 'Nice try, Straker. Again.'

Clay pulled in the slack.

Cobra stood, signalled thumbs-up to the white Chevy. 'If you're going to try to disappear, you should be more careful,' he said. 'Not a good idea, your little doctor friend dumping all those bandages in the bin out back. But you already know that, don't you?'

The arc light of realisation shot through him, blinded him. '*Fok jou,*' he croaked, the words weak, without purchase.

Cobra smiled. His teeth were strong and straight, the colour of an old bull elephant's tusks. 'Not a bad idea,' he said, 'getting her to do it, *ja.*'

Clay tensed, felt the anger come now, the welcome familiar fury. 'I should have killed you right there.'

'*Ja*, probably,' said Cobra. 'An easy shot through that kitchen window.'

Clay's heart valves fluttered, hung a moment. He swallowed hard, remembering those same eyes staring at him in the back of the Hercules.

Cobra smiled and looked away. He was a step away, no more, looking off towards the far end of the park, the houses beyond, vulnerable. 'Go ahead, Straker. I know what you're thinking. Try.'

At this distance, he might be able to take Cobra down. A round kick to the side of the knee might put him off balance long enough to get in close, do some damage. But with hands tied and his side still only partially healed, he had little chance of getting the gun. What he needed was time. Time to think his way through this. Clay said nothing, held his position.

Cobra still hadn't moved, just stood there with his back turned, looking down the hill. 'What are you waiting for Straker?'

Clay knew now that Joseph wasn't coming to meet him, and that Vivian was now either dead or in some BOSS prison somewhere, her Torch colleagues by now exposed and in the process of being rounded up and tortured.

'I'm not playing,' said Clay. Not with witnesses in the Chevy ready to testify that Cobra had acted in self-defence, had had no choice but use his weapon.

'No. You're not.'

Cobra moved so quickly Clay barely had time to raise his hands. There was no warning, no discernible lowering of the hips or tensioning in the shoulder. One moment Cobra was looking down the hill, and the next his booted right heel had whipped through a three-sixty arc and slammed hard into the side of Clay's ribs.

Clay grunted with the impact, crumpled to the ground.

Cobra was standing above him, that same smile on his face. His handgun was nowhere to be seen. 'That was for fucking with me, Straker,' he said.

Clay was doubled over in pain. Cobra had hit him in his undamaged side, but the wrenching impact sent blades of pain screaming through his torso. He closed his eyes as the white shock exploded inside him, ripped through his consciousness so that for a long moment he was gone, unaware of his surroundings, of Cobra standing near him, of anything except the pain, those exquisitely evolved signals.

An arm threaded under his shoulder, thick and powerful, pulling him up, steadying him. And then a voice, far off, distorted: 'Just behave, and this will be a lot easier for everyone. Come on.' And him walking now with knee-jerking steps, groggy, his vision returning, vaguely aware now of the white Chevrolet pulling away, trundling down the street, everything coming through a rain-swept lens, the trees and the rich people's houses and the clouds in the sky, everything liquid and uncertain.

Cobra was leading him down the hill, away from the road. Clay watched his own feet, the desert boots that had until recently belonged to Vivian' husband, shuffling through the coarse grass.

'Where are we going?' Clay managed.

'We have business to do, you and I,' said Cobra, switching to English now for the first time.

Cobra's car was in a lay-by on the other side of the park. He opened the passenger-side door, put his hand to the back of Clay's head, pushed him down and in. The seat was too far forwards and Clay's shins jammed up against the dash. Cobra walked around to driver's side, opened the back door, threw in Clay's pack, and then got in behind the wheel. He pulled out and unfolded a black cloth, about the size of a shopping bag.

'Sorry to have to do this, Straker,' he said, opening up one end of the bag and pulling it over Clay's head.

Even the darkest night is blessed by stars. And up high, where the air is cold and pure and untroubled by the light of cities and the smoke of a million fires, it is as if darkness itself has been banished to some distant edge of the universe, and the stars fill every hole in the firmament. Nights in Ovamboland, when the new moon came and they were given a few hours to rest, he and Eben would lie on their backs and look up at the wonder. Eben would talk about relativity, about time and magnetism, about the vast improbability of life. He'd point to a star – always a different one – Rigel, there, so blue; Aldebaran, there, the red giant, do you see it? And he'd place Clay on that planet. Do you realise, he'd say, that if I saw you wave to me right now, right this instant, you'd have been dead for ten thousand years?

Then he'd go quiet for a long time and they would just lie there staring up into spinning infinity, and it was as if at any moment gravity would just let go and they would plunge into it, as if into a cold, midnight river. And lying there, close but not touching, so close that Clay could feel the heat coming from his friend's body, it was as if they had shared the same womb, brothers now, that closeness that comes only when we finally understand and accept our own isolation.

Do you know what that means, *bru*? Do you *understand*?

Time isn't an arrow. It's not a flowing river. Space and time are like a block of ice. Every moment is frozen in place, forever: your first kill, your first kiss, swimming in the Cunene that day Wade gave us the afternoon off and we took turns on the bank with an R4 in case of crocodiles. And then he would smile that beautiful smile of his and say something like: 'It's the ultimate conscience, *bru*.' And in a way that Clay could still not grasp, and was destined to never fully understand, he *was* standing on that planet, each fraction of a second of unending time there and so real as if nothing could ever take it away from him. And much later, with more time behind him than ahead and cold eternity beckoning, he would again consider the harsh physics of Eben's philosophy and in it search for some kind of explanation for all he had done.

But now there was nothing. The darkness was absolute. It was hard to breathe. Fear poured into him, the terror of loneliness, of knowing that there was no one left to care.

The engine started, the transmission engaged. A snap and burn and then the sharp tang of tobacco as Cobra lit a cigarette. The rumble of backstreets, the car's suspension groaning over the rough surface.

Clay considered options. Hands tied, blind, he had little chance of overpowering Cobra inside the car. There is always an opportunity, always something you can do, in any situation – that's what Crowbar always told them. He would have to be patient, wait until they arrived wherever Cobra was taking him.

After a few minutes, Cobra slowed the car and brought it to a stop. He swung open his door, got out, walked around to Clay's side and opened the door.

'Get out.'

Cobra walked Clay a few metres across a hard surface, then stopped. Another car door opened. The sound it made was of wrenching metal, as if part of the car's skin was being ripped away. A hand cupped the back of Clay's head, pushed him into a seat. A door closed behind him, that same grating wrench. A powerful odour flooded the inside of Clay's hood. A shudder boiled up in his diaphragm and quivered down through his guts to his sphincter. The smell was strangely familiar, like a forgotten nightmare – vaguely antiseptic, as if someone had tried to clean away something especially foul and had been only partially successful.

And then they were moving again, accelerating into second gear, the car lurching over a stretch of bad road, the shocks bottoming out as the wheels hit a succession of potholes. It was a different kind of vehicle, larger, it seemed, heavier, with a bigger engine. After a while the road smoothed out and the driver geared up into third and then fourth gear.

The sound of a lighter snapping open. The smell of burning tobacco cut through shit and disinfectant and rotten meat.

'How did she contact you, Straker?' Cobra said over the noise of the engine. 'Was it during your first hospitalisation?'

Clay said nothing.

'Are you a member of Torch Commando, Straker?

'Jesus. No.'

'Bullshit. What were you doing on that C-130?'

'The question is what were *you* doing?' said Clay. 'Murdering bastard.'

He heard Cobra laugh under his breath, take a deep pull on his cigarette. By the change in the engine's hum and the hiss of the tyres on the road, they'd now joined a major thoroughfare.

'Clever of the doctor to fake your death like that,' said Cobra.

The car decelerated and then came to a stop. Diesel fumes wafted through the car, the smells of the street coming through the open windows. Somewhere in the distance, the sound of children playing – a school? And then they were moving again, the street sounds drowned by the air buffeting through the open windows, the tyres on the road.

'Too bad about your friend, though. Barstow, isn't it?'

'You bastards,' hissed Clay. 'We're out there fighting and dying for our country. And you're busy doing what? Running some kind of warped experiments? Getting rich?'

'I'm too old for the righteous soldier bullshit, Straker.'

'Fuck you.' Clay strained at the ties around his wrists, wrenched and pulled against the sharp plastic.

'You'll just cut yourself,' said Cobra.

'Is it really going to matter?'

'That's up to you.'

'You better hope I don't get out of these things,' Clay breathed.

A sharp turn, the acceleration pushing Clay into the car door, and then the vehicle slowing, out of the city now, or on the outskirts, the air cleaner, the smell of fields and green coming through the thick cloth of the hood.

'You killed Wade, didn't you? You and Botha.'

Cobra was quiet for a long time. Clay could hear him there next to him, working the pedals and the gears, lighting another cigarette, breathing in the smoke, exhaling long and deep, all this, too, locked away forever, to be viewed in ten thousand years from some distant star.

'Not me.'

'You're BOSS, aren't you?'

Cobra laughed. 'Me? Hell no.'

'Who the hell do you work for, then?'

'Does it really matter?'

Clay could feel the rage growing inside him, the reactions firing, a dawning realisation of just how badly they'd all been duped. He felt as if he were going to be sick. 'You, or Botha, or whoever you work for, you fucked up Eben's operation, didn't you?'

Just road noise for a long time. And then: 'They shouldn't have done that.'

'So, it's true.'

'I'm sorry, Straker. I had nothing to do with it.'

'Sorry?' screamed Clay through the hood. 'What the fuck is that supposed to mean? Fucking sorry?'

'Take it easy.'

Clay whipped his head towards Cobra with as much force as he could muster, trying for contact with Cobra's face. He met only empty air. Cobra was too fast, had moved back and away. Clay grunted as his side lit up. He collapsed back into his seat.

'Keep that up and those stitches she put in you are going to open up.'

'*Fok jou.*'

'Your choice.'

And then the car slowing, the sound of gravel under the tyres, ruts in the road, the suspension groaning, the car lurching over potholes. The car stopped and Cobra turned off the engine.

It was suddenly very quiet.

Birdsong came on the breeze. The engine block ticked as it cooled.

Cobra lit another cigarette.

'What the hell is going on?' said Clay, his voice muffled.

'Sit tight, Straker.'

And then the car door opening and closing, footsteps on the gravel, moving away, the background stench of the vehicle re-establishing itself. After a moment, the murmur of voices, the words indistinct across the distance: another man, his voice deeper than Cobra's, and then, a woman's voice, raised, scared.

Clay raised his hands, grabbed the hood and tried to pull it off. The thing wrenched under his neck. He searched the edge of the bag with paired hands. Some sort of drawstring knotted near his throat, soft, like a shoelace. Clay fumbled with the knot, sought an edge, a loop to exploit. He could hear the men talking, and now the woman again, tension in the voices, heavy in the crushed vowels.

And then, an opening. The knot unravelled. He yanked at the hood, pulled it from his head. The light was blinding. He squinted at the shapes beyond the windscreen. There were three of them, standing about twenty metres from the car. They were in a small clearing, surrounded by trees; a woodland of some sort. He fumbled for the door handle. The figures were walking back towards the car now, Cobra in the back, handgun drawn.

'Get out, Straker.'

Clay pushed open the door, stepped to the ground, everything overexposed.

A white man with thin shoulders and a sparse beard strewn with grey stood behind Cobra. He wore a blue-and-red tracksuit, white training shoes, and a white headband over thinning hair. His face glistened with sweat. Beside him was the woman. She looked at Clay.

'I think you two know each other,' said Cobra.

☾

Commissioner Barbour: Tell us, Mister Straker, about Torch Commando.

Witness: I really didn't know much about it at the time. I was never part of it.

Commissioner Barbour: We understand that, son. But tell us what you, ah, what you know about it, for the record.

Witness: It was an organisation devoted to overthrowing the apartheid regime. It started, I think, in the military, in the 1950s; members of the armed forces who disagreed with the way the country was being run, with the subjugation of the blacks and the coloureds. They wanted a true democracy. It was an underground movement, a loose affiliation of independent cells. Whites. I'd heard of it, but had no idea it was still active.

Commissioner Ksole: And your Captain Wade, was he a member?

Witness: I think so. That would make sense.

Commissioner Lacy: And BOSS had him killed?

Witness: I can't prove it, but yes, I think so.

Commissioner Lacy: Is that why your friend, Mister Barstow, dug up the notebook? Do you think he suspected a connection with Captain Wade's death?

Witness: I don't know, ma'am. He must have done it just before we left for Operation Protea. I can only guess that he thought it safer to keep the notebook with him than to leave it in camp, especially with Botha wandering around. Maybe he wanted to take a closer look at it, see what he could figure out. He was like that, Eben. Sucker for a book. He never got the chance to tell me.

Commissioner Barbour: And this organisation, Torch Commando, was the doctor, ah, the young lady, was she involved?

Witness: Yes, sir.

Commissioner Lacy: She was a very brave young woman.

Witness: Yes she was, ma'am.

Commissioner Lacy: So much has been lost.

Witness: Sorry, ma'am?

Commissioner Lacy: You must understand, young man, that this commission has already spent months hearing the stories of witnesses from across the country; stories

of the hate and destruction and loss that has torn our
country apart. So much has been lost.

Witness: Yes, ma'am. Much.

Commissioner Ksole: And on the other side, the Broederbond
network. Were you aware, at that time, of the existence
of this organisation?

Witness: No, sir. I'd never heard of it.

Commissioner Ksole: And later?

Witness: Yes, sir. I was … I was made aware.

Commissioner Barbour: Tell us what happened, son.

28

This Forgotten History

Some things are not as they seem.

Garbed in misdirection, cloaked in confusion, what lies beneath is hidden to us. But no camouflage is perfect, no ruse without flaw. Could you have detected those rips in the fabric sooner? And if you had, could you have seen through them? And then, much later, when the essence of the thing is stripped bare, naked and shivering before you, are you able to see it for what it is? For the real truth is that memories fade, and what may have seemed clear and self-evident at the time browns in the sun, erodes with the winds and rain of seasons, thins and grows frail as the body weakens and motives grow suspect.

Counterfactual: Sometimes things are exactly what they appear to be.

Thus does a decade of looping reconstructions and endless replays, conscious and subliminal, grow in a troubled mind. His. After all this time, he just wasn't sure anymore.

At first, Vivian hadn't moved. She just stood there with her mouth open in that little 'o' of hers, staring at Clay, at the ties around his wrists, and then past him to the vehicle he'd arrived in. Then she focused on Cobra and tightened her skilled fingers into delicate little fists.

'Where is Joseph?' she shouted, anger and fear sending visible tremors through her body.

'Waiting for us at the RV,' said Cobra.

Clay could see her swallow hard, choking on the confusion. 'That wasn't the plan,' she managed.

'Bullshit,' said Clay, looking at Vivian. 'He's BOSS.'

'No,' said Cobra. 'Please, listen to me.'

Clay took a step towards Cobra, lowered his hips, brought his wrists up over his right shoulder, his elbows together in front of his jaw, and prepared to charge.

'Don't Straker,' said Cobra, whipping out a *karambit*. The knife's ugly curved blade gleamed in the sun slanting low through the trees.

Clay froze. Vivian stood where she was, staring at Cobra.

'I know what you're planning to do,' said Cobra.

'You don't know anything,' said Clay.

The guy in the tracksuit started backing away.

'Stay where you are,' barked Cobra.

'Whatever is going on here, I've got nothing to do with it,' the man in the tracksuit blurted, waving his hands in front of his chest. 'I'm just out jogging, that's all.' He opened his arms as if to say, 'look at me'.

'Shut up,' said Cobra. 'I know exactly who you are.'

'How did you get that?' said Vivian, pointing past Clay, at the vehicle.

'Joseph,' said Cobra. 'He told me to take it.'

Clay looked over his shoulder. The vehicle he'd come here in. It was an ambulance.

'That's how we're going to get in,' said Cobra. 'All of us.'

Silence. The possible meanings of this whirring in three brains.

'I don't know what you're talking about,' said the guy in the tracksuit. 'I'm leaving.'

'Alright,' said Cobra. 'You go ahead and finish your run, *bru*,' said Cobra. 'Go back to your wife and kids. Harriet and David and June, isn't it?'

The guy in the tracksuit looked like someone had just severed his carotid artery. He staggered, blood draining from his face.

'Give us what you came here to give us,' said Cobra. 'Then you can go.'

With a quick glance at Vivian, the guy unzipped his tracksuit top, reached inside and pulled out some kind of laminated card on a blue lanyard and a red plastic pass.

'Give them to the doctor,' said Cobra.

The guy complied, stepped back a few paces, stood hunched and uncertain.

Cobra waved his hand. 'Go,' he said.

'You're going to shoot me,' said the guy. 'Oh, God.'

Cobra looked bored now, that same look Clay had seen outside the bunker that day in Angola with the mortars raining down and the Hercules powering up.

'If I'd wanted to shoot you, you'd be dead already,' said Cobra. 'Now piss off.'

The guy turned and started walking towards the trees. After a few steps he started to run. In a few seconds he vanished into the woods.

'*Dof*,' said Cobra. He was smiling. Smiling. He looked at Vivian. 'Now you have what you wanted. A way in.'

Vivian stood mute, uncomprehending.

'Torch Commando,' said Cobra.

'Don't listen to him, Vivian,' said Clay. 'He works with Botha, with Doctor Death. He was there in Angola when they were injecting those blacks. It was his men who were throwing them into the ocean. He's got nothing on you. Don't say anything.'

Cobra hung his head. 'Look, I'm trying to help you. Can't you see that?'

Clay raised his wrists.

'Would you have come with me otherwise?' Cobra took a step towards Clay, stopped striking distance away, brandishing the *karambit*.

Clay stood his ground.

'Those BOSS types in the Chevy,' said Cobra, 'it was for them, Straker. All of it. I had to make it look good.'

'I don't believe you,' said Vivian, recoiling now.

It was then that Cobra struck. The movement was so fast that Clay barely registered it. One second he was standing there, wrists bound, watching Vivian trying to process what she was seeing and hearing, and the next he was free, the tie cut clean. Three small drops of blood bloomed on the outside of his left wrist where the *karambit*'s tip had grazed the skin.

Cobra grinned, rubbed his jaw with his free hand. 'Look,' he said. 'I've been working inside COAST for six months now. I'm Torch, like you. Joseph was the overlap in my cell. When you started hatching this plan to get into Roodeplaat, he came to me. We've been working this thing for too long for you to come in and screw it up.'

Clay shook his head, unable to reconcile this with what he'd seen. 'No,' it can't be true.'

'Why do you think I let you go, that day in the back of the Herc, Straker? You and Barstow. I didn't have to. Could've killed you right there. Too easy.' Cobra sheathed his knife. 'And who do you think tipped off Wade about the RV with UNITA that night in the first place? Someone had to have. There was no way you could have found us otherwise.' Cobra paused, staring into Clay's eyes. 'That's right. It was me.'

'It could have been anyone,' said Clay, still reeling from all he was hearing. 'Zulaika. It could have been her.'

'No way, Straker. You're reaching. How could she have known?' Clay shook his head.

'And before that, out in Angola, when that psycho Mbdele wanted to kill you; who stopped him? I've been looking out for you, Straker. You're our star witness, *bru*. When this all comes to trial, one day, when all this bullshit is over, we're going to need your testimony.'

'No,' said Vivian. 'Joseph would have told me.'

Cobra took a step towards Vivian, leaned in close so that his face was inches from hers. Then he said something that Clay could not make out.

Vivian's reaction was immediate. Her eyes opened wide, as if in wonder at hearing for the first time some great and secret truth, and then, as quickly, her face crumpled and tears were pouring down over her turgid lips, falling from her chin and jaw. She hid her face in her hands and sobbed.

Cobra pulled out his handgun and checked the action. 'We're running out of time,' he said. 'Lab staff go home at five. That leaves only night guards front and back, and a night clerk. But they only accept deliveries until 6 pm. We've got less than twenty minutes.'

'Vivian?' said Clay.

She looked up at him through tear-strewn eyes. Then she nodded.

Cobra was already walking towards the ambulance. He opened the driver's-side door, pulled out a set of white coveralls and threaded them over his clothes. From one of the pockets he produced a sealed badge and clipped it to his front pocket.

Clay took Vivian by the hand. 'Are you sure?'

'Yes, Clay. He's telling the truth.' She squeezed his hand. 'But you can't come with us. There is only one badge. You should go. Try for the border.'

'I'm not letting you go alone, Vivian. Not with him.'

Cobra was in the driver's seat now, tapping the face of his wristwatch.

Vivian put the badge around her neck. 'Don't worry about me, Clay. Please, go. Get to safety.' She started towards the ambulance.

Later, much later, in any one of half a million realisations, the results were different. Perhaps if he'd had more time to think about it, if he'd picked up on some of the hundreds of clues, if he'd simply been more aware, things might have turned out differently. But he didn't, and with each decision, each action, icy reality was frozen into place forever. He did get into the back of the ambulance. He did ignore Vivian's pleas to go. Cobra's suggestion that he lie on one of the stretchers and feign incapacitation had seemed a good one, so he did it. And so, by the time the ambulance pulled up to the back gate of the Roodeplaat Research Laboratories on the outskirts of Pretoria just before six o'clock in the evening in September of 1981, at the height of apartheid, with the war on the border raging, the dead and the dying were already lining up to take their places in this forgotten history.

29

Structure and Function

Clay lay on a stretcher in the back of the ambulance, feeling the vehicle rumble over the gravel. The same foul odour filled his nostrils, worked its way into his mouth and throat. It seemed to seep from the vehicle's ridged metal floor and the canvas weave of the stretchers, that bitter cut of biocide barely masking the intestine stench of shit and blood and something else he thought he knew but didn't acknowledge.

Vivian and Cobra were up front. Vivian had donned a white lab coat and pulled her hair back into a work pony tail. He could hear them talking, muffled voices over the groan of the engine and the complaints of the suspension. The tone was businesslike, determined. They had decided they were working together, that was clear.

But Clay couldn't make the shift. Cobra, a member of Torch Commando? Undercover all this time, infiltrating Operation COAST, getting close to Botha and *O Medico de Morte*? It seemed ludicrous, more than far-fetched. And yet it was clear to him now that this thing was widespread, and big. Captain Wade – his own CO – had surely been part of it. Brigade, too, most likely. Who else? There was no way to tell. It could be anyone. So why not Cobra? Everything he'd said was true. At each previous encounter, he'd been instrumental in helping Clay and Eben escape or continue unscathed. And he'd convinced Vivian. Whatever he'd said to her back in the woods had instantly removed any doubt from her mind.

The ride smoothed out, sealed road under them now, back in the *platteland*. Through the rear windows, Clay could see the lights of

Pretoria, the taller buildings of the central district standing above the flatland like beacons in the darkness.

The ambulance slowed.

'Here we go,' came Cobra's voice from the front. 'Remember, Straker, you're unconscious, drugged up. Keep quiet.'

You'd know all about it.

'Straker?'

'*Ja*, good,' said Clay.

The ambulance rolled to a stop. A voice from outside, the gate guard. And then Vivian replying, her voice professional, even – something about an unexpected patient, the need to conduct immediate tests. Unscheduled. They would be about an hour. And then quiet, Cobra lighting a smoke, the engine idling, rocking Clay in his cradle.

They waited a long time. Perhaps the guards were telephoning someone for confirmation. Checking the register, Vivian's pass, the vehicle's registration number.

And then Cobra's voice, clipped and urgent: 'Straker, they're coming.'

Clay closed his eyes, lay still.

The rear doors opened with a crash. Cold, evening air flooded the compartment. A light flashing over him, around him. Voices. And then the beam steady on his face so the insides of his eyes lit up red and swimming and he could feel his lids twitching in the glare. He didn't breathe. He lay still and quiet and empty like all those dead men he'd looked down upon in this latest and perhaps last year of his life. He imagined fatalism. The kind of acceptance that so frequently overcame Eben, that seemed to punctuate his normal rebel insanity. Everything frozen forever, just like he'd said, there for eternity. What the hell.

And then the light was gone and the doors were closed again and the smell re-established itself and the ambulance was moving. Clay opened his eyes. Through the rear windows he could see the arc-lit razor wire coiling the lip of the wall, a candy-striped barrier descending, and then the corner of a building as the ambulance veered left and slowed. A few seconds later they stopped again and the engine died. The front doors opened and closed and then the rear doors opened again and someone was clambering inside. Clay felt himself being lifted, let his head slump to the side with the move-ment, playing his role. And then he was being carried. The evening air flowed clean over his face and the smells were altogether famil-iar: the sweetness of far off veldtgrass and the dendritic majesty of the city's two million jacarandas. New doors opened, closed behind him, and then it was as if a blanket had been thrown over him, a close, smothering warmth and with it a new and more powerful set of odours: hospital, yes – he knew that – but something else, too; oddly agricultural: silage and farm machinery and the stench of shit. And then the sound of footsteps echoing along some sort of corridor, peeling from linoleum flooring, another set of doors creaking on dry hinges. More voices – close by. A man with a squeaky voice saying something Clay could not distinguish. Another man saying: 'Sign here.' The distinctive scribble of pen on paper. A chair scraping over the floor. Now Vivian speaking, professional, calm, the sound of her voice like a rescue. 'One hour,' the squeaky voice said. 'Thank you.' Vivian again. And then, quiet. A door closing.

'Okay, Straker, up.' Cobra, hand on Clay's shoulder.

Clay opened his eyes. They were in some kind of examination room: stainless-steel work benches, seasick-green walls, glass cabi-nets. He stood

'One hour,' said Cobra. 'No more.'

Vivian nodded.

'What are we looking for?' said Clay.

'Anything,' said Vivian. 'Anything that will help us understand what they are doing in here.'

Cobra looked around the room. 'The longer we stay, the higher the chances of something going wrong. They have cameras outside the building and covering the entire perimeter, but nothing inside.'

'That tells us something,' said Clay.

'No records,' said Vivian.

Cobra glanced at him, then her. 'The minimum, Doctor. Get what you need, no more.'

'Well there's nothing in here,' she said with a final glance around the room. 'Let's go.' She walked to the door, pulled it open a few centimetres and peered out.

Nodding to them she started down a dimly lit corridor. Clay followed, aware of Cobra behind him, wary. She slowed outside the first door they came to, scanned the wall plaque, kept going. They passed a second door without looking inside. They were halfway down the corridor when Vivian stopped. She turned and faced them. 'In here,' she whispered. A small plaque to the right of the doorframe said: 2A Sequencing.

She tried the handle. 'It's locked.'

Cobra bid her move aside, reached into the pocket of his coveralls and pulled out what looked like a small knife. He bent to the handle, inserted the blade into the lock. In a few seconds he had the door open. They stepped inside, closing the door behind them. Cobra found the light switch. Fluorescent tubes clicked overhead, strobed, then steadied, harsh and clinical.

It was some kind of laboratory. Various instruments ranked along opposing sets of polished, stainless-steel benches. A high-powered microscope, precision scales, glassware, pipettes and rows of test tubes in plastic racks. A dormant computer screen, a keyboard: HP – American. But what attracted Vivian's attention almost immediately was none of these. It was a strange-looking thing – a box about the size of a packing crate, festooned with wires and tubes which entered the casing at different points. She made straight for it. Clay followed.

The device seemed to be hooked up to a clear-plastic cylinder pump about the size of a car engine's piston. Beneath it was a long row of more than a dozen small, steel doors, each with a vertical handle, what appeared to be a temperature gauge, and a timer. They looked almost like small household ovens. Vivian pulled out her camera, adjusted the lens and clicked off a few photos.

'What is it?' said Clay, leaning close.

'A mass spectrometer,' she said, without dropping the camera from her face. 'And this is an HPLC – a liquid chromatograph. Down here, ovens for hydrolysis.'

'What are they for?'

'Peptide sequencing would be my guess. This equipment is very expensive, hard to come by. It's all from America.' She let the camera rest on its strap around her neck. 'It's for isolating proteins so you can study their structure and function. It allows you to understand cellular processes, for instance, and devise ways to manipulate specific metabolic pathways.' She paused, glancing around the room, then opened a drawer under the lab bench, flipped through a stack of papers and withdrew a spiral-bound report. 'Look at this,' she said, handing it to Clay.

It was about the thickness of a paperback. The cover was emblazoned with the now familiar SAMS logo, and Operation COAST in thick black letters. Below, a secondary heading: *Swarts Bom: Voorlopige Verslag*. Clay flipped it open, scanned the first page, the next, the one after that. Three words stood out amongst the formal Afrikaans and the scattered technical English, words that surprised him: *eiers*, *sperm*, and *embrios*.

Vivian glanced at him. She'd seen them, too.

'*Swarts bom*,' said Clay. 'Black bomb?'

Vivian shrugged her shoulders. 'It's important,' she said. 'Take it.'

Clay closed the cover and made to stash the report inside his jacket.

'No,' said Cobra. 'Don't take anything. We don't want to leave any evidence that this was anything other than a routine delivery.'

'You heard her,' said Clay. 'This is important.'

'Nothing leaves here,' said Cobra.

'Not even us?' said Clay.

Cobra grinned, pointed at the open drawer. 'Put it back, Straker.'

Clay looked at Vivian. She took the report, placed it on the desk and photographed the cover and the first twenty or so pages, then replaced it in the drawer. Then she opened another drawer, flipped through the documents, took more photos.

'Could this equipment be used for developing drugs?' whispered Clay.

'Definitely.'

'What kinds?'

'Any.'

'13B?'

'Undoubtedly.'

Clay's insides tumbled. He took a couple of shallow breaths and followed Vivian towards the door. Cobra was already out in the corridor, waiting.

Clay grabbed Vivian's elbow, pulled her close. 'What did he say to you, Vivian, back in the clearing?'

She stared at him wide eyed, but did not answer.

'What did he tell you that made you change your mind?'

'Come on,' she said. 'We don't have much time.' She had just reached for the light switch when Clay glimpsed something at the edge of his vision. It was the colour that caught his attention. Three racks of identical sealed tubes set side by side on the bench, ten or more tubes in each rack. Each tube contained the same red liquid. Each rack was labelled, thick black marker pen on white card: *Blanke*, *Swaart*, and finally, *Primaat*.

Clay rocked back, realisation pulsing through him like a cold dose of adrenaline. He grabbed Vivian's arm, and pointed to the bench. She stood there for what seemed like a long time, staring down at the tubes and the white cards. And then she turned off the light.

'Holy Mother of Jesus,' she whispered under her breath.

It was the stench that led them onwards.

Vivian covered her face with the sleeve of her lab coat, as she pushed open a set of double doors into another corridor. This one was longer, set at right angles to the first, the spine of a second wing to the complex. At the far end of the corridor a large set of doors was painted in thick yellow-and-black chevrons. Biohazard signs flanked the doorway on both sides. With each step they took, the smell grew more powerful.

Clay tried to breathe through his mouth. The stench lodged in the back of his throat, seemed to coat his tongue. He knew this taste, this bitter corruption, knew it intimately, wished it was not so. It was the smell of fear, thick and heavy, like staring into the worst nightmare, the one that's real. And suddenly the walls of the corridor were closing in on him, the ceiling falling, the floor under his feet turning to cloying mud. Blood and shit swirled around his feet. Acids and solvents welled from pores in the walls, dripped from hairs that seemed to have sprouted from every surface, living follicles that swayed like the tentacles of anemone in the counter-currents of some deep-sea vent. His eyes streamed. He gasped for air, retched back the foul vapours. His head was spinning. His heart hammered inside his chest, a full-out sprint. He staggered a few steps, aware of Vivian moving away, Cobra following her, both mere blurs. He stopped, fell to his knees. What was happening to him? He was a combat veteran, for God's sake. This was nothing. He'd been through so much worse. Why here, why now?

He closed his eyes, felt himself moving towards a blurred edge, fought against the tide. He gasped in the toxic air, gagged, put a hand on the floor. And then a voice, a hand under his shoulder, coaxing him up.

'Clay, what's wrong?' Vivian's voice hollow, submerged.

'I ... I don't know,' he gasped.

'Come on,' she said, pulling him to his feet. 'We don't have much time.'

Clay staggered forward, unsteady. 'I'm sorry,' he said. 'I don't know...'

She took his face in her hands and kissed him on the cheek. 'Shush,' she said. 'After what you've been through, I'm amazed you're even walking.' And then she smiled at him. 'Come on. Almost there.'

And then, as if with a mother's kiss, it was gone. The vertigo, the pulsing choking panic. Clay stood, straightened, checked his limbs. Everything there. Everything working. He started after Vivian.

Cobra was waiting for them at the door.

Much later he would come to see, after many years of reflection, that what lay behind those big yellow-and-black striped doors would change the way he looked at the world forever.

Cobra pushed them open. A cold stench pushed them back like a shove in the chest. They peered into the darkness.

It was a big room, like an aircraft hangar, or some kind of warehouse. The air was cold, but strangely humid. There was no light. Cobra switched on a torch and played the beam across a smooth, concrete floor. Dark liquid ran in channelled open gutters that spined the middle of the floor and ribbed out to the walls. A forklift truck hulked next to a stack of wooden pallets.

'What's that?' said Vivian.

'What?' said Clay.

'Can't you hear it?'

The place was deadly quiet.

'No.'

'Breathing,' said Vivian.

Clay recalibrated. She was right. It was if the walls were alive, inhaling, exhaling. 'Jesus,' whispered Clay. 'What is this place?'

Cobra switched off his torch.

'What are you doing?' said Clay.

'There's nothing here. It's just a warehouse.' Cobra turned back towards the door.

'No, wait,' said Vivian. 'Let's look.'

'We're running out of time,' said Cobra. 'If we get caught…'

'Not like you to panic, *bru*,' said Clay.

'I've worked too long on this cover to blow it by being stupid,' snapped Cobra, anger in his voice.

A light flashed on. 'You stay, then,' Vivian said, stepping into the darkness. She'd brought her own torch. Clay followed as she penetrated the darkness, painting the floor with her beam.

After a few steps, she stopped. The beam of her torch was weak, short range.

'This way,' said Clay, guiding her by the elbow. 'Towards the wall.'

Cobra was not with them. Was he still waiting at the door? They kept going, bubbled in the torchlight.

She stopped. 'Look.' She scanned the beam across a wall.

At first Clay wasn't sure what he was seeing. Compartments, a latticework of horizontal and vertical steel beams, like the frontage of an apartment building, two, three storeys high. In each opening, where the windows might have been, were a series of vertical bars, equally spaced. The light was too weak to penetrate beyond.

A second beam swung across the bars. 'Jesus,' muttered Cobra, approaching from behind.

Vivian let out a gasp, held her breath, grabbed for Clay's arm.

Pinpoints of light. Dozens of pairs of them, reflected back at them from the depths of each compartment. Eyes.

Cobra stepped towards the wall, played the light through the bars of one of the cells. A pair of chimpanzees huddled together in the back of a cage.

'Live animal testing,' said Vivian. 'What I suspected.'

Cobra went ahead, his torch swinging amongst the cages. 'Gorillas,' he said, 'Orangutans. Perfectly legal.'

'Disgusting,' said Vivian. 'The poor things. They're terrified.'

Cobra turned off his torch, started back towards them. 'We need to go,' he said. 'If we don't get back soon, the night clerk will come looking for us. Nothing more to see here.'

Clay reached for Cobra's torch. 'May I?' he said.

Cobra pulled it away. 'We need to go,' he said. 'I don't intend to get caught in here.'

'Give us five more minutes. Please,' said Vivian. 'We've come this far.'

Cobra looked at his watch. 'No,' he said. And then: 'I'm sorry. We must go.'

Clay took two steps towards Cobra, stood beside him. 'He's right,' he said. 'Come on, Vivian.'

Vivian turned and started towards them. As she approached, Clay shot his hand out, grabbed the torch and wrenched it from Cobra's hand.

'What the *fok*?' barked Cobra.

Clay flashed the beam into Cobra's eyes. 'Thanks, *bru*,' he said, grabbing Vivian's hand. 'Won't be a moment.'

'Straker,' shouted Cobra. 'Idiot. Come back.'

But Clay was already moving deeper into the warehouse, swinging the beam before him. The place was deathly quiet, the animals silent, brooding, hiding. He shifted the beam to the opposite side of the room. At the limit of the beam's illumination they could make out ranks of what looked like storage sheds with big metal doors. Between them, stainless-steel benches like the ones they'd seen in the sequencing lab shone dull molybdenum.

'What are we looking for?' Clay whispered.

She didn't answer, just kept walking, close to the cages now, splaying her light into each cell, one after the other, some empty, some not, the animals huddled, terrorised.

And then she stopped dead, her torch shaking in her hand, its beam trembling over the bars and into one of the cages. 'My God,' she whispered.

Clay turned his beam in the same direction. The occupant of the cage stood grasping the bars, staring out at them with wide, bloodstained eyes. There were deep red wounds on its head and limbs. Its dark skin and heavy, naked breasts glistened with sweat.

It was a woman.

30

Going To Die Anyway

When the lights came on the place erupted.

It was as if the sudden illumination, the flooding of the chamber with a million-and-a-half candle power of electric light, broke the spell of terrified silence that had held the place gagged and huddled since they'd arrived. Screams filled the air, every frequency saturated, decibels pulsing from heaving lungs and snarling, fang-toothed mouths. It was the sound of rage. Rage fuelled by fear and desperation.

And then above it all, the sounds of language.

Clay shielded his eyes and looked instinctively back towards the doorway. Vivian grabbed his arm. Clay froze, his torch shining use-lessly on the floor by his feet.

A man was standing in the doorway, his left hand still on the main light switch. He wore a surgical facemask that hid his nose and mouth. His white lab coat hung open, revealing a blue-shirted girth beneath. He held a black handgun in his right hand.

'*God dam,*' muttered Cobra.

'I often work late on Tuesdays,' the man said in English, the face-mask and his thick Afrikaner accent clogging the vowels, shredding the consonants. His words were barely audible above the screaming of two dozen primates and God knew how many human beings. He started walking towards them, gun levelled.

'It's him,' said Clay.

'Botha?' said Vivian.

'No. The one I told you about. *O Medico de morte.*'

He felt Vivian's hand tighten around his forearm.

'Stay exactly where you are,' shouted the man above the cacophony. He had closed the twenty or so metres that separated them from the doors, herding Cobra back to where Clay and Vivian stood. He now stood a few paces away, holding the handgun level at his waist. It was trained on Clay.

'You,' he said. 'You killed Shwartz, didn't you? In the dunes. He never came back.'

Clay said nothing, held his ground.

Veins throbbed at the man's temples, bulged over his balding scalp. 'Tell me, what happened to him?'

Clay remained mute, unmoving.

'Murderer,' he shouted, jabbing the handgun towards Clay.

'Be careful with that thing,' said Clay. 'Might piss yourself again.'

The man the Angolans called *O Medico de Morte* snapped the pistol forward, aimed for Clay's face. Hate burned in his eyes.

Vivian took a step back. 'Doctor, please,' she said.

Her voice seemed to calm him. He steadied, filled his lungs, exhaled.

'Doctor Grasson,' she said. 'You are a medical doctor.'

He seemed deflated now, as if she had tamed something inside him.

'Please,' she said. 'Lower the gun. Consider what you are doing.'

The doctor seemed to think about this a moment, his eyes flicking up and to the left before settling back into their lambent stare. Then he frowned. 'What I do is necessary,' he said.

'What you are doing is illegal,' she said. 'And immoral.'

The man's chest swelled. The window of connection was gone. 'Quite the opposite. Everything we do here is perfectly legal.'

'What about them?' shouted Vivian, pointing back towards the far cages, the ones containing blacks, human beings.

'Those blacks are diseased.' Then he smiled and said: 'This is a high-level quarantine area. I am afraid you have all been exposed.'

'Exposed to what?' said Clay.

'Anthrax. Cholera. Botulism. Take your pick.'

'*Fok jou*,' said Cobra.

'And you,' said the doctor, pivoting slightly to bring his handgun to bear on Cobra. 'Have you decided to side with the kaffir lovers and communists?'

'What are you doing to them?' shouted Vivian. She let go of Clay's arm and took a step towards the doctor. The movement caught him by surprise and he stumbled back. He had just started swinging the gun around towards her when Cobra struck.

He covered the metre and half between them in a fraction of a second, parrying the doctor's gun hand with his left so that the weapon was pointing uselessly at the far wall. At the same instant, his open right palm smashed into the doctor's face. As the doctor's head snapped back, Cobra's right hand joined his left on the gun, and with a tearing motion, he ripped the pistol from the doctor's hand.

A scream cut the din. The doctor crumpled to the ground, clutching his hand. Blood poured from his nose. His bent and bleeding trigger finger hung limp from its knuckle. Cobra stood above him with the handgun aimed at his head.

'Go, Straker,' Cobra hissed, handing Clay his own weapon. 'Both of you. I'll catch up. Don't leave without me.'

Vivian gasped. 'What are you going to do?'

'What do you think?' said Cobra, raising the handgun.

She put her hand on Cobra's forearm. 'No, wait,' she said. And then to the doctor: 'What are you doing with the peptide sequencer?'

The doctor looked up at her through tears of pain.

'And the embryos? Tell me. Is it some kind of genetic engineering?'

The doctor looked down at his broken hand. 'Don't, *poppie*,' he barked.

'Go,' said Cobra. 'We're out of time.'

Clay grabbed Vivian's hand. 'Let's go. He's right. If we don't leave now, we never will.' He started pulling her towards the door.

She pulled back. 'No, Clay. This is why we came. I need to know.'

'For Christ's sake,' said Cobra. 'I'm not telling you again. Go. You don't want to see this.'

Clay wrenched Vivian by her elbow, manhandling her towards the door. Any doubts he might have had about Cobra were gone.

But Vivian twisted herself around and looked back at the doctor. 'What is the *swarts bom*?' she shouted. 'You're going to die anyway, you sick bastard. You might as well tell me.'

The doctor bared his teeth. 'Traitor,' he shouted.

'Straker.'

No matter what the situation, no matter how many voices overlap, you can always hear someone calling your name. Again it came, over the noise of chattering monkeys and chimpanzees, the wail of a dozen caged voices. His name. Loud, clear, familiar.

Clay stopped, turned, faced the sound. It was coming from the far cages. His name again, clear now. He let go of Vivian, started towards the far end of the room. Everywhere, naked black men and women pushed themselves up against the bars, their fists clenched around the steel uprights. They were staring at him.

'Where are you going, Straker?' called Cobra.

'Straker.' The voice again, hoarse, desperate.

'God damn it, come back,' shouted Cobra.

Clay shivered, cold suddenly, despite the dripping exhalations of three dozen mouths. He stepped towards the cage, within touching distance of the bars. A black arm reached out for him, its fingers like twisted mopane roots. The face was swollen, deeply discoloured around both cheekbones, the eye sockets caved.

'Jesus Christ,' said Clay.

'Straker. Get me out of here.'

'My God. Brigade. What have they done to you?'

☾

Commissioner Rotzenberg: Are you aware, Mister Straker, of the requirements for the granting of amnesty by this commission?

Witness: Yes, sir.

Commissioner Rotzenburg: Let me restate them for you. First and foremost, you must relate the entire truth, to the best of your ability, no matter how difficult.

Witness: Yes, sir. That's what I'm trying to do.

Commissioner Rotzenburg: And then you must show real contrition.

Witness: I understand.

Commissioner Rotzenburg: The witness maintains he wants amnesty, that he is here to tell the truth, and yet he systematically withholds important information.

Witness: I don't understand.

Commissioner Rotzenburg: The witness claims that after hospitalisation, he began working with Torch Commando to uncover a conspiracy to use engineered drugs against the enemies of the regime. But his account of events systematically contradicts those of other witnesses. You say Doctor Grasson, the man you have been calling Doctor Death, was there, the day you supposedly broke into Roodeplaat Research Laboratories.

Witness: We did get into the laboratory. He was there.

Commissioner Rotzenburg: And yet official records place Doctor Grasson in Libya at the time. Over the course of that entire month, in fact. We have documentary evidence of this. Airline records, hotel receipts.

Witness: I'm telling you, he was there. He had us at gunpoint, for Christ's sake. Why would I lie?

Commissioner Rotzenburg: Are you lying, or are you simply remembering incorrectly, as you have at various points throughout your testimony to this commission?

Witness: Look, I'm telling you what I saw, what I heard.

Commissioner Lacy: Could it have been someone else you saw, Mister Straker? Perhaps because of the mask you say this man was wearing?

Witness: I'm sure it was him. He recognised me, from the plane. That's why he accused me of murdering his assistant. Who else could it have been?

Commissioner Rotzenburg: Indeed. Who else?

Witness: What are you saying? That I'm lying? Making this up? _____ you.

Commissioner Barbour: The witness is warned that further outbursts will not be tolerated. You say you want amnesty, Mister Straker, that you want forgiveness for the things you have done – the *terrible* things you have done. We are here to get to the truth. Attacking members of the commission will do you no good.

Witness: I'm … I'm sorry. This isn't easy for me.

Commissioner Lacy: Nor for us, young man. We are all South Africans.

31

Just Like You

Clay paced back to where Cobra stood with Doctor Grasson, shoved the muzzle of the handgun Cobra had given him into Grasson's mouth and pushed his head back.

Grasson gagged, choking on the metal.

'Keys,' barked Clay. 'Now. Or believe me, it will be my pleasure to blow your head off.'

Grasson reached into his pocket and withdrew a heavy ring of keys.

Clay grabbed the keys and held them up in front of Grasson's face. 'Which one?'

Grasson reached up and touched a large key with a red plastic rim on the bow. His hand was trembling.

'Take off that lab coat.'

Grasson complied. Clay grabbed the coat, pulled the gun out of Grasson's mouth and pushed him back hard with a palm to the solar plexus.

'What are you doing?' said Cobra.

'I'm going to let those people go.'

'You can't do that, Straker,' said Cobra, moving so that he was now standing between Clay and Brigade's cage. 'Let them go and my cover is blown, *broer*. I won't last a week. We still have a chance of getting out of here, if we go now.' Cobra glanced at Vivian. 'I'm not going to be able to help anyone if I'm dead.'

Vivian frowned, let go of Clay's arm. 'He's right, Clay,' she said.

'We have to do something, Vivian,' said Clay. 'We can't just leave them here.'

'You'll start an epidemic,' she said. He could barely hear her over the clamour.

'I don't believe a word that asshole says. That's exactly what he told me over the Atlantic. That those men all had cholera. It was complete bullshit.'

'You're not thinking straight,' said Cobra. 'Even if they're not infected, how are we going to get them out? We don't have room in the vehicle. The guards aren't just going to let us walk out with them. They'll be killed before they get five steps out the front door. And so will we.'

'He's right,' said Vivian. She grabbed his hand. 'Come on.'

'One of my brothers is in there,' said Clay. 'I'm not leaving without him.'

'What the *fok* are you talking about?' said Cobra.

'Brigade. A 32-Bat scout. A friend. He's here.'

'This is bullshit,' said Cobra, glancing at Grasson. 'We have to go now. Stick to the plan, Straker.'

'Straker.' Brigade calling to him again, his name so clear against the shrill background, an island rising out of a storm-lashed sea. 'Straker, don't leave me.'

Vivian took Clay's arm and hugged it to her chest. 'Clay, please. Don't.'

Clay peeled away her fingers. Then he turned and ran to the cell. He'd just put the key into the lock when Brigade's hand reached through the bars and grabbed his and pulled him towards the bars.

'Straker,' Brigade whispered, his lips close to Clay's face. 'That man.'

'The doctor.'

'No. The other one.'

'He's with us.'

'No, Straker. Not.'

'Get back. Let me open the door.'

Brigade held fast, stopped Clay from turning the key. 'He's bad.'

'He was pretending. He's with us.'

'No. I've seen him. Here.'

Clay pushed the gun into the waistband of his trousers, and with his free hand pried Brigade's fingers away from the key. 'I don't have time to explain,' he said. He opened the cell door, handed Brigade the lab coat.

'What about them?' said Brigade, motioning towards the other cages.

'Come on,' Clay said, turning away and starting back towards the others.

If Cobra knew Brigade, he gave no sign of it. 'Fucking amateurs,' he said, shaking his head. 'You think we can just walk back out of here, with one more body than we came in with?'

'What are we going to do?' said Vivian.

'Change of plan,' said Clay, levelling his pistol at Grasson. 'The doctor here is going to call the night clerk and authorise a special shipment. He's going to authorise us to take one black subject out with us, to be delivered to another laboratory.'

Cobra glanced at Clay and nodded. Then he jabbed his gun into Grasson's side, started pushing him towards the door. 'Okay Straker. I'll take him to his office. He can make the call from there. You three meet me at the back door where we came in. Two minutes. And make it look good. Tie the black's hands. Straker you will have to be on the stretcher again.'

They started towards the door. Thirty-eight voices, man and beast, screamed in desperation as they left. And then the lights were out and Clay and Brigade and Vivian were walking back along the night-lit corridor and through the double doors into the east wing.

They retrieved the stretcher from the examination room where they'd left it, reaching the back door a moment later. Clay looked out through the window, across the floodlit tarmac towards the rear gate. The compound was quiet, the ambulance parked where they'd left it. There was no sign of the guards.

Clay pulled a lace from one of his shoes. 'Turn around,' he said to Brigade.

Brigade held out his wrists. 'Thank you,' he said.

Clay tied Brigade's wrists tight, then lay on the stretcher and pulled the blanket up to his neck.

'Do not trust him,' said Brigade, looking down the corridor.

'He's good,' said Vivian. 'He is Torch Commando. Just like me.'

Brigade shook his head. 'No.'

Just then, Cobra appeared at the end of the hall. His gait was steady, even, empty-handed and powerful. 'Okay,' he breathed as he reached them. 'Here's what we're going to do. Grasson has kindly initiated quarantine protocol for the receiving area of the facility. The clerk and the guards have moved to the safe area at the front of the complex. I've disabled the exterior cameras, and I have the codes to unlock the rear gate. Forget about the stretcher, Straker.' He looked at Vivian, his pale eyes flat and expressionless. 'Ready, Doctor?'

She nodded. 'What about Grasson?'

Cobra held her gaze. 'What about him?'

'What did you do?'

'Me? Nothing.'

'What do you mean?' she said.

Cobra stared at Brigade a moment. 'He was killed by a lone black prisoner who subsequently escaped.'

Clay could have sworn he saw Vivian's eyes light up.

32

He has a decade and a half to replay it in his mind.

Sitting on the veranda of that same seaside hotel in that decid-edly foreign port, and nothing much has changed. The old man who came by every morning thirteen years ago selling roasted groundnuts in little paper scoops is still there, his gait a little stiffer, the stoop in his back a little more pronounced. And every morning, just before dawn, the molybdenum sea still lies flat and expectant all the way across to Madagascar, as it will long after he is gone.

Clay is in the back of the ambulance. Brigade is there with him, his face battered and swollen so that Clay barely recognises him. They sway on the stretchers as Cobra hurtles the vehicle through the night. Vivian is up front with Cobra, and when Clay leans towards the driver's side of the rear compartment, he can just make out her slender right forearm, bare in the pale illumination of the instrument panel, tresses of now-black hair snaking loose across her shoulder.

Brigade clasps his hand around Clay's knee, looks straight into his soul. What they did, he says. What they are doing. There are tears in his eyes. Clay says nothing, tries to look back into the place from which the other man is speaking, but cannot. He knows then, but does not realise why until much later, that he lacks some essential quality indispensable for this task. A starting point, an anchor, some point of comparison. Belief.

The miles flood by, are frozen in place the moment they pass. The vehicle's suspension groans as they leave the paved main road for the potholed gravel track leading to the township. Brigade hides his face in his hands and drops his head to his knees. This hardened warrior, child of repression, cries. His shoulders shake. The smell of his tears comes thick over the other smells of the ambulance. All of this like prehistory, locked in permafrost. Eben was right.

After that, everything accelerates. It's as if time decides to double up, run ten minutes in five, compress itself in some sort of quantum rearrangement, a last sprint towards its final prison. The ambulance stops. They step out into cold night. There are lights. Open fires. Wood smoke drifts in the narrow lanes between rows of flotsam shacks. Oil lamps shine through makeshift windows. The house is grander than most, has a concrete foundation, glass in a few of the windows. The owner appears. He is a big man. His face is kind. He smiles at Vivian, hugs her tight. His sons hide the ambulance in a makeshift garage. This is the rest of her Torch cell.

The owner ushers them inside. No one is introduced. Names are not used. There is a thickness to everything, a palpable sense of loss pressing down on them. Clothes are brought for Brigade, bandages. Vivian hovers close to Cobra, seems not to want to leave his side.

In another place, in another time, perhaps events might have unfolded differently. Perhaps motivations, upbringings, the fundamental reckoning people have of the purpose of their own existence, of what life should mean, could have catalysed a different outcome. If you believed in that shit.

He remembers dogs barking. A single mournful cry at first, somewhere in the distance. And then others joining in, a wave coming closer, crashing towards them. Cobra hears it, too. Clay sees him shift towards the wall, away from the door. He reaches for his weapon, grabs Vivian's arm with his free hand.

The owner, too, has noticed, and starts towards the front door. He is standing two paces from the door when the thin sheet metal blows apart. The owner is thrown back as if hit by a wave, toppled. His chest is full of holes. Clay dives behind a table, pulls out the Beretta Cobra gave him. Something clatters off the far wall, spins across the floor, a silver canister. Clay recognises it immediately. It explodes somewhere to Clay's right. The room starts to fill with smoke. Clay takes a deep breath of clean air. The last thing he sees before he closes his eyes is Cobra crouching near the far wall. Vivian is gathered in his arms.

Clay waits, prone, eyes closed tight, not breathing. He hears Vivian coughing, spluttering. Then a bang as what is left of the front door is kicked in. Footsteps. Clay opens his eyes. The first man through the door is wearing a gas mask. Clay aims, fires twice. The man crashes to the floor in a heap. Someone is screaming outside, a woman. Clay's eyes burn. Tears stream across his face. Another man appears at the door, a shadow through the smoke. Blind, Clay raises the gun, pulls the trigger. Nothing. A jam. He pulls back the action, tries to clear the round by feel, pushing his finger into the chamber. The gun is empty. He is out of ammunition.

Clay scrambles to his feet, reaches out for the wall, feels his way towards where he remembers seeing a doorway, a kitchen beyond. His lungs are screaming. He starts a slow, deliberate exhalation. Soon he will have to breathe and the CS will flood his lungs. He stumbles along the wall. Gunshots crash outside, the buzz of an Uzi, screams.

And then he is hit hard in the stomach. Clay doubles over, gasps. The chlorobenzalmalononitrile hits his lungs. He retches uncontrollably. It is as if he has been turned inside out, doused in acid. Something jerks at his collar, and he is being dragged across the floor, out into the night. He tries to open his eyes, cannot. He is thrown to the ground. The air here is clean, and he gulps it in, tries to purge his lungs.

That's when he hears the voice. That same plaintive growl Clay had heard first in Ovamboland, that day at the airstrip, then again in the hospital. I have to thank you, Straker, says the voice in Afrikaans, close by. I am grateful to you both, he says. We have been trying to eliminate this cell for a long time. If the doctor hadn't saved you, we would never have been able to do it.

33

A Distant Port

The dose of CS gas he'd received was relatively small, one half-breath, a blink – enough to align the Z88's barrel with the intruder's chest. They'd been gassed with CS during training, the day before his nineteenth birthday, all of them crowded into that room and then a couple of canisters tossed in, the sergeants watching them through the glass, laughing. After that they knew why it was called tear gas.

But Vivian hadn't been so lucky. She lay in the dirt beside him, spluttering and retching, her eyes streaming.

He reached out and squeezed her hand. 'It won't last long,' he said. 'An hour at most.' Clay blinked his eyes open for a moment and caught sight of two figures standing nearby, a twin blur against a swirling night-lit surface. He pushed himself up to his knees and faced the figures.

'Where is the other one?' he heard one man say. 'The black.' It was Botha. Jesus. He must have followed them from the laboratory.

In the distance, a shouted reply in Afrikaans. 'Can't find him, *baas*.'

'*Kak*,' said Botha.

'Don't worry about him,' said the other man. 'We've got what we wanted. Let's get out of here.'

Clay's throat tightened up, realisation cascading through him. 'You bastard,' he spluttered.

The other man laughed. 'I thought it would be harder, convincing you. One broken finger and a little blood was all it took.'

Vivian shuddered then spewed vomit into the dirt. 'No,' she hissed.

'Yes,' said the second man.

'John?' she gasped.

The second man laughed. Clay did not know his name. It was the man in his own mind he called Cobra.

'What do you think, *poppie*?' Cobra said.

Vivian slumped to the ground. Desperate sobs shook through her body. It wasn't the CS.

'Search the ambulance,' shouted Botha. 'Retrieve any documents and the camera.'

'Time to go,' said Cobra. 'On your feet, Straker. Help the doctor.'

Clay wasn't going to ask what they were going to do. They would find out soon enough. He stood and lifted Vivian to her feet. She leaned unsteadily against him.

'Turn to your left,' said Cobra. 'Walk.'

Clay started forward, snatched a blink. His eyes were already recovering. He could keep them open for almost a second at a time now, enough to scan a quick arc of liquid ground. They were approaching a vehicle of some sort.

A loud bang cut the night. A shotgun going off, somewhere close. Clay crouched instinctively, pulling Vivian down with him.

'What the hell was that?' he heard Botha say. And then a moment later. 'Keep going, Straker.'

Clay straightened, made as if he was fumbling with Vivian, let her fall to the ground.

'Get the *fok* up,' barked Botha.

And then, closer this time, another blast – very loud so that the concussion slammed through his chest. And then all around, close, the sounds of gunfire, a 9 mm handgun banging off six, seven quick shots – Botha's? – then, very close, the same shotgun; the shot ripping through metal.

Clay pushed Vivian to the ground, dropped and rolled his body over hers. He heard a vehicle door slam shut, an engine starting, revving wildly. Then wheels spinning on gravel, stones spraying wooden doors, clattering from tin sheeting, and then the sound of the engine slowly fading in the distance.

As soon as he rolled off Vivian he knew something was wrong. At first he thought it might be the mucus that still streamed from her nose from the CS, a heavy wetness that seemed to cover his chest and arms. He opened his eyes. It was like looking out across the dark water of a rippled sea, the lights of a distant port playing out across the waves, prisming from a million surfaces, gas-flame blue, kerosene yellow, standby red, and the harsh white neon of overhead tubes. And spreading across her abdomen, a hot black stain.

'We must go.'

Clay looked up. It was Brigade. He was holding a pump-action shotgun.

'Help me,' Brigade said, slinging the shotgun over his shoulder, stooping to pull Vivian to her feet.

'Clay?' Vivian's voice was hoarse from the gas, weak. 'Is that you?'

'I'm here,' he said.

'Clay, I must tell you something.'

'Quiet, now,' said Clay. 'We're going to get you to a doctor.'

'Please, listen to me,' she whispered. 'I know what they are doing. You must listen to me and remember.'

'You can do it yourself.'

'No, Clay. We don't have much time.' She winced in pain, coughed. 'The equipment we saw in the lab. It's for isolating specific proteins – for discovering their structure and function within a living organism.' She powered out, lay gasping for breath.

'Vivian, please. This isn't the time for a biology lesson.' Clay and Brigade started to lift her. The front of her blouse was wet with blood.

She spasmed with the pain, pushed him away. 'Then you can develop drugs to target specific metabolic pathways. Do you see?'

Clay shook his head, tried to open his eyes. 'No,' he said.

'Those files we photographed. They explained how they were hydrolising protein samples into constituent amino acids. That's what all the ovens were for. You saw the test tubes. Blood from apes, from men.'

'Black and white.'

Vivian panted, grabbing Clay's arm. 'Get the camera.'

Clay looked at Brigade. 'Where is it?'

'In the house,' said Vivian, weakening rapidly. She clawed Clay close. 'You must remember what I am telling you. It was there in the files. You saw them.' Her voice was no more than a thread now.

'I remember,' he said. The pages he'd seen were in his head, but the words meant nothing to him.

'They're searching for a racially specific gene, Clay. They want to make a "black bomb." That's what they call it in the files: *swarts bom.*

Clay glanced at Brigade, back at Vivian. 'I don't understand,' he said.

'A chemical or biological agent they can release into the environment that will selectively kill black people, Clay. Blacks, but not whites. Kill, sexually sterilise, anything. And if they can't find the gene, they'll do it by direct delivery.' Vivian collapsed, the effort of speaking too great.

'Jesus Christ. A population control programme?'

'No, Clay. Genocide.'

Part V

34

Suicide Continent

4th October 1981,
Latitude 24° 43'S; Longitude 29° 37'E,
Gauteng Province, South Africa

They carried Vivian to the car. Brigade drove.

She'd been shot in the stomach. Clay tried to staunch the flow of blood, but no matter what he did, it kept coming, welling up from deep inside her until it covered his hands and arms, and his clothes were soaked in it.

At the main road, Brigade turned north.

'What are you doing?' shouted Clay from the back seat. 'Turn around. You're going the wrong way. The closest hospital is in Pretoria.' An hour away.

Vivian grabbed his hand. 'No, Clay,' she breathed.

Brigade kept going, north.

'Turn around, damn it,' Clay yelled.

Vivian looked up at him in the darkness. The whites of her eyes shone briefly in the light from a passing car. 'It will never work.'

'What won't work, Vivian?' said Clay.

She laughed, a thin rattle. 'We are all the same.'

He could barely hear her. 'I don't understand,' he said.

She closed her eyes, lay there, rocking limp and bloody in his arms as the car hurtled through the darkness. Sometime later she gasped and opened her eyes, stared right into him. Then she whispered something he could not make out, and she was gone.

He sat there for a long time, her head in his lap, feeling her go cold in his arms, the road unwinding before them in the pitiful illumination of the headlights, the platteland dark and deserted as they struck north towards the border.

It wouldn't be until much later that any of his would become real to him, as if only in recollection, by processing through memory, might the events of this time in his life attain some measure of tangibility, become actual.

Now, he felt nothing. Just a vague sense of detachment, a moving away from himself and his surroundings, from the cold night air buffeting through the car windows, from the smell of blood, from the solemnity of death.

It was then that he realised he'd become used to it.

After a while he tapped Brigade on the shoulder. 'She's gone,' he said.

Brigade nodded, kept driving.

Clay lay Vivian's head on the seat and stared into the myopia of the headlights. Cobra had played them. Whatever he'd said to Vivian to convince her, there in the woods outside the laboratory, had been a lie. Something about her husband, John. It must have been. Cobra had played with the most delicate part of her, the most desperate. Had he perhaps rekindled in her some hope that John was still alive, that he might help her find him again? That would explain her behaviour in the laboratory, the urgency with which she'd agreed with him, made of him an ally.

That Cobra was dead, shot by Brigade, by now covered over in a shallow grave somewhere in the township, was of no consolation. But there was synchronicity there, a measure of justice.

After a while, Brigade slowed the car and turned onto an unpaved road. A few kilometres in he stopped the car and turned out the lights.

'We have to leave her,' he said, opening the door and stepping out into the night.

By now, the effects of the CS had largely worn off. Clay's throat still burned, and it felt as if he'd sucked a cup of bleach up through his nose, but his head was clear and he could see. Standing next to Brigade, he looked out over the flat darkness of the veldt. Stars filled the sky so that there was no part of the firmament left unoccupied by some wavelength, some dead or dying history. He shivered. But the cold air felt good flowing over his cornea, across the scored flesh of his throat.

Brigade handed him a shovel.

They carried her away from the road, laid her on the ground and started digging.

When they lowered her into the grave, they did it gently, laid her face up. They stood a moment looking down at the shape of her, the starlight just touching the pale angle of her jaw, the rest of her in shadow. The first few shovelfuls were the hardest, the dirt a violation against the once-warm flesh, covering the pale skin, a crime being done. Once the body was covered, it got easier. Just more digging. Soldiers did a lot of that.

But he wasn't a soldier anymore.

Now, he wasn't anything.

When the job was done he leaned against his shovel and looked up at the stars. There was the proof. The irrefutable evidence of his utter insignificance, of hers. The scale of it, the futility, shocked him. He looked down at the mound of fresh soil. One of so many similar mounds scattered across Africa, a continent committing suicide.

'You heard what she said, before she died, about genocide?'

Brigade nodded.

'I never would have believed it.'

'The devil's work.'

'I didn't know. None of us did.'

'Some did,' said Brigade, standing there with one foot on the blade's shoulder, the shovel's shaft balancing against his upper arm. 'Many.'

'Do you believe me?'

Brigade looked hard into Clay's eyes. 'If I did not think it,' he said, 'I would not be here.'

'I'm sorry,' said Clay.

'So am I.'

Clay glanced at the grave. 'She fought.'

'Yes.'

'Not much of a place.'

'We had to do it.'

'I know.'

'If they stop us.'

'I know.'

Soon they were back in the car, heading north-east.

'We must try to reach the park before dawn,' said Brigade, staring straight ahead into the tunnel of light angling from the tarmac. 'We will keep to the small roads. It will take longer. But it is safer.'

'Mozambique,' said Clay.

'Yes. Through Kruger to the border.'

'Botha will have the word out. They'll be watching for us. We can't go into the park by road.'

'We will walk in.'

Clay nodded. They were still at least six hours away from the park. Between them and that twenty-thousand-square kilometre wilderness were hundreds of miles of farm and scrubland, villages and police stations, prying eyes and citizens eager to help the patriotic cause of white South Africa. Who knew what resources Botha might now deploy to hunt them down? Roadblocks? Spotter planes? Helicopters? Once the sun came up, they would be in trouble.

As they drove, hesitantly at first, Brigade related what had happened to him since they'd last seen each other.

After Clay and Eben had secreted themselves onto the C-130 that night at the makeshift airstrip, Brigade had left Zulaika to return to her village and he'd exfiled back to 32-Bat's Caprivi base on foot. He could only assume that Clay and Eben were dead. He'd reported what he'd seen to his Battalion Commander, as ordered, who passed on the report to Wade. Not long after, he'd heard that Wade had been killed. That was when they realised that the Broederbond was going to make sure they went back to the village near Rito to take out everyone who knew what was going on. Brigade had been sent, with two others, to warn the villagers to clear out before the parabats arrived. But his team was ambushed by UNITA before they were thirty kilometres inside Angola. They'd been waiting for them, knew exactly where they'd be and when. The Broederbond had people everywhere. His two companions were killed and he was captured. UNITA marched him around for a few days, and then one night he was drugged and flown south, eventually ending up at the Roodeplaat facility. 'I prayed for someone to come,' he said.

'I was trying to tell you,' he continued. 'The one I killed in the township tonight, he was there, at the laboratory, many times.'

'Cobra.'

'Yes,' said Brigade pointing to his own bicep. 'The snake.'

'I heard him speaking to the other one, the doctor. They were testing chemicals to make the women not able to have babies. Different ways of sterilising them. I heard them.'

'Jesus,' said Clay.

'I tried to tell you.'

Clay put his head in his hands. 'I'm sorry, Brigade. I thought...' But there was no point. It was done.

'It was good to kill him,' said Brigade.

When the sun rose over Mozambique, they were still an hour from the park boundary.

Commissioner Barbour: Mister Straker, your service records, which we have here before us, say that you were dishonourably discharged.

Witness: Yes, sir.

Commissioner Barbour: And are you aware of the accusations that accompanied this discharge?

Witness: I am now, sir.

Commissioner Barbour: Have you seen the records?

Witness: No, sir.

Commissioner Barbour: Then how can you know what they say?

Witness: A friend told me.

Commissioner Barbour: I am not sure you were told everything, Mister Straker.

Witness: I'm not sure what you mean, sir.

Commissioner Rotzenburg: He means, Mister Straker, that if you did know what was contained in those records, you would not have come back.

Witness does not answer.

Commissioner Rotzenburg: In your earlier testimony, you implied that Operation COAST was conducting experiments on human beings. Did you see such experiments occurring in the laboratory?

Witness: What was in my record, sir?

Commissioner Rotzenburg: The witness will answer the question. Did you see such experiments occurring?

Witness: Please, sir. You chose to bring up the issue of my record. Surely you can tell me what it says.

Commissioner Barbour: You were accused of war crimes, murder, and crimes against humanity.

Witness: Sir?

Commissioner Barbour: Of course, those charges were never brought to trial or proven, but they appear on your record. They formed the basis for your dishonourable discharge. There is the massacre near Rito, which you have testified about, and the murder in the dunes. There

are also accusations that you assisted in conducting
illegal medical experiments on prisoners of war.

Witness: That is total _____.

Commissioner Rotzenburg: So I ask you again, Mister
Straker. Did you see such experiments occurring in the
lab?

Witness: I don't know who made those accusations, but I had
no part in it. I was trying to stop it.

Commissioner Rotzenburg: How do you know that what you
claim transpired in that laboratory, actually did?

Witness: Brigade was there. He told me. It was clear what
they were doing. The samples we saw, the men and women
held in cages.

Commissioner Rotzenburg: I did not ask for your medical
opinion on what might have been happening. I asked you if
you had seen such experiments occurring. We are not here
to deal in conjecture. The witness must understand this.

Witness: I already told you about the experiments I saw,
that night at the airstrip in Angola. Dozens of them.

Commissioner Ksole: This colleague of yours, the one who
you say was held in the facility, did he witness such
experiments occurring within the facility?

Witness: I don't know if he actually saw them occurring.
But he heard them talking about it.

Commissioner Rotzenburg: So it is entirely possible that
these people you say you saw in the facility, were in
fact simply prisoners, and that no tests occurred at all.

Witness: Why keep prisoners in a secure medical testing
laboratory? It makes no sense.

Commissioner Rotzenburg: Or is it that these are simply the
recollections of a deluded, unstable mind?

Witness: No, I … I remember it. It happened, God ___ it.

Commissioner Rotzenburg: You have already admitted to
murder. Not only the South African citizen you killed
in the dunes, but a member of the security team sent to
bring you to justice in Soshanguve Township. This confirms
what we know from your records. Does the witness believe
that those murders were justified?

Witness: No, sir. Nothing can justify … What I mean is, it
was wartime. I've already told you, they were trying to
kill us, kill me. They killed Vivian.

Commissioner Barbour: Is that why the witness is here,

testifying to this commission? To seek forgiveness for
these murders?
Witness: Yes, sir. It is. For that, and for everything
    else. This country needs to know what happened, what our
    government did, the wrongs that were done, the terrible
    things. I am here for more than just reconciliation, or
    amnesty. I'm here to speak for those that can't.

35

Anything Other Than a Human Being

'*Merda*.' Brigade pulled over to the side of the road and stopped the car behind an old baobab that had somehow survived all these years on the road verge.

'Word got out fast,' said Clay, slumping down in his seat.

About three hundred metres ahead, a small column of vehicles was drawn up at the outskirts of a smoky early-morning village. Uniformed policemen moved among the vehicles. A Buffel armoured car watched over the scene, its hulk protruding from behind a corrugated-iron shack. Whether the roadblock was for them, he had no way of knowing. It was wartime. South Africa was under attack. Terrorist infiltrators were everywhere. Roadside checkpoints and random inspections were common.

'We can go around,' said Brigade.

'How far are we from the park?'

'Ten kilometres, for a bird.'

'We're not birds.'

'I don't know the roads.'

'We can't chance the roadblock. We walk.'

Brigade nodded. 'South first. We go around Phalabowra.'

Clay opened his door, stood in the red laterite of the roadside, this blood earth of his native land. He thought of Vivian lying cold in this same ground not so far from where he stood now. That same hollowness opened up inside him, and for a moment he stood staring into it and it was Vivian's grave, the one he had dug and then refilled. So much easier to fill than dig.

The sound of the car boot opening, a hinged cry, and the grave was gone, closed over.

Brigade slung a canvas pack onto his shoulder, handed Clay a steel water bottle, shouldered the sawn-off shotgun and started into the bush. Clay scanned the road ahead and back a moment then crouched, unfastened the car's rear registration plate and pulled it off. Then he removed the front plate and followed Brigade into the bush.

A hundred and fifty kilometres to the border, through some of the world's wildest country. No head start. A canteen, a handgun with nine rounds, a single diamond. Evidence that would rock the nation to its foundations. And if they did manage to reach Mozambique, then what? He had no passport, no identification, no money. By all accounts, the country was a shambles, riven by civil war. The usual scenario: one side supported by the Russians, the other by South Africa, and until just a couple of years ago, Rhodesia. He'd heard the stories of draft dodgers and deserters seeking refuge in Mozambique, they all had. Whether they were just stories, he had no idea. But he had no doubt that BOSS would pursue him wherever he went. One thing was sure: whatever happened, he would have to disappear, for a long time. Crowbar had been right.

They moved through the day, taking it in turns to carry the pack Brigade had managed to assemble before leaving the township. It contained some food, a couple of water bottles, a machete, and half a box of shells for the shotgun. Keeping to the footpaths and bush trails, they skirted villages and avoided roads, guided by Brigade's unerring sense of direction. By early afternoon they were striking resolutely east, the main Phalabowra corridor far enough to the north now, through a country of low scrub bushwillow and copper-leafed mopane, the long grasses dry and brittle here, the occasional jackalberry towering over them, its branches reaching arms of shade across the landscape, summer nearing its end, the promise of the first rains in the air, the smell of woodsmoke drifting on the breeze, the twittering of birds. And in this walking he was for a time detached, transported. Long minutes passed when he did not think of Eben or Vivian or the war or any of it. But then a sound would jar him from his reverie – a distant cry, a dog's bark – and he was back on patrol,

and each footstep was a descent into uncertainty, and he longed for
the familiar weight of his R4, the turgid potency of its long, curved
magazine, that feeling that, with this instrument, he was, for the first
and only time in his life, somehow *in control*.

Sometime later, when the sun had reached its zenith and started
its slow decline towards another meridian, the distant buzz of an
aircraft engine sent them running for the cover of a thicket of buffalo
thorn. They crouched at the base of one of the trees, looking up
through the branches as the sound grew louder. And then there it
was, close enough, perhaps a thousand feet up, a tiny single-engine
plane, sideslipping across the high, blue, cloud-strewn African sky.

'Bosbok,' said Clay. 'Military.'

Brigade nodded, watched the thing circle lazily and then disappear below the tree line.

They kept walking.

Later they skirted a small kraal. Three thatched rondavels clustered inside a circle of stacked thornbush. A woman with a baby at
her breast stood watching them through an opening in the palisade.
They nodded to her and moved on.

Evening came, the sun slanting long and yellow behind them,
casting long shadows across the dry grass clearings, two ghosts
warping over the landscape. As the light faded a herd of springbok
emerged from the bush and crossed their path. They stopped and
watched the animals pass, over a hundred and fifty of them, small
and lithe, quick footed.

'Hungry?' said Brigade.

Clay nodded, took out his Z88 and downed one of the stragglers
from thirty metres. The gun's retort sent the herd scattering for the
safety of the tree line. Soon they were alone again.

They stood over the carcass.

It was a beautiful animal, young, its fawn skin soft and supple. The
bullet had blown open its neck. The flesh glistened in the evening
sun. They carried it to the edge of the trees. Brigade worked with
deft strokes of his bush knife, slicing out the choicest cuts of meat,

skewering them on sharpened mopane sticks. Soon they had a fire going. Stars appeared, shining through the bare dry-season boughs of the trees like some distant reminder. They drank, checked their weapons; habit. The fire burned down to coals. They roasted the meat in silence, the lean flesh sizzling as night and all of its fiery beacons ascended around them.

The park boundary was close. Brigade reckoned a couple of kilometres at most. They would eat, catch a few hours of sleep, wait for the moon to rise, and then slip through the game fence soon after midnight. By the time the sun rose again they would be halfway to Mozambique.

☾

Sleep came quickly.

But it did not last. The events of the past days, the revelations complete and partial, the unanswered questions, trampled through Clay's mind. Pain gnawed at his side. He shifted on the cold ground, moving closer to the fire. As a boy, on the nights he could not sleep, he would lie in his bed under the eaves and listen to the wind rattle the casement windows and count to himself. He couldn't remember ever getting past twenty. Innocence sleeps. Now, by one hundred and fifty he was still wide awake, covered in sweat.

Three hours later, Brigade's boot sole rolled over Clay's shoulder. As he turned and raised himself up, a sharp pain creased his side. He reached for his ribs. His hand came away wet.

'Okay?' came Brigade's disembodied voice.

'*Lekker*,' said Clay, getting to his feet. There was no point inspecting the wound in the dark. They buried the coals and the car's registration plates and moved off in silence.

Less than an hour later they reached the park boundary. A single three-metre wire fence ran compass straight for as far as they could see through in both directions. On each side of the fence the bush had been hacked away to create a firebreak. They waited a while, shivering in the cold, watching. But the country here was bereft of men. Brigade cut the wire with a pair of pliers and they slipped through into the park.

A three-quarter moon rising low and oversized above the trees sent living shadows skittering across the landscape. Gone were the colours of the day, the russets and sky blues, the waxed tawn of the grasses and the grey naked limbs of trees. They moved through the black and moon-silvered territory like cats, navigating by the stars and planets, aware that they had entered a different world, one where they were no longer the masters, despite the weapons they carried and the skills they'd learned. Predators watched them, moonlight glinting from their dilated pupils. Big cats circled, wary, then moved on. A group of spotted hyenas, bolder, more dogged, caught their scent and started tracking them. Clay could feel them, pacing behind, keeping distance, could smell their powerful soapy secretions. Every time he turned to face them they would halt, watching him, noses twitching, eyes aflame, only to continue their shadowing as soon as he turned away.

By now, Clay knew that the wound in his side had opened up again. He could feel the blood spreading cold and wet down his side. With every step the pain worsened. He clamped his elbow down hard against his ribs and tried to keep up, but Brigade was setting a determined pace. As Clay fell back, the hyenas, emboldened, got closer. He could hear them, close behind now, moving through the bush, chattering, sniffing the air, tracking him. Again he stopped, turned to face them, brandished the Beretta as if this would have some meaning for them, that they might associate this small black object with danger. They were close, ten metres away, half a dozen of them, spread in a loose semi-circle, hunched low, close enough that he could see their cold eyes, the hunger, the anticipation, the complete lack of fear. Coarse hair bristled across their muscled shoulders. Moonlight glinted from big, exposed canines and bone-crushing carnassials. Tongues lolled. Noses twitched. Clay charged at them, shouting, waving the gun. They bolted into the night.

Brigade appeared. 'What are you doing?' he whispered. 'You must be quiet.'

'Hyenas,' Clay said. Moonlight drifted over them.

Brigade glanced at Clay's side. 'You are hurt.'

Clay said nothing.

Brigade inspected the ragged bandages then pulled Clay's shirt back down. 'Why did you not say?'

'Would it have changed anything?'

Brigade shook his head. 'We must keep going while it is dark.'

Clay nodded.

They continued on. Brigade slowed his pace now, stayed with Clay.

It wasn't long before the hyenas were back, wary of Brigade, standing off, circling.

'They can smell the blood,' said Brigade. '*Kom ons gaan.*' Let's go.

The hyenas were still with them as the moon rose and the sky cleared. And then, sometime deep into the night, they broke off and did not return, and for a while they were alone, sliding like upright phantoms through the pale and darkened bushland. And in the pale light of the constellations and the wan brightness of the moon, there was no dissemblance between them.

They kept to the open country when they could. The thicker bush made slow going. Thorns tore at their clothes and skin. Dry branches caught at their limbs and raked their faces. Above, the stars turned. And as had happened sometimes on the long night patrols he'd done in Angola, particularly during his second tour, a feeling came to him that this wilderness that he travelled through was a place of prehistory, a relic, at odds with the new reality of human ascendency, of wars and politics and the manifold machines of death. To him the wild had always been a place of dreams, of a past when humans were few and their hold on life precarious, when time was ruled still by the seasons and the rains, the triggers that launched the great continental migrations, when the herds were not constrained or channelled by fences but wandered a timeless Africa. But it was also a dream of his childhood, of long days spent wandering the bushland behind his uncle's summer house in Cape Province, of the rocks and trees and all of the creatures of that place, of walking with his parents in the rock-strewn alpine of the Cedarburg mountains, the dark crags of the Draakensburg. But all of these things were gone now, existing only within that elusive and unreliable dimension of memory.

Sometime during the night they turned north, crossed the Olifants River and the main east-west park road that followed it and then swung east towards the Lembobo Mountains, the long, rifted volcanic margin that marked the border with Mozambique. Brigade kept a painted dog's unrelenting pace, which Clay struggled to match, his body unused to the exertion after weeks of convalescence, the pain in his side growing. With every step he could feel his strength draining away. He put his head down, bit into the pain and kept walking.

As the sky lightened from starlit black to deep-ocean blue, shallowing over sand as the first hint of dawn touched the horizon, the mountains rose up dark and jagged before them. By the time they reached the base of the first broad talus slope, it was morning. The steep cliffs threw kilometre-long shadows across the slope and the bushveldt beyond. They found a cleft in the boulders, shaded by a clutch of acacia, where they could rest out of sight.

Brigade removed Clay's blood-soaked dressing and inspected his wound.

'At Rito?' he said, as he poured water across the place where the FAPLA shrapnel had torn through Clay's side.

Clay grunted an affirmative.

'Some of the stitches have come out,' said Brigade. 'Not all.'

'Do you have a needle?'

Brigade shook his head. 'Only this.' He held up a military field compress.

'Put it on and tie it tight,' said Clay.

After Brigade has applied the bandage, Clay stood, ran his hand along his side. The bleeding seemed to have stopped, for now. 'Let's *ontrek*,' he said. And then, looking into Brigade's eyes: 'Thank you.'

It took them more than two hours to reach the cliffs. Still in shadow, they stopped to rest and drink. They were almost out of water. Clay looked back the way they had come. All of the veldt lay below him, the mountain's black shadow retreating over the parched shrubland as the sun rose. And away past the farthest western horizon, still in darkness, the Okavango, the Caprivi Strip, and Angola, where the war was.

Monkeys watched them from rocky crags and the branches of ancient trees rooted into dark clefts in the cliffside. A Verreaux's Eagle, messenger of the Shona ancestors, circled high in the distance. And then, coming on the wind, the faint drone of an aircraft. They searched the sky. There, to the west, a speck on the horizon, a Bosbok spotter plane. They watched it for a while, then turned east and kept going.

The climbing was difficult. Clay sweated over blocky volcanic tuffs and sharp cuesta ridges, working from one handhold to the next, from ledge to rock face, up splayed gullies, climbing steadily despite the pain that pulsed through him each time he stretched or twisted his torso. And yet, he was alive. Without Vivian's efforts, he would have died. A graveside emptiness swept through him. Ice shivered through his vertebrae, skull to tail. Vivian.

A couple of hours later they stood at the apex of a rocky ridge. Half a kilometre below, Africa spread away flat and blue and hazy.

Brigade pulled the pack from his shoulder, handed it to Clay. 'The border,' he said, scuffing the ground with his boot heel. 'No fence. No line you can see. But it is here. You are in Mozambique.'

Clay looked out along the ridge.

Brigade reached into the pocket of his trousers and handed Clay an American twenty-dollar bill.

'What's this?' said Clay.

'All I could get.'

Clay shook his head, not understanding.

'I leave you here,' said Brigade.

Clay swallowed. He'd assumed Brigade would stay with him, that they would escape to Mozambique together. 'Where will you go?' he said.

'I will try to free those people. And then, if I am lucky, I will go back to my family.'

Clay caught his breath, wiped the sweat from his eyes, looked into Brigade's dark retinae. He towered over the other man, outweighed him by at least thirty kilos, but he felt suddenly very small in his presence. 'I run, you fight,' he said. He felt like a coward.

'No,' said Brigade. 'Now, our fighting is different. Please, take the money.'

Clay pushed the bill away. 'Keep it, *broer*,' he said.

Brigade resisted a moment, then relented, pocketed the note.

'They will be looking for you,' said Clay.

Brigade smiled, ran his hand across the coiled stubble of his chin. 'I have a disguise,' he said.

'I should go back with you,' Clay said. Part of him believed it.

'No,' said Brigade. 'You must tell the British and Americans what is happening here. If they know, they must do something.'

'Do you think they will?'

Brigade reached into his pocket and placed something in Clay's palm. It was an undeveloped canister of 35 mm film. 'From Doctor Vivian's camera,' he said. 'You must go. And you must put it in the newspapers.'

He wanted to tell Brigade how inadequate he felt for this task. Instead he nodded, closed his fist around the canister.

'You will do it?' Brigade said. 'You will tell them?'

'I will try,' said Clay, looking out over the rumpled green ridges to the darker blue of the Limpopo plain. He had never felt so alone.

'Take the shotgun,' said Brigade.

Clay pushed the weapon away. 'Keep it,' he said. 'You'll need it.'

'You must go to Maputo,' said Brigade, swinging the shotgun over his shoulder. 'There is a British Embassy there.'

Clay nodded.

Brigade put his hand on Clay's shoulder. 'Be careful. They will be hunting you. Even there.'

Clay looked into Brigade's eyes and offered his hand. Brigade took it, held it a long time. And then, without another word, Brigade turned away and started back down the mountain.

Clay stood and watched him move away through the steep ridged country, picking his way through the rocks, descending quickly. Soon he was gone, disappeared into the bush. After a while Clay caught sight of him again, farther down, very small now as he traversed another ridge, but soon he vanished again, this time for ever.

And he realised that it had been two days since he'd thought of this man as anything other than a fellow human being.

36

That Periphery of Darkness

He was far too young to understand.

Everything he had been taught to hold true lay shattered and broken as the rock beneath his feet. All those black-and-white certainties that had underpinned his life lay dead. Colour, crazed rainbows of uncertainty, flooded his cortex. He had nothing. No home, no country, no one to stand by.

The breeze was warm, blowing in from the east now, from Mozambique and the dark volcanic plain. There was ocean in it, too, humidity and faint whiffs of salt and iodine and the spice of the trade winds. He filled his lungs with it, let all of this provenance flow into him as if to replace all that he had lost.

Despite everything, he had survived. How many deaths had he witnessed? Kingfisher and Cooper, the piles of FAPLA dead at the airstrip, the poor unfortunates dosed and dying on the cargo deck of the Hercules, Vivian's face slowly vanishing behind that veil of red earth. And how many had he slain? Murdered with his own hands? Faces and moments he would never forget, was destined to replay in his dreams for the rest of his life. Sin enough to drown in.

Jesus, help me.

His heart was pounding. The ground shifted under his feet, knocking him off balance. Clouds spun into cruel vortices. His throat tightened. He fought for breath, dropped to his knees, dug his fingers into the riven, degraded rock of this new country, sank his forehead to the ground. Sobs shook his body, shivered through those places in him that had been rent open and then, somehow, miraculously repaired.

For what seemed a long time he remained there, a supplicant prostrated before infinity, terrified of looking up into that blue-and-white depth. Tears streamed down his face, permeated the rock.

Slowly, his breathing eased. Panic receded. He stood, looked out across the folded rift to the forest stretching blue and unbroken to the eastern horizon. The sun glowed warm on his face. He was alive. And suddenly, it was beautiful. All of it. The dry and burning bushland, the blue horizon of an unknown country, the African sky spread above him like the promise of a different future, the as-yet invisible path down the mountain and across the plain to the coast and all that life might yet bring. He was young, and the world entire lay there, ahead of him.

☾

It took him the rest of the day to leave the mountains behind and cross the dry bed of an un-named river to move into the flat, open mopane country north of Lake Massingir. He kept away from roads and major tracks, skirting any signs of human settlement or travail. This was a country at war. FRELIMO, the Marxist and ANC-leaning ruling party who'd taken over after the defeat of the Portuguese in 1972, were now fighting guerrilla opposition of their own, the supposedly South African-backed RENAMO. A civil war he wanted no part of. He was done with fighting. He would make his way east as far as the Rio Singuedeze and then strike south, skirting the eastern edge of the lake, and then south to the dam at Massingir. He estimated a little over a hundred and fifty kilometres by foot through the wilderness, allowing for the meanderings of the country. His knowledge of the geography of this new place was limited to what he remembered from school and Brigade's crude directions. From Massingir, there was a paved road all the way to Maputo. If he couldn't find some kind of transport, he'd walk. Once in the capital, he'd go straight to the British Embassy, quit Africa as soon as he could, leave the war behind, get to the UK. Maybe in London he might find some peace, learn a trade. In school he'd always been good at maths and physics, had thought he might be an engineer one day, like his father. Fix things. Build things rather than tear them down. Maybe. Maybe one day.

With the sun low in the sky behind him, he stopped under a sprawling mopane and pulled up his shirt. Blood slicked his side. He loosened the compress and inspected the wound. A gash about three centimetres in length had opened up at the lower end of the scar. The rest looked to be holding, but blood was seeping from the open part of the wound. It still looked clean, and there was no sign of infection. A few stitches, however crude, would close it up. Even a roll of tape, wound tight around his torso, would do. But he had no implements for the task, nothing to stop the slow loss of blood.

Clay waved away the flies, tightened the compress down onto the wound and kept going.

Shadows lengthened.

As the sun set he moved into more heavily wooded country. Mosquitoes came, ravenous squadrons of them. Waving them away put even more strain on his side, so he trudged on, tried to ignore them. With the sun's disc edging the treetops, he came upon a family of leopards, three of them draped in the limbs of a sprawling fire-blushed jackalberry. The pink and bone-white carcass of a zebra hung lifeless nearby, carried up in powerful jaws and slung hoofs-down across a branch. The cats watched him pass, eyes narrowed in watchful repose. He was so close he swore he could hear them purring. In school he'd been taught that leopards and the other big cats couldn't purr. So much for school.

Darkness came fast.

Clay gathered some wood, a few dry twigs, and using the matches from Brigade's pack, started a small fire. He huddled to the warmth, took stock. Bedsides the Beretta and half a clip of ammunition, he had the matches, a bush knife, the diamond, the notebook and the film. There was half a bottle of water, but no food, and he was bleeding again. He guessed he'd covered twenty kilometres since parting with Brigade at the border. If he could cover forty kilometres a day, he was still at least three days from Massingir. Normally, that pace wouldn't have been a problem. But weakened from loss of blood and with the danger of infection looming, it would be a tough go.

In the firelight, he searched inside the pack, checked the pockets for anything that might have been of use, found nothing. He pulled off his shirt, unstrapped the sodden compress and dropped it into the fire. It hissed and steamed in the flames. Using the knife, he cut strips from the hem of his shirt and used them to bind his side. It was crude, but by cinching down hard he was able to staunch the leakage of blood. He threaded what was left of the shirt over his shoulders and huddled up to the fire.

The sky was clear. Stars appeared. He knew he should keep going. Find water. Kill something for food. Make progress towards his destination. The stars were there, a multitude, so bright now, pointing the way. East, then south. Away from this place, this doomed continent. But exhaustion beckoned, bid him stay. All he needed was a few more minutes. A little more rest. A few moments more to warm himself, then he would go.

He lay panting by the fire, fighting back the dark edge of sleep. And that periphery of darkness was the forest itself, the collapsing cocoon of firelight that defined his world. Eyes peered in at him, a double semicircle of flashing, glinting faces. And then the laughing came, that mocking, hysterical bark.

Clay reached for the Beretta, chambered a round, pushed himself up to one knee, tried to stand. The first hyena burst towards him. Off balance, he fired.

☾

Commissioner Ksole: What are these, Mister Straker?

Witness: These are prints of the documents we photographed at the Roodeplaat laboratory.

Commissioner Ksole: The quality of some of these prints is very poor.

Witness: Yes, sir. By the time I had the film developed, it was badly degraded.

Commissioner Barbour: But some of them are quite clear.

Commissioner Ksole: Tell us, Mister Straker, in your own words. Tell us what these photographs show.

Witness: The first photo is of a document. It is dated 5th March 1981. 7th Medical Battalion, SAMS. Operation COAST. Experimental Suite GR7-B. Objective: Development of a genetically specific targeted sterilisation agent to control and reduce the black population of South Africa and neighbouring territories. Chemical and biological options to be investigated.

Commissioner Ksole: Go on, Mister Straker.

Witness: SAMS is authorised to use whatever means needed to acquire necessary chemical and biological agents and other required technology overseas.

Commissioner Rotzenburg: How do we know these so-called photographs are not elaborate fakes? It would not be difficult to create such documents.

Witness: If the commission would formally investigate COAST and its operations, these photos could be compared to actual documents. You would see that they are authentic.

Commissioner Ksole: Please continue, Mister Straker.

Witness: Yes, sir. The second and third photos are of documents from the same dossier. They state: Human testing is essential. Authorisation to test promising formulations on enemies of the state. If genetic targeting cannot be developed in time, direct delivery methods are to be sought.

Commissioner Rotzenburg: If these documents are real, as the witness claims, then the question again arises, as it has before, of the witness's own involvement in these activities.

Commissioner Barbour: Is that all, son?

Witness: No, sir.

Commissioner Barbour: Proceed.

Witness: Photograph Four: by authorisation of the President
   of the Republic.

37

Heavenward

The face was young, the skin like polished wood.

Clay narrowed his eyes against the day. Light streamed through the trees in thick woolly beams, haloing the boy's head.

'*África do Sul?*' the boy said.

'*Sim,*' said Clay. Yes.

The boy pointed at Clay's side. '*Hiena?*' he said.

Clay looked past the boy. A spotted hyena lay motionless on the ground, not far from the dead ash of the fire. Its coarse fur was matted with blood.

Clay nodded.

The boy handed him a gourd. '*Agua,*' he said.

Clay raised himself, drank, collapsed back to the ground.

The boy stood, spoke something in Xitsonga that Clay could not understand. Then he stooped to pick something up. It was Clay's Berretta. The boy held the weapon in his little hands, gazing at it as if it were some precious treasure.

Clay reached out a hand, grunting in pain. '*Por favor,*' he said.

The boy stared into Clay's eyes a moment, handed him the gun, then turned and ran barefoot into the trees.

Clay reached for Brigade's pack, checked its contents. Nothing was missing. He must have passed out right after the hyenas attacked. He only remembered firing one shot, but he counted three 9 mm shell casings scattered about him. The pain in his side had bloomed into a constant aching roar, and he could feel the fever pulsing through his body. Every movement drove spikes of pain into his side.

Sometime later, the boy reappeared. An old man was with him, his skin like weathered hide. He had a small white beard and carried a wooden spear. The old man and the boy helped Clay to his feet, gathered his things, and started walking him through the forest.

It was slow going. Clay was much bigger than the villagers, and they struggled to support him. Every few metres they had to stop, panting, glistening with sweat, and prop him against the trunk of a tree. After a few minutes of rest they would wedge themselves beneath his shoulders and hoist him up again, coax him forward.

Clay fought to stay conscious, to keep moving. His legs felt like stone columns, rigid and impossibly heavy. Every step sent exquisite shards of pain slicing through his torso. Fever raged through him. He was bleeding again, and the old man kept looking down at Clay's side, pushing his withered bony hand against the wound. Had something ruptured inside, where the shrapnel had torn through his insides? Infection had set in. He could feel it. What he needed was a doctor. He needed Vivian. She was a doctor. Where had she gone? She'd been with him in the car. Yes. With Brigade. Maybe she'd gone to pray. Someone call for a casevac. Where the hell was Eben? Call for a casevac.

Light strobed through the trees. Emerging into some sort of clearing, he stumbled, fell to the ground. And then voices, a sensation of being lifted, carried. The sounds of gunfire, close now, the whump of the Puma's rotors, the arc cut of metal rupturing air, confusion, dust swirling in the wash, the whine of the turbines, the magnetic chop of the door guns. The casevac was on the way. They were coming for him.

When he opened his eyes he was looking up into the vaulted ceiling of a cathedral. It was Saint Giles, in Edinburgh. He'd only seen it once, as a boy, on his only trip 'home' with his parents. He'd been nine years old. Stone pillars of ancient mopane towered above him. Spreading boughs arched across the sky. Sun streamed through the golden leaves of medieval stained glass. He turned his head, looked out across the dry earthen nave. A thornbush palisade. A thatched rondavel pulpit, another beyond. Wood smoke wisping heavenward.

A small black girl emerged from behind one of the huts. She wore a colourful skirt and her hair was elaborately braided. She toddled out towards him, distracted by something in the trees, a bird or a butterfly. Suddenly she stopped, swaying on unsteady legs, looking at Clay, eyes wide. She blinked once, twice. Her mouth fell open in a silent cry. Then she turned and ran screaming back from where she'd come.

Sometime later, two men came. They carried him into one of the huts, lay him on a bed of dry grass covered in a coarse woollen blanket. Inside, it was dark, close. The boy appeared, the one who'd first found him in the bush. With him was the old man.

'*Médico*,' the boy said in Portuguese. Doctor.

'*Sim*,' said Clay. Yes.

'He will fix.'

The old man kneeled in the earth beside Clay. He was bare chested and wore some kind of headdress. There were deep scars across his torso, three parallel troughs, as if he'd been raked by a set of claws. He inspected Clay's side, bent his head to the wound and sniffed it.

'*Hambanisa*,' he said, frowning.

Clay looked at the boy. 'What does he say?'

'A bad spirit,' said the boy in Portuguese, tapping his own chest. 'Inside.'

'Jesus Christ,' said Clay. Yes.

The old man spoke again.

The boy translated. 'He says, this is the country of spirits.'

The old man rocked back on his heels and said something to the boy, who immediately disappeared. With a surprising gentleness, the old man cut away the strips of material that Clay had used to bind the wound, and dropped them into a small, wooden bowl.

'*Hlantswa*,' said the old man, pointing to the wound. His voice was soft, like a woman's. Then he reached into a small bok-skin pouch and withdrew a small spike of polished bone. '*Rhunga*,' he said. '*Rhunga*.'

Clay shook his head. 'Don't understand you, old man,' he said in Afrikaans. And then in Portuguese: '*Não entendo*.'

The man smiled, made a dipping motion with the spike, holding it between his thumb and index finger.

The boy reappeared with two steaming bowls, one in each hand. He set one of the bowls down and handed the other to the old man. The old man reached his hand behind Clay's head and brought the bowl to his lips.

'Drink,' said the boy in Portuguese. 'It will make you sleep. Then he will clean and sew you.'

Clay drank. 'Ask him, can he make the spirit go away?'

The boy spoke. The old man listened, rubbed his chin, looked into Clay's eyes. Then he smiled, said something in Xitsonga.

'My grandfather says no. He says you must learn to live with it.'

Clay let his head sink back onto the straw and closed his eyes.

☾

Thirteen years later, back in that same country again, he would come to see that the old man had been right. He was possessed. For more than a decade he had tried to apply mathematics and the laws of physics to something that no logic could explain. Later, after he'd met Rania, he'd even tried religion, in his own way. How or exactly when the spirit had entered his soul, if that was where it resided, and indeed if such a place existed, he could only guess. What were the origins of this visitant? Was it perhaps the essence of one of those he'd murdered? What, exactly, did it want of him? For more than a decade, he'd done as the old man had counselled – tried to live with it, locked in an uneasy truce. But he'd always held to the hope that one day exorcism might be possible. That's why he'd come back.

When he woke, it was dark.

A small flame glowed in the hut's stone hearth. He pushed back the blanket. Underneath, he was naked. The wound was closed, packed with some kind of poultice. The bleeding had stopped. His fever was gone. The pain was still there – his side throbbed – but the jagged white heat of before was gone. Beside him, set on a piece of hide, were his few things: the Beretta, the small pouch with the diamond, the film, the notebook, and Brigade's backpack.

Clay tried to sit up, but the pain in his side sent him back. He closed his eyes. He knew that he needed to rest now, to let the wound heal properly. That's what Vivian would have said. What she had said. A vision of her face came to him, pale in the bottom of the grave he'd dug for her, the red earth raining down on that beautiful, flawlessly freckled skin.

He jerked his eyes open.

The boy was standing above him, holding a small oil lamp. Flame light danced across the thatched weave of the hut's walls.

'You shouted,' said the boy.

'I was dreaming.'

'It is the spirit.'

'No.'

'Yes. This is what my grandfather says.'

'It was a dream.'

'You have been shouting all night, all day.'

'How long?'

The boy held up two fingers. Two days. Then he placed a steaming bowl on the ground beside Clay. 'Eat.'

Clay pulled down the blanket, pointed to the poultice covering the wound. 'What is this?'

The boy pointed to the ceiling. 'Mopane leaves.' He raised his fingers to his mouth, made a chewing motion. 'It heals, and cleans.'

Clay nodded. 'Thank you. And thank your grandfather.'

The boy looked down at the gun. 'Where do you go?'

'Maputo.'

'There is war.'

'There is war everywhere.'

'And you are a soldier?'

'No. Not now.'

'Soldiers come here sometimes. But they are not like you.'

'Which soldiers?'

'Black men. From the coast.'

'Government soldiers?'

'No. Not.'

'RENAMO?'

The boy nodded. 'They take things.'

'Take things?'

'Yes. Goats. Fruit. They wanted to take my sister, but my father stopped them.'

Clay said nothing, pushed back everything that came flooding at him.

'My sisters are very afraid of you.'

'I am not like those soldiers.' He said it, heard the words leave his mouth and inhabit this small place, felt the falsity echo back towards him.

'That is good,' said the boy. 'Miringo is sixteen. I know why the soldiers want to take her.'

'Please tell your family not to worry.'

The boy nodded. 'But my littlest sister will still be afraid.'

Clay glanced at the Beretta. 'Because of this?'

The boy shook his head. 'No. She thinks you are *fantasma*. A ghost.'

'The evil spirit.'

'No,' said the boy. 'She has never seen a white man before. As children we learn, white man is ghost. Walking dead.'

Clay swallowed hard, took a few shallow breaths. 'The shouting.'

'Yes.'

'Tell her I am not dead.'

The boy smiled. 'Grandfather says eat and sleep.'

The boy made to leave.

'Wait,' said Clay.

The boy turned back to face him.

'What is your name?'

'Matimu. It means history.'

'Matimu. History. This spirit. Inside me. What does it want?'

The boy frowned. 'Bad things.'

'How do you know?'

'Grandfather has been speaking with it. While you are sleeping.'

Clay took a shallow breath. 'What does it say?'

'It is attached to you very strongly, Grandfather says.'

'What does it want?'

'It wants to kill.'

Clay looked away. The boy didn't move. 'Please bring me some of that drink, Matimu,' Clay said. 'The one that makes you sleep.'

38

Nothing Here Is Yours

When he awoke it was to shouting.

But it wasn't a dream, and it wasn't his own screams that tore him from the deep, dreamless sleep he'd fallen into. For the briefest moment, he thought he was back on Fireforce standby at Ondangwa, and the shouting was the senior NCOs rousing the men, sending them to the waiting helicopters. And then it registered: the slivered shafts of sunlight streaming through the gaps in the thatching, the smell of charcoal and mopane leaves, the bleating of goats, the feel of the wool blanket against his skin. And now, the screams of women, adding to the crescendo.

Clay pushed himself up onto his knees, grabbed the Beretta, chambered a round. He swayed a moment, breathing hard, letting the pain move through him. The hut was too small for him to stand upright, so he crawled to the entrance and peered through a gap between the thatch and the flap.

Two black men in jungle camouflage uniforms stood in the middle of the kraal, facing Matimu, his father and grandfather. One of the soldiers – if that's what they were – was older, heavier and carried an R4. The other, younger, taller, appeared unarmed except for a knife in a scabbard at his belt. His hand was clasped around the wrist of a young girl. She looked to be about sixteen, and was naked except for a short skirt fashioned from some kind of hide, and colourful beaded anklets.

Clay crawled to the other side of the flap, surveyed the rest of the kraal. There were no other soldiers that he could see. The rest of their unit couldn't be far, though. Perhaps they were waiting outside the kraal, in the clearing, or in the forest beyond. If they were RENAMO – and judging by the R4 the guy was carrying, they were – then they were ostensibly friends, supported by South Africa in their fight against the communists. Were these the soldiers Matimu had spoken of, the ones who came to take?

A high-pitched scream sent Clay scuttling back to the other side of the flap. The girl was struggling, trying to pull her arm free of the soldier's grasp. The father was pleading with the men now in rapid Xitsonga, waving his hands. Suddenly, Matimu broke from the group and ran towards the inner kraal. He emerged a few moments later with a pair of goats on twine leads. He led the animals to where the men stood, handed the leads to his father. His father stepped towards the soldiers and offered them the animals.

The younger soldier laughed, pulling the girl to him, and wrapped his hand around her waist, grabbed for her breasts. She wailed, struggling to free herself. The soldier held her a moment, but she was strong. She whipped her head to the side and sank her teeth into the man's ear, jerking her head back. The soldier screamed and fell to the ground, one hand raised to what was left of his ear. The girl spat something to the ground and ran to her father, blood pouring from her mouth.

The other soldier glanced down at his companion and levelled his rifle at the family. The girl was sobbing, clutching her father. They all stood there – the soldier, the father and grandfather, the girl, Matimu – staring at each other. No one spoke.

Clay froze. This was not his war, not his country, perhaps not even his continent anymore, now that he had determined to leave it behind. Certainly, these were not his people. They had offered him succour, probably saved his life. But they were of a different race. A race he'd been taught to consider as inferior, as not quite human, not like *us*.

It was, in the end, the final unveiling. And as he stepped from the hut, naked but for his scars, Beretta steady in his right hand, the left supporting the base of the pistol and his right hand as he'd been taught, careful to keep the left thumb down to avoid the recoil of the slide, he knew that everything he'd been told, everything he'd learned in school, his whole life, had been a lie. And it wasn't the brutality of the war, or the banality of the things that he'd grown up with every day, or the chemicals, or the experiments, or even the way Vivian had died in his arms. It wasn't any of that. It was this. Right now. This poor family who'd taken him in, rather than leaving him to the hyenas.

'*Pare*,' Clay shouted, advancing towards the soldiers. Stop.

The soldier with the R4 swivelled towards him, rifle at his hip. He looked surprised, upset at being interrupted. But immediately his countenance changed and he lowered his weapon. 'My friend,' he said in Afrikaans, smiling as he looked Clay up and down.

Clay kept his pistol trained on the man's chest.

'South Africa?' the soldier said.

Clay nodded.

'Special Forces?'

'That's right, *bru*.' He'd heard that special units of the SADF were operating inside Mozambique, but he'd always considered it to be rumour, like so much of the other bullshit the men passed around on a daily basis.

'We are RENAMO,' said the soldier. 'Allies.'

'This is my village,' said Clay. 'Please leave.'

The soldier glanced at the young girl. A smiled creased his face. 'Yes, I understand.'

'Understand whatever you like.'

'*Fok jou*,' screamed the younger soldier.

Clay stood impassive, gun aimed at the armed man's chest.

The elder soldier frowned, hefted the R4 in his hands, as if assessing its power in this situation. By now, his younger companion had staggered to his feet, hand clamped to the side of his head. Blood flowed through his fingers and dripped onto his uniform. He glared at the girl, muttering to himself.

'We will be back,' said the elder soldier.

'I'll be here,' said Clay.

The soldier shrugged, shouldered the R4, took his injured colleague by the arm and started guiding him towards the palisade. Clay exhaled, lowered his pistol, watched them go.

The soldiers were almost to the gate when the younger man stopped and turned and faced Clay.

'Nothing here is yours, white man,' he shouted in Afrikaans, fists clenched at his sides. 'Do you hear me? Nothing.'

39

You Could Show Me How

Slowly, Clay healed.

Every morning Matimu's grandfather would come and clean his wound, check the stitching, apply more of the chewed mopane poultice. Matimu would bring him food and water, sit with him long hours, and Clay would tell him about the Scotland he knew briefly as a boy, about the ocean, about the planets and the stars. Matimu soaked it all up, his eyes flashing with wonder.

Clay kept the Beretta close, but after a week the soldiers still hadn't returned. He could have killed them, but the risk of reprisal was too great. Either the RENAMO unit they belonged to had moved off, or the threat of tangling with South African Special Forces was enough to keep them away. But he couldn't stay here forever.

One morning, rain came. Matimu sat with him listening to the thick droplets tapping on the thatch of the roof, the water guttering to the ground outside the entrance.

The boy glanced outside. 'The rain is early.'

Clay nodded.

'My mother and sisters will be glad,' said Matimu after a long time. 'Their crops will grow.' Small talk.

'Your Portuguese is good,' said Clay. '*Muito bom.*' Better than mine.

Matimu smiled.

'Do you go to school?'

'School is very far.'

'How did you learn?'

'My father teaches me.'

'Good.'

Thunder rumbled like artillery in the distance, walked out across the plain in big booming footsteps. The boy glanced outside then pointed at the place where his wound was. 'The hyenas did not do this.'

'No.'

The boy considered this a moment. 'If the soldiers come back…'

'They won't.'

'But you will leave.'

'Yes. There is something I must do.'

'If they come after you leave?'

'They won't.'

'How can you be sure?'

'I'm sure,' he lied.

Matimu directed his big-eyed gaze at the handgun. 'Teach me to use it,' he said.

'No,' said Clay.

'If you give it to me, I can protect my family.'

Clay closed his eyes, opened them again. 'What do you think would happen if you shot them?'

'They would be dead.'

'Others would come.'

The boy frowned, sat a long time saying nothing. The rain had stopped. Sunlight lit the hut. Outside, the ground steamed.

'What must you do?' said Matimu after a while.

It was a question Clay was unprepared to answer. He was running. That's what he was doing. He was saving himself. While Brigade and others stayed and fought against the lie, while so many others had died fighting – Zulaika, Wade, Vivian – Clay was running. He'd promised Brigade and Vivian that he'd tell the world about Operation COAST. But what did he actually know? And, more importantly, what could he prove?

All he had was fragments, isolated glimpses of something which he could not quite grasp. A black bomb? Was it even possible? What kind of warped mind could even conceive of such a thing? No one would believe it. And what had Vivian meant when she'd said: *We are all the same?* Her dying words. The possibilities circled in his head, collided and dissipated like the steam rising from the parched earth outside the hut. How could he ever hope to explain any of it to the press, let alone some foreign authority, if he couldn't make sense of it himself? And all he had was his word. The word of a deserter. A traitor. A murderer.

And he knew they would come for him.

'The same thing you must do,' said Clay, putting his hand on the boy's head. 'Live.'

'Then live here,' Matimu said after a time. 'With us. You could marry my sister.'

Clay smiled at the thought.

'I could teach you how to hunt, how to keep the goats safe. You could show me how to shoot. I would be uncle to your children.'

'I'm sure she wouldn't want me,' said Clay.

'Oh, yes. She does. She could have copper babies.'

Clay rumpled his brow. 'Copper?'

'White and black together. She says they come out copper coloured.'

'She does?'

The boy nodded. 'She told me yesterday. She wants you to stay also. We all do.'

☾

Commissioner Ksole: Are you sure that the men you saw in Mozambique were RENAMO?

Witness: Yes. Definitely. They were armed with South African-made and supplied weapons. They specifically mentioned SADF Special Forces.

Commissioner Ksole: Are you sure?

Witness: Yes, sir.

Commissioner Barbour: This is extremely important, Mister Straker. If you are correct, this is the first time we have had first-hand, eyewitness accounts of government-authorised incursions into Mozambique.

Commissioner Ksole: On this basis, a full investigation of the SADF and its activities is warranted.

Commissioner Rotzenburg: That is premature, and not in the power or mandate of this commission.

Commissioner Barbour: Son, is there anything else you can tell us, about, ah, about what happened to you in Mozambique.

Witness: I didn't stay with that family. I left two weeks later. I walked to Massinga. It took me ten days. From there I went overland to Maputo, by bus mostly. Some I walked. But I did go back.

Commissioner Barbour: Back? To the village, the family kraal?

Witness: Yes, sir.

Commissioner Barbour: When did you go back, son?

Witness: Last week.

Commissioner Barbour: A few days ago?

Witness: Yes, sir. Before coming here to testify. I went back to that same place.

Commissioner Barbour: And? Is there something you would like to share with us?

Witness does not answer.

Commissioner Barbour: Son? Are you alright?

Commissioner Lacy: Perhaps we should recess.

Witness: No. I … I went back to see, to see if…

Commissioner Barbour: And what did you find?

Witness: Nothing. There was nothing there.

Commissioner Barbour: It was a long time ago. They

probably, ah, moved on. Most in that region are
itinerant.

Witness: It was hard to find. Scrub trees had taken over.
Mopane and bushwillow. But it was definitely the spot. I
found a patch of melons, gone wild. The skulls and bones
of goats. And I found something else. Scattered all over
the place where the kraal had been. 5.56 millimetre shell
casings. Dozens of them. Old. South African made.

40

117 Days

November 1982,
Maputo, Mozambique, one year later

The civil war dragged on. For Maputo it meant continuing shortages of everything, frequent lengthy power cuts, and the never-ending inefficiencies of the workers' committees and state-run services. Like everywhere, life below the official surface continued.

November was a time of unsettled weather, the heavy rains of December and January looming in the towering, anvil-topped cumulonimbus massing over the western plains, the distant echo of thunder. Clay peeled his shirt away from his back, wiped his brow, and climbed the two flights of crumbling cement stairs to the one-bedroom flat he'd rented above a tailor's shop in the old town, just off the recently renamed Avenida Vladimir Lenin. He stopped a few steps short of the door, pushed himself up against the wall, palmed the handle of the Z88 in his belt. He crept closer to the door. Before he'd left that morning he'd dusted the door knob with cement powder. He kept a small bag of it inside the flat, near the doorway. The lightest layer was enough to reveal any handling. It was undisturbed.

He let go of the handgun, pulled out his keys and opened the door. Inside, it was dark, despite the tropical sun blazing outside. Clay closed and locked the door, threw the keys onto the table set against the wall near the only window and flung open the shutters. The stink of the harbour wafted through the room, the smell of rotting fish from the docks, rubbish piled in the alley below, woodsmoke from a thousand braziers and open fires.

It had been another morning of frustration at the British Embassy. Obtaining a passport without proof of citizenship was proving impossible. He'd put his name on a list of asylum seekers, had filled out the forms months ago, but apparently processing was slow, and there was a glut of South Africans clogging up the system, so many of them here fleeing the war and the regime. Be patient, the embassy staff told him. Meanwhile, every day was an exercise in paranoia. The communist government seemingly paid him no attention. He was, after all, just another South African draft dodger, one of the hundreds of young, bearded, bedraggled white men floating around the city, congregating in the same bars and clubs.

A few days after he'd arrived in the city, he'd been interrogated by what could only have been a KGB agent – thick Russian accent; leather jacket despite the heat; pallid Arctic Circle skin stretched over Mongol cheekbones; cheap plastic sunglasses. The man had jotted a few things down in a notebook – Clay's name, unit, the fact that he was a deserter – and warned him not to leave the city without notifying the police.

Since then, Clay had moved around the city, never staying anywhere longer than a few weeks. He shunned other South Africans, stayed away from their haunts, wary of informants. That BOSS was here, too, he had no doubt.

After a few weeks he'd found a fence for his diamond. Clay was sure the guy had ripped him off, but it gave him enough money to survive, even occasionally have a couple of cold beers and a plate of grilled prawns by the pool at the Polana hotel, listening to the bikini-clad Uzbek singers slaughter Dylan under the watchful eye of their KGB minders. Otherwise, he kept a low profile, bought food from local markets, stayed clear of trouble. At least his Portuguese was getting good.

The only friend he'd made was an elderly Jewish lady who lived not far from the Polana in a rambling colonial-era house. South

African originally, she'd been exiled for anti-apartheid activities in the early 1960s, after the Sharpesville Massacre. A devout communist, she'd come to Maputo in 1978 and taken a post lecturing at the university. He met her one day at the university library. Clay had gone to see if there were any engineering or mathematics textbooks, hoping to spend a few hours learning, dreaming of a new, different kind of life. They'd met at the sign-out desk. Old enough to be his mother, she had a sharp, angular face, a thick head of dark hair and deep, penetrating eyes. Clay had been refused a library card. She'd picked up the books, glanced at the titles, smiled at him, and offered to take out the books on his behalf.

She introduced herself as Ruth. They agreed to meet back at the library two weeks later. From then on, their regular meetings had been the highlight of Clay's fortnights. She was witty, vivacious, and hyper-intelligent. Sometimes they'd have coffee together in a local café and talk about politics, the situation in Mozambique. She never probed Clay about his past, never asked him about the scars he carried.

About a month after they met, she gave Clay a signed copy of one of the books she'd written. It was in English: *117 Days*, it was called. Clay read it in a single day, deep into the night, a harrowing account of her detention, imprisonment and torture at the hands of South Africa Police Special Branch in the 1960s. After finishing it, he took a long walk along the beach, north out of the city, and watched the sun rise over the Indian Ocean.

And then in September, Ruth stopped showing up at the library. At first Clay had thought it might have been because of work, or sickness. Twice more she missed their rendezvous. Finally, Clay had gone to the faculty building where she taught. Her colleagues told him that she'd been killed back in August. She'd received a letter in the post. When she'd opened it, it had exploded, killing her instantly.

Clay cracked the fridge and grabbed a beer. The power was off again and the beer had warmed. He opened it anyway, drank half the bottle down. Two months he'd been in this flat, now. Too long. He was getting lazy. It was time to move. Tomorrow, he'd find another place.

Clay had just settled back on his cot, cracked open his disintegrating copy of *War and Peace* – one of the few books in English he'd managed to find in the city – when there was a knock on the door. Clay dog-eared the page he was on, closed the book, slipped the elastic back around the volume and palmed the Beretta.

Seconds passed.

The knock again.

'*Senhor? Por Favor.*' It was his landlady, Senhora Lizabet.

Clay swung his feet to the floor, slid the Beretta into the belt of his trousers at the small of his back, flipped his shirt over it, and walked to the door. It was unusual for Senhora Lizabet to come to his door. If she wanted to speak with him, usually about the weekly rent, she'd catch him near the front door of the building.

'*O que é isso, Senhora?*' Clay called out. What is it?

A pause, and then the same words as before. Sir. Please. Clay took a step back. Something was wrong.

'*Agora não,*' said Clay. Not now. 'I'm busy. Come back later.'

Whispering outside, the sound of footsteps. 'A friend is here to see you,' she said in Portuguese.

'What friend?' asked Clay.

'Just open the *fokken* door, Straker.' A man's voice, in Afrikaans.

And then the sound of a key being thrust into the lock.

Clay stepped away, oblique to the door, drew the Z88, chambered a round. Just as he did the door flew open.

It was the first time Clay had seen him out of uniform.

'Put the gun down, Straker,' said Crowbar.

41

Orders

Crowbar closed the door behind him and stood surveying the flat. He wore blue jeans, a white, collared shirt and a tan canvas jacket, none of which disguised his obvious military bearing. 'Nice set-up you've got here, *broer*,' he said. And then, glancing at Clay's weapon: 'Expecting company?'

Clay slid his Beretta back into his waistband. 'Jesus Christ, *Koevoet*. You scared the *kak* out of me. I thought it was BOSS coming to get me.'

Crowbar walked to the fridge, opened it, grabbed two beers. 'Power's off,' he said, popping off the tops against the windowsill, handing one to Clay. 'They're warm.'

'This is Africa, *bru*.'

'*Ja, ja*. TIA.'

'What the hell are you doing here, *Koevoet*?'

'I thought you'd be glad to see me.'

Clay raised his bottle. 'Jesus, *Koevoet*, I am. I am. It's just you're the last person I would have expected to walk through that door, that's all. I almost put a slug through you.'

Crowbar smiled, drank, wiped his mouth with the back of his hand. 'You always were a jumpy one, Straker. I guess I should have called ahead.'

Clay smiled. 'It's good to see you.'

Crowbar frowned, finished his beer. 'It's taken me a while to find you.'

A fizz ran through Clay's legs, echoed in his ankles. 'How long?'

Crowbar waved this away. 'Doesn't matter, Straker. Not now.'

Clay drank, his mind spinning. How long had *Koevoet* been here, looking for him? And why? He was the one who'd told him, all those months ago back at 1-Mil, to leave South Africa, run as far away as he could.

'But I *did* find you, Straker. You should be more careful.'

'Why are you here?'

Crowbar reached into his jacket, produced a manila envelope, and threw it onto the table. 'This is for you.'

Clay opened the envelope and slid the contents out onto the table. A British passport, a birth certificate, and his military ID card. The passport was out of date, the picture unrecognisably young, the face innocent, smiling – a younger version of him. Clay leafed through the passport, examined the birth certificate. Now, finally, he could get out.

'*Dankie, Koevoet*,' he said. 'Jesus. It couldn't have been easy getting these.'

'It wasn't.'

When Clay looked up, Crowbar had a gun in his hand.

Clay wasn't surprised. He'd rarely seen Crowbar without a weapon. But why had he drawn it now? 'What's wrong?' he said.

'Nothing, Straker.' Crowbar levelled the gun at Clay's chest.

'What are you doing?'

'This isn't easy, Straker.'

'What are you talking about?'

'Reach back and lay that Z88 on the floor for me, *bru*. Nice and steady.'

'What the *fok*?'

'Just do it, Straker.'

Clay did as his *Liutenant* asked. By now, his insides were tumbling.

'Kick it over.'

Clay sent the gun skidding across the floor. Crowbar stooped and picked it up, stashed his own gun in his jacket pocket, and levelled the Z88 at Clay's chest.

'What the hell is going on, *Koevoet*?' said Clay, scared now, angry. 'What the *fok* are you doing?'

Crowbar scuffed the floor with his boot, took a deep breath. 'I was ordered to come here and find you, Straker.'

'Since when does the army send field officers to track down deserters?'

'It wasn't the army.'

'Who then?'

'It doesn't matter,' said Crowbar. 'What matters is that some very powerful people thought it important enough to send someone like me all the way here to find you.'

'Talk sense, for Christ's sake, *Koevoet*.'

Crowbar shook his head. 'What did you do, *seun*? I told you to leave, to get out. Instead you go and get yourself mixed up in something you don't even understand.'

'I understand enough.'

Crowbar shook his head again. 'No, Straker, you don't.'

'You came all this way to tell me that?'

'No, *seun*, I didn't.'

'For what then?'

Crowbar frowned. 'Haven't you figured it out yet?'

'You're here to take me back.'

'No, Straker. I'm sorry. I'm here to kill you.'

42

Live Your Life

Is the universe random, without coherence or purpose? Or is there order underlying the chaos? Does an individual life have meaning, or are we as disaggregated plasma, spinning in vortices we neither control nor understand? And when, if there is meaning to it all, will our purpose be revealed?

As Crowbar's words registered in Clay's brain, sending a shock wave of adrenaline thundering through his body, a philosophy was born. He didn't know it then of course, and wouldn't be able to articulate the basic principles of this new belief until many years later, but this was the moment when it all started to coalesce in his mind.

If you don't care, it can't hurt you.

Simple enough. And certainly not new. But for him, at twenty-two, looking down the mouth of a loaded gun held by the last person on the planet he'd still trusted, a revelation. And, in the nullity of its meaning, the parallel and opposed mirror-image negatives, the seeming cancelling-out of everything he'd been raised to believe, to trust, there was a measure of the order and balance the universe seemed no longer to contain.

Crowbar stared at him, the gun steady in his hand.

'Why you?' said Clay. It came out as a croak, a hoarse half-whisper.

'I volunteered.'

'No,' was all Clay could manage. Everything was coming down around him, every last part of the rotten scaffolding that had propped him up, every crutch and prop of delusion built up since childhood.

'Understand, Straker. If what you know gets out, some very powerful people will end up looking very bad. More importantly, they could lose a lot of money. I told you to leave it, but you wouldn't listen. And a lot of people are dead now because of it.'

Clay swallowed back the bile rising in his throat. 'What they're doing is wrong, *Koevoet*. You know it is.'

'It isn't a question of wrong or right. You can't think that way. That was Barstow's problem – a *fokken* idealist. These people, they have the power, Straker. So they make the rules. We are nothing.'

'No, you're wrong. All you have to do is decide.'

Crowbar laughed, walked to the fridge, keeping the gun levelled at Clay, took out another beer. 'You think so?' he said. 'Look around you. Can't even get a cold *fokken* beer in this place.' He cracked the top against the butt of the weapon.

'That's not what I meant.'

'Shut up and listen, Straker.' Crowbar turned the chair around and sat with his legs straddling the chair-back. 'This war, the one we've been fighting, it's not about the *Rool Gevdar*, or protecting our precious way of life.' What Wade had said.

Clay said nothing. He hadn't believed that for a long time.

'Why do you think we're supporting UNITA?'

'Because they're supporting us.'

'Wrong, Straker. Deals have been made. UNITA doesn't give a shit about South Africa. The reason we're in Angola fighting the commies is so that when UNITA wins, with our help, they'll hand over control of the country's resources to *us*.'

'Who is *us*?'

'*Them*.'

'Same question.'

'The people who want you dead, Straker. The people who sent me here. This isn't about politics, ideals. It's about money, *seun*, plunder. Oil leases, diamonds like the ones you took from that asshole Mbdele, wood, ivory, whatever. There are no *sides*. There is only who gets what.'

'And what does UNITA get?'

'Power. Control. The means to exact revenge. That's what they think they're getting, anyway.'

'But they're not.'

'No, they're not. Part of COAST's job is to flood Angola with highly addictive drugs. *Kak* like MDMA. COAST manufactures the stuff and ships it into Angola by air. UNITA distributes in-country, and in the process become addicts themselves.'

'That day at the airstrip with Colonel Mbdele.'

'Right. They pay with ivory, diamonds, anything they can get their hands on.'

'And with human beings.'

'Exactly. Symbiosis. It's the perfect set-up.'

Clay stared at his commander, his mentor, his enemy. 'And these people you work for, is it BOSS?'

Crowbar laughed, tilted his head back. 'That bunch of *dofs*? Hell no. They work for *us*.'

'Then who?'

Crowbar tipped the bottle to his lips, swallowed. 'You don't understand, do you? Here it is, Straker: these people, the ones who pull the strings, they don't have sides.'

'And COAST?'

'Does pretty much as it likes. Grasson works for them.'

'And the *swarts bom*?'

'A more efficient means of subjugation.'

'What is that supposed to mean?'

'These people don't care about the nation – my nation. As long as it can be used to serve their interests, they will tolerate it. If they can subjugate and control it, so much the better.'

'The Broederbond.'

Crowbar nodded, tapped the muzzle of the Beretta on the edge of the table. 'Apartheid is just a way to make sure the bastards don't have to share.'

'And anyone who gets in the way, they kill.' Clay hung his head.

'That's right. Kill, or torture, or imprison, or more often than not just scare into compliance. Most people just shut up and do what they're told. The brave ones, the ones who stand up and fight, those they kill.'

'The village near Rito.'

'*Ja,* them.'

'You knew.'

Crowbar inclined his head.

'Why? Why did you do it, *Koevoet*?'

'To save you, Straker. You and Barstow.'

Clay choked back tears. 'Bullshit. Don't say it.'

Even here, in the dim light of a tropic afternoon, Crowbar's eyes shone a deep glacier blue. 'It's the truth,' he whispered.

Clay covered his face with hands.

'It was them, or you. The bastards knew what you'd done, what you'd seen, out there over the Atlantic. Those villagers were dead anyway. That woman Zulaika wasn't going to back down. I convinced them that I could keep you quiet. I was wrong.'

'And now you have to clean up the mess.'

Crowbar finished his beer. 'Someone had to. I don't send others to fix my mistakes.'

'They killed Wade, didn't they? These people of yours.'

Crowbar tapped the Beretta's muzzle on the table top in a slow heartbeat. *Tap-tap. Tap-tap.*

'I said, they killed Wade.'

'I tried to warn him.'

'It was Botha.'

'*Ja.* But you don't need to worry about it. Botha's dead.'

'Good. How?'

'Very unfortunate. He was killed by a stray bullet to the head. About two months ago during one of his buying trips into Angola.'

Clay sat staring at Crowbar, at the gun in his hand, tried to contemplate his end, but could find no way of starting.

'I'm sorry, *seun*,' said Crowbar after a time. 'I didn't want it to be this way. Any of it.'

Clay looked into Crowbar's eyes. 'I trusted you.'

'But you didn't *listen* to me.'

'*Fok jou.*'

'One day, Straker, this whole pile of shit will come crashing down. And when it does, then maybe the story can be told. I hope I'm around to see it. But now is not that time.' Crowbar stood. 'Do you have the photographs?' he said. 'The ones you took in the lab?'

Clay nodded.

'And the notebook?'

'What difference does it make?'

'Without them, there isn't much of a story, is there?'

'What do you mean?'

'Without proof, it's just your word.' Crowbar lowered the weapon, dropped the mag, ejected the live round and put the gun on the table.

Clay's heart lurched.

Crowbar took a step back. 'Give me the film, Straker. And the book.'

Clay looked at the gun, up at Crowbar.

'You left the country before I could find you.'

Clay glanced down at the documents on the table.

'Decide, Straker.'

Not much of a choice. Live, and bury the story forever; or die here, and the truth dies with you. Clay made to reach behind him for Brigade's backpack.

'Do it slow,' said Crowbar.

Clay had no illusions about Crowbar's capacity to kill him instantly. He reached into the backpack's outer zip pouch, pulled out the film canister and the notebook and put them on the table.

Crowbar regarded the objects for a moment, as if he, too, was making a decision. Finally, he picked up the canister and the blue, hard-covered notebook and stashed them in his jacket pocket.

'Go, Straker,' he said, straightening up. 'Get out of here. And this time, take my advice. Live your life. Keep quiet. If you don't, they will kill you, I promise you. Consider that a direct order.'

'What will you do?' managed Clay, still reeling.

'My job. Try to keep salt-dick amateurs like you alive long enough to see something good come out of this Godforsaken country.' Crowbar put the empty beer bottle on the table and started towards the door.

'*Koevoet*, wait.'

Crowbar stopped, one hand on the doorframe.

'Did you kill Botha?'

Crowbar smiled. It was a big, toothy grin that creased deep lines around his mouth and eyes. 'What do you think, *seun*?' Then he reached into his pocket and pulled out a small envelope. 'Almost forgot,' he said, flipping the envelope to Clay. And then he was gone.

☾

Commissioner Ksole: This van Boxmeer, Crowbar as you call him, do you know what has become of him?

Witness: No, sir. I do not.

Commissioner Ksole: You have not had any contact with him since?

Witness: No, sir. I never saw him again.

Commissioner Ksole: Then how did you get possession of the photographs, Mister Straker? The ones you have shared with this commission.

Witness: The film came in the post, a few months ago. No return address.

Commissioner Ksole: From him?

Witness: I can only assume so.

Commissioner Ksole: And the notebook. Do you have this also?

Witness: I have photocopies.

Commissioner Ksole: Are you willing to provide them to the commission as evidence?

Witness: I am.

Commissioner Ksole: Do you know what became of the original document, Mister Straker?

Witness: No, sir, I don't.

Commissioner Barbour: And you never went to the press, the authorities in the United Kingdom?

Witness: No, I didn't.

Commissioner Ksole: Why not, Mister Straker?

Witness: I don't know, exactly. I mean, I thought about it. But after a while I guess I just wanted to forget. I had no proof, and no one would have believed me anyway.

Commissioner Rotzenburg: And Mister Straker, what was in the envelope he left you, that day in Maputo?

Witness: Diamonds. Five of them.

Commissioner Rotzenburg: The diamonds you took from UNITA, the ones you hid?

Witness: Yes. They were all there.

Commissioner Rotzenburg: And what did you do with them?

The witness's answer is unintelligible.

Commissioner Rotzenburg: Speak up, Mister Straker. What did you do with the diamonds you stole?

Witness: I squandered them.

Commissioner Barbour: Do you have anything else to say, son, before we conclude?

Witness: No, sir. Except to ask when I might expect to hear back from the commission about my amnesty.

Commissioner Barbour: It will be several weeks, at least, Mister Straker. You will be notified as soon as there is a ruling. The commission thanks you for your honesty, and your willingness to come forwards to help in the process of healing our country's wounds. I know it has been very difficult for you.

Witness: Thank you, sir.

Commissioner Lacy: There is one last thing, Mister Straker, before you go. We are able to share some information with you, facts that have come to light as part of this process. As you know, all of the transcripts of these hearings will be made available to the public in due course. This is an open and transparent process.

Witness: I understand.

Commissioner Lacy: In your testimony you mentioned a doctor, Vivian.

Witness: Yes, ma'am.

Commissioner Lacy: Her name was Doctor Vivian Russell. Her husband was Captain John Russell, SAAF. Official government records, now declassified, show that John Russell was arrested by the Bureau of State Security on 3rd August 1980, for suspected acts of treason. He was held in detention and died in custody of apparent suicide on 7th October 1981.

Commissioner Rotzenburg: We will be in contact, soon, Mister Straker. Until then, please do not try to leave the country.

Epilogue

15th November 1996,
Maputo, Mozambique

'*Allo?*'

'Hello, Rania.'

'Claymore. How are you?'

'I saw my friend today. I went to her grave.'

'Your friend?'

'A lady I knew when I was here before. A long time ago.'

'*Je suis desolée*, Claymore.'

'You would have liked her, Rania. She was a lot like you. A writer.'

Silence on the end of the line, her breathing.

'I tried, Rania. I told them everything.'

'The commission?'

'They're not going to give me amnesty.'

A deep breath. 'I am sorry, Claymore.'

'They're going to charge me. They want to put me in jail.'

'*Mon Dieu*, Claymore. I am so sorry.'

'You knew.'

Silence on the end of the line.

'You knew, Rania. Why didn't you warn me?'

'What are you talking about, Claymore?'

'Back in Yemen when we first met, you told me you'd seen my SADF service record. Do you remember? It wasn't that long ago, Rania.'

'Yes, I did. But—'

'Then you knew I'd been dishonourably discharged. That they had linked me with COAST, had accused me of war crimes.'

She was crying, now. 'I saw the dishonourable discharge report, but that is all. There was nothing else. Nothing about the reasons why. Claymore, I didn't know. *Je te jure.*'

Clay breathed, listened to the sound of her tears.

'*Mon Dieu*, if I had seen something like that, do you not think I would have mentioned it?'

Clay said nothing, stood staring into the depths of his memory.

'Claymore?'

'I'm sorry, Rania. I just assumed ... I shouldn't have.' Again, he'd been too quick to judge, to lash out.

Silence, for a while, and then: 'What will you do?'

'Run.'

'No, Claymore. Stay where you are. Please. I will come to you, *chéri*. Give me a few days. It will take me some time to organise a babysitter, flights. It will be so good to see you again.'

Clay grabbed the balcony's handrail, steadied himself against the distant blue of the horizon, that unperturbable line between ocean and sky that stretched to the ends of the world.

'Claymore?'

'You have a child.'

'I should have told you. I did not know how to reach you. I am married, Clay. I have a son.

All that this meant washed through him, a torrent.

'*Chéri*, are you there?'

That word of hers: *chéri*. He closed his eyes, said: 'I'm happy for you, Rania.' He was.

'You would like him, Clay. You would like them both.'

'I wrote to you.' He shouldn't have said it.

'I know, Claymore. I am sorry.'

Clay watched a family, a couple with two young children, walk hand in hand through the hotel garden towards the beach.

'I can be there by the twenty-eighth,' she said.

Clay filled his lungs, exhaled until there was nothing left. 'I'll write it out for you instead, everything. I'll post it to you. There are photos, too, notes and documents. Proof. I kept the originals. You can use it any way you like. Just tell it.'

'Claymore, *chéri*. I will. But I want to see you. There is so much we need to discuss. I should never have left it as I did.'

'No, Rania.' No. He would write it. He would write it as truly and completely as he could. And then maybe she would understand.

She was crying now, deep sobs coming across the line. 'I can be in Maputo in three days. Just give me three days. Please, *chéri*. Please.'

'I won't be here when you arrive.'

'*Non*, Clay. Please.'

'It's okay, Rania. It's too dangerous. You have your family to think of. This is best. I shouldn't have asked you. I'm sorry.'

Rania sighed. All the energy that had crackled through the line a moment ago was gone. Her voice came flat and resigned. 'What will you do?'

'Try to keep going.'

'Where? Will I ever see you again?'

'I don't know, Ra. I don't know.'

'Claymore, *please*.'

'Will you write it, Ra?'

'You know that I will, *chéri*.'

Clay put down the phone, walked to the table and picked up the handgun, felt its weight in his hand and stared out at the sea. He had done what he had said he would. He had kept his promise. Rania would write the story, and the world would finally know the truth. And then, maybe one day, the dead and their wandering spirits would rest, and there would be peace.

But now, it was time to run.

Historical Note

Operation COAST was established in 1981 by the apartheid government of South Africa as the nation's secret chemical and biological weapons programme. COAST was seen as a vital part of the war effort against the communist insurgencies in neighbouring countries, and against domestic enemies of the regime, including the African National Congress (ANC) and its sympathisers. From its outset, COAST was run by one man (who the press later dubbed 'Doctor Death'), with little or no oversight. Within a short period of time, several hundred researchers and equipment from around the world were assembled and put to work within a number of shell companies set up by COAST, including the Roodeplaat Research Laboratories (RRL).

Soon after, Doctor Death was alleged to have orchestrated the killing of more than two hundred SWAPO prisoners using a lethal cocktail of muscle relaxants, clandestinely disposing of the bodies at sea. Over the course of the 1980s and early 1990s, allegations surfaced of Operation COAST's involvement in the assassination of anti-apartheid activists, including members of the SADF, and of attacks using chemical weapons in South Africa and against FRELIMO troops inside Mozambique. At the same time, COAST began producing large quantities of non-lethal drugs such as ecstasy and mandrax, which they sold into target areas at significant profit. In 1996, the Truth and Reconciliation Commission (TRC) began to investigate the activities of the SADF during the war, including Operation COAST. The international press picked up the story and gave it wide exposure. Partly due to pressure from the USA and Great Britain, Doctor Death was arrested in Pretoria in 1997. At the time, police found a thousand ecstasy tablets in his car, along with classified Operation COAST documents. Subsequent investigations suggested that he had been selling COAST's chemical and biological weapons secrets to Libya and Iraq. In 1998 Doctor Death testified to the TRC. He refused to seek amnesty from the commission. The TRC concluded that he should be put on trial.

In October, 1999, Doctor Death was tried in Pretoria for two hundred and twenty-nine counts of murder and sixty-seven other charges including embezzlement, drug trafficking, fraud, conspiracy to murder, and theft. The trial lasted thirty months. During that time, the prosecution called one hundred and fifty-three witnesses. Doctor Death called only one – himself. He gave evidence for forty days. In April 2002, Judge Willie Hartzenberg dismissed all charges and granted the defendant amnesty, ruling that a South African court could not prosecute crimes committed in other countries. Doctor Death was released.

In 2003, the state tried to appeal the judgement, but the Supreme Court of Appeals ruled that there would be no retrial. In 2005, the Constitutional Court of South Africa overturned the Court of Appeal's ruling, finding that a South African court could prosecute for crimes committed abroad. Since then, no further legal action has been taken by the state, and Doctor Death has travelled the world as a highly-paid guest speaker.

Between 1996 and 1998, the Truth and Reconciliation Commission considered seven thousand, one hundred and twelve applications for amnesty. Only eight hundred and forty-nine were granted.

The human genome was sequenced in 2000, proving definitively that attempts to create a genetically targeted 'black bomb' were always destined to fail. We are all the same.

Acknowledgements

This book owes much of its existence to my father, who instilled in me early a thirst for knowledge and travel. As a boy, our house was always filled with visitors and friends from abroad, including many South Africans fleeing apartheid. Sources of inspiration and details of the times and places in the book also came from *19 With A Bullet*, by Granger Korff (30 Degrees South Publishers); *Buffalo Battalion: South Africa's 32 Battalion, A Tale of Sacrifice*, by L.J. Bothma (Dr L.J. Bothma); and *Under Our Skin: A South African Family's Journey Through South Africa's Darkest Years*, by Donald McRae (Simon & Schuster). Thanks as always to my fabulous publisher Karen, my editor, James, my agent, Broo, to Heidi, Zac and Dec, my crazy sister Camilla, and to readers everywhere.